Maggie's
War

ALSO BY TERRIE TODD

The Silver Suitcase

MAGGIE'S WAR

TERRIE TODD

Waterfall
PRESS

Bible Scripture taken from the New King James Version, public domain.

Hymns referenced: "Jesus Loves Me," Anna Bartlett Warner (1859); "'Tis So Sweet to Trust in Jesus," Louisa M.R. Stead (1882); "Silent Night," Joseph Mohr (1818); "If Jesus Goes with Me," C. Austin Miles (1908)

Published by Waterfall Press, Grand Haven, MI

www.brilliancepublishing.com

Amazon, the Amazon logo, and Waterfall Press are trademarks of Amazon.com, Inc., or its affiliates.

ISBN-13: 9781503941335
ISBN-10: 1503941337

Cover design by Laura Klynstra

Printed in the United States of America

In loving memory of Shane

"God sets the lonely in families . . ."

Psalm 68:6

CHAPTER 1

M aggie Marshall awakened to a sense of relief unlike anything she'd experienced before. Her husband was dead.

Did she dream it or had it really happened? She swung her legs over the side of the bed and reached for the telegram that still lay on her bedside table. Moving to the window, she raised the blind and looked out at the Winnipeg skyline. She'd opened the window a crack the night before, and a slight breeze now kissed her cheek and stirred the paper in her hand. Across the street, the Union Jack fluttered gently from the overhang of Anderson's Drugstore. Sparrows twittered in the hedges below, and the aroma of fresh bread wafted over from McClellan's Bakery down the block. Looked like it was going to be a sunny day.

A perfect day to begin my new life of freedom.

She looked down at the precious paper that had arrived yesterday afternoon. The news seemed surreal, but there it was in black and white:

MRS. MARGARET MARSHALL

2411 HAWTHORN AVENUE, WINNIPEG, MANITOBA 1942
AUG 23 AM 8:19

10711 MINISTER OF NATIONAL DEFENCE DEEPLY REGRETS TO INFORM YOU THAT A107405 PRIVATE DOUGLAS THOMAS MARSHALL HAS BEEN OFFICIALLY REPORTED KILLED IN ACTION ELEVENTH AUGUST 1942 STOP IF ANY FURTHER INFORMATION BECOMES AVAILABLE IT WILL BE FORWARDED AS SOON AS RECEIVED.

DIRECTOR OF RECORDS

Maggie turned from the window and began pulling on her dress and shoes. Doug had been among the first to enlist when Canada went to war three years earlier, following his buddy's drunken dare. Now that she knew he would not be coming home, her heart felt lighter than it had since the day he left, when she could only hope for this outcome. Maybe there really was a God after all. Maybe now the nightmares would end, the memories could truly fade.

But first, there would be much pretending to do. A memorial service to attend. She could play the role of widow convincingly, she knew. After all, she had played the role of loving and beloved wife for nearly five years before Doug joined the Royal Canadian Army. To her knowledge, no one had yet guessed the truth. And if she pulled off her performance in this last act, no one ever would.

But she would summon the tears later. First things first. She checked in on Charlotte, who was asleep in the room across the hall, and studied the youthful face resting on the pillow. She'd looked so exhausted the night before. How long until the girl delivered her baby and left forever? Six weeks? Maggie swallowed a lump in her throat. *No point getting attached.* Might as well let her get her rest, though. She picked up a stray sweater from the floor and laid it gently across a chair, then closed the door quietly.

Downstairs, Maggie found an empty cardboard box and tore off one flap. Using the thickest nib of her fountain pen, she carefully drew the letters across it and hung it in the front window of the restaurant, then stepped outside to view her workmanship. She stepped back as close to the street as she dared and surveyed her sign: **CLOSED.** Then, in smaller print: Bert's will reopen on August 26, following the funeral of Douglas Thomas Marshall, killed in action.

There. That announcement not only gave her a few days off, but it also might generate some sympathy as well. Sympathy was good for business. Maggie stepped inside the restaurant and locked the door. She surveyed the dining room, chairs stacked on top of tables where she and Charlotte had placed them last night before mopping the floor. She pulled the blinds down on the front windows to thwart the curious, then stepped into the kitchen, where she lit the stove and put on a pot of coffee.

Once she was settled at the kitchen table with a fresh cup in hand, Maggie began her list. Everyone she could think of to contact had received a phone call from her last evening, so she'd had plenty of practice in sadly relaying the news of her husband's passing. *I should go to Hollywood and be in a picture,* she thought. *I certainly know how to act, and no one would miss me much here.* Well, except for some of her regulars like old Lawrence Winston, whose coffee no one but Maggie could get right.

Reverend Fennel. Reuben. Had anyone informed him yet? It had been years since Maggie had darkened the door of Reverend Fennel's church, but she still considered him her pastor, even if they were no longer the chums they'd been as children. She knew her husband's parents would arrange with their own minister to lead the funeral at their big highfalutin church, and Maggie was just fine with that. The less she had to do, the better. Just show up and play the role.

But something in her wanted Reverend Fennel to know. She was a widow, after all. Wasn't the church supposed to look after widows and orphans? With the war on, though, she knew she wasn't exactly unique in her position. Thankfully, her restaurant did all right, even in these hard times. And she had no children, like some.

At the thought of children, Maggie's throat constricted and she struggled to get her next swallow of coffee down. Blinking hard to ignore the memories, she focused on the paper in front of her and tried to think about who else she should notify.

But the memories refused to be choked back this time. If she hadn't miscarried, her baby would be four years old now. Would Doug have stopped hitting her if he'd known she was pregnant? *Why didn't I just tell him?* She flogged herself again with the same old question. If only she hadn't been so foolish. She had truly thought she could pack up and get away from Doug without his ever finding out about the baby. But although the opportunity finally came one night while he went out drinking, her plan fell apart when Doug came home early. He'd been gone long enough to get good and drunk, but not long enough for Maggie to get packed and out the door.

The roar of his questions when he caught her, suitcases in hand, still echoed painfully in her mind, as did the feeling of the blows to her body that ended her baby's life, without leaving a mark on her face. Within minutes, Maggie had been cramping and bleeding, and by the next morning, she knew there would be no baby. No doctor was consulted. No friends or family members were called. No one, including Doug, ever knew there was a baby.

No one but Maggie.

"Mornin', Mrs. Marshall." Maggie heard Charlotte Penfield lumbering down the stairs as swiftly as her pregnancy would allow. "Sorry I overslept." Without looking up at the girl, Maggie knew Charlotte was following her daily routine—that she'd grabbed an apron from the hook behind the door and was moving toward the stove.

"Stove's already lit," Maggie said. "Some people aren't such slackers as others."

"I'm really sorry," Charlotte repeated. "Thanks for lighting the stove. Why didn't you wake me?"

Maggie stayed focused on her list, knowing Charlotte's big blue eyes would melt her heart if she ever looked long enough at them. She couldn't let that happen. "Doesn't matter now. Just get some porridge going for the two of us. We won't be opening the restaurant today."

This announcement was met by silence. Maggie finally glanced up at the girl. She stood there, tall and slim, except for the mound at her midsection. Her straight blond hair was neatly gathered at the nape of her neck, in contrast to Maggie's unruly red frizz.

"I'm really sorry about your husband, Mrs. Marshall. This must be so hard."

"Life is hard, that's all." Maggie went back to her paperwork. "Now don't be thinking you can lollygag around in your room just because we're closing for a few days. It'll be the perfect opportunity to clean out the pantry and give the stove a good polishing. Maybe even wash some windows."

"Yes, ma'am."

"Maybe we can get those new curtains sewn for the front, too. The fabric's been sitting there for six months already, since before you ever came."

Maggie looked up at Charlotte once more, but the girl hadn't budged. If she was off in dreamland, it wouldn't be the first time by any stretch.

"Well, don't just stand there, get that porridge going. I already brought the milk inside and put it in the icebox, since somebody was being a lady of leisure this morning."

The girl moved into action, rattling pots and scooping the rolled oats out of a covered metal bin under the counter. While she waited for the porridge to bubble, she poured herself a cup of coffee and warmed up Maggie's. Then she cleared her throat. "Will there—will there be a funeral . . . or anything?"

"I believe they call it a memorial service when there's no body to bury." Maggie kept adding tasks to her list without looking up. "It's set for one o'clock on Wednesday."

Maggie swept the paperwork off the kitchen table and carried it into her office to finish making her list there. By the time she returned, Charlotte had the table set and two steaming bowls of porridge were waiting. The two ate in silence, Charlotte fidgety and Maggie as calm as she'd been the morning before.

"Mrs. Marshall?" Charlotte said.

Maggie looked up.

"Are you okay? I mean, it's almost as if nothing's happened."

She's right, Maggie thought. *But shouting about my newfound freedom from the rooftop would be frowned upon.*

"I closed the restaurant, didn't I?"

"Well, yes, but . . ." Charlotte chewed a fingernail. "It seems like people are usually grief-stricken at times like this. I'm just . . . well, I wonder if it has really hit home yet. You know?"

"You grieve your way and I'll grieve mine," Maggie said, taking another spoonful of porridge. "This is undercooked."

"Sorry, Mrs. Marshall."

The two finished their meal without further conversation. Maggie drained her coffee and stood to clear the dishes. "I'll take care of these," she said. "You go on down to Ogilvie's and buy some stove blacking, a spool of white thread, and a can of Bon Ami for the windows." She reached into a canister on the end of the kitchen counter and pulled out her ration book and some cash. "Make sure it's the paste. Don't let them try to sell you some newfangled product."

"Yes, ma'am." Charlotte took the book and the money and headed out the back door.

Through the window above the sink, Maggie watched the girl's pregnant frame waddle across the tiny yard, through the gate, and around the corner. Then she slipped her hand into her apron pocket and pulled out the note card she had kept for two years. Of the dozen girls she had seen come and go over the past three years since Douglas left, only one had ever sent a thank-you note. Probably the only one who'd ever seen past Maggie's tough exterior, and the only one Maggie had allowed herself to care about. And what had that brought her? Only more loss. She wouldn't make that mistake again.

She'd memorized the note long ago. That didn't stop her from reading it almost daily, though. She ran her fingers over the illustration of two tiny sparrows on the front, then opened the well-worn card to view the careful penmanship inside.

> Dear Mrs. Marshall,
>
> I just want to say thank you for everything you did for me during my time with you. The money I earned has also made it possible for me to continue my education, and I am pleased to say I am now doing well in normal school and will be a full-fledged teacher next fall. Working in the restaurant was great experience and has helped me get a good job on campus.
>
> More importantly, thank you for never shaming me for my situation. It means a lot. I will continue to pray for you and for your husband overseas. I pray that God will bless you and make his face shine upon you and grant you peace.
>
> Sincerely,
> Cornelia Simpson

Maggie slumped into her chair, placed her head over her arms on the table, and wept like a baby.

CHAPTER 2

Charlotte waited until she rounded the corner of Bert's Restaurant before muttering aloud, "Grouchy old thing."

Glad for this trip to the store—or any reason to get away from Grumpystiltskin, her nickname for Mrs. Marshall—Charlotte could breathe a little more freely. She took her time, looking into store windows along the busy city street and watching young mothers pushing baby carriages or herding toddlers alongside. It was hard to believe a woman could lose her husband one day and be all business the next, but if anyone could do it, Charlotte figured, it was Maggie Marshall. The woman didn't harbor a single human emotion in her body. Why she had ever started taking in unwed pregnant girls was still a mystery to Charlotte. Cheap labor for the restaurant, maybe? It certainly wasn't out of any sense of compassion. But then, what would a woman like Maggie know about being young and in love? She had to be at least thirty, maybe even thirty-five.

The heat of the morning caught up with Charlotte, and she stopped to sit on a bench. *So what if I'm late getting back?* She wiped a handkerchief across her brow. *Mrs. Marshall will accuse me of taking too long whether I'm late or not.* A streetcar rattled by, and Charlotte watched with longing the passengers riding to wherever it was they were going. *How I'd love to climb aboard and take the streetcar all the way home.*

Home. It seemed a lifetime since she'd been there, safe and secure in her parents' upper-class neighborhood, hundreds of miles away in Toronto. That her parents had hunted so long to find this placement for her spoke more of their pride than of their love for Charlotte, but she wouldn't hold it against them. Her situation was of her own doing. She'd willingly given herself to Reginald, and she'd do it again in a heartbeat. She loved the man with everything in her.

She had come to Mrs. Marshall's with only her parents knowing the truth. Even Reginald believed she was spending six months in Winnipeg to help an aunt whose husband was fighting overseas. Charlotte wished it were true. Assisting an aunt with three young children couldn't be any more challenging than working in Mrs. Marshall's restaurant.

Five more weeks and it would all be over. The baby would be born, adopted out, and Charlotte could return home and resume life at her private girls' school as if nothing had happened. She had already stuck it out here four months; five more weeks would not kill her. And if she seemed different to her friends when she returned . . . well, this crazy war was changing everyone. With any luck, it, too, would be over by then, and Reginald would be relieved of his duties. She was glad he'd not been sent overseas yet, but was serving as a cook at Camp Petawawa.

How she longed to write to him. Her parents had strictly forbidden it. "Worthless piece of trash," her father had called him, forbidding him to contact Charlotte again, and she him. Even her friend Ruby had advised Charlotte to keep the pregnancy secret from Reginald, if she hoped to ever hear from him again.

The absurdity of it all grated on Charlotte as she resumed her walk to the store. Why shouldn't he know about his own child? He wouldn't abandon her. He wouldn't! He wanted to marry her, and a child would only hurry the marriage along.

I know he loves me, Charlotte reasoned. *I know it.*

Still, the nagging question remained. Why had Reginald made no attempt to write? Surely if he truly cared, he'd send letters to Ruby, who would forward them to her. Perhaps he was just busy, she concluded. It had to be nerve-racking, feeding a military camp full of hungry men. Helping in the restaurant, Charlotte was only beginning to appreciate the challenge of preparing mass quantities of food, especially when supplies were often unavailable and food was rationed.

The store window displayed a decal showing three Canadian soldiers, saluting. Do your bit. Back us with your money, it read. Buy Made in Canada Goods. Behind the lettering was a Union Jack with a yellow maple leaf in the center. Charlotte put her thoughts aside as she pushed the door open. Inside, she found the needed items easily. In the dry goods section, where she'd gone to pick out a spool of thread, she was drawn to some ready-made baby clothes. Tiny nightgowns, flannel receiving blankets, and knitted sweaters were on display together. She allowed herself the luxury of running her fingers gently over the little garments, savoring their softness. Then, with a deep sigh, she squeezed her eyes shut a moment, then moved quickly to the counter to pay for her items. No sense thinking about what was not to be. Someone else would be swaddling her baby.

By the time Charlotte returned to Mrs. Marshall's, the sun was high and she was damp with perspiration. She laid the bag of items on the kitchen table and poured herself a tall glass of water, then sat down at the table to drink it.

"Took you long enough." Mrs. Marshall stepped in from the dining room, carrying an armload of faded white curtains. "Drink your water, then get started on those front windows. I'm going to wash these, and when they're dry, you can take them down to the Red Cross. Soon as they're on the clothesline, I'm going to stitch up the new curtains. This place will be looking right spiffy when we reopen."

Charlotte pulled the window cleaner out of the bag, gathered some rags from beneath the sink, and pushed her way through the curtain that separated the kitchen from the dining area. *Trust Mrs. Marshall to pick the hottest day of the year to wash windows.* At least the windows were still on the shady side of the building. For now.

A knock at the kitchen door stopped her. She paused and held the curtain back to watch Mrs. Marshall open the door. A man in a clerical collar stood on the other side, hat in hand.

"Reverend. I didn't expect to see you so soon," Mrs. Marshall said.

The man nodded. "Hello, Maggie. May I come in?"

"Uh . . . sure."

He stepped inside and Mrs. Marshall looked over her shoulder. "Go on about your business, Charlotte," she said. "I want those done before lunchtime."

"Yes, ma'am." Charlotte let the curtain fall into place and began her task, telling herself she didn't care about the conversation coming from the kitchen.

"Have a seat, Reverend Fennel." Maggie placed her load of curtains on the counter and waved a hand toward a kitchen chair. Part of her wanted to tell him he was a sight for sore eyes. "I guess you heard the news already?"

"I did."

"I meant to call you. It's on my list." Maggie sat down across from the man, trying to remember the last time she'd seen him. His dark brown hair and eyes were just like she remembered from their teen years, but the spindly adolescent had matured into a well-built man.

"Word travels fast. I thought I'd come by to see how you're doing and offer whatever support I can."

"Well, that's very kind. Especially since I haven't been to church—well, at least not to *your* church—"

"Maggie, that's not what this is about. Just . . . forget all that. How are you?"

Maggie hung her head. "It's hard. As you know, we married very young . . ."

"I remember."

Maggie had attended Sunday school with Reuben Fennel when they were both youngsters at the small church he now pastored. Her parents were faithful members, and as a child she'd had no reason to doubt any of the teachings about Jesus and God she'd learned there. But after Douglas Marshall came into her life, it was all too easy to slowly drift away from the little corner church with the white clapboard walls and get swallowed up in the large one Doug's family attended, with its fancy stained glass windows, pipe organ, and steeple. It was there that Maggie had walked the long aisle in a gorgeous white dress on her father's arm, while Doug's parents looked on with an impressive imitation of approval.

The tension had begun within days of the picture-perfect wedding. Maggie would never forget Doug's first outburst. How had she failed to see this side of her fiancé before it was too late? With her father still occupying the living quarters at the restaurant, Douglas and Maggie had rented their own little apartment above Sam's Shoe Repair. That night, she'd finished her restaurant shift and was turning the key in the lock at the front of the building when Doug jerked the door open, grabbed her by the arm, and roughly pulled her inside and up the stairs to their apartment. Maggie had to take two steps at a time to keep from stumbling.

"Get in here, woman," he said.

"Ow! Doug, you're hurting me. Let go!" Maggie tried to wrench her arm away as the whiff of alcohol invaded her nostrils. Who *was* this man she'd thought she knew? He hung on tight, and when they got to the top of the stairs, he pulled her inside and slammed the door shut. Without letting go of her wrist, he braced his back against the door.

"Where have you been all night?"

"All night? I've been working! It's only—"

"Don't tell me what time it is, woman. The restaurant's been closed for more than two hours."

Maggie was surprised when she glanced at the clock and saw that he was right. "I—I was visiting with my father. We haven't had any time to chat since the wedding and I—"

"Shut up! I saw that Melvin Bloom eyeballing you when you waited on his table. He hung around, didn't he? You were with him, weren't you?"

"*What?*" Maggie couldn't believe what she was hearing. She ignored her gut reaction to say "you're crazy," though she certainly thought it.

"Don't lie to me, woman." With a grunt, Doug shoved Maggie sideways so that she completely lost her balance and hit the floor, knocking over a floor lamp on her way down. The glass globe over the bulb shattered with a sickening crack, spewing shards around the room.

The breakage seemed to halt Doug's violence for the moment.

"I'm going out," he said. "You better have this mess cleaned up when I get back. And listen to me. If you ever, I mean *ever*, mess around like that again, it will go so much worse for you. You'll only wish I was as easy on you as I was tonight."

He ran a hand through his hair to smooth it down and walked calmly out the door.

Maggie picked herself up, carefully swept up the broken glass, righted the lamp, and crawled into bed, where she cried herself to sleep. When she awoke in the middle of the night, Doug lay snoring next to her.

In the morning, he was gone. It was Maggie's day off, and later, as she prepared a late breakfast, Doug came in the door clutching a handful of daisies and black-eyed Susans.

"I'm sorry." He sounded truly remorseful. "If we had any money, I'd bring you two dozen red roses, you know I would. I don't know what got into me last night, Maggie. You know I love you, right?"

Maggie slowly nodded and took the flowers, trying not to dwell on the fact that she'd seen these same flowers in the neighbor's garden next door.

"I'll never do it again, Maggie, I promise."

Maggie sighed. "Sit down and eat some porridge."

Looking back now, Maggie knew something had changed in her that very day. A bitter, cold shell had begun to form over her soul ever so slowly, an unconscious attempt to shelter the compassionate and loving girl who still resided somewhere inside her. She knew now she should have left right that minute, after the first time. She should have run straight to her father. Bert Sutherland would not have been pleased with his daughter's brief marriage, but he would have believed her and sheltered her. Now there was no father to run to.

After that, regular church attendance had become less of a priority as Maggie and Doug got busier in Bert's Restaurant. Following her father's retirement just six months later and his unexpected death only three months after that, the job of running Bert's in lean times had fallen on the two of them.

"Maggie? Are you all right?" Reuben Fennel was asking.

"Sorry, Reverend. Just lost in memories is all." Maggie knew this was as good a time as any to practice her new role. She wiped her eyes with the corner of her apron.

"You can quit with the 'Reverend' stuff, Maggie. It's me, Reuben. The kid who stuck your braid in Reverend Donnor's inkwell when you weren't looking, remember?"

Maggie couldn't resist a side grin as she glanced up at the man. "Did I ever forgive you for that?"

He smiled. "Did I ever ask you to?"

When she didn't respond, he continued. "How are the plans coming along for a memorial service? Can I help?"

Feeling chagrined, Maggie told him Doug's parents were handling the arrangements at their own church. "But I'd love for you to be there," she added.

"Of course. Who will sit with you?" he asked, almost too softly for her to hear.

Maggie hadn't thought of that. Truthfully, all she had really thought about was her life beyond that service and her new freedom. Such as it was. With her parents dead and gone and her only brother serving overseas, and given her knack for keeping people at a distance, Maggie found that she had no one she would consider a close friend.

She hesitated. "I suppose I could ask Freda from up the street. Although with school out for the summer and all her children home, she might not be able to get away in the middle of the afternoon."

"I'd be happy to sit with you if you like."

The thought struck both caution and longing into Maggie's heart. How wonderful it would feel to have someone be there just for her, someone strong and good and kind. Someone who had known her before her heart grew cold. But stubbornness won out.

"I imagine I'll sit with Doug's family."

"Of course." Reuben shuffled his feet beneath his chair. "Maggie, would you like me to pray with you before I go?"

"If you like."

Reuben leaned forward, elbows on knees, and bowed his head. Maggie folded her hands in her lap and looked down at them.

"Heavenly Father, I lift Maggie to you and ask for your gracious hand upon her in the difficult days ahead. Bring her comfort, peace, and courage. Help her feel your presence and your love. Provide for her in every way, Lord. Bring people around her to support and help her. In Jesus' name, amen."

When Maggie looked up, she saw that Reuben continued to sit with his head bowed. She didn't know what to do. Was he done? She watched in wonder as he pulled a handkerchief from his pocket and wiped his eyes. He was crying? For *her*?

"I didn't even offer you a drink," Maggie said, hoping to break the awkwardness. "How about a glass of cold water?"

"Sure, that would be great."

Maggie poured the water and set it on the table in front of him. She decided to remain standing.

"What will you do now, Maggie? Have you had a chance to think about it?"

It took Maggie a moment to understand what he was even asking. Why would she do anything different than what she'd been doing?

"Guess I'll keep running the restaurant, like always. And taking in girls who need a place."

"It's a real ministry you're doing, you know." Reuben's voice cracked slightly.

"Ministry?" Maggie gave a dismissive sniff. "That's got nothing to do with it."

"You might not think so, but it is. Regardless of how you see it."

Maggie didn't know how to respond. She wished he'd leave. This was becoming increasingly uncomfortable.

"Well, I used to keep two at a time. But with all the boys gone to this wretched war, fewer girls need what I offer now, if you get my drift. But then, with the war on, we don't get as much restaurant business either. So it all works out."

Reuben smiled. "That's one way to put it. How many young ladies have you lodged here?"

Maggie let out a snort. "If they were ladies, they wouldn't need me in the first place."

"Now, Maggie."

Maggie started counting on her fingers, but gave up. "Oh, I don't know. Twelve, I think."

"Do you keep in touch with any?"

"No."

"Any one in particular stand out?"

Maggie knew the correct answer was a resounding *yes*, but launching into a description of Cornelia Simpson's excellent work habits, cheerful attitude, and abundant faith would only delay Reuben's departure. Not to mention that the girl had studied her way through high school courses by correspondence all the while.

"Not really," she said.

"Well, I'm proud of you. I'm sure they'll always remember you."

No kidding, Maggie thought. *They'll remember me as an old shrew.*

He stood and placed a hand on her upper arm. "You take care of yourself. And please, if there's anything you need, be sure to call me. Will you?"

"Sure." Maggie escorted him to the door and showed him out without a good-bye, then closed the door and placed her forehead against its surface.

Playing the heartbroken widow was going to be harder than she'd imagined.

CHAPTER 3

Charlotte had worked harder all day than she did on days when the restaurant was open. After washing the windows, she'd cleaned out the enormous pantry and helped Mrs. Marshall inventory their supplies, all before lunch. In the afternoon, she spent hours scrubbing the inside and blacking the outside of the cast-iron kitchen stove while Mrs. Marshall cut and sewed new curtains for the front windows. *No sense giving the pregnant girl the easier job,* she thought as the scratch of her scrub brush drowned out the whirring of the sewing machine's treadle.

Just when Charlotte was sure they'd finally be calling it a day, Mrs. Marshall had her bring the old curtains in off the clothesline, pack them into a box, and carry them the ten blocks to the Red Cross Thrift Shop. By the time she got there, they were closed for the day, and Charlotte dropped the box by the door, not caring whether they ever received it.

By the end of the day, she'd been too tired to eat supper, let alone prepare it. But upon her return, Mrs. Marshall placed a plate of steamed vegetables, a loaf of bread, and a tall glass of milk in front of her. Another typical wartime meal.

"Eat. That baby needs it even if you don't."

Charlotte had swallowed the food without tasting any of it, then climbed the stairs and pulled on her nightgown.

There had to be a way out of this place. So many times, Charlotte had dreamed of catching a train and leaving town. She had enough money socked away in her dresser drawer to buy a one-way ticket to Petawawa and find Reginald. She played the scene out in her mind nightly, the appropriate background music as spectacular as any picture show: She makes her way to the military camp where someone gives her directions to the mess tent. She enters the tent and her eyes adjust to the dim lighting. Then she spots him in his khaki uniform with a white apron tied round his waist and a white cook's hat on his head. He doesn't see her at first, because he's busy stirring a large pot of something. Steam rises from the pot. Charlotte stands still, watching him, taking in the details of his new life. She sees a faraway look in his eyes and knows he is thinking of her. Then he glances up, for only a second. He turns to speak to one of his buddies, then stops midsentence and looks back. He stares. She smiles. The light dawns in his eyes.

He can't even speak. He comes around the corner, dodging around tables and knocking over benches to get to her as fast as he can. Then he stops short.

"Char? Is it really you?"

Charlotte nods, and Reginald moves forward, taking her in his arms and swinging her all the way around.

"I can't believe it's you!" he says. Only then does he notice the mound of her stomach between them. Surprise lights up his face.

"Char? Oh my goodness, Char! Are you . . . ? Are we . . . ?"

Charlotte only nods and smiles.

Reginald is overcome with joy. He wraps his arms around her once again.

"Marry me, Char," he says. "Right this minute! Please marry me."

"Yes!" she shouts.

The war ends that same day. Reginald is discharged and marries Charlotte before the weekend is over. They set up housekeeping in a cute little cottage with a white picket fence, and Charlotte spends the remaining months of her pregnancy sewing and knitting tiny clothes in preparation for the baby's arrival.

"Charlotte? You still up?"

Charlotte was pulled out of her fantasy by the sound of Mrs. Marshall's voice at the bottom of the stairs. What could she possibly want now? Was there one last chore left undone? Perhaps if she didn't answer, Mrs. Marshall would assume she was already asleep and hadn't heard. She lay quietly on the bed, closing her eyes.

Eventually she heard Mrs. Marshall climb the stairs, go into her own room across the hall, and shut the door. *Guess it couldn't have been too important.* She sighed with relief and tried to resume her fanciful daydream about Reginald, but sleep took over and she was helpless to order the dreams of her slumber. They would come as they willed.

Charlotte was surprised when Mrs. Marshall allowed her to sleep in two mornings in a row. She dressed quickly, intent on starting breakfast before having to be told. But when she got down to the kitchen, all was quiet. A note on the kitchen table informed her that Mrs. Marshall had errands to run and would return by noon.

Charlotte decided this was a golden opportunity to have eggs and toast for breakfast instead of the usual porridge. Mrs. Marshall no doubt knew the precise number of eggs in the pantry and would scold Charlotte later, but it would be worth it. She fried her eggs with care, placed them on a plate with two slices of toast, and carried her meal into the restaurant so she could sit down and eat in leisurely style. No longer the waitress, she was now the patron.

Seated across from her is her beloved Reginald. While they enjoy their food, he gazes into her eyes and tells her how beautiful she is and how much he adores her. Other customers look on in envy, but she and Reginald have eyes only for each other.

A rattling at the front door yanked Charlotte out of her imagination. With all the blinds pulled, she couldn't see who was on the other side of the door. Couldn't they read Mrs. Marshall's sign? The restaurant wouldn't be open until after the funeral tomorrow afternoon. She watched the person's shadow step away and carry on down the street.

The funeral. A spark of an idea began to burn in Charlotte's mind. Would she be expected to attend? Surely not. She'd never even met the deceased man. How long would Mrs. Marshall be away? Easily long enough for Charlotte to catch a bus to the train station and get out of town. She could leave a note saying she was out for a walk. By the time Mrs. Marshall reached Charlotte's parents by telephone or telegram, she could be halfway to Petawawa, maybe even farther.

Oh, but that's crazy, her more logical side argued. One way or the other, they'd catch up with her and then what? Bring her back here? Or would they take her home? Knowing her parents, they would refuse to let her return home lest she be seen in her pregnant state by anyone they knew.

Still, even if they sent her straight back to Mrs. Marshall, maybe she could stay ahead of them long enough to see Reginald first. At least then he would know about the baby. Surely if he knew, he would put a stop to her parents' ridiculous insistence that she keep her pregnancy a big secret and give the baby up for adoption. Even if the war didn't end soon, even if Reginald couldn't get a discharge, he would promise to marry her as soon as he possibly could. She knew he would.

Charlotte cleaned her dishes and started in on the list Mrs. Marshall had left for her. Scrubbing down tables and chairs, refilling salt and pepper shakers and napkin dispensers were mindless tasks. She'd be able to think about her escape plan while she worked. She would call it "Operation Finding Reginald."

Maggie sat in front of the big oak desk in the reception area of Jones, Brighton, and Jones, Attorneys at Law. Across from her, the young woman who had invited her to sit now tapped at a typewriter with mesmerizing speed. Maggie watched in fascination, wondering what it would be like to work one of those machines.

Theodore Jones opened his office door and poked his head out. "I can see you now, Mrs. Marshall." He disappeared inside and Maggie followed.

"Have a seat." The lawyer waved a hand in the general direction of two chairs facing his desk. "I presume you're here about your husband's will."

"Yes. Well, more specifically, my father's will," she said. "When my father, Bert Sutherland, died, he left his restaurant to my husband and me. It has been in our names, jointly, ever since. Now that my husband has passed, I would like this changed so that Bert's is fully mine."

"Yes," he replied. "You explained that over the telephone, and I was able to pull all the needed papers from the files. I'm afraid, however, you might be disappointed with what I've found."

"What do you mean?" Maggie had thought this would be simple. Once the paperwork was done, she planned to move ahead with plans to renovate the restaurant. Oh, completing a renovation might not be that easy in wartime, but the sooner she jumped through all the legal hoops, the sooner it could happen. Besides, the war could end today. She wanted to be ready.

"You are correct in that the restaurant is in both your names. However, before he shipped out, your husband revised his own will. Were you aware of this?"

Maggie shook her head, a sense of foreboding suddenly triggering a twitch in her left thumb. What on earth had Douglas done?

"I'm sorry, Mrs. Marshall. Your husband's new will indicates that his portion of Bert's Restaurant is bequeathed to his brother, Earl."

Maggie's mouth dropped open. She tried to speak, but no words would come out. *Earl?* As despicable as Douglas was, he was a model citizen compared to his younger brother. While drunk at Doug and Maggie's wedding, Earl had flirted openly with Maggie and teased her about her legs. She, along with the entire wedding party, had heard the loud, slurred words: "Nice solid woman ya got yourself here, Duggie. Good sturdy legs on 'er."

Douglas had laughed and thrown an arm around his brother without giving so much as a glance in Maggie's direction.

Now, Maggie swallowed whatever was trying to come up her throat. "He can't . . . he can't actually do that, can he? The restaurant was my father's before it was ours."

"It all appears to be legal from what I can see. I can investigate further if you'd like."

"How much would that cost?" Maggie's head was starting to spin. Even given all the battering she had suffered at Doug's hand, this was the worst thing she had endured. What had he been thinking? Was this his final trump card, a way to continue to abuse her in the event he never returned? *How could he?*

"Our usual rates would apply," the lawyer said.

Maggie placed one hand on top of the other in her lap, willing them to stop shaking. But she could do little about her voice, and it quivered as soon as she spoke. "There's got to be a way to fight this, doesn't there? But I have no money for lawyer's fees, Mr. Jones."

"It will need to be probated in any case. If you like, I can recommend a lawyer who might consider taking your case pro bono." He flipped through some cards on his desk. "But to be frank with you, Mrs. Marshall, I don't see that you really have a leg to stand on here. In my opinion, you would be wasting your time and money. Especially as a woman, trying to run a restaurant on her own. I'm sure your husband believed he was looking out for your best interests. Now that he's passed away, I think any judge would see it that way too."

Maggie felt glued to her chair. *Earl?* There was no way she was going to partner with Earl on the restaurant. Or on anything else.

"Perhaps your brother-in-law would be willing to sell you his share?" The lawyer folded his hands on his desktop.

Maggie sighed. "That would require that I actually speak to the man, wouldn't it?"

Theodore Jones looked at her. "It's like that, is it?"

"I'm afraid so."

"Well, unless you're willing to pay lawyers to do all the negotiating, yes. You would have to speak to him. Perhaps it will go better than you think."

"Anyway, I can't afford to buy him out."

"Then perhaps he would buy you out?"

Maggie had no intention of selling to anyone, and she certainly couldn't imagine handing off her father's legacy to the likes of Earl Marshall.

"Is there anything more I can do for you today, Mrs. Marshall?" The attorney seemed eager to get on to his next appointment.

"N-no. I guess not." Maggie managed to get to her feet. She left the legal office clutching her purse, a carbon copy of Doug's last will and testament in her other hand and a cloud of fog in her head. Walking along the sidewalk, she found a bus stop bench and sat down to clear her mind. An elm tree provided restorative shade, and Maggie closed her eyes.

How could he do this to me? Was the restaurant the reason Doug had married her in the first place? That made no sense. It wasn't like it was worth a fortune or anything.

"Ma'am? You getting on?" A bus had stopped and the driver was looking at her, the door swung wide. Maggie hadn't even noticed.

"Uh . . . no, thank you. I think I'll walk." Maggie decided the twenty-block walk would do her good. She could use the time to think. But the farther she walked, the angrier she became. Her sturdy black shoes pounded harder against the concrete with each step. The worst of it was, she didn't know who she was angrier at—Doug or herself. *What a fool I was to marry that man!* If only she'd left him the very first time he smacked her. The divorce would have been final long ago, her father's will would be clearly laid out, and the restaurant hers alone. Even the stigma of divorce would have been better than the hell she'd lived with that man, and the mess he'd left behind.

How would she ever get through the funeral now? How was she supposed to play the grieving widow, pretend she missed and mourned Doug?

And how on earth was she supposed to face his brother, Earl?

CHAPTER 4

Charlotte turned over the last of the restaurant chairs in order to wipe it down. Mrs. Marshall had returned from her errand even crankier than usual, if that were possible, only to turn around and leave again.

"That garden isn't going to tend itself, girl," she'd announced. "I want to see some progress made on the weeds when I get back, and the beans need picking again. See to it. It's a much more pleasant day today; it will do you good to get some fresh air. I have some more business to take care of. Oh, and forget about opening the restaurant after the funeral tomorrow. We'll wait an extra day."

Charlotte stuck her tongue out at the door as it slammed behind the bitter woman. What was wrong with her, anyway? Did she bring young pregnant girls into her home just to torture them because she'd never had any children of her own? Maybe now that she was a widow, she'd get a new husband and have her own babies instead. She wasn't *that* old. But who on earth would ever marry such a battle-ax?

Well, there's no way I'm working in that garden this afternoon, Charlotte told herself, even though she knew in the end she'd probably do whatever Mrs. Marshall asked. It felt good to be rebellious. Her resolve to carry through with her plan had just become even stronger. If Grumpystiltskin had decided not to open the restaurant after the funeral, perhaps that meant she'd be staying away longer now, mingling with relatives and such. This would all work in Charlotte's favor.

Operation Finding Reginald was carefully penned across the top of a blank sheet of paper in Charlotte's mind, where no one else could see it. Step One: Pack. She would pack her bag tonight after bedtime and stash it under her bed. Step Two: Write note. If she had a note written ahead of time, all she'd have to do is leave it on the table the moment Mrs. Marshall left the premises, saving her precious time. She would wait until tonight to actually write the note, but she composed it in her mind while she continued to fill salt and pepper shakers.

Dear Mrs. Marshall: I hope the funeral went well. I decided to go for a long walk. I will lock up when I get in, so don't feel you need to wait up.

That could buy her until morning, as long as the ol' girl didn't wait up.

Step Three: Find out the train schedule.

Oh, now's my chance. Charlotte brushed her hands together and headed for the telephone on Mrs. Marshall's desk in her tiny office off the kitchen. On the bulletin board above the desk was a long list of telephone numbers frequently requested by customers, including those of the bus depot and train station. Charlotte took a quick glance out the window before picking up the receiver and dialing.

A young woman's voice answered. Charlotte tried to sound as grown-up as she could.

"Yes, I'm anticipating an excursion to Petawawa, Ontario. Can you tell me which trains I should take? I'll need the schedule and ticket prices as well, please."

Charlotte was shocked to learn that Petawawa Military Camp was over twelve hundred miles from Winnipeg, and the train trip would take more than thirty-six hours! Still, she scribbled down everything she needed to know. If she could just make it to the station by three thirty tomorrow afternoon, she would be on her way.

The schedule would not give her enough time to walk from Bert's Restaurant to the station, which meant she'd need to catch a bus . . . which meant dipping even deeper into her meager stash of cash. Charlotte did the math in her head. She would have enough to do it, but there'd be little if anything left to buy food on the journey.

Step Four: Pack a lunch. After another glance out the window, Charlotte opened the icebox and took a quick inventory. With the restaurant closed, the perfectly good roast chicken she found in there was going to waste. Mrs. Marshall never let food spoil.

"It's not like I'm stealing," she reasoned aloud. "I would get to eat this if I stayed behind, so why shouldn't I be entitled? Besides, the way I slave around here every day for the mere pennies she doles out, I can consider it fair wages."

She assembled two sandwiches, one with a thin slice of chicken, the other with peanut butter. With the garden carrots, apples, and small package of soda crackers she added, she knew she could get by until she reached Reginald. She'd be hungry, but it would be completely worth it! She wrapped the food together and ran upstairs, where she stashed it under her bed.

As soon as all this was done, she went outside and pulled weeds from Mrs. Marshall's garden as though her life depended on it. The woman had been right. The weather had cooled and rain clouds appeared to be gathering on the horizon.

"Thank you for another fine meal, Mrs. O'Toole." Reuben Fennel wiped his lips with the napkin his landlady had provided and laid it neatly beside his plate.

"I'm wishin' it could be more than wee potatoes and beans, Rev'rend," the elderly woman said, gathering dishes and moving to the kitchen. "You should have tasted the dishes I could turn out before the war. Before I had to make this into a boardinghouse, back when me children were all still home."

"Well, if anyone can make something tasty out of beans and potatoes, it's you. And I do appreciate it." Reuben patted his stomach and rose from the table, hoping Mrs. O'Toole would detect in his tone the closing of the conversation. If there was anything the woman did better than cook, it was chatter.

"Oh, but you haven't had your coffee yet, lad. Sure and they're goin' to be rationin' it soon, just like sugar. Better enjoy it while you can."

"Well, who can argue with that?" Reuben smiled and sat again, sighing inwardly. He knew this meant another session of listening to Mrs. O'Toole ramble on and chided himself for his reluctance to engage further. *You're a pastor. This is what you do, remember? Listen to people.* Besides, her coffee was undeniably good.

"Sure and they're goin' to ration coffee and tea. Our boys are needin' to get theirs first." Mrs. O'Toole took a seat across from Reuben, relishing her audience of one. "Oh, I wouldn't care for meself, mind you. But how a body's supposed to run a boardinghouse on so little is beyond me. Course, you're my only boarder who stays for lunch. Miss Renfrew and Mr. Broadford are here only for breakfast and supper. Except weekends, of course. Although Miss Renfrew generally goes home to her parents on the weekend. I'm not sayin' I mind it, mind you. I like that you're here for lunchtime, love. Breaks up my day."

"It's admirable, what you're able to do." Reuben took a swallow of coffee.

"Well, I'll just rise to the challenge, I will. But Lord knows how the cafés and restaurants manage to stay afloat. I guess many of them are closin' their doors, too . . ."

At the mention of restaurants, Reuben's mind drifted to Maggie Sutherland. Maggie Marshall, now, though he rarely thought of her by that name. How was she managing to keep Bert's Restaurant going in these hard times without a spouse around? And now she truly would be alone.

It was difficult to believe Maggie was the same person Reuben had known when they were kids. So full of life and laughter then, she'd had a lot more boys than just Reuben pining for her attention. Did she have any idea how interested he'd really been?

The day he dipped her braid in the inkwell, he'd been acting on a dare from Eddie Junket. Carefully, he'd rolled the tip of Maggie's braid between his fingers, feeling its softness against the calluses on his ten-year-old fingertips. He used extreme caution to get only the tip in the ink, lest she be forced to cut off any of her lovely red tresses.

Maggie had acted mad that day, of course. She'd called Reuben a nincompoop and stuck out her tongue. But within minutes, she'd returned to her good-humored self, laughing with the other girls and looking just as pretty as a boy could imagine.

What happened to her? Reuben could remember the ache he felt the day he learned she was engaged to marry Douglas Marshall. But seeing now what Maggie had become, he supposed he was better off alone. As much as he admired her for taking in unwed mothers, he couldn't help but pity those poor girls for having to put up with the likes of her. Well, at least there'd be no nonsense under her protection. Of that, he was certain.

Even with her new hard edge, though, he'd noticed that she was still a beautiful woman. Or surely would be, if she'd only smile. And maybe wear something besides those thrift-shop dresses designed for sixty-year-old grandmothers. Maybe Douglas hadn't known what he was really getting, either.

Or was it Douglas Marshall who'd blown the candle out in Maggie's heart to begin with?

Mrs. O'Toole's voice rose, bringing Reuben's thoughts back into the room—". . . and so I told her, you catch more flies with honey, love. Now I know that's in the Bible somewhere, am I right, Rev'rend?"

"Um. Actually, Mrs. O'Toole, I don't really think that one's—"

"Not that I'm the sort who goes around thumpin' people over the head with the Bible, mind you. No sir, not me. I don't believe in that. Just drives folks away, it does. That's what I appreciate about you, Rev'rend. You don't shove anything down anyone's throat. You just live what you know is right. I respect that. We're all knowin' what you stand for, what you believe. But you're not hammering us with it, no sir."

"Well, thank you, ma'am. I try to live what I believe. And right now I *believe* it's time I returned to work." He drained his coffee cup and rose.

"Oh, you." Mrs. O'Toole laughed. "And you've got a jolly sense of humor too!"

Reuben thanked her again and made his escape. It was only a short walk to the church, where he planned to work another hour on Sunday's sermon before heading out to visit a sick parishioner. *Sick* seemed like a stretch. Bonnie Cartwright was a first-class hypochondriac who requested weekly visits from Reuben for the sole purpose of describing to him, in excruciating detail, her every ache and pain. She replayed the scenes of her many doctor's visits, to Reuben's embarrassment, and regaled him with show-and-tell presentations of her many medications. The one time Reuben had been able to sneak a word in edgewise, he'd commented about how miraculous it was that, in spite of her numerous ailments, Mrs. Cartwright was still able to faithfully attend her bridge club and host it with renowned flair whenever it was her turn.

Okay, Lord, I admit I am low on compassion where Bonnie Cartwright is concerned, he confessed as he reached for the doorknob. From the back door of the church, he could hear the telephone jangling in his office. He ran to grab it.

"Smith Street Community Church, Reuben Fennel speaking."

Silence. Reuben decided the caller had given up before he'd answered and went to replace the receiver in its cradle, but then he heard the familiar voice.

"Reverend? Reuben?"

"Yes." He could have sworn the voice was Maggie Marshall's, but he figured his ears were playing tricks on him because she'd been on his mind.

"It's me. Maggie."

Reuben sat. The sudden addition of weight started his wooden office chair's wheels turning. The chair scooted backward, dragging the telephone halfway across Reuben's desk and knocking a heavy concordance to the floor—but only after it hit the edge of the metal wastebasket, tipping it over with a crash.

"Uh. Maggie! I was just—uh. Good to hear from you."

"What's the commotion? Did I call at a bad time?"

"Uh, no. Not at all, uh . . . Maggie. What can I do for you?"

"Well, if your sermons are as well delivered as your phone conversations, I haven't been missing much."

It was Maggie, all right.

"Sorry about that, I just, uh . . . dropped something. No problem."

"Anyway," Maggie continued. "Looks like I need to take you up on your offer. You know, when you said to call if I needed anything."

"Of course!" Reuben pulled the chair closer to his desk and sat. "I'm glad you called. What is it you need?"

"Well, it's kind of complicated. I was hoping to make an appointment and talk to you about it in person."

Reuben stood his wastebasket upright and returned the concordance to his desktop. "Certainly. When would you like to come?"

"The sooner, the better."

Looking down at his appointment book, Reuben picked up a pencil and neatly stroked out Bonnie Cartwright's name. "A slot just opened up, in an hour. Can you get here by then?"

"Back door?"

"That's best, yes."

"I'll be there." Maggie hung up without a good-bye.

"Forgive me, Lord," Reuben muttered. "But if I said 'I'm sorry,' we both know I'd be lying."

CHAPTER 5

After calling Bonnie Cartwright to reschedule, Reuben completed precisely three sentences of his Sunday sermon in the hour he waited for Maggie Marshall's arrival. What was it she needed? As strong-willed and independent as Maggie seemed, he'd never dreamed she would look to him for help, no matter how many times he offered. It must be something serious for her to have swallowed her pride and asked. Would he be able to help her? Finally, he brushed aside his paperwork and rested his forehead against his hands, his elbows on the big oak desk.

"Lord, who am I to counsel a new widow when I've never even been married? Whatever it is Maggie's coming to me for, equip me to help her. Please give me wisdom. I don't want to let her down."

Reuben heard the door open and close, as if on cue. He went to his office door and saw Maggie shaking water out of an umbrella and wiping her shoes on the mat. When had it started to rain?

"Hello, Maggie. Don't worry about your shoes. Come on in."

"It's really coming down out there." Maggie grabbed one edge of her full skirt and gave it a flip to shake out the water, then walked toward Reuben.

"Let's hope this doesn't continue for the funeral tomorrow, eh?" Reuben said.

Maggie raised one eyebrow, making him wish he could retract his words. What had made him say such a thing? What difference did it make what the weather did? Perhaps a rainy day was perfect for a funeral. But instead of trying to backpedal and risk making things worse, he changed the subject.

"Have a seat, Maggie. Can I get you some tea? We even have a little sugar, I think."

"Oh, that isn't necessary." Maggie sat in one of the two chairs facing Reuben's desk.

"Well now, I didn't ask if it was *necessary*. But you got yourself rained on out there, and I bet you'd like a nice hot cup of tea. It's all ready."

"I'd like to come right to the point, if you don't mind." Maggie pulled some papers out of her purse and flattened them across her lap.

"All right." Instead of sitting behind his desk, Reuben turned the other chair to face Maggie and sat in it. "What did you want to see me about?"

"Remember when you offered to sit with me at the funeral tomorrow?"

"Of course."

"Well, I'd like it if you would."

"Oh? Well, certainly. I'd be happy to sit with you. But you didn't have to come all the way down here to ask me that. You could have said something on the telephone." Reuben's curiosity was definitely piqued.

"There's more."

"I thought there must be."

Maggie shuffled the papers in her hand. "Reuben, did you know my father left the restaurant to both Douglas and me when he died?"

Reuben remembered Bert Sutherland as a levelheaded, hardworking man. "Well, I never really thought about it, but I guess that makes sense . . . if your brother wasn't interested in the business."

"He wasn't. I was."

Reuben waited, but Maggie's gaze drifted to the window, where the rain still formed rivulets. He felt himself wanting to stare at her, knowing full well doing so was inappropriate.

"I've had some wonderful meals there, Maggie, before and since your father passed."

Maggie sighed. Then her voice took on an angry tone and she spoke through a clenched jaw. "This morning I found out that Doug changed his will before he shipped out. He left his half of the restaurant to his brother." She held the papers out for Reuben to see.

He took the will and sat back in his chair, skimming the document. It all looked completely official and legal, as far as he could tell. What on earth was Maggie going to ask of him? And why did he suddenly want so badly to be able to do it, whatever it was?

"I see. Is that a problem?"

"A problem? Yes, it's a problem." Maggie's tone made Reuben feel like a moron. "That was my father's restaurant. He and my mother worked hard to build that place up and grow its clientele. It should be mine."

Reuben called upon his most soothing pastoral voice. "It still will be, Maggie. It will be half yours, just like it has been since your father died. Am I misunderstanding something?" Reuben checked the signature at the bottom of the page.

"It will be half Earl Marshall's." Maggie's fists were clenched in her lap. "And that's just unacceptable. Daddy would never have wanted this."

"It's a challenging thing for a woman to run such an establishment all on her own. It seems to me that your husband was trying to protect you by arranging for his half to pass to his brother. He didn't want to burden you with the sole responsibility of—"

"Responsibility? Don't talk to me about responsibility!" Maggie's face was turning red. "I've been running that place alone since my father died, Reuben Fennel. And let me tell you, the job became a far sight easier when my dear husband went off to Europe." She all but poked Reuben in the chest with her pointer finger.

Reuben knew he was staring, but he couldn't help it. The fire in Maggie's voice nearly restored the youthful amber glow to her hair instead of the faded beige it had become. But this new piece of information was something he had wondered about—just what kind of relationship had Maggie and her husband had? Had Douglas merely been too passive to match Maggie's ambitious work ethic, or was it worse?

"I'm sorry, Maggie. I didn't realize things were so difficult for you. I mean, before."

Maggie looked him straight in the eyes for a moment, then spoke quickly. "Maybe I shouldn't have come." She reached for the papers, but Reuben hung on to them more tightly.

"No. I'm glad you came."

"So you could talk some sense into me? Help the little woman understand how it is?" She rose to her feet, still reaching for the papers.

"No. I apologize, Maggie, I just . . . Help me understand the full story here. Tell me about your brother-in-law."

Maggie focused on a point on the far wall for a moment, then finally lowered herself back into the chair.

"Let's just say I don't trust the man, Reuben. I wouldn't want to partner with him in a three-legged race at the Sunday school picnic, let alone a business. Let alone my father's business!"

Reuben sighed. He didn't know much about married life, but he had to wonder: How could a man make such an important decision without consulting his wife? Still, there wasn't a lot to be gained in agreeing that Maggie had been wronged in this. Surely there was some bright side to be found.

"Have you spoken with your brother-in-law about it yet, Maggie?"

"I have not." Maggie played with the snap on her purse.

"Well, there. How can you be so sure he's not to be trusted?"

She sighed and snapped the purse closed with a firm click. "Let's just say I know."

"All right. Let's say your assessment is correct. You still need to speak with him and find out what he intends to do with his share, right? Perhaps he would sell, either to you or someone you feel you *could* work with."

Maggie's head was shaking before Reuben finished his speech. "I want to fight this, Reuben."

"Okay. What did your lawyer tell you?" He looked at the papers in his hand again, trying to decipher the legal lingo.

"That I don't have a prayer."

"Well, perhaps we need a second opinion."

"That's just it. I can't afford lawyer's fees. I can barely afford to keep the restaurant open, and I certainly can't afford to buy Earl out."

Reuben sighed. He wanted to help Maggie, but her troubles were completely outside his realm of expertise. And, while the whole thing did seem unfair, he couldn't shake the feeling that she might be overreacting.

"What was it you were hoping for from me, Maggie? I'm not an attorney. I really don't know anything about the legalities of such things."

"I know." She sighed. "I guess I was hoping you'd go with me when I talk to Earl. Just for support, or . . . oh, I don't know." She took the legal documents from Reuben's hand and folded them into her purse. "I'm sorry I bothered you with this."

"Maggie, you're not bothering me. I want to help you. And of course I'll go with you. I'll do whatever I can."

For the second time since she'd walked in the door, Maggie looked straight into Reuben's eyes. He tried to ignore the warmth that stirred in his heart. "Let me sleep on this, Maggie. Do you mind if I ask around a bit? Without giving your name, of course."

"I'd appreciate it." She snapped her purse shut.

"In the meantime, I can tell you one thing your lawyer was wrong about, with absolute certainty."

Maggie looked up, a faint glimmer of what might be hope in her eyes.

"When he said you don't have a prayer, he was badly mistaken. I'll be praying for you like crazy. And I will see you tomorrow."

"Thank you." Her voice had softened to nearly a whisper.

When he showed Maggie out the door, the rain had stopped and the sun was out. As they stepped outside, they were hit with a wall of hot, muggy air. He watched until Maggie reached the bus stop half a block down the street, then he came back inside, perspiration forming on his upper lip.

"Lord, I have no idea what to do for Maggie." He spoke the words aloud as he returned to his desk. "This one is way too big for me. But thank you. Thank you that she asked."

CHAPTER 6

Charlotte picked the last bean in the row, just as the rain started. *Fresh rain on a neatly weeded garden ought to make Mrs. Marshall happy.* She welcomed the cool raindrops on her face as she took her time putting the tools away in the tiny garden shed, then gathered up her basket of beans and carried them inside. By the time she'd washed up and settled herself at the kitchen table with a glass of water and a knife, the downpour had subsided and the sun shone again. She was glad to be done outdoors, knowing how humid the air would feel after the rain. *I won't get a wink of sleep tonight in that stifling upstairs bedroom.*

She was halfway through trimming and cutting the beans when Mrs. Marshall appeared. Without a word, the woman hung her umbrella on its hook and walked past Charlotte, as though she weren't there.

Maybe she won't even notice when I'm gone.

When Mrs. Marshall came back downstairs, she had changed out of her good gray dress into her everyday gray dress. The woman dressed like a nun. Charlotte watched her tie an apron around her trim waist, find another knife, and take a seat next to her. She started in on the beans, working at twice the speed Charlotte worked.

"Shall I get the canner going?" Charlotte asked, breaking the silence.

"No. It's too hot to can. Let's put these in the icebox and serve them when we reopen."

I won't be here when we reopen, Charlotte mused. By late Thursday, she would have found her way to Reginald and everything would be right again. Mrs. Marshall would have to find another slave to serve her beans.

"Leave out a good bunch for our supper," Mrs. Marshall said. "There's still some chicken in the icebox. After supper, we should turn in early. Big day tomorrow."

Charlotte looked up. *Oh no.* Surely she wasn't expected to attend the funeral, was she? That would ruin everything! She had to think of something, quick.

"I know you'll want to spend as much time as possible with friends and family tomorrow," Charlotte began, ignoring the snort that came from the other woman. "So I thought I'd stay here and get things set up for reopening. Maybe do the laundry, too. And with this weather, there's sure to be more things to pick in that garden by tomorrow—"

"Relax. You don't have to go to the funeral."

The woman had read her like a book. How did she do that? They continued working together quietly until only a handful of beans remained in the bottom of the basket.

When Mrs. Marshall broke the silence, Charlotte nearly jumped. "Things may soon be looking a little different around here."

Charlotte waited for her boss to continue. What was that supposed to mean? Was there a new girl coming? That would work out well, actually. Charlotte really wouldn't be missed.

"I've been thinking of renovating the restaurant."

"Oh?" This was not what Charlotte had expected, but it was nice to hear the woman talking about something besides more tasks to be completed.

"This war has got to end sometime soon, and when it does, I want to be ready. The boys will be coming home, and there will be celebrations galore. Folks will want a nice place to go for a good meal." Mrs. Marshall took Charlotte's knife and carried both knives to the sink.

"Yes, I suppose that's true." Charlotte didn't give a fig about renovations, but she might as well keep the woman talking.

"We've got good meals already. What we need is more space." Mrs. Marshall began walking around the room, and Charlotte could almost see the gears turning in the woman's head as she envisioned her plan coming to fruition.

"How would you create more space?"

Mrs. Marshall stood at the window. "My father bought the lot next door and had it appended to this one, thinking to expand one day, but it never happened. I figure we could add more dining space on the south side, knock that wall out."

Charlotte tried to picture it. "Sounds ambitious."

"Oh, I don't suppose it'll affect you any. It'll be at least a couple of months before I can get everything organized for the work to start. You'll be gone home by then, I imagine."

"My baby is due in five weeks."

To Charlotte's surprise, Mrs. Marshall gazed at her with a look that might almost be called tender. Then she scooped up the empty basket and walked over to hang it by the door. "Start some of the beans cooking for our supper now, and put the rest in the icebox. You can pull that chicken out of there, too. I'll go down to the cellar and fetch apples."

Charlotte did as she was told, amazed. It was the first time Mrs. Marshall had offered to go down to the cellar herself. She always sent Charlotte. Had the reminder of Charlotte's due date finally sparked an ounce of compassion in her?

Glad for the chance to cut more chicken meat away from the bones so Mrs. Marshall wouldn't notice the bit that was already missing, Charlotte placed generous slices onto two plates while the green beans steamed on the stovetop. She added a handful of freshly pulled carrots to their plates and filled two glasses with water. While Mrs. Marshall cleaned and sliced the apples, Charlotte drained the beans and divided them between the two plates. The pair sat down to eat in silence.

As she contemplated her plan for the next day, Charlotte felt too excited to swallow much.

"Too hot to eat?" Mrs. Marshall focused on Charlotte's full plate.

That was as good an excuse as any. "I guess so," she said.

"Better eat up. That baby needs nourishment."

Charlotte knew she'd need to keep her own strength up for the trip ahead, and kept coaxing the food down her throat. By the time they'd finished their chicken and beans, the apple slices went down more easily.

After they finished, Mrs. Marshall disappeared into her little office off the kitchen. Charlotte could hear the rat-a-tat of the adding machine while she washed the dishes. Mrs. Marshall was no doubt figuring out what her renovation plans were going to cost. How could she be thinking about such things when her husband had just died? Charlotte didn't understand.

I'm never going to have that kind of marriage, where I don't even care one whit about it when my husband dies, she decided. *I'd rather not marry at all.*

Drying the dishes provided a perfect opportunity to daydream about Reginald and the life they'd have together as soon as this horrid war was over. She wished she'd had the nerve to escape sooner, before she'd become so awkward and fat. *Reginald will be surprised, but I know he loves me. We'll get married just as soon as possible and it will all be okay. I know it.*

"I'll be taking a bath tonight," Mrs. Marshall announced from the other room. "Feel free to take one yourself when I'm done."

"Yes, ma'am." Charlotte decided a bath was a good idea. It would help her sleep and, with a little effort, she could manage to still be clean and fresh when she reached Reginald—despite the fact that Mrs. Marshall insisted they share bathwater.

She climbed the stairs to her room and closed the door, then opened her window as wide as it would go. The air was now cooler outside than in, and she welcomed the refreshing breeze. When she heard Mrs. Marshall running her bathwater, she pulled her duffel bag out of the closet and filled it with everything she'd brought with her from home, save the clothes she would put on in the morning. When she was done, she shoved the bag under the bed with her feet and draped the sheet down low to make sure it couldn't be seen.

Next, she went to work on the note she would leave behind. That's when it dawned on her that the moment Mrs. Marshall started to suspect something, she'd search Charlotte's room for clues. Perhaps if she left a few things, it wouldn't be so obvious that she wasn't coming back.

Out came the bag again. Charlotte pulled out a dress that was getting much too snug, a brown sweater she hated, and the work dress she'd been wearing almost daily since her arrival. *I won't miss this thing,* she thought as she returned it to the closet with the other items.

That would have to do. She couldn't very well show up at Reginald's base empty-handed. After she heard Mrs. Marshall leaving the bathroom, she carried her nightgown in with her, hung it on a hook behind the door, and settled into the warm water for a good soak. Between her exhaustion following her efforts that day and her excitement for tomorrow, Charlotte felt almost too exhausted to climb out of the tub when she was done.

When she finally crawled under her sheet, blankets off and window open, she fell asleep in minutes. For the next several hours, she dreamed of train rides, chicken sandwiches, green beans, and Reginald Wilson.

CHAPTER 7

The pipe organ droned on. Maggie recognized the melody of "Amazing Grace" and agreed it would be pretty amazing indeed if the likes of Douglas Marshall had made it through the pearly gates.

"The family" was ushered in last and took up the first three pews on the right side of the church. Maggie sat in the front row with Reverend Fennel. If people thought that odd, so be it. She appreciated that Reuben's presence created a buffer between Doug's family and her. On the other side of Reverend Fennel were Douglas's parents and Earl. Behind them sat Douglas's sister, Thelma, with her husband, George, and their six children, whose names Maggie could never remember. The third row was filled by various Marshall relatives.

Doug's family had been against his marriage to begin with, although Maggie could only speculate about the reasons. She'd once heard his mother mention Mildred, an old girlfriend who seemed to stand in high favor. Unlike Maggie's parents, Mildred's were well-to-do. Both families had sailed to Canada from England on the same ship a generation before, while Maggie's four grandparents had immigrated from Italy, Austria, Norway, and Ireland!

In addition, Doug's father had interrogated Maggie about her church. It seemed the church in which they now sat was the only right one. Or at least the only church from which his offspring should choose a mate. Even though Maggie had been inside this church numerous times since her marriage, it was the memory of her wedding day that sprung to mind now. How could she have been so happy and so blind?

Maggie could hear her mother-in-law weeping on the other side of Reverend Fennel and, though she didn't feel any closer now to the woman who'd never accepted her, she couldn't help but feel sorry for anyone who lost a child. It was not the natural order of things. Maggie decided she should take a cue from the woman's genuine grief. She reached into her purse and pulled out a hankie. Lowering her head, she dabbed at her eyes and cheeks in her best ladylike imitation.

The organ music stopped and the pastor got up to speak. He read first from Psalm 23 and then recounted the story of Jesus raising Lazarus from the dead. Maggie glanced up at Reuben Fennel and saw him nodding his head in agreement to the words of Scripture, his eyes closed. When Doug's mother let out another sob, Maggie again raised her hanky to her own eyes. Reuben patted her hand.

Maggie figured she could get through the funeral just fine. It was facing Earl later and being confronted with his joint ownership of the restaurant that would be tough. As the pastor rambled on and more hymns were sung, Maggie tried to figure out what she would say to the man. Reuben had suggested taking a civil approach, going into the conversation with the assumption that Earl had only good will toward Maggie and no desire to see her unhappy. Perhaps even no desire to be a part owner of a restaurant. What Reuben advised made sense, she knew. Following his recommendation would be hard, but Maggie decided she'd put down her boxing gloves until she knew for certain they'd be needed.

Then she'd fight to the finish.

"I am the way, the truth, and the life," the pastor quoted, bringing Maggie's focus back to the present. "No man cometh unto the Father, but by me."

Maggie had memorized those words so many years ago, she could rattle them off as easily as counting to ten. It had been a pretty bold statement for Jesus to make about himself. As a little girl, she'd always assumed he really was who he said he was. It was later, when life began to get so difficult, that she started to doubt. Oh, it's not that she wrote Jesus off as a liar. She figured he'd just been a bit misguided or confused. Still, she admitted, he had spouted an awful lot of wisdom and pulled off some amazing feats. Eventually, Maggie had just drifted away from thinking about God or church at all and made her own way. Deep down, she still believed God was there and that Jesus had died for her sins, like she'd been taught. She just wasn't quite as convinced that he cared about the day-to-day business of her life. If he did, wouldn't he have spared her such cruelty at the hands of her own husband? The man she pretended to grieve today, just for the sake of propriety.

When the organ started up again, the family was ushered downstairs, where a reception would take place and refreshments would be served. Maggie found herself leaning hard on Reuben's arm as they walked down the aisle, without having to fake the necessity of it one bit.

She spent the next half hour shaking hands and even receiving hugs from people she barely knew and some she was certain she'd never met. Where had they all come from? The Marshall family had more connections than she realized. Most said kind words about what a fine young man Douglas had been and how they would be praying for her. Their comments only confirmed what she alone already knew: that Doug had been an expert at playing the dual role of model citizen outside his home and controlling tyrant within it. She felt grateful when Reuben steered her toward a chair and brought her a cup of weak tea.

Maggie sat sipping her tea and nibbling a cheese sandwich. As she brushed some crumbs off her skirt, a pair of shiny black shoes appeared on the floor in front of her. Before she even looked up, she knew who they belonged to. As her eyes moved up the dark gray double-breasted suit, her heart began to pound. Earl Marshall stood before her, grinning and holding out his right hand.

"So I understand you and I are going to be partners, Maggie."

Maggie swallowed hard. Earl had refrained from using his old nickname for her, but the tone of his voice still held the same contempt. She set her sandwich and teacup down on the table to her right, but did not accept Earl's hand. Eventually he put both hands in his pockets.

"I guess this isn't the time to discuss it," he said. "When would be a good time, Maggie?"

Finally Maggie looked Earl in the eye. The resemblance to his brother sent shivers down her spine. She could almost feel the slap of Doug's hand across her cheek again, could hear the filthy curses spewing from his drunken lips. Though she opened her mouth to speak, no words came out. She scanned the room until she made eye contact with Reuben, who stood cornered by the pastor who had led the service.

"Not going to talk to me at all, Maggot?" There it was. Earl leaned across Maggie's chair, one hand on the wall behind her. He bent low to speak directly into her ear. "I figured you'd want to go over details as quickly as possible, get things squared away. I've got some great ideas for improving the place."

When Maggie looked up at him, he took it as an invitation to continue. "Like hiring real cooks and pretty, slim waitresses, for starters. I don't know whose idea it was to take in those unwed mothers. It might be cheap labor, but they're never gonna pull in more business."

"I'm the cook," Maggie managed to say.

"I rest my case. What we want is a real professional chef—"

Suddenly, he stopped and stood upright again.

Maggie looked up and saw Reuben standing there. He held out a hand to shake Earl's, introducing himself as Maggie's family friend.

"How do you do, Rev'rend," Earl said, pumping Reuben's hand. "I was just telling Maggie here about the improvements I got planned for the restaurant, now that we're partners."

Reuben smiled. "See, Maggie? I bet Earl here has some of the same ideas you have for renovating and expanding."

Earl waved his drink around while he talked. "The way I see it, it's all about people. You get quality people doing the job, you attract quality customers. And they attract their friends. No more of this do-it-yourself, hire-the-cheapest-help-you-can-get nonsense. You get what you pay for. And, of course, you need to start serving liquor. That goes without saying."

This was followed by the same sickening laugh Maggie had heard in her own home for seven long, dreadful years.

Maggie sat staring at her own knees. She could feel Reuben's eyes on her. No doubt he was wondering why she wasn't speaking up. On the inside, she fumed. How dare Earl presume he knew anything about running a restaurant, or any business? He'd moved around from one unskilled job to the other for as long as Maggie had known him. The restaurant was *hers*! *She* was the cook, and her faithful customers told her every day how much they enjoyed the food. If they wanted some fancy chef, there were plenty of other places they could eat. As for the help . . . well, Earl would never understand in a million years.

But her tongue felt glued to the bottom of her mouth. What was it about these Marshall men that reduced her otherwise feisty self to a meek shadow of the woman she used to see in her mirror? She raised her eyes to Reuben's, and he seemed to hear what she was saying without her saying it.

"Perhaps this isn't the time to be discussing business, Earl," Reuben said at last, his brown eyes on Maggie's. "I think it might be best if you gave Maggie a little more time to absorb . . . everything."

"Oh, of course, of course. Didn't mean to rush you into anything, little lady. But I hope you'll start thinking about what I said. That sorry little place oughta be pulled clear down, if you ask me. But the location we got there could be a real gold mine. 'Specially once this doggone war is over."

"Well, we're all praying for that." Reuben reached to shake Earl's hand again and thumped the man on the back a little harder than necessary, clearly encouraging Earl to move along.

"I'll call on you in a few days, Maggie." Earl waited for a minute, apparently anticipating a good-bye of some sort, but Maggie didn't have it in her. He turned on his heel and drifted into a circle of people gathered near the food.

Reuben watched him walk away, then turned. "You all right, Maggie?" His gentle expression nearly did Maggie in, but she was unwilling to give in to emotion.

"I think I'm ready to go home." She picked up her purse and stood, taking a deep breath. Along the hallway that led to the stairs, a row of childish drawings graced the wall. One particularly well-done picture caught Maggie's eye. In a rainbow of crayon, it said *God loves you.*

Stepping out into the late afternoon sunlight, Maggie couldn't help but think God had a strange way of showing love. Just when she thought she'd finally been released from her nightmare life, it seemed she was being ushered into another.

CHAPTER 8

From the kitchen sink, Charlotte watched Mrs. Marshall go out the door and walk around the corner with the reverend who was escorting her to Mr. Marshall's funeral. She counted to ten, then dashed upstairs, grabbed her duffel bag and lunch from under the bed, and hurried back down to the kitchen. She pulled the carefully penned note from her purse and laid it on the table, then weighted it down with a saltshaker for good measure. One more quick glance out the window and around the room, and then she was out the door, remembering to lock it behind her.

It was only a block and a half to the nearest bus stop, but between the heat of the day, the load in her hand, and the other in her belly, Charlotte felt winded by the time she arrived. She waited only a minute before the bus pulled to a stop and she climbed aboard. She gave the driver fifteen cents and deposited the second ticket in her purse, although she had no intention of ever returning to Winnipeg to use it. She only bought it because the drivers always sold tickets in pairs.

Settling into a sideways-facing seat, Charlotte placed her bag by her feet and looked around. A young mother with two toddlers and another baby on the way smiled at her in camaraderie, recognizing their common condition. Wishing she could hide it, Charlotte gave the woman a halfhearted grin and looked away. Two uniformed soldiers occupied a pair of seats, reminding Charlotte of her mission. An elderly couple sat in the seat behind the soldiers, carrying on an animated conversation that it seemed neither husband nor wife could hear. Just an ordinary day in the lives of ordinary people, but to Charlotte the day represented freedom, adventure, and romance unlike any she'd ever known.

In less than thirty minutes, they were at the train station, and in another twenty, Charlotte was on board the CP Rail car that would eventually end up at the East Coast. She could feel her heart pounding with the excitement of leaving this wretched city for good, of running away, of finally being reunited with Reginald. The train car was much more comfortable than the bus. The air was cooler, the seats bigger and softer. She sat back and tried to relax. That she had made it this far undetected was almost too good to believe. Once this coach started off, there'd be no catching her.

A brown-haired woman with a young girl took the seats facing Charlotte.

"Hello. Mind if we join you?"

The words were obviously just a courtesy. Who could stop her from taking any seat in the car? Charlotte smiled, and the pair settled into their seats. Maybe having company wouldn't be such a bad thing. It would help the time pass.

"How far are you going?" the woman asked.

"Petawawa."

"That's a funny name," the little girl piped up, and the two women chuckled.

"And you?" Charlotte said.

"All the way to Toronto. My parents will pick us up there. They live just outside the city. Is your husband stationed in Petawawa?"

"Yes." The lie came out so quickly Charlotte had no time to reconsider her words. But even if she'd taken the time to think before answering, she might have concluded that pretending to be married was for the best. Besides, Reginald would be her husband soon enough.

"Mine is overseas—in France, last I heard. I'm Marlajean, by the way. This is Trudy." The little girl smiled.

"I'm Charlotte."

The train began to move, and the trio watched through the window as folks on the platform waved to other passengers. Surprised by how fast her heart was pounding, Charlotte wiped damp hands on her skirt and tried to relax.

As the train sped up, Charlotte took a deep breath and rested her head against the seat. She was on her way! Now all she had to do was ride. It would be a long trip, but so worth it. Marlajean pulled a book out of her purse and began to read. Trudy curled up in her seat, her head on her mother's lap. Charlotte pulled out a small pillow from a compartment above her seat, tucked it up against the window, and leaned her head on it. The afternoon sunlight made her so sleepy, she dozed off in no time.

When Charlotte awoke, her tummy was rumbling and she was desperate for a toilet. The sunny skies had turned to dull gray. "What time is it?" she asked.

Before Marlajean could provide an answer, a steward came through the car announcing that the 6:00 p.m. meal was being served in the dining car.

"Care to join us?" Marlajean asked, standing.

"Oh. Thank you, no." Charlotte said. "I'll just stay here. I brought a lunch."

Once her seatmates had left, Charlotte maneuvered to the on-board lavatory at the back of the car and used it. There, she found tiny cone-shaped paper cups next to a crock of water with a spout. She helped herself to a drink and splashed a little water on her face. When she returned to her seat, she pulled her lunch bag out and decided the chicken sandwich should be eaten first. It was dry, but she was hungry enough not to care. She wished she had thought to bring a jar from Mrs. Marshall's to fill with water from the lavatory. Eating an apple helped her thirst a little. Although tempted to eat the second sandwich as well, she knew she had better save it for later.

Had Mrs. Marshall returned home yet and found her note? With any luck, the woman would be worn out and go straight to bed, and not realize until morning that Charlotte was gone. The more distance she could put between herself and Winnipeg, the better. Now she could focus on the mission ahead: get to Petawawa and find a way to Reginald's army base.

Marlajean and Trudy returned looking energized and happy. Marlajean settled her daughter with a coloring book and crayons and began chatting with Charlotte.

"It's going to be a long trip, but I'm so glad we're on our way. Trudy and I are going to wait out the war with my parents. Hopefully, when we return home it will be as an intact family, with my Frederick back safe and sound."

"I hope that for you, too." Charlotte didn't know what else to say.

"When is your baby coming? I would guess . . . November?"

"The end of September."

"That soon?" A look of motherly concern came over Marlajean's face. "It's late for you to be traveling—do you have your doctor's blessing?"

The thought had not occurred to Charlotte. She'd seen Dr. Olson only one time. He had confirmed the baby's approximate due date and Charlotte's general good health. Before that, her family doctor back in Ontario, Dr. Bruce, had first confirmed the pregnancy. Now, she supposed, she would need to find a new doctor.

"Not exactly, but I'm sure I'll be fine."

"I assume you're going to visit your husband?" Marlajean's eyebrows were raised high and a wide smile broadened her pretty face.

"Yes." Charlotte smiled back and nodded enthusiastically. "I can't wait."

"How long has it been?"

Charlotte thought about the day her beloved Reginald boarded the troops' train in their hometown, before even she knew about the coming baby. "Too long," she said. "Seems like a lifetime."

"I know what you mean."

The evening passed pleasantly enough. It being too dark to read, Marlajean continued chatting with Charlotte until they both dozed into a restless night as the train kept chugging along.

In her dreams, Charlotte ran through a crowded train station, dodging soldiers and old women and children as she fought her way through the throng. A sense of urgency engulfed her, and she looked over her shoulder every few steps. Her legs felt like they were trying to carry her through knee-deep water, making progress nearly impossible. Each time she awoke to the rocking motion of the train, a sense of relief washed over her—only to return to the same dream. The entire thing was overshadowed with a vague sense of guilt, but she refused to let her mind dwell on that. She was doing what she had to do.

At some point in the middle of the night, Charlotte awoke to stomach cramps. She lumbered to the rear of the car to use the lavatory, but her discomfort only grew. She returned to her seat and tried to relax. Had the chicken in her sandwich gone bad? She shifted her position every few minutes, but sleep would not return. Another two trips to the lavatory didn't help.

The sun was peering over the eastern horizon when Marlajean awoke, rubbing her eyes and stretching her limbs. After just one glance at Charlotte, motherly concern swept across her face again.

"Are you okay, honey? You're looking awfully pale."

Charlotte groaned. "No, I'm not. I think I ate some bad chicken last night."

"Did you throw up yet?"

"No. It's not really that kind of sick."

"Diarrhea?"

"No. Just pain. It comes and goes." Charlotte laid her hand across her abdomen to indicate where the pain was.

"Oh no." Marlajean placed her hand over Charlotte's. "When did you say this baby was coming?"

"Not for five more weeks."

Marlajean sighed. "Okay. Try to relax, honey. This is probably just false labor."

"Labor?"

"*False* labor. It might come and go for weeks." She pulled a blanket over Charlotte's shoulders. "I'm taking Trudy to the lavatory. You try to relax. I'll bring you some tea to sip."

Charlotte felt weak as she watched them leave, as if a lifeline were being pulled away from her. How could she get sick now? By the end of this day, she'd be with Reginald! She couldn't show up sick, she just couldn't. Maybe Marlajean was right. Whatever this "false labor" was, it would soon pass.

"I'll be okay," she whispered. "God, let me be okay." Charlotte could not recall the last time she'd called upon God for anything, but she had no sooner done so than a gush of warm water soaked the seat beneath her. It took her a minute to realize it was coming from her body.

"Marlajean?" Her call came out in a distressingly weak croak. She tried again. "Marlajean?"

CHAPTER 9

Reuben had accompanied Maggie home from the funeral before returning to his office, where he spent several hours writing Sunday's sermon on "Comforting the Mourning."

There seemed to be enough mourning within his congregation to merit a year's worth of sermons. Someone had left a note on his desk saying the Richards family had received word their son was wounded. His life was out of danger, but he'd be returning home with no legs. Reuben made a note to visit the boys' parents first thing in the morning.

And the needs didn't end with his parish. Hardly a home in the city was untouched by some sort of disaster, it seemed. Even today, he'd felt a pang of guilt over spending so much of his time ministering to Maggie Marshall because she was not officially part of his congregation. No one had complained yet, but he knew it was only a matter of time.

"Your flock pays your salary, Reverend Fennel," Walter Mitchell had told him late one night after a lengthy board meeting. "We're happy to have you reach beyond, as time allows, of course. But not at the expense of our own."

If only he could convince his people of the need to minister to one another and help carry the load. Even Jesus had a team of disciples to help distribute the loaves and fishes he provided. Reuben based the sermon he was writing on Galatians 6:2: "Bear ye one another's burdens, and so fulfill the law of Christ."

When he was finally satisfied with his work, he looked up and was surprised to see the sun had gone down. With a sigh, he turned off his desk lamp and walked to Mrs. O'Toole's boardinghouse. One lamp in the entry remained on, and his landlady's calico cat rubbed up against his leg in greeting.

"Good evening, Sheila. Are you the only one still up?" He crouched down and stroked the black, orange, and cream-colored fur until the purring began. On the dining room table, a plate of food sat covered with a dish towel. He lifted the edge of the cloth and peered beneath. Some sort of potato-and-ham dish with a side of sliced carrots filled the plate. Even the wonders that typically flowed from Mrs. O'Toole's kitchen couldn't fuel his appetite tonight. But, knowing he'd never hear the end of it if he left the food untouched, he carried the plate upstairs to his room and laid it on his desk. Perhaps he could eat the meal later.

After peeling off his jacket and clerical collar, he splashed a little water on his face at the sink in the corner of the room. He lay across the bed, staring up at the ceiling, hands behind his head. It had been a long day and he had accomplished so little.

He couldn't get his mind off Maggie Marshall.

The woman was simply not the same person he'd once known. When she wasn't being grouchy or downright mean, she acted like a frightened sheep, looking to him for help he felt completely inadequate to provide. Somewhere beneath that bitter mask, though, the joy-filled girl he had once known must still be hiding. He felt sure of it, but how on earth did one begin to find her?

The jangling of the telephone downstairs caused him to stir, and Reuben realized he had fallen asleep still fully clothed. He glanced at the clock on his dresser. Four a.m. How long had he been asleep? Was that a parishioner in need of his services? *Please, Lord. Not tonight. I'm so tired.*

When a knock sounded at his door moments later, he knew the call was for him. Mrs. O'Toole stood in the hallway in her robe and slippers.

"Telephone for you then, Rev'rend."

"I'm so sorry your sleep was disturbed, Mrs. O'Toole."

"Nonsense. I was readin' in bed, I was. Couldn't sleep anymore. And if it's the Lord's work you're bein' called to, I consider it a privilege to be a part of it."

"Thank you." Reuben plodded down the stairs and picked up the phone, praying it was not Bonnie Cartwright on the line.

"Reuben Fennel here."

"Reuben? It's Maggie."

"Maggie? Is everything all right?"

"That darn girl has run off."

Reuben's brain couldn't shift gears fast enough. "What girl?"

"Charlotte. My waitress. I wasn't concerned at first. When I got home, I found a note saying she'd gone walking and might visit her friend Rose. Rose's family runs the bakery up the street, and the girls have gotten acquainted. I was exhausted and went to bed."

"What do you mean, she's run off?"

"She's still not back. When I went to check her bedroom, it was stripped of her belongings. Well, almost. She left a few items, but I haven't seen her wear any of them since she first came."

"Did you check with Rose?"

"Yes, I walked over there and woke up the whole family. They were none too pleased, let me tell you. Rose said she hasn't seen Charlotte for a week or more."

"Have you called the police?"

"I did. They said they don't consider someone missing until it's been twenty-four hours."

"Did you tell them she's pregnant?"

"No. Didn't think it would make a difference."

"What about her parents?"

"Charlotte's parents are not . . . how can I say this?" Maggie sighed. "They're off on a holiday. When I called their home and got no answer, I remembered Charlotte mentioning that they were traveling through the western states, then back up to Canada, and would pick Charlotte up on their way home to Ontario. Guess they figure she'll have had the baby and given it to the adoptive parents, and it will all be over by the time they get here."

Reuben shook his head. What kind of parents treated their daughter that way?

"I have a hunch, though," Maggie continued. "Someone scribbled some numbers on my ink blotter, and it wasn't me. Sure looks like a train schedule. I think she might be trying to go see that boyfriend of hers in Petawawa."

"Is he the father of her baby?"

"Yes, but he doesn't know anything about it. Looks like he's about to find out, though. Unless I can track her down first."

"I'll do whatever I can to help you, Maggie." Reuben couldn't imagine what he could do, but he was fully awake now.

"Know anybody who's got a car and would consider loaning it to me? I figure maybe if I leave right away, I can find out the train schedule and get to one of the stops before her train does."

Reuben knew that was nearly impossible. The roads into northern Ontario were rough gravel at best and boggy trails everywhere else. "Have you traveled much? The roads—"

"I wasn't calling for your opinion. I'm looking for a car to borrow."

"But Maggie, you'll never—"

"I have a regular customer who makes the trip all the time in his delivery truck. Says he can get from Fort William to Winnipeg in a day." Reuben could picture the stubborn set of Maggie's jaw.

"You'd never catch up with a train."

"Besides, the train has to stop at every town along the way. I don't."

"Still. She's way ahead of you, Maggie."

"I'll drive all the way to Petawawa if I have to. She's bound to get off there."

Reuben could hear the determination in Maggie's voice, but the idea sounded ludicrous to him. "Surely if you wait, the police will be able to help you."

"*I'm* responsible for that girl, Reuben. If you can't help me, I'll keep asking elsewhere. Good-bye."

"Maggie, wait!" Reuben sighed. "I have a car. It's been parked for months, ever since they started rationing gas. You can use it."

"Thank you. Can you meet me at the train station so I don't lose any more time?"

"Wait! What about fuel?"

"I'll figure that out as I go along. We're just wastin' time yammering on the phone."

There was no way Reuben was willing to see Maggie or any woman taking off cross-country without adequate fuel rations, and it would take nearly a year's worth to make the round trip she was considering. "Listen. One of our deacons works for the oil controller's office, and he got me one of those Special Class A ration cards for church emergencies. I, um . . . was supposed to turn it in if I put my car in storage, but . . . it's not technically in storage. If you insist on going, then I insist that you take the card."

Silence.

"Maggie? You there?"

"Thank you, Reuben." Was that a catch he heard in her voice? "I'm leaving for the train station the minute I hang up this telephone. I'm going to find out if anyone saw her. No sense going off on a wild goose chase if she didn't actually get on a train."

"I'll meet you there as soon as I can. But for the record, I really don't think this is a good idea."

The phone went dead without a good-bye from Maggie. Replacing its receiver, Reuben tossed up a quick prayer for help and took the stairs two at a time. He changed his clothes, threw a few items into a bag, and looked out the window to where his car had been sitting for months. The light from his bedroom window reflected off its hood. Would the thing even run properly?

Mrs. O'Toole stood in the hallway wringing her hands.

"Has something awful happened, Rev'rend? Have we lost another one of our boys?"

"No, nothing like that. I'm going to help a friend, that's all. I may be gone a day or two, Mrs. O'Toole, and I'm taking my car. You can help by praying it'll start right off."

By the time Reuben got the 1938 Plymouth running and a thick layer of dust washed off the windshield, the sun was coming up and Mrs. O'Toole had pulled together a bag of sandwiches. He accepted it gratefully when she handed it to him with a somber "God bless you."

He didn't know whether he'd need the lunch, but he knew one thing for sure. He was not letting Maggie Marshall go on this quest without him.

CHAPTER 10

Maggie took one step inside Union Station on Main Street and was bowled over by memories. The scents of luggage and floor cleansers and the sounds of train whistles and destinations being called out over the public address system took her right back. Suddenly it was 1926 and she was sixteen years old again.

At first, she'd been excited about the plans to accompany her mother to Calgary to visit her aunt Audrey. It was her first train trip, and she and her mother would not return for three weeks. The station was still relatively new then and was bustling with activity and travelers. The magnificent dome overhead and the elaborate circular design in the marble tiled floor filled her young heart with awe. But though she gawked long and hard at all the unfamiliar sights, her heart was heavy.

Maggie's best friend, Susan Cuthbert, was carrying a secret burden no girl should have to shoulder. Maggie and Susan had become playmates as preschoolers. Susan lived just four doors down from Maggie and once they started school, they grew inseparable. People teased them about being Siamese twins, but they loved it. They shared everything—clothes, books, and secrets. Even when Susan started going out with Bobby Lodge, and Maggie was still years from having her first boyfriend, their friendship remained strong.

It had been a month since Susan confided her fear.

Maggie had tried to convince her to see a doctor to confirm the pregnancy, but doing so would mean telling her parents, which Susan refused to do.

"They're going to find out sooner or later, Suze," Maggie said. "I'll go with you. It'll be okay."

And so she had. But it was not okay.

Even as Maggie packed her bag to accompany her mother on this trip, she knew Suze was packing her own bags. Her parents were sending her on a trip too—not to some place where she could have the baby, but some place where they would "take care of it." Susan would return in a few days, no longer pregnant. The nightmare would be over, no one would be the wiser, and her parents would make sure Suze never saw Bobby Lodge again.

Three weeks later, Maggie and her mother returned to this same train station. She couldn't wait to visit Susan. Her father met them and carried their baggage, but was unusually quiet. Maggie immediately began peppering him with questions. Was Susan home yet? Had he seen her? Could Maggie go see her?

"We'll talk when we get home" was all he said.

Before Maggie could even carry her bag upstairs, her father sat her and her mother down at the kitchen table. Until the day she died, Maggie would never forget the expression on Daddy's face nor the wave of nausea that overcame her when he told her Susan was dead.

"What did they do?" her mother demanded. "Take her to some filthy backstreet witch doctor who—"

"No, Martha. Susan never even left home." He swallowed hard. "She took her own life."

Maggie could only stare. It had to be a mistake.

Daddy opened the drawer where they kept scissors and string and pulled from it a sealed envelope with *Maggie Sutherland* written on the front. When he handed it to Maggie, she immediately recognized Susan's handwriting.

"I would appreciate it if you could read that here, with your mother and me, Maggie. But if you want to wait—or take it to your room—I understand."

Maggie looked at both her parents. She could read in their faces their concern for her and knew they had loved Susan like their own daughter. With a massive sigh, she opened the envelope but did not read aloud. Doing so would have been impossible. Her parents waited patiently while she read in silence, disbelief flooding her heart with every sentence Susan had written.

Maggie,

By the time you read this, you will know what I have done. I am so sorry, my dearest friend in all the world, my sister, my kindred spirit. I know if you were here, you would try to talk me out of it and I would probably listen to you because I always do. That's why, in the long run, it is best that you are away.

I made the grave mistake of telling Bobby about the baby. I thought he would be on my side, that he would rescue me somehow. Instead, he agreed that my parents' solution is the only way. It hurt me, but I prepared my heart to follow through with the plan everyone agreed was best. I took comfort in knowing Bobby would still be there for me and we would have more children after we married. But when I went to Anderson's Drugstore on an errand for my mother yesterday, I saw Shirley Fox and Bobby laughing together at the soda fountain. When I confronted him, Bobby told me it was over between us and I should quit being such a child.

You are the only one who has not condemned me. For that alone, I am grateful. But I cannot bear the pain of all this, Maggie. Maybe I am taking the coward's way out, but how can I face the rest of my life—sixty or seventy years—living with this pain, guilt, rejection? It's too much. You understand, don't you? I hope you can find it in your heart to forgive me.

You have been the best thing in my life and I love you with all my heart. I am so sorry, my dear friend.

Suze

Maggie slid the letter across the table toward her father. Her mother leaned into his shoulder and they read it together, in silence. By the time they were done, Maggie's mother was sobbing.

Not a single tear formed for Maggie. She quietly picked up her suitcase and carried it upstairs to her room, where she undressed, pulled a nightgown over her head, and crawled under the covers. That night, sleep refused to come. The words of Susan's letter, however, stayed with Maggie, one line in particular repeating itself mercilessly:

I know if you were here, you would try to talk me out of it and I would probably listen to you because I always do.

Like the waves that had rolled off Lake Winnipeg when she'd gone to Grand Beach once as a little girl, the words continued to rise to her mind, unbidden. But instead of refreshing coolness, they brought only pain.

I will find a way to make it up to you, Suze, Maggie thought at the time. *I should have been a better friend.*

Maggie paused only briefly after entering the station. It was not the first time she had been to this place since Susan's death, but she'd forgotten the effect it always had on her. With a quick intake of breath, she tightened her grip on her purse and marched to the ticket counter. At this hour of the morning, the place was relatively quiet and only one window was open. A man who looked old enough to be Maggie's grandfather sat behind it.

"Where to?" he asked.

"Oh, I'm not buying a ticket." Maggie leaned in so she could speak as softly as possible. "I'm looking for someone. Would you happen to know if a young woman came through here yesterday afternoon, buying a ticket for Petawawa, Ontario?"

"Ma'am, we probably saw hundreds of young women come through here yesterday."

"I realize that," Maggie said. "But this one would be hard to miss. Nearly eight months pregnant. Only seventeen years old. Blond hair."

"You her mother?"

"I'm her guardian."

"Run away, did she?"

"Please. Do you take names of passengers?"

"No, ma'am. But if she wanted to get to Petawawa, she would have taken the 4:50 to Ottawa."

"Where is that train now?"

The man flipped some pages in a thick book off to the side. Maggie could see it was a train schedule but couldn't make out the details.

"Should be pulling into Fort William station in about an hour." He turned back to Maggie. "Got a picture of her?"

"No. I—she hasn't been with me that long."

"You call the police?"

"Yes. They can't help me. Not yet."

The man sighed and leaned toward Maggie. "Look. I've raised kids myself. I don't know if your girl came through here or not, but the last ticket I sold before I got off duty yesterday was to a young blond lady. I remember because when she walked away, she dropped her purse. I watched her pick it up and that's when I noticed her condition. Expecting, like you said."

"Do you remember what she was wearing?"

"Can't say I recall. But her ticket was for Petawawa and she paid with exact change."

"Can the railroad have her detained in Fort William?" Maggie felt sure she was grasping at straws.

"No, ma'am, we can't do that. Not unless she tries to go further than her ticket allows."

"Where would I have to drive to in order to intercept her train?"

"Can't be done. You'd have had to leave yesterday, ma'am."

Maggie felt a hand on her arm and turned around. Reuben Fennel stood there, concern on his face.

"Reuben! Thanks for meeting me. I think my hunch was right." They walked away from the booth and Maggie told him what the ticket vendor had said, except for the part where it couldn't be done.

"How long do you think it will take me to drive all the way to Petawawa if I have to?" she asked him.

The sincerity of Reuben's next words matched the warmth in his brown eyes. "I'm going with you, Maggie."

Maggie stared at him. Although part of her sighed with relief at the thought of having company, she couldn't ask this of him.

"I can drive, Reuben. I just need to borrow your car."

"This is not up for discussion. Come on, we're losing time." He headed for the front doors with a determined march.

Maggie half-ran to keep up. "Reuben, you can't just take off halfway across the country—"

Reuben stopped and turned. Was that the hint of a grin on his lips? "It's a huge country, Maggie. This jaunt is not even close to halfway across it."

"That's not the point. What about your job? You can't just take off—with me—on what could turn out to be a wild goose chase. Your congregation will never—"

"Technically, my congregation is funding the trip." He held the door open and Maggie walked through.

"The gas ration card. You told me. And I appreciate it, but—"

They had reached Reuben's car. "The card's got my name on it, therefore I have to go. Get in."

"I can't let you do this, Reuben."

"Then I can't loan you my car."

Maggie glared at him. They were losing time with every argument she raised.

"Fine." She climbed inside and slammed her door shut. "No skin off my nose if they fire you for inappropriate conduct."

Reuben ignored the comment. "I'm going to pray before we take off."

"Make it quick."

"Lord, you know where Charlotte is. Please help us find her. Keep her—and us—safe. And thank you for your provision of gas rations for the journey. Amen."

Maggie stared straight ahead as Reuben started the Plymouth and headed east out of the city.

CHAPTER 11

The early morning sunlight had turned to gray fog by the time Charlotte managed to hoist herself off the soaked upholstery of the train seat and walk to the lavatory. Marlajean and Trudy were no longer there. Only one other passenger hadn't left the car for breakfast, and he appeared to be fast asleep.

Closing the door behind her, she looked at her white face in the mirror. She dried off her body as best she could, doubling over whenever another wave of pain enveloped her. She splashed cool water on her face and was just drying it when she heard an urgent-sounding rap on the door.

"Charlotte? You in there?"

Marlajean. *Thank God.* Charlotte opened the door to see her new friend standing there, concern written all over her face.

"What's happening to me?"

"Charlotte, I want you to come back to your seat. We'll try to make you comfortable. Then I'm going to go speak to the conductor. We need to get you off this train as quickly as possible."

"I can't get off the train," Charlotte protested. "I've got to get to Reginald."

Marlajean spoke with the same tone she used on her little girl. "Sweetie, you need a doctor. If we're really lucky, there may be one on the train, but they're going to want you off as soon as possible, one way or the other. For now, I've rounded up a couple of blankets." She took Charlotte's arm to steady her and nudged her down the narrow aisle toward their seats. Trudy was busy with her coloring book. A cup of steaming tea sat in the holder by Charlotte's seat. Marlajean spread a blanket on the seat and eased Charlotte onto it.

"Try to take long, slow breaths. Do you think you can take a sip of this tea?"

Charlotte could feel the tears welling up and squeezed her eyes shut. She would not behave like a child, not after all she'd gone through to make her escape.

"Is the baby coming, Marlajean? Is that what this is?"

"Yes, honey, I think so. But try to relax. It could be a long time yet."

"But it can't come now! I have to get to Reginald!"

"Stay here, Charlotte. I'm going to go find help." Then Marlajean whispered softly to Trudy, who nodded and watched her mother walk away.

Charlotte looked at the little girl and tried to imagine what it would be like to have a child. Trudy was a sweet one. Brown curls framed a tiny face that seemed half-filled by big brown eyes. Charlotte had not heard her whimper or fuss once.

"Would you like me to sing you a song?" Trudy asked. "Mommy said I should."

Charlotte nodded as another contraction gripped her. She tried to breathe slowly like Marlajean had instructed while Trudy's soft voice filled the space between them.

> "Jesus loves me! This I know,
> For the Bible tells me so;
> Little ones to him belong;
> They are weak, but he is strong.
> Yes, Jesus loves me!

Yes, Jesus loves me!
Yes, Jesus loves me!
The Bible tells me so."

Charlotte knew the song from her childhood, but those years seemed an eternity away now. Her parents had taken her to Sunday school and attended church themselves, but God was not something they ever talked about between Sundays. *If Jesus loved her like the song said, why had he let her get into this mess?* But even as she thought this, she recognized that the mess was her own work and really couldn't be blamed on anyone, not even God.

"Keep singing, Trudy." Any distraction was welcome. The little girl sang the song through two more times, coloring while she sang.

Charlotte sipped the tea and tried to focus on the words Trudy sang as she gazed out at the hazy world. They were traveling through heavy forest now, but even the nearest trees were hard to see through the fog. She tried to sing along.

". . . little ones to him belong." *Little ones.* Like her baby? For the first time, Charlotte began to consider that the child inside her was more than just a part of her. A little one, who belonged to God. *Oh, my poor baby!* Would he or she be born on this train? What had she done? This child was supposed to be adopted. The lady who had come to talk to her about it already had a family picked out.

But she couldn't think about that now. As another contraction gripped her, Marlajean returned with a large red-faced man in a uniform.

"Charlotte, this is Mr. Scott, the conductor. He says there are no medical personnel on board, but we'll be in Fort William in about twenty minutes. He's already wired ahead and there will be an ambulance waiting to take you to the hospital."

"No! I don't want to go to a hospital, I have to get to Reginald!"

"We can send your husband a telegram, too, ma'am, if you like. But we can't let you stay on this train," the conductor said.

"It will be okay, sweetie," Marlajean said. "They'll take good care of you."

Mr. Scott scurried away. Just before reaching the end of the car, he turned and called back to Marlajean. "Stay with her, please. I'll take another walk through all the cars and ask one more time if there are any nurses or doctors aboard. Just in case we missed someone."

Marlajean sat down across from Charlotte and fished paper and a pencil out of her purse.

"Charlotte, if you give me your husband's name, I promise I'll do everything in my power to contact him and let him know where you are. But you have to realize he may not be granted leave anytime soon. Is there anyone else I can contact for you?"

Charlotte wiped at the tears that refused to be held back. "No. There's no one."

"What about your parents?"

"My parents are traveling. The baby wasn't supposed to come yet!"

"I know, honey, but we can't always predict these things. There must be someone I can call."

Charlotte thought of Mrs. Marshall, who was no doubt furious with her by now. No point in trying to call her. Even if she wanted to help, which was highly unlikely, what could she possibly do from so far away? She was probably glad to be rid of Charlotte.

"Please just send word to my—to Reginald. Private Reginald Wilson at Petawawa Military Camp. He's a cook."

Marlajean moved to Charlotte's seat and took her hand with a gentle touch. "You're not alone, Charlotte. You'll get through this. It may not all happen the way you hope, but eventually your husband will be free to come to you, and the three of you will be reunited as a happy family. You'll see."

At this, Charlotte's tears came in a torrent.

"You're wrong. You're so wrong, I can't even begin to tell you how wrong you are," she wailed.

But Marlajean only grew more persistent, patting Charlotte's hand and rubbing her arm. "In the meantime, I'm here with you. When we get to Fort William, there will be help waiting."

"You don't understand!"

"And no matter what happens, God is always with you. He loves you, Charlotte."

"He's not my husband!" Charlotte groaned.

"Of course God isn't your husband," Marlajean said. "Don't you see? A husband can leave, sometimes willingly and sometimes not. Sometimes a husband even dies. But God has promised to be with us always."

"*No!* I mean Reginald is not my husband. We're not married. He doesn't even know about the—"

Another contraction cut Charlotte's confession short. Marlajean stared at her, but Charlotte was in too much pain to explain further. When the pain had finally passed, she realized little Trudy was staring at her, too, her massive brown eyes looking bigger than ever.

"You're not married?" Marlajean said softly.

"No. My parents sent me to Winnipeg to stay until the baby comes. It's supposed to be adopted out. What's going to happen now?"

Marlajean pressed her lips together. "Sweetie, you've got to believe everything is going to work out. Right now you just need to focus on bringing this child into the world as best you can, okay?"

Charlotte looked into Marlajean's eyes and nodded. Was this how it felt to receive compassion from a mother? It was a new feeling, and she wished she could experience it under less urgent circumstances.

"Now, take a big breath and let me wipe those tears from your cheeks." As Marlajean did, Charlotte felt like a baby herself. How had she ever thought she was all grown up?

"I don't know if I can do this," she confessed.

"Of course you can. Women have been doing this since creation."

"Will you stay with me?"

Marlajean sighed. "I can't, honey. Trudy and I need to stay on the train and get where we're going. My parents are waiting. But let me write some things down first."

Between contractions, Charlotte gave Marlajean all the information she could think of: Maggie Marshall's name, address, and phone number. Her parents' contact information and expected time of arrival home. Even Reginald's parents were added to the list, though Charlotte begged her to save that information to use only if she became desperate, since neither Reginald nor his family knew about her pregnancy. Marlajean wrote it all down twice, on two separate slips of paper. She tucked one into her purse just as the train began to slow.

"Fort William," a voice rang out as a steward made his way through the car.

"I'll help you get off," Marlajean said. She began gathering Charlotte's things when the conductor, Mr. Scott, returned.

"There's an ambulance waiting, ma'am," he said. "We'll unload you first."

Charlotte felt like so much unwanted freight at the idea of being *unloaded*. She didn't know whether to be relieved or fearful, but she knew she somehow had to be brave. With one hand, Mr. Scott carried Charlotte's bag, and with the other, he tried to steady her. Marlajean gripped her other elbow and did her best to support her as they made their way along the aisle and down the steps. As she stepped onto the platform, another contraction struck, and Charlotte leaned heavily into Marlajean until it passed. A nurse and a driver, both dressed in all white, jumped down from a big white car with a red cross on the side. They helped Charlotte into a wheelchair.

"This is Charlotte Wilson," Marlajean said to the nurse, handing her one of the sheets of paper. The two women spoke together quietly while Mr. Scott and the man in white escorted Charlotte to the waiting ambulance. She suddenly realized she hadn't given Marlajean her own last name, and amidst the confusion, she overheard her friend mistakenly providing Reginald's. Just as she was about to try to correct the situation, another labor pain hit her.

In less than a minute, Charlotte was settled in the vehicle and covered with warm blankets. The nurse sat beside her, checking her blood pressure and pulse, before the ambulance pulled away from the station. Charlotte looked up at the young woman. Her blond hair was pulled neatly into a bun beneath a securely pinned white nurse's cap. Her reassuring smile helped Charlotte feel more at ease.

"How far is it?" she asked.

"It will only take us a few minutes to get to the hospital. I'm Nurse Bailey, and they sent me specifically because I'm a maternity nurse. You'll be just fine."

"Did Marlajean tell you—?"

"The lady who was with you? She gave me a list of names and addresses. We'll do our best to locate someone from your family."

"But did she tell you that I'm not . . . that the baby is supposed to be—"

Another contraction swept over Charlotte then, and suddenly nothing else mattered.

CHAPTER 12

Maggie had fallen fast asleep on the passenger side of Reuben's car, a light jacket rolled into a ball under her cheek. Reuben saw a sign for Oxdrift and could use a break, but decided to drive right through so Maggie wouldn't wake up. His gas station road map told him he could follow the route he was on as far as Fort William, and the gravel road had not been as bad as he feared. As long as it didn't rain, they might be able to make pretty decent time.

Please keep the car running, Lord. Help us find Charlotte.

The girl was so young. He'd seen her only briefly the few times he'd stopped at Bert's for coffee or lunch. He knew Maggie wasn't easy on the girls she employed and lodged, but he had to believe her heart was soft toward them. He'd heard the panic in her voice over the telephone and seen her near tears at the train station. Why did she work so hard to not let it show? Did Charlotte have any idea how much Maggie truly cared?

Again, his mind returned to the Maggie he had known years before. Maybe things could have turned out differently for her if only he'd had the courage to declare his feelings then. She'd have made a wonderful pastor's wife. *Back then.* He tried to imagine her winning over his congregation now, with her cold demeanor and sarcastic wit. He chuckled aloud at the thought of his board confronting Maggie's forthrightness. It would be an all-out war.

At the sound of his laugh, Maggie stirred, and he watched her settle into sleep again. Though the years had added a hardness to her features, the beauty beneath it remained. If only that wild head of red hair could receive a little tender loving care instead of being yanked into a fierce bun all the time . . .

Forgive me, Lord. Reuben disrupted his thought with a prayer. *The woman hasn't even been widowed a week. Help me keep my mind on the mission, to not try to pick up what I let go way back then.*

Maggie stirred again, this time stretching her arms and giving a massive yawn. "Need me to drive awhile?"

"No, I'm okay. I'm sure I got more sleep last night than you."

"Well, I'm awake now." Maggie sat up straight and began smoothing her hair.

"Need a stop?"

"No, not unless you do. We need to get as far as we can as fast as we can."

"Agreed." Reuben glanced into his rearview mirror, then at Maggie. "I've been thinking. How much do you know about Charlotte's boyfriend?"

Maggie was pulling pins from her hair and re-twisting her bun. With her hands thus occupied, she spoke around the bobby pin between her lips. "Just his name and that he's stationed at Petawawa. Why?"

"Any idea how he might react if she makes it there?"

"He'll be shocked out of his khaki pants, that's what. He doesn't even know about the baby." Maggie pushed the last pin through her hair.

"You're kidding." How could such important information be withheld? It didn't seem right.

"Charlotte's parents forbade her to see him. Said no boy, including that one, would ever marry her if she didn't keep it a secret."

"And she hasn't contacted him in all this time?"

"Not as far as I know."

Reuben shook his head. "I'm trying to put myself in that boy's position."

"Well, first of all, that boy isn't you. You wouldn't have gotten a girl in that way in the first place. Secondly, Charlotte is twitter-pated."

"Twitter-pated?"

Maggie waved one hand around in the air. "Always got her head in the clouds, imagining who knows what. She probably thinks Reginald will be waiting with arms wide open, regardless of her condition."

Reuben couldn't help giving a soft chuckle. "And you don't think he will be?"

"I think she's setting herself up for the biggest heartache of her twitter-pated life." Maggie looked out her window and Reuben was sure he saw her swallow hard.

"And you'd like to spare her if you can."

Maggie just pressed her lips together.

"Why does it matter, Maggie?"

"I took responsibility for her, didn't I? Her parents expect me to see this through until the baby comes. I need to make good on that. That's all." She looked out her window again.

"Well, I sincerely doubt your commitment included chasing across the country after a runaway."

"It's a big country, Reuben. We're not going to cross it. Remember?"

Reuben chuckled and shook his head. The sunny day was disappearing into a light fog, and he prayed it would not slow them down.

"Sure hope Charlotte's train stops at every little settlement along the route." Maggie was studying the road map. "If we can just get ahead of it, then it's only a matter of waiting at one of the stops, and when she gets off to stretch her legs, we've got her."

"What if she refuses to come home with you?" Reuben took his eyes off the road to study Maggie's face and saw her looking at him out of the corner of hers.

"That's why you're along."

Reuben grinned. "You counting on my powers of persuasion, my charm, or my brute strength?"

"All three."

They rode in silence for a while. Despite the serious nature of the trip, Reuben felt glad to be with someone he could relax around. It seemed these days he spent all his time with either needy or critical parishioners, or with Mrs. O'Toole and Sheila, her cat. The other two boarders were closer to his age than was his landlady. Nettie Renfrew was a schoolteacher and Robert Broadford worked for the Greater Winnipeg Victory Loan Organization, around the clock sometimes. But Reuben rarely saw either one of them.

Reuben thought back to the previous winter, when Winnipeg had organized "If Day," a mock Nazi invasion that educated people on what was happening in Europe, promoted the purchasing of war bonds, and raised three million dollars for the war effort. Reuben still had a copy of the *Tribune* from that day, February 19, 1942, tucked somewhere in his filing cabinet. The paper's name was crossed out on the front page and *Das Winnipeger Lügenblatt* (*The Winnipeg Lies-sheet*) appeared instead.

They had all hoped the war would be over by now.

"Visibility's getting bad." Maggie's words pulled Reuben back to the present. "Don't suppose the fog slows the trains down any, eh?"

"It's doubtful. Don't worry, Maggie. We'll catch up with her eventually, even if we have to drive all the way to Petawawa. We know she's not going any further, right?"

"I suppose there's a chance she'd try to carry on to Toronto once she realizes she can't just waltz into a military training camp like some kind of princess and walk off with her prince. Will that gas card of yours take us that far?"

"I think so."

Maggie pulled apart the drawstrings of a small pouch and counted whatever was inside. "I'm surprised she had enough money to even buy the ticket she did. With what I pay her."

"So you admit it."

"What?"

"You're stingy."

"Who said anything about stingy? My girls get room and board. That should be enough for the easy bit of work I ask of them. Their pay envelopes are just gravy."

"Uh-huh."

"Don't give me that judgmental 'uh-huh' business. You know they're getting a good deal."

"I'm pretty sure you are too."

"It's a mutually beneficial arrangement, what can I say? Look out for that skunk!"

But it was too late. In an explosion of black and white fur, Reuben's Plymouth instantly ended the skunk's life, which in turn filled the car with a powerful stench.

"Oh no." He drove another half mile to get away from the source, then pulled over to the side of the road. The two of them opened the doors wide and left them that way while they climbed out, still coughing. Maggie, who'd been holding a handkerchief over her nose and mouth, now waved it around as though the motion could miraculously clean the car, the air, and them. Her attempts to improve things only brought on another fit of coughing, which made Reuben snicker.

"Sorry," he said. "But sometimes you just have to laugh."

"You don't look so sophisticated yourself. But you look a dang sight better than you smell."

Reuben and Maggie locked eyes, but he had no comeback. Trying to contain his laughter only made it worse.

"Aw, go ahead. May as well laugh. It beats cryin'."

He let loose then, and Maggie joined in. It felt good to laugh hard, but it felt even better to see Maggie surrender to it, her face lit up with laughter. When the mirth finally diminished, Reuben produced the bag of Mrs. O'Toole's sandwiches from the trunk. "If these aren't completely ruined, we might as well eat them now."

Thankfully, the food had been tightly wrapped and secured inside Mrs. O'Toole's metal Beekist honey pail with a snug lid. They sat on a car blanket on the side of the road and relished the sandwiches, chuckling again every once in a while. When the picnic was over, there was nothing to do but climb back inside the smelly car and carry on down the road.

"We'll stop at the next town and see what we can do about the stink," Reuben said. "I could use something to drink anyway."

They didn't have far to go. But when they pulled into the little gas station in Dryden, it seemed their odor had arrived before they did.

"Hoo-ee! Smells like somebody tangled with a nasty one," the attendant said. "There's a hose around back if you want to spray her down."

"My car or my traveling companion?" Reuben said, loud enough for only Maggie to hear. She gave him a look that would shrivel a green apple and climbed out of the car.

"If your wife would like to use a nicer facility, she can go on over to the house next door," the attendant said, pointing. "The boss owns it, and his wife insists the ladies shouldn't have to use our station toilet."

"Oh, thank you, but she's not—" Reuben looked up in time to see that Maggie had caught the man's words and was already headed over to the house. "Never mind."

He hosed down the car after the tank was filled.

At the local grocery store, Maggie stayed in the car while Reuben endured more looks of disdain as his scent greeted the people inside before he could even open his mouth.

"Can I get a couple of Cokes?" Reuben asked at the counter. "I'll take two apples, too."

The cashier wasted no time in putting the order together and taking Reuben's money. When he returned to the car, Maggie was in the driver's seat.

"Figured you could use a rest," she said. "You couldn't have slept much last night either."

Reuben didn't argue. They drank their Cokes in silence, and before they'd gone twenty miles, he was fast asleep.

CHAPTER 13

Maggie hadn't driven a car in years, and she was one of the few women she knew who had learned at all. When she was still going out with Douglas, he had proudly taught her to drive his 1920 Hudson. He still had the car when they married, but didn't keep it for long. He told Maggie he'd sold it, but she never saw any evidence of the proceeds. When one of his poker buddies drove by in it the very next week, her suspicions were confirmed. Douglas had lost it in a game.

Maggie's brother had also taken her for a few rides in his car before he went off to war, and he'd let her have a turn at the wheel now and then. She missed Bert Junior. He was a musician and had spent most of his adult life before the war on the road. In his last letter, he'd written that he was hoping for a transfer to the entertainment unit called the Tin Hats. Their father's dying wish had been that Bert Junior would take an interest in the restaurant like Maggie had, and that he would one day be a partner. But her brother had made it perfectly clear he had no such inclination.

Thoughts of the restaurant reminded Maggie of Earl and his insistence that he was now her partner. It would have broken her father's heart to see his beloved restaurant fall into the hands of a man like Earl Marshall. It was just as well he'd never know.

Maggie supposed there was one good thing about getting side-tracked by this road trip. At least she hadn't had time to worry about her problems with her brother-in-law. At least, not until now. With Reuben asleep and nothing but the road stretching out before her, she found herself wondering what would transpire when she returned to Winnipeg. There had to be a way to keep Earl out of her business.

She hit a bump in the road and Reuben startled awake.

"What was that?" He looked around.

"Just a bump. What's the matter? Don't trust a woman driver?"

"Would I have let you drive if I didn't?"

Maggie grinned. "I'll try to be more careful. You can go back to sleep."

But Reuben's eyes stayed open, though he kept his head resting on the seat. After they'd sat in silence for a while, he said, "Next town, I think we should find the train station and see if we can learn where Charlotte's train is now. Don't you?"

"Sure."

Some time passed before he spoke again. "I've been wondering something."

Maggie waited until her patience gave out. "That's it? You've been wondering something?"

Reuben sighed. "If Charlotte decided to get off somewhere along the way, how would we know?"

"Why would she do that?"

Reuben didn't answer, and his silence unnerved Maggie. "Huh, Reuben? Why would she get off early? You know something I don't?"

Still, the man was slow to answer. And vague, once he did. "I . . . might."

"You might? What's that supposed to mean?"

"I can't be sure."

"Listen, mister, if you have more information, you better speak up." *How infuriating.*

Reuben appeared to be chewing on the inside of his cheek. "Okay. This might sound kind of crazy to you, Maggie, but . . . well, do you believe God speaks to people? Through dreams and such?"

So that's it, Maggie thought. *I'm traveling with a kook. I should have known he was too good to be true.* "I don't know. I haven't talked to God much lately, and he's never talked to me that I know of. What are you saying? Did he talk to you?"

"While I was sleeping before. How long was I out, anyway?"

"I dunno. An hour or so, I guess." *What on earth did he think God said?* "Did God tell you Charlotte got off the train?"

Reuben hesitated. "It's not so much what he told me." Another infuriating pause. "It's more like—an impression. No, more than that."

"A vision?"

"Maybe. I don't know how to explain it, but it's happened to me before."

Maggie wanted to believe him. "Has it ever been wrong before?"

Reuben grew strangely quiet while Maggie waited.

"No," he said finally. "Not even once."

"Well, that would come in kind of handy, wouldn't it? Can you just ask him stuff, like—say, what the stock market's going to do or who's going to win the playoffs?"

Reuben shook his head and looked out his window. "I knew I shouldn't have said anything."

As soon as she saw Reuben's lips clamp shut, Maggie regretted her teasing. "No, come on. I was only joking. I take you seriously. I do. You're a man of the cloth, for heaven's sake. Get it? For 'heaven's' sake?"

Maggie laughed, but Reuben only looked out the window. Chagrined, she decided to try a more serious tone. "So what was this 'impression'?"

Another sigh. "Let's just say I feel strongly that we won't need to drive any farther than Fort William."

"Well, that's pretty specific. You think she got off there?"

"I don't know. I just—maybe I'll know more when we get there."

Maggie let that sink in before she spoke. "How much farther to Fort William?"

Reuben studied the map. "We should be able to get there late tonight if the roads don't get any worse and the car keeps running."

Maggie tapped the steering wheel. "C'mon, car. Nice car."

When Reuben said nothing more, she decided to press him. "So, tell me about these dreams of yours. How often do they happen?"

"Very seldom, actually. Only a handful of times before. They're . . . not like regular dreams. But they're not like being awake either." He shook his head. "I can't explain it."

"Do you have regular dreams too?"

"Oh, sure. All the time. That's how I know these are different."

"What other things has God shown you, if you don't mind my askin'?" Maggie swerved to miss a hole in the road and hit some loose gravel. The Plymouth shimmied a little, then straightened out.

"If I tell you, it'll be the first time I've told anyone."

"Ever?"

Reuben nodded, but said no more. Maggie decided not to press. He would tell her in his own good time.

And if he didn't, it didn't matter.

The truth was, Reuben's dream had shaken him. Fifteen years had passed since his last one, and he'd thought those days were behind him. He figured they were an anomaly of his youth. Now that he had been to Bible college and was a fully ordained minister of the gospel, surely God expected him to search out truth for himself, from God's word. And he had. He spent long hours hunched over his Bible, reading and rereading, pulling out spiritual nuggets for his congregation and, sometimes, for himself. He memorized long passages of Scripture. He double-checked each verse against the original Greek or Hebrew to help him fully understand the text. He prayed before he wrote every sermon and prayed again before he delivered them. He asked God to cause him to forget anything he was supposed to leave out and to inspire him with anything he was supposed to add in. That way, when he sat down to lunch on Sunday afternoon, there would be no kicking himself over anything he'd forgotten. He took God at face value and trusted that what he had asked for, God had granted—and would continue to grant as long as Reuben prepared well.

He would just as soon not have the dreams. Or visions, or whatever they were. They were too unsettling. The thing is, he knew no way to describe them. He couldn't remember seeing or hearing anything in particular afterward. He only woke from them knowing something extraordinary had happened and feeling aware of a clear action he must take. Perhaps the reason their existence felt so painful to him was because of the one he'd chosen to ignore and the devastating results.

How much should he tell Maggie? She was so unpredictable, seemingly fierce in her independence one day, then entreating him for his assistance the next. In any case, she seemed to have lost the relationship with God she'd clearly had when they were young. Back then, Maggie talked about Jesus in a way that made it seem like she had coffee with him every morning.

He knew this might not be a good time to broach the topic, but they still had a long stretch of road ahead of them, hours to be filled with conversation. He turned and studied her face, seemingly intent on the road ahead. A strand of red hair had fallen loose from her hastily constructed bun, and she tucked it behind her ear.

"Can I ask you something?" he ventured.

"If you're wondering who taught me my stellar hairdressing skills, it's top secret."

Was Maggie's humor some kind of shield? He could play that game too. "Oh. In that case, I'll think of a different question."

"Shoot."

Reuben cleared his throat. "Unless my memory's failing, you had a really close connection with the Lord when we were teens."

Maggie paused. "That's not a question."

"I'm getting to it."

But he'd underestimated her depth of perception. "You wanna know what happened, don't you?"

"Well . . . yes. I *am* curious. If you want to tell me, that is."

Maggie sighed. "I guess I kind of owe it to you."

"No, not at all. You don't owe me anything. I'm just . . . It's hard to tell where your faith is now. I'd love to help you with that if I can. And if not, well . . . maybe something you've learned would be helpful to me."

Maggie sighed and gripped the steering wheel tighter. "I don't know, Reuben. Life is what happened, I guess. It's not that I don't believe in God anymore. I just . . . There have been some tough times, you know? And God wasn't there for me like I thought he'd be. Guess you could say I got disappointed with him and learned to get along on my own."

"I'm sorry."

"Not your fault."

"Maybe not. But when someone says 'God wasn't there for me,' it usually means God's people weren't there when the person needed help. Somebody was not obeying what God was asking them to do."

Maggie chewed on her bottom lip as she put another quarter mile behind them without speaking.

"Maybe that somebody was me," she admitted. "The week before my wedding, I had this feeling in my gut that I should break things off with Douglas. I brushed it off. Now I wonder if God was trying to tell me not to marry him."

"Why did you brush it off?"

"Oh, who knows?" Maggie's hands gripped the steering wheel, but her thumbs wiggled back and forth. "The invitations were already out, for one thing. I didn't want to face the humiliation. I guess you could say my pride got in the way."

Pride was something Reuben understood. "Did you talk to anyone about it?"

Maggie nodded. "A little, to my dad. He assured me it was normal to feel pre-wedding jitters. So I went ahead."

Reuben waited, wondering if she would say more or let it drop. He decided to prompt her. "You've sort of . . . indicated . . . that the marriage wasn't the best."

Maggie let out a snort. The car hit another bump in the road that made both of them smack their heads on the roof.

"Ow!" Maggie rubbed her head with her right hand, still gripping the steering wheel with her left.

"Ready for me to drive?"

"How far to the next town?"

Reuben studied the map again. "We should hit Ignace in thirty minutes or so."

"I'll be okay until then."

"At least the skunk smell is gone."

Maggie made a face. "We're probably just used to it."

"I guess we'll know next time we stop." Reuben sighed and looked out his window at the passing scenery. The prairie fields with their ripening crops had long since given way to lakes and trees, as far as he could tell through the fog. He figured Maggie was through discussing her personal affairs, but she surprised him.

"Got any more burning questions?"

He chuckled at her directness. "Yes, actually, I do. About Earl. He didn't seem all that threatening the day of the funeral. I can't figure out how a spunky woman like you was rendered silent by him. Shoot, I've given you more grief than he has and you've given it right back."

"You ain't seen nuthin' yet." Her words were light, but Reuben detected a layer of something else beneath them: anger, maybe. Or was it fear?

"I believe you. So why can't you do the same with Earl?"

"Reminds me too much of his brother." Maggie said nothing else for a long time, but then her three-word answer broke through the silence, delivered in little more than a whisper. "He beat me."

Reuben thought he hadn't heard correctly at first. *Who* had beaten her? Earl? That didn't make sense. But if she'd said what he thought she had, it had probably taken all the courage Maggie could muster to say it once. Asking her to repeat herself would be cruel. He looked at her, waiting for her to continue. He could see Maggie's eye dart sideways at him, then quickly back to the road. When she didn't speak, he sent up a quick prayer for wisdom and tried again.

"Douglas beat you?"

"Yes. Maybe you'd figured that out already."

Reuben tried to match Maggie's hushed voice by speaking as gently as he could. "No. I just want to be clear. Was it a one-time thing, or . . . ?"

"No." Maggie cleared her throat, and then spoke with more volume and conviction. "It should have been. I should have cleared out after the first time." She waved one hand away from the steering wheel as if dismissing the thought. "Don't ask me why I didn't."

"I wasn't going to." Reuben looked out the window again, hoping Maggie would feel more inclined to keep talking if she didn't feel scrutinized.

"I suppose you think I'm pathetic."

Reuben's head jerked to the left as he looked at her. "Pathetic? Maggie, I could never think of you that way. Do you want to talk about it?"

To Reuben's surprise, a tear began to run down Maggie's cheek and she brushed it away with her hand. "I'd rather not rehash the details." She sniffed. "But it is good to know someone else finally knows. Part of me wanted to stand up at the funeral and shout it out for everyone to hear, you know? Right when they were going on about what an upstanding guy he was."

Reuben looked down at his hands and saw that they were curled into fists. He couldn't stand the thought of any man becoming violent with a woman, but the fact that it had happened to Maggie felt like a personal offense.

"I wish I could have been there for you then." Reuben wasn't certain he'd even said the words aloud until Maggie responded with a resigned sigh.

"Guess you could have been, had I asked. Not your fault."

"What made you decide to tell me now?"

Maggie shrugged. "You told me a secret, I figured I could tell you one too. Anyway, he can't hurt me now. And I've learned I can get along just fine without a man around. In fact, I'm a lot better off. Looks like we're in Ignace."

Sure enough, a billboard displaying WELCOME TO IGNACE greeted them. Maggie slowed the car and they cruised into the main street of the small town. A gas station boasting the Imperial Oil brand stood on their right, and Maggie pulled up to the tank like an expert. Though their conversation was laid aside as they climbed out to stretch their legs, Reuben felt a stirring in his heart that made him want to wrap his arms around Maggie Marshall and never allow anyone to hurt her again.

CHAPTER 14

Charlotte hadn't known such pain was possible. Surely she was going to die. She would perish right here, no one back home would ever know where she was, and the people here wouldn't even know *who* she was. She'd probably be buried under some tree with a misidentified marker. Or no marker at all.

But every time she tried to tell someone her real last name, she was overcome by another contraction. This continued until her name no longer mattered. She just wanted the whole thing over, and if she ever laid eyes on Reginald Wilson again, all she wanted to do was punch him in the nose. He would never touch her again!

When they had arrived at the hospital (was it only hours ago? It felt like weeks), the medics had rolled Charlotte inside on the stretcher. Each bump felt unbearable. She had no idea where she was or what direction they were taking her. When they wheeled her alongside a bed and instructed her to move herself onto it, she refused to budge.

"We need to get you onto the delivery table, Mrs. Wilson," someone was saying. "As soon as the next pain subsides, lift your hips and scoot onto the table. You can do it."

"I'm not Mrs. Wilson!" Charlotte shouted. "I'm Charlotte Penfield!" With that, she gripped the sheets and wadded them into balls with both hands, hollering the whole time.

Nurses were undressing her and putting a hospital gown on her, as if that was going to help. After some pushing, lifting, and shoving from the medical staff, Charlotte found herself on the delivery table, her knees bent and her feet pushed into some sort of cold metal stocks. She felt like an animal. Or worse, a criminal.

"What are you doing to me?" Charlotte screamed. No one had prepared her for such indignities.

"You need to scoot down a bit, Mrs. Wilson, so the doctor can examine you."

"I told you I'm Charlotte Penfield. Penfield!"

"Sorry, Mrs. Penfield. Can you please scoot down just a little more?"

"Not *Mrs.* Penfield—*ooowww!*" Charlotte was certain she was about to black out, and truly hoped she would.

"Try to calm down, Mrs. Penfield. Your baby is going to come soon, but it will go much better for you if you can relax." The woman's voice came from behind her head somewhere.

Then a male voice. "Good afternoon, everyone. Who have we got here?"

"This is not one of your prenatal patients, Dr. Thompson," the nurse said. "She was passing through by train and went into early labor. Five weeks early or so, from what we can gather."

"First pregnancy?"

"Yes!" Charlotte shouted. The next thing she knew, the most uncontainable urge to push overcame her, and she didn't resist. Whether hours went by after that or merely minutes, she couldn't tell. It was all a blur of pain and pushing and bright lights and white-masked heads floating above her. After she managed one final push, the voices above her cheered. A baby wailed.

"You have a little son, Mrs. Penfield." Charlotte looked up at the smiling eyes above the mask. Her own eyes followed the doctor's gaze to the howling, naked infant in the nurse's hands. Then just as quickly, the baby was whisked away again. She closed her eyes tight and tried hard not to think about what was being done to her. Perhaps now she could die in peace. She'd never been so exhausted, not even after a whole day of waiting tables and washing dishes for Mrs. Marshall.

"Five pounds, ten ounces," a nurse announced. She brought the blanket-wrapped baby to Charlotte and held him out for her to take. "He's a little one, but he's perfect. Either you were further along than you thought you were, or this is an especially robust little man you have here."

Charlotte had never held a baby in her life. She didn't even like babies. They made her nervous.

"I'm not—I'm not supposed to—"

But the nurse was shoving the bundle into her arms. That's when Charlotte caught a glimpse of his tiny face. He had stopped crying, and now he squinted as though trying to focus on something. She took him in her arms.

"Hello, Baby."

The child squirmed, then relaxed. He looked up at Charlotte, and she felt suddenly overwhelmed by awareness of how utterly vulnerable he was.

"Oh, my goodness." Charlotte had thought she'd never cry again, after all the tears she'd shed in the last twenty-four hours. But she felt tears of a different sort welling now. Looking at her tiny son, she realized the magnitude of what she had done, who she had been carrying all these months, and the decisions that had already been made for his future.

"I've never seen a smaller human being," she whispered. "Anyone could do anything to you, and you'd be completely helpless. *Anything.*" This child would have to go wherever people carried him, consume whatever nutrition was offered him or die of starvation. He had no say at all. He was at the mercy of anyone who chose to pick him up, anyone who chose to love him or hate him, meet his needs or destroy him. She couldn't bear the thought.

"Mrs. Wilson, we need to contact your husband." A nurse stood next to Charlotte's bed, clipboard in hand. "Do you have a number where he can be reached?"

"My name's not—" Charlotte began. Then she looked down again at her son. He'd fallen fast asleep, a mere featherweight in her arms. "M-my husband is in the service."

"Overseas?"

"Yes," Charlotte lied. Panic rose in her throat. Surely if they knew the truth, this child would be ripped from her, and she'd never lay eyes on him again. "I'll be on my own until he returns, or until the war is over."

"What about your parents?"

Before she realized what she was saying, Charlotte gave the nurse Maggie Marshall's name and telephone number in Winnipeg. "My father is dead," she added. If they called Maggie, at least Maggie would know what had happened to her. She'd never come after her in a million years, and with her parents traveling, it might be weeks before they could be reached. By then, Charlotte and her son would have found their way to Petawawa and Reginald. Everything would be all right then.

The nurse left, and Charlotte studied her little boy some more. "You need a name, don't you, little guy? Yes, you do." Though she was tempted to name him after his father, something held her back. "What name do you like? You won't always be little, you know. You're going to grow so, so big and be a man just like your—"

For the first time, niggling doubts about Reginald's acceptance picked at her heart, though she wasn't sure why. If he were truly the love of her life, the hero she'd painted him to be, wouldn't he have found a way to write to her by now? Maybe Reginald didn't deserve to know about this little boy after all. Maybe Reginald didn't deserve *her*. She shook the thought off and turned to the baby, talking to him as if to an adult.

"I've always hated my own name. My mother would have died if she knew the boys at school called me 'Charlotte the Harlot.' I suppose I lived up to it, didn't I? There's a Charlotte in my favorite book, too—*Pride and Prejudice*. Charlotte was not an attractive young woman in that book. Unfortunately, my mother never read Jane Austen's book before she named me. I could name you after Mr. Darcy, but Mr. Darcy's first name was Fitzwilliam. I can't very well call you Fitzwilliam, can I? I suppose we could just call you Darcy. And Fitzwilliam for a middle name, since you were born in Fort William? Would you like that?"

The nurse returned. "I tried to place a telephone call to your mother, but the operator tells me there is no answer at this number. Should we try again later?"

"Yes." Charlotte's ruse had worked, granting her a reprieve. The baby started to fuss.

"He's getting hungry," the nurse said. "Have you fed him yet?"

"No." Charlotte had only a basic understanding of how mothers nursed infants. She'd never seen anyone do it, but a tingling sensation overtook her breasts all the same.

"Relax. I'll help get you started," the nurse said. "I'm Nurse Rhoden, by the way. You have a lovely little boy. So strong for a preemie."

Within ten minutes, baby Darcy was nursing hungrily and Nurse Rhoden busied herself with Charlotte's chart. "Change sides in five minutes or less," she said. "Otherwise, you'll regret it. I'll be back in ten." She left the room, humming.

Charlotte switched sides as instructed, but after only another minute on the second side, Darcy was fast asleep again. Charlotte stroked his hair, ran a finger over his velvety cheeks, and counted his tiny fingers and toes.

How could she have ever imagined she could give away her child?

"I'll fight for you, Darcy." Charlotte's voice was fierce. "No matter what my parents try to make me do. It's you and me, you hear me? You and me. No matter what."

CHAPTER 15

It was dark when Reuben and Maggie pulled into Fort William. Maggie had fallen asleep again after their last stop, their conversation unfinished. It wasn't difficult to find the train station. Reuben pulled up in front and turned off the engine with a tired sigh.

"We're here, Maggie."

She opened her eyes and yawned. "Fort William?"

"Yes. I came straight to the train station."

"You think she's here?"

"I don't know. Let's go inside and see what we can find out."

The lobby was deserted, one lone light hanging above several empty wooden benches. A middle-aged man with a boyish cowlick sat at the wicket.

"No more trains comin' or goin' tonight, folks."

"That's fine, we're not here to catch a train," Reuben explained. "Possibly to meet one, though. We're looking for a young woman who may have come through here today."

"You her parents or what?"

Maggie jumped in. "Guardians." She wished Reuben had worn his clerical collar. It might give them more credibility. "A blond girl, seventeen years old and pregnant. Her ticket was from Winnipeg to Petawawa."

"That train went through, all right. This morning. Won't be another one 'til Friday. What's that smell?"

"Sorry, we had a little run-in with a skunk," Reuben apologized. "Do you happen to know if she might have gotten off here?"

"Why would she do that if her ticket was for Petawawa?" The man leaned forward, as though he hoped for a piece of juicy gossip worth passing along.

"Just a hunch," Reuben said.

"Seems like a pretty silly hunch to me." The man leaned back again and flicked through the stack of tickets in his hand, licking his finger about every fifth one.

"We weren't asking for your opinion. Did you see the girl or not?" Maggie's foot tapped on the marble floor.

"Maggie," Reuben said quietly. This ticket vendor might be their only lead to Charlotte. There was no point in provoking him.

"Sorry," she mumbled.

"Look, I only came on duty at six o'clock tonight. Barney Lyall is the one you want to talk to. He would've been here when that train came through."

"Where can we find him?" Maggie asked.

"Oh, I wouldn't go bothering Barney this time of night if I were you. He's gotta be up by four in the morning to feed his chickens and goats before he comes to work at six. He can be a real bear."

Reuben looked up at the big clock behind the man. It was after midnight. Somewhere along the route, they'd crossed into a different time zone, and it was even later than he'd thought.

"He'll be here at six sharp, though. Always is. You're welcome to wait, just as long as you sit as far away from me as you can git." The man gestured to the hard wooden benches and returned to his ticket flicking.

Reuben looked at Maggie. She looked at the benches, then back at Reuben.

"Guess we gotta rest sometime," she said and shrugged. "But what if she's still on the train? We might be wasting precious time."

"She's not on the train anymore." Reuben moved to the farthest bench and sat down.

Maggie followed. "Then why isn't she here? Where would she go?"

"I don't know. Does she know anyone here?"

"I have no idea. Possibly. But how can you be so sure she got off here?" Maggie sat on a bench across from Reuben, a low table covered with newspapers between them. The headline on the top one read "Fed Judge Upholds Detention of Japanese-Canadians."

When Reuben only sighed, Maggie asked the question he'd dreaded. "These dreams of yours. Tell me how they work."

Reuben leaned in closer, and Maggie followed suit. "I wish I could. I don't really know how they work, and they don't always happen the same way. But I can tell you about one, just as an example."

"It's about time." Maggie pulled her shoes off and dropped them on the floor. Then she pulled her feet up onto the bench and rubbed them. "I'm all ears."

Reuben looked around. He'd never shared this with anyone before. If Maggie decided he was a lunatic after this, it was going to be a long trip home.

"The first time it happened, I was twelve. My father had helped me build a tree house in our backyard, and I used to spend my summer afternoons up there, after chores were done. Sometimes my buddy Clarence Kalbright joined me, and we had all kinds of adventures. But this time I was alone, reading and daydreaming. I fell asleep."

Reuben sighed again. How to describe it? There were no words. "I don't know exactly what happened. I don't remember seeing anything specific in my dream. Possibly a light, a bright and colorful light. But somehow, that description seems inadequate. And if I heard anything at all, it was instructions to go to the brown house on the corner, two blocks away—though I don't remember hearing anything, exactly.

When I woke up, I just knew that's what I had to do. I could see the house in my mind."

"Who lived there?"

"I didn't even know. It had been vacant quite some time, but we had noticed a new family moving in a week or so before. We hadn't met them. I climbed down from the tree house and walked the two blocks. When I first saw the brown house, nothing looked unusual, and I was tempted to turn around and go home."

Maggie's eyes were focused intently on Reuben's, shining in spite of her fatigue. "I'm guessing you didn't."

"I did turn around, actually. But the compulsion was so strong. I thought I could never live with myself if I didn't check further, even though I felt as silly as all get-out. So I went back and opened the gate and headed up the sidewalk to the front door. I was about to knock, when I heard something around the side of the house."

Reuben brushed his fingers through his hair. He leaned his elbows on his knees and looked down at his feet. "When I went around to the side of the house, I discovered a pile of collapsed boards. I pulled some of them away and discovered an old well. From where I stood I could hear whimpering. At first I thought it might be a puppy, but then I heard *Mommy* coming faintly from below. My heart was racing, I can tell you. It was too dark in the well to see the child, but I figured it couldn't be that deep if I could hear him whimper. I yelled for help as loud as I could, then started to climb down the well, bracing myself on both sides. Not the smartest move, in retrospect."

"Well, you were just a kid yourself." Maggie's eyes were wide.

"I was able to reach the child easily enough," Reuben said. "He'd landed on a ledge of some sort. In the darkness, I couldn't tell if he was hurt, but I stayed on the ledge and talked to him. He was only about two years old, I think. Thankfully, his mother had heard my cry for help and appeared at the top of the well.

"Long story short, I waited down there with the little guy until they could let down rescue ropes and pull him up, then me."

"So you're a hero." Maggie grinned.

"My father asked later how I happened to be walking past the brown house that afternoon, but I just shrugged. 'The Lord led him there, of course,' my mother said. 'And I pray every day that he will lead you, always.' Guess that sounds kinda corny. It made an impact on me, though."

"I don't think it's corny. I'm glad you told me."

Reuben could see the sincerity in Maggie's eyes and sighed with relief.

"Me too. Now I think we'd better try and get some sleep." Reuben wadded up his jacket and tucked it under his head as he lay down on the bench. He was just dozing off when Maggie asked one more question.

"Any idea whatever happened to that kid?"

Reuben smiled up at the ceiling. "He's twenty-three years old now and already a captain in the Royal Canadian Air Force."

"Dropping bombs on the bad guys?"

"His mother promised to let me know the minute he gets home."

With that, the conversation ceased. But even through his sleep, Reuben remained intensely aware of the woman who lay only a few feet away.

CHAPTER 16

Bright sunshine hit Maggie directly in the eyes at the same moment she realized every one of her joints and muscles was aching. The night had brought little rest, and when she had slept she dreamed she was on a merry-go-round at the carnival. She could see a girl on a pony up ahead and felt desperate to reach her, but no matter how hard she tried to hurry her horse, she always stayed the same distance behind. Whether the girl was Charlotte or Maggie's old friend Susan wasn't clear.

The big clock in the lobby said 5:45. Soon the ticket-counter clerk who might have seen Charlotte would be in. Maggie sat up and looked around. She saw only one other passenger, a man who looked like a traveling salesman or possibly a politician. She carried her bag with her to the ladies' room and freshened up the best she could. She gave her spare clothes a good sniff and was relieved to detect no whiff of skunk.

When she returned to her bench, Reuben was gone. She went out to the car and saw him walking toward her with two paper cups and a brown bag.

"'Morning." He held out a cup toward her. "Coffee."

As they sat on a bench on the platform Reuben opened the bag and took out a muffin that he gave to Maggie. It looked like a feast to her, and she'd devoured it before Reuben had his half-eaten.

"Should I have brought you two?" he asked, raising an eyebrow.

Maggie felt sheepish as she brushed the crumbs off her skirt. "Well, we did skip supper last night. You suppose that's the guy with the chickens and goats?" She nodded toward a man who approached the side door of the station, wearing the same CP Rail uniform the ticket seller wore.

"Barney Lyall?" Reuben said to her.

"You've got a good memory for names."

"Hazard of the occupation."

"Speaking of that, you got one of those fancy collars in your bag? Might come in handy on this little mission." Maggie stood. "I'm going in to find out if Mr. Lyall saw Charlotte yesterday."

Inside, the traveling salesman was already in line at the window, and Maggie fell in behind him. By the time it was Maggie's turn, Reuben was behind her, a clerical collar neatly in place. She grinned.

"Where to?" the agent asked.

"We're looking for someone," Maggie answered. "Why don't you tell him, *Reverend*?" She nodded toward Reuben. Might as well gain whatever advantage the collar might afford.

Reuben stepped forward and explained the situation in a much more serene fashion than Maggie would have. She kept her eyes on the ticket seller's. She'd hung around Douglas and his friends enough that she could usually tell when someone was hedging.

"Pregnant, you say? Yeah, she came through all right. I'd venture to guess she's not pregnant anymore, though. It was quite the hoo-ha around here when that train pulled in."

"What do you mean?" Maggie's determination to stay quiet was short-lived.

"The conductor wired ahead for us to have an ambulance waiting for a woman on board who was in labor."

Maggie's hand flew to her mouth.

"I called right over to McKellar Hospital, and they had a car here in no time. It's just up the street, you know." He pointed with his thumb, like a hitchhiker.

"Is that where they took her?" Reuben asked.

"I suspect so. I haven't heard any more about it."

"Thank you," Reuben said. "You've been very helpful." He turned to go.

"Wait," Maggie said. "This woman in labor. Was she a blonde? Young?"

"I didn't really get a good look, ma'am. They took her on a stretcher."

Reuben thanked the man, and he and Maggie headed toward the door.

"And tell her the rest of her ticket is good for thirty days if she wants to carry on to Petawawa," the man called after them as the door swung slowly closed. "Babes in arms travel free."

Spurred to action by the man's words, they ran for Reuben's car. He started it and Maggie jumped in on the passenger side.

"Oh, that poor girl. What are the odds of a baby this early making it?" Maggie rubbed her forehead.

"I don't know. Maybe better than you'd think." Reuben backed out and pointed his car in the direction the man had indicated. "I was premature myself. Do you see anything that looks like a hospital?"

Just a few blocks down, Maggie spotted a three-story building, one side decked with wide porches on the first and second floors. "McKellar General Hospital," she read aloud. "Let's pray she's here."

Reuben took her literally. After finding a spot in the parking lot, he turned off the engine and bowed his head. "Lord, you've brought us this far. Please help us to locate Charlotte and keep her and the little one safe. Amen."

Maggie swiped at the tear in her eye before Reuben had a chance to open his own. It had struck her that if it weren't for Reuben's dream the day before, they'd still be on their way to Petawawa.

"Seems like this was almost too easy," he muttered.

"Of course, it could have been a different pregnant woman," Maggie said. They climbed out of the car and walked up the steps to the front door.

Again, Reuben explained to the receptionist that they were looking for Charlotte Penfield, who would have arrived by ambulance yesterday and was probably taken to the maternity ward.

The receptionist looked in her book. "I'm sorry, sir, we have no one registered by that name."

"How about another ward?" he asked.

The young woman looked again, turning the page and checking the names slowly.

"No, sir. No one."

"Is there another hospital in the area?"

"No, sir. McKellar General serves a very wide area." The telephone rang and she turned to answer it.

Reuben looked at Maggie and sighed. "I knew it seemed too easy."

"Let's sit down over here where we can think." Maggie led Reuben to a row of stiff wooden chairs and sat. "These dreams of yours. You say they're never wrong?"

"Oh, Maggie. Please don't think I haven't asked that question a million times before I even told you about this one. So far, no. They have never been wrong."

"Well, maybe you missed a piece of information then, because the woman they brought here from the train station must have been someone else."

Reuben said nothing. He leaned forward, resting his elbows on his knees and looking at his feet. Praying, probably.

Maggie spotted a door with the word *Ladies* on it and excused herself. She wrestled with the question of Charlotte's whereabouts as she washed and dried her hands, but when she walked out, something caught her eye that convinced her they were on the right track. She marched straight to the front desk again, waving Reuben over as she walked.

"She's here, Reuben." She turned to the receptionist again. "Excuse me, miss, but would you happen to have a Charlotte Wilson registered?" A nurse standing a few feet away studied a clipboard. She glanced over the top of her glasses at Maggie.

The receptionist gave Maggie a skeptical look, but by this time, Reuben and his beautiful collar had stepped up behind Maggie. She checked her list again.

The nurse's eyebrows suddenly shot up. "Yes. Charlotte Wilson, room 103."

"Bingo!" Maggie said, giving Reuben an ear-to-ear grin.

The receptionist didn't smile. "I'm sorry, but visiting hours don't start until this afternoon at one o'clock."

"Is she okay? Is the baby all right? Is it a boy or a girl? When was it born? How big?" Maggie spoke so quickly she sounded like an auctioneer.

"I really can't answer all those questions, ma'am."

The nurse nearby spoke up. "Are you family?"

"We're the girl's guardians," Maggie said.

"Then perhaps you can clear up the confusion about her name. Is it actually Wilson? In all the chaos when she arrived, we were given at least two names."

"How'd you know she was here, Maggie?" Reuben said in a low voice.

Maggie grinned. "From the door to the ladies' room, I could see a chalkboard outside the maternity ward. On the top, it says 'Welcome,' and below that it lists Baby Brookes, Baby Jenkins, and Baby Wilson!" Then she turned to the receptionist. "Wilson is the baby's father's name. It would be just like Charlotte to use it."

The receptionist sighed. "You'll still have to wait for visiting hours. Feel free to wait in our waiting area."

"But we drove all the way from Winnipeg," Maggie complained.

"I'm sorry, Mrs. . . ."

"Marshall. Maggie Marshall."

The nurse made a note on her clipboard. Reuben took Maggie's elbow and led her back to the seating area.

"Wilson is a pretty common name," he murmured. "How silly will we feel if it's not her?"

"Who's doubting now, dreamer?" Maggie couldn't resist teasing.

But Reuben didn't take the bait. "All right. Assuming it *is* her, what happens next? We can't exactly take her back with us. Don't they usually keep mothers in the hospital for a week after delivery?"

"Yes," Maggie agreed. "But it's the baby I'm wondering about. Plans are in place for it to be released for adoption immediately upon birth. Do you suppose Charlotte told them?"

"You could ask, but I doubt it would do any good."

"*You* could ask. *Reverend*." Maggie wiggled her eyebrows.

Reuben stood. "Let's be patient, shall we? C'mon, it's a beautiful day out there. I'll buy you a proper breakfast while we're waiting."

They walked three blocks to a diner, where they both ordered bacon and eggs and toast and coffee, and where Maggie complained through the entire meal about the slow service, the overcooked eggs, and the dusty windowsills.

CHAPTER 17

Though Charlotte was needled with worry, her exhaustion had allowed her to fall asleep immediately after Darcy was taken to the nursery. Twice during the night and once this morning they had brought him to her for feeding. Each time, she talked to him for the length of his stay. And each time they took him away, she felt the tugging pain of separation more keenly. When she slept, a black-hooded figure entered her dreams and tried to steal a treasure chest from her. Although she didn't know what was inside it, she fought fiercely to keep it.

She had just eaten a lunch of lukewarm tomato soup and a dry cheese sandwich when a nurse brought Darcy to her again. It took less than ten minutes for him to fill his tiny stomach and fall asleep in her arms. She was sleepy, too, but didn't want to waste one precious minute of their time together. She stroked his hair and kept speaking softly to him.

"You're my little boy, yes you are. You're the sweetest little boy in the whole wide world, yes you are. Yes you are." The song of the little girl from the train came to mind and Charlotte sang softly every line she could recall of "Jesus Loves Me." The scene would have been idyllic if not for what happened when the nurse waltzed back in.

"Good news, Mrs. Wilson," the nurse announced. "You're going to have company this afternoon. Your guardians have arrived from Winnipeg."

Charlotte gaped at her. "My—my what?"

"Your guardians. The Marshalls. They'll be in as soon as visiting hours start."

"But—" How on earth had Mrs. Marshall found her? And who was with her? Mr. Marshall was dead. *Wasn't he?*

"Is this little guy ready to return to the nursery?" the nurse asked.

Charlotte's head was spinning. If Mrs. Marshall was here, she'd explain everything about Darcy being born out of wedlock and how he was supposed to be adopted. They'd take him away! She couldn't let that happen.

"Can I keep him awhile longer?" She gave the nurse the most serene smile she could muster.

It must have worked, for the woman smiled back. "Sure. Ring your bell if he gets fussy or when you're tired. We need to make sure you're getting adequate rest."

As soon as the nurse left the room, Charlotte got up. Weak and dizzy, she felt her heart racing at a steady clip. She left Darcy in the middle of her bed while she found her clothes and put them on. Miraculously, the bag she had carried onto the train lay at the bottom of the tiny locker beneath the clothes she'd worn. *God bless Marlajean!*

She removed just enough clothing from the bag to be able to nestle the sleeping baby on top and then left the bag as wide open as she dared. Poking her head out the door, she peered down the hallway. A doctor was heading toward her, but she ducked back inside until he passed. When she stepped out into the hallway, she had no idea which direction to go. At the first corner, she turned right. From there, she saw a door across the hall. It had a window in it through which she could see blue sky. Once the coast was clear, she dashed across the hall and out the door as quickly as her aching body would allow.

She found herself in a grassy courtyard, hemmed in on all four sides by hospital walls. When she tried to duck back inside, she heard footsteps coming toward her at a sharp clip, and closed the door again.

Charlotte checked on Darcy, who was still sleeping contentedly in her bag. She crossed to the opposite side of the courtyard, where there was another door. She opened it with caution and peeked inside. A cafeteria, deserted except for some kitchen staff busily wiping down counters. *Good.* She slipped in and tried to look like she belonged. Head held high and with as much confidence as she could muster, she walked close to one wall until she reached a set of double doors. To her relief, they led to an open veranda.

Outside, Charlotte carried her precious cargo around to the opposite side of the building, where a parking lot was filling with afternoon visitors. She turned the corner just in time to see Maggie Marshall and that minister friend of hers walking in the front door. She was free!

Now where? Charlotte had no time to think. As she made her way across the street to get as far from Mrs. Marshall as possible, the only thing she knew for sure was that she was already exhausted. Her body ached, and she had no idea how long Darcy could hold out. The only logical place to go was the train station. Once she was on the train, she could rest. She could be in Petawawa by morning. Reginald would take care of everything, if she could only find him.

She shook off the nagging thought that perhaps this wasn't true.

But where was the train station? She remembered little about her ambulance ride, but she was certain it had taken only a few minutes. A woman approached.

"Excuse me." Charlotte tried to appear calm. "Can you tell me where I might find the train station?"

"Oh, sure. It's just up that way a few blocks. You can't miss it. You can hear the trains from here."

Charlotte thanked the woman and carried on as fast as her stamina would allow. Once she reached the station, she had to sit on the platform bench to rest before she could go inside. She hoped the train to Petawawa hadn't left.

She lifted Darcy out of the duffel bag. He stirred, but didn't appear hungry yet. A new thought occurred to her, though. He'd be due for a diaper change soon, if he wasn't already. And she had nothing. Not even one diaper! What was she going to do? Digging around in her bag, she contemplated how she might use some of her own clothing—undergarments and otherwise—to fashion diapers until she could come up with something better.

Carrying the bag in her right hand and snuggling Darcy close in her left arm, she entered the station. Thankfully, there was no lineup at the ticket counter.

"Good afternoon." She did her best impression of a grown-up. "I have a ticket from Winnipeg to Petawawa but, unfortunately, I was detained here and had to delay my excursion. I would very much like to continue my journey now. Can you arrange it, please?"

The man looked from her face to the baby and back. Then he spoke so slowly, she thought he might be intellectually stunted.

"Uh . . . yeah. We can get you on a train to Petawawa. Sure thing." He took Charlotte's ticket stub. "Why don't you have a seat over there? I'll just have to run this past the station manager."

"What time will I be boarding?" she asked.

"Depends, ma'am. Soonest would be the three o'clock coming from Dryden, but . . . uh . . . only if the seats aren't all booked. Servicemen take priority, of course. And the baby travels free as long as you're holding her."

"Him."

"Oh. He sure is a new little feller, ain't he?"

Charlotte turned away from the ticket window and looked at the large clock on the wall. It was only 1:15. She needed to be on that train before Mrs. Marshall found her. "I'll just go have a seat. Please call me the second I can board. My name is Charlotte Penfield."

Charlotte felt ready to collapse and wished the benches weren't so hard. She fished a sweater out of her bag and folded it to sit on. But when she adjusted the baby in her arms, she felt something soaking her sleeve. *Oh no.*

In the ladies' room, she discovered a long vanity with chairs in front of it. She busied herself with the baby until the only other occupant left the room. Upon examination she found that Darcy's diaper, nightgown, and blanket were all wet. The towel dispenser offered long strips of fabric that rolled around as you pulled fresh sections down. Charlotte gave several firm tugs and tried to tear the fabric off, but it was too strong. With one of Darcy's diaper pins, she managed to work enough threads loose at the selvage edge of the material to make a small tear. Starting there, she ripped the cloth in half, and then with one mighty yank, wrenched the fabric free from the dispenser. Charlotte used it to fashion a diaper, which she pinned on her little boy. He was starting to fuss.

"Shh, little pumpkin," she crooned. "Mommy's gonna get you fixed up."

She pulled one of her own nightgowns out of the bag and tore it in half. She swaddled Darcy in the soft flannel and stuffed the wet things into the bottom of her bag. She could deal with those later.

A woman with a little girl came in to use the facilities, and Charlotte studied her own reflection while she waited for them to leave. She was so pale, it was hard to recognize herself. As she swayed back and forth trying to keep Darcy quiet, she wondered who that girl in the mirror could be.

After the woman and little girl left, Charlotte tore another long strip of toweling off the machine and stuffed it into her bag. There would be time on the train to rip it into diaper-sized pieces. By this time, Darcy was wailing to be fed. She sat down on one of the chairs to nurse him, thankful they were padded. Every muscle in her body ached, her mouth felt like parchment, and the room was beginning to wobble.

CHAPTER 18

Maggie led the way to room 103. Though the other rooms each bore the names of two patients, only one name appeared on this door: *Charlotte Wilson.*

"Why don't you go on in?" Reuben said. "I'll wait here for a bit."

"Afraid you might see somethin' inappropriate?" Maggie teased.

"Yes, actually," he said.

Maggie turned and gave a quiet knock on the door, then another when she heard no answer.

"Thank you for helping me find her," she said, without glancing Reuben's way. She pushed the door partway open and stuck her head in the room. "Charlotte?"

No answer. Maggie walked in, Reuben following. The room was deserted. One bed still had its hospital corners tightly tucked. The other looked recently occupied, but no one was in the room.

"Where do you suppose she could be?" Maggie flipped open the locker-style closet.

"Careful, Maggie. We still don't know for sure it's her."

"It's her all right." Maggie held up a blue sweater. "She lived in this thing for weeks, even after it got too snug."

They made their way back to the maternity ward nursing station, and Maggie asked where Charlotte might be. A nurse with a nametag displaying *R. Dobson* gave Maggie a blank stare and then confirmed the room number from her chart.

"I'm telling you, no one's there," Maggie said.

Nurse Dobson led Maggie and Reuben back to the room. "Mrs. Wilson?"

She took in the sight and then practically flew to the nursery, instructing Maggie and Reuben to wait in the hallway. When she came back, her face was ashen and she asked them to take a seat.

It was Reuben who spoke up. "Wait a minute. Are you telling us you don't know where she is?"

"Please just have a seat. She couldn't have gone far." When they didn't budge, Nurse Dobson sighed and turned to her co-workers. A younger nurse explained that she'd gone to Charlotte's room to return the baby to the nursery after his last feeding, and while she was there had given Charlotte the good news that her guardians had arrived.

Nurse Dobson glanced toward Maggie, then back again. "Where's the baby now?"

The younger nurse looked down at her shoes. "I didn't bring him to the nursery. Mrs. Wilson asked if she could keep him with her for a while. I didn't see any harm in it."

"How long ago was all this?" Reuben asked.

Before she could answer, the front-desk receptionist rushed in, a slip of paper in her hand. "Excuse me, Nurse Dobson, could I speak to you please?" she asked. The pair of them stepped aside, out of earshot.

When she returned, Nurse Dobson dismissed the younger nurse and turned to Maggie and Reuben. "A man from the train station called. It seems a young woman with a newborn just showed up there inquiring about a ticket to Petawawa. He said he thinks you folks might be looking for her."

Maggie bolted for the door and heard Reuben toss a *thank-you* over his shoulder as she raced through it. Why hadn't she and Reuben waited here instead of going out to eat? What was that crazy girl thinking? How had Charlotte gotten out without being stopped?

"We can't let her get on that train, Reuben." Maggie opened the passenger door and climbed in.

"I have a hunch they'll manage to detain her." Reuben started the car and raced to the station.

"Was that part of your dream, too, or just a regular hunch like normal people have?"

Reuben ignored her cynical tone. "Just a regular hunch."

They pulled up in front of the station and ran inside. The place had filled with travelers since that morning, and they both scanned the crowd—made up mostly of servicemen in uniform. "See her?" Maggie asked.

"No. I'll go talk to the ticket agent. Why don't you check the washroom?"

Maggie headed in that direction, but just before she reached the door, a pale figure emerged, carrying a duffel bag and a tiny infant.

"Charlotte!" Maggie's arms instinctively reached out toward the girl as relief washed through her.

Reuben heard her cry out and came running over. Recognition dawned in Charlotte's eyes as she saw Maggie.

"Are you okay?" Maggie stepped forward, her arms still outstretched.

Charlotte relinquished the baby to Maggie, then dropped her bag just in time for Reuben to catch her in his arms.

She had passed out cold.

CHAPTER 19

When Charlotte fully awoke, she realized she was in her hospital bed. She had only the vaguest recollection of having been carried somewhere. Had she dreamed the entire escape? The train station washroom had seemed so real. Where was Darcy?

"You awake?"

Charlotte turned toward the stiff voice. Mrs. Marshall sat in the chair while her preacher friend stood by the window, looking out. He turned at the sound of her voice.

"Where's my baby?"

"He's fine. He's in the nursery. The staff took care of his wet things from your bag." Mrs. Marshall sounded matter-of-fact. Was she angry?

"I want to see him." Charlotte looked down at her hand and noticed an IV.

"They're just getting some fluids into you, that's all," Mrs. Marshall said. She sounded just like she often did at the restaurant, disgusted and impatient. Yet there was something different there too.

Charlotte suddenly remembered the look on Mrs. Marshall's face when she'd spotted her at the train station and cried out her name—panic and relief rolled into one. "Why did you come?"

Mrs. Marshall glanced at the preacher, then back to Charlotte. "Why did you try to run away? That was quite the Houdini stunt."

Charlotte blinked back tears. What had she been thinking? She hadn't even had enough strength to get herself on a train, let alone to make the rest of the trip and take care of a baby with no supplies, no money.

"I just—I can't give up Darcy, Mrs. Marshall. I can't do it." Though she wanted to sound strong, her voice was little more than a pathetic squeak.

"Darcy?"

"Is that your son's name?" The preacher man had turned around. "It's a nice one. Irish, I think." He looked at Mrs. Marshall. "Like you, Maggie."

Charlotte looked up at the man. "What's yours?"

"I'm sorry." The man took a step toward the bed, holding his hat in both hands. "Reuben Fennel. I'm an old friend of your—of Mrs. Marshall's. I've seen you at the restaurant."

Mrs. Marshall let out a huff of air. "Now that everybody knows who everybody is, perhaps we can start sorting out this mess. For starters, Charlotte, the note you left behind was hardly truthful."

With one stern comment, Mrs. Marshall could turn Charlotte into a little girl again. "I'm sorry. I never dreamed you'd come looking for me."

"Where were you going? I was frantic. If it weren't for the reverend here, we'd still be on the road to Petawawa. Then we finally find you only to discover that you've taken off again."

Charlotte could hear the frustration in Mrs. Marshall's voice and hung her head. They would never let her keep Darcy now, not when she'd behaved like such a child. "It was stupid. I see that now. But Mrs. Marshall, you can't let them take Darcy. Please!"

Mrs. Marshall stared back and let out a huge sigh. "It's not for me to say, Charlotte. Your parents will be passing through Winnipeg in a few weeks and you had better be there, ready to go home with them like they planned. Alone." She stood and headed for the door.

Charlotte could feel desperation rising. "Where are you going?"

The woman didn't turn around. "I'm going to see what the staff can tell me about adoption regulations in Ontario." She headed directly out the door without slowing down, even after Charlotte began to sob.

The preacher pulled the one chair in the room closer to Charlotte's bed and sat on it. He reached across and put one hand on Charlotte's arm and with the other, handed her a handkerchief. He waited until her sobs subsided.

"I imagine you must feel very alone."

Charlotte looked up into the kind eyes. No judgment or impatience registered on his face. She sniffed and nodded.

"You know Mrs. Marshall cares about you, Charlotte. Don't you?"

Charlotte rolled her eyes.

"It's hard for her to show it, but believe me. I heard the panic in her voice when she called me to help."

"That's only because she's going to be in big trouble for losing track of me," she said bitterly. When the preacher didn't respond, she finally looked up into his face and sighed. "I guess she cared enough to come all this way. Did she contact my parents?"

"She tried, several times. If we hadn't caught up with you, we'd have tried Camp Petawawa next. That's where the baby's father is, right?"

"Yes." Charlotte was surprised Mrs. Marshall had remembered those details about her life. She'd mentioned Reginald and where he was only once, shortly after her arrival.

"Would you like to talk about him?"

Charlotte gazed out the window. "It's not fair that he doesn't even know he has a son, is it? Shouldn't he know?"

Reverend Fennel paused. "I'd have to agree with you there. He should have the chance to make his own decision about how to handle his responsibilities."

"Yes, that's what I mean." Did Charlotte finally have someone on her side?

"But he might choose to not be involved. Then you'd have to accept his decision, whichever way it goes."

Charlotte turned onto her side, facing away from the preacher. What did he know anyway? And what did Grumpystiltskin know? She'd never had a baby, she couldn't possibly understand Charlotte's torment. Reginald would be a good father, once given the opportunity. Why shouldn't he get the chance?

"Everything will work out. You get some rest." The preacher patted Charlotte's shoulder and started toward the door. But she didn't want to be left alone.

"It's not like I imagined," she said in a tiny voice.

She sensed the man stop and turn around. "What isn't?"

Charlotte played with the pilled threading of her blanket and still kept her back toward the preacher. "If I had known what it's like to bring a baby into the world, I never—I never would have let them arrange the adoption."

She could hear Reverend Fennel walking back toward the bed. "What did you think it would be like?"

Charlotte rolled over onto her back and looked at him with a sigh. "I don't know. I thought I could just go back to my old life. Finish school. Marry Reginald as soon as this awful war is over. Then have *real* babies that we could keep."

"But . . . ?"

"But Darcy *is* a real baby. My life will never be the same, no matter what happens. If I never see Darcy again"—her voice caught in her throat. "I will still always know he's out there, somewhere, with someone else. Always."

Reverend Fennel sat down again. "There's a verse in the Bible about that."

Charlotte raised her eyebrows. "There is?"

He nodded, twirling his hat in his hands. "Somewhere in Isaiah, I think. It says, 'Can a woman forget her child, that she should not have compassion on the son of her womb? Yea, they may forget, yet will I not forget thee.' It was God's promise to his people that He would never forget them."

Charlotte thought about that. Maybe someone did understand after all. "Isn't there some way out of this?" she asked.

"I don't know, Charlotte," he said softly. "Maybe the better question is, what's best for Darcy?"

At this, Charlotte began to sob all over again.

"May I pray for you?" When Charlotte nodded, Reverend Fennel placed his hat on the bed and took Charlotte's free hand between his own. "Lord, you know how difficult it is to be separated from your child. You know Charlotte's heart. You've made her a mother, and a good mother always wants what is best for her children. Please flood Charlotte's heart with peace right now so she can get the rest she needs to heal. Help her, Father. Amen."

Without another word, the man gently wiped a tear from Charlotte's cheek with the back of his fingers, then turned and left the room.

CHAPTER 20

Reuben found Maggie at the nurses' station in heavy debate with Nurse Dobson. As he approached, he had to grin at the contrast between the two. The nurse was a good six inches taller than Maggie, and her shiny, nearly black hair looked like she'd just walked out of a salon—especially when seen beside Maggie's mass of unruly red curls. Even so, it appeared the little spitfire was managing to intimidate the head nurse.

"This is incompetence, that's what this is." Maggie had both hands on her hips.

"Ma'am, please do not blame this on my staff. She told us she was married. We could not possibly have known this baby was supposed to be withheld from her. She didn't exactly volunteer that information!"

Maggie's volume rose a notch. "You didn't find it the least bit odd that this mere child—?"

"We see seventeen-year-old married girls in here all the time, Mrs. Marshall." In contrast to Maggie, Nurse Dobson's voice got quieter but firmer. "We were flooded with them about nine months after Canada entered this senseless war."

Maggie pressed her lips together, her face red. "She was traveling alone. In her condition. That should have tipped someone off."

Another nurse approached. "Excuse me, but I couldn't help overhearing. I'm Nurse Bailey. Maybe I can help. I went with the ambulance to meet Charlotte at the train." She reached out to shake Maggie's hand and explained briefly about how the railroad had wired ahead and what Charlotte's condition had been when she got off the train car.

"Another passenger had kindly taken Charlotte under her wing and made sure we had her belongings and her name. Although in the end, I guess we had that wrong, too." She looked up at Reuben. "Are you her parents?"

"No. We're—I'm—her guardian." Maggie answered. "Her parents brought her to me in Winnipeg, where she was supposed to stay until the baby was born. Arrangements were in place for his adoption. Instead, she took off on her own without a word while—"

She stopped short before finishing her sentence.

Reuben thought Maggie had been about to say "while I was at my husband's funeral" and thought better of it. When she didn't continue, he placed a gentle hand on her arm and spoke for her.

"Her parents are traveling and we haven't been able to reach them. Thank you for taking such good care of Charlotte. She and the baby are safe now, which is the main thing. And we have all of you to thank for that." He looked at Maggie, hoping she would follow his cue and show the staff some gratitude. Instead, she took a deep breath and let it out slowly. Not what he was hoping for, but at least she was calmer now.

Nurse Dobson had moved behind the desk and was sorting papers. "This baby will have to be returned to Winnipeg. Our hands are tied, other than to release him to his mother or, in this case, his mother's legal guardian."

"Her parents are still her legal guardians," Maggie said quietly. "I don't know what to do."

"There is also the matter of the hospital bill." Nurse Dobson's eyes darted from Maggie to Reuben and back again.

"Her parents will cover it." Of that, Maggie sounded confident.

"In any case, neither Charlotte nor the baby is ready to be released yet. We generally keep all our mothers a full week, and we have no way of knowing how much this afternoon's little escapade may have set her back. Her doctor will be in to see her in the morning."

"And until then?" Maggie asked.

The nurse sounded as puzzled as Maggie, and Reuben knew this must be a highly unusual event. "Until then, I suggest you keep trying to get a hold of her parents. If the baby isn't leaving with his mother, we need to start feeding him in the nursery and keep them separated. It will go a lot harder on her now that she's been nursing him."

Reuben remembered the Bible verse he had just shared with Charlotte. Though he would never experience her pain, he found himself wanting to cry for the poor, lonely girl.

"She even gave him a name," Maggie said sadly. "Something Irish. What was it, Reuben?"

"Darcy."

"Oh yeah." Maggie sighed again. "So? Which of us gets to tell her?"

Reuben took Maggie's elbow and led her away from the nurses' station. "She's resting. Let's go get a cup of coffee."

Maggie relaxed into the padded seat of the restaurant booth and sipped her coffee. This place was a definite step up from the one they'd eaten breakfast in, and she spotted a couple of decorating ideas she might be able to use at Bert's, like the slowly turning overhead fans. Reuben had excused himself to make some telephone calls, and she could see him through the restaurant window as he stood inside the booth, looking up numbers in a thick book. As he bent over his task, she couldn't help but notice how capable and determined he looked. He'd be almost handsome if it weren't for that goofy clerical collar. And he was in desperate need of a shave.

Maggie pushed away her thoughts about her traveling companion. Reuben's appearance didn't matter. What mattered was, what was she going to do next? If she'd known this was going to turn into such a mess, she never would have approached Reuben for help in the first place. The poor man had had no idea what he was getting into, yet he acted like the problem was his own to solve. He'd been a real peach about it all, but she couldn't ask any more of him.

She could wire enough funds from her bank in Winnipeg to get her through the next few days, then bring Charlotte back to Winnipeg on the train. Perhaps she could find a boardinghouse to stay in here in Fort William, something more affordable than a hotel.

Meanwhile, every day that she was away, Bert's sat empty. She worried that her customers would find other places to eat, maybe even form new dining habits that would keep them from Bert's even after her return. *Darn that Charlotte!*

Then again, Maggie admitted to herself, maybe Charlotte was not the only one to blame. Maybe if Maggie hadn't been so hard on her, she wouldn't have been so determined to run off. Maybe if she'd shown more kindness, the girl would have confided in her. Still, it was maddening. Of all the childish, idiotic things to do! Clearly, this girl was not ready to be a mother. She had way too much growing up to do.

The seesaw ride between indignation and self-blame was giving Maggie a headache.

Reuben returned to his seat. "We've got a place to stay." He picked up his coffee and took a sip, but it must have been cold. He made a face, put the cup down, and waved the waitress over for the check.

"What do you mean?" Maggie asked, surprised. "You need to get in your car and head home."

He looked up. "Why would I do that? I can't abandon you and Charlotte here."

"Why not? I'm half-tempted to abandon her here myself. You've done more than enough. Your congregation needs you. I'll stay until she's discharged and then bring her back with me by train. The rush is over. She's safe now."

Reuben acted like he hadn't heard her. "I called a couple of churches in the area. Pastor Cooper at St. Paul's Anglican answered. When I introduced myself and shared our dilemma, he said they have folks in their congregation who are willing to billet people in emergencies just like this."

Maggie stared at him. "This dilemma is not *ours*, Reuben. It's mine."

"Of course, we'll be in two separate homes, for the sake of propriety."

"Did you not hear me? This is not your problem. And I think propriety went out the window when I climbed into your car and rode halfway across the country with you."

He grinned. "Not nearly halfway. It's a big country, Maggie."

Maggie rolled her eyes, but smiled in spite of herself. "Are you being stubborn, Reverend? Because let me tell you, it ain't pretty."

"Look who's talking. You invited me along on this escapade, remember? I intend to see it through."

"I did no such thing! I asked to borrow a car. You're the one who butted your way in."

Reuben did not dignify this with a response. "We're meeting Reverend Cooper at the church in fifteen minutes. Our hosts will meet us there; we can settle in and freshen up." He pulled a wallet from his pocket. "Then I think we'd better head back to the hospital and have a good long talk with Charlotte, don't you?"

Maggie didn't know what to say. It had been years since anyone had "taken charge" with her, and the last time someone had, it had not been a good thing. This was so much different. Reuben's actions made her feel cared for, provided for. As much as she wanted to send him on his way and solve her own problems, she had to admit, this felt awfully good. She had felt alone for so long.

"I think I'm glad I roped you into this, Reverend." She swallowed the last of her coffee and stood, without looking him in the eye. But as he was laying some coins on the table, she stole a glance back at him.

The fool was grinning from ear to ear.

CHAPTER 21

Maggie tossed her bag onto the bed and looked out the window in time to see Reuben's car driving away, following after the Anglican minister. He and Reuben had dropped her at the home of an older couple whose names were Peter and Pansy Flannigan. She learned that the couple had an unmarried son who was fighting overseas and a married daughter who lived just across the street with her husband and four children.

"We just want to help out however we can," Mr. Flannigan had said. His wife had shown Maggie to this room and pointed out the bathroom just across the hall. Reuben had promised to return for her in forty-five minutes. Now she pulled her one remaining clean outfit out of her bag and hung it over the tub while it filled, hoping the steam would rid it of wrinkles. After taking a short soak, she tossed her dirty clothes into the tub and swished everything around. That would have to do. She wrung them out as tightly as she could and hung them around her room from chairs and bedposts.

By the time she was dressed again, she felt much better. At the bottom of the stairs, Mrs. Flannigan offered her lemonade, and they chatted at the kitchen table while waiting for Reuben to return.

"The reverend told me about your husband," the woman said. "I'm so sorry. It must have been a real blow to you, dear."

Maggie nodded. No need to explain to this stranger.

"Do you have children?"

"No."

"Well, you're young yet. There's time." Mrs. Flannigan's soft gray curls flattered her round face. "I hope and pray for my boy's safe return every day. His father was in the great war."

"The war to end all wars," Maggie murmured.

"Wasn't that the biggest lie?" She gave a resigned sigh. "Maybe this one will finally be the last."

"Maybe it will."

"But if not, may you never have to go through the agony of saying good-bye to your son, wondering if you'll ever lay eyes on him again. It's a heartache I wouldn't wish on anyone."

The doorbell rang and Maggie followed Mrs. Flannigan to the entryway, where the sight of Reuben on the other side of the screen door made her heart do a little flip. *I must be nervous about having this talk with Charlotte,* she reasoned.

"Feel better?" Reuben asked as they got into his car.

"Much."

"Me too." They both pulled their doors shut.

"Not sure I'm ready for this next task, though." Maggie could picture Charlotte's sad face, her sobs still clear from the last time they'd parted.

"Me either." As he had done before on their trip, Reuben bowed his head and prayed aloud. "Lord, thank you for helping us find Charlotte and the baby. Please give us wisdom as we speak with her. Show us how to handle this. Help us get in touch with her parents, somehow. Amen."

Maggie mumbled an *amen.* How could Reuben talk to God so easily, about anything? He really seemed to expect answers, too. And the crazy thing was, he got them.

She turned her attention to the matter at hand. "Tomorrow I should try to contact the adoption agency in Winnipeg and see what I can learn."

"Tomorrow's Saturday," Reuben reminded her. "We may have to wait until Monday."

Maggie had completely lost track of the days. It seemed months, not a mere week, since she'd received the telegram informing her Douglas had been killed in action. How could she have grown so comfortable with Reuben Fennel in such a short time?

Then it struck her.

"Wait a minute. If tomorrow's Saturday, don't you need to get back to your church and preach on Sunday?"

"It's already arranged," he said. "I telephoned Deacon Ellis, who fills in for me when I'm away. Turns out he had a sermon all ready to go the last time I was scheduled for a holiday and was quite disappointed he never got to use it."

"Why didn't he get to use it?"

"The war broke out. I didn't take the holiday."

Maggie gave a snort. "Guess you're taking it now instead."

Reuben grinned. "I also asked Deacon Ellis to let my landlady know I'd be a few more days."

"You think of everything. I don't suppose you checked up on my restaurant while you were at it?" Maggie's face held a mischievous grin.

"Yes, I did. It said to tell you it hardly misses you at all and is enjoying the peace and quiet."

Before heading to Charlotte's room, Maggie and Reuben stopped by the nurses' station in the maternity ward. Nurse Dobson was gone for the day, but had instructed her staff to begin bottle-feeding Darcy in the nursery. It was not going well, the ward nurse told them, but their orders were to keep trying. When he was hungry enough, he should accept the bottle.

They found Charlotte picking at a supper tray of meat loaf and mashed potatoes when they got to her room.

"May we come in?" Reuben asked from the door.

Charlotte looked up. Her face was drained of color except for red tear streaks that remained, though her cheeks were dry. A Bible lay open beside the food tray on her over-bed table. "I thought you'd left town."

"We're not leaving without you," Maggie said.

Charlotte raised her eyebrows. "When will that be?"

"When you're ready to be discharged."

"Are we leaving Darcy here?" The girl's voice sounded flat.

Reuben spoke up. "We don't know all the details yet, Charlotte. Right now your job is to get your strength back and rest. Try to trust that everyone involved will do everything in their power to do what's best for Darcy."

"I've been doing some thinking about that." Charlotte laid her fork on the tray. "Mrs. Marshall, I owe you a big apology. I can see now how foolish and selfish I was, taking off like I did. I was only thinking of myself. And then running away again today. I don't know how I could have endangered Darcy like that."

Now it was Maggie's turn to raise her eyebrows. Had the girl grown up that much in just two days?

"Can you forgive me?" Charlotte looked her straight in the eye.

"It's water under the bridge now." Maggie shrugged. "Like the reverend said. You need to concentrate on getting strong enough to leave here."

"But that doesn't answer my question," Charlotte looked ready to burst into tears again. "I need to know if I'm forgiven."

Maggie glanced at Reuben, who slowly nodded.

"All right." Maggie cleared her throat. "I forgive you."

"I can make it up to you," Charlotte said. "I'll work as long as necessary, help you make those changes to the restaurant you want. Anything."

"That won't be necessary." Maggie picked some lint off her skirt. It would have been easier to stay mad at the girl.

"And you, Reverend Fennel. I'm sorry for all the inconvenience I've caused."

"You're forgiven, Charlotte." He stepped over to the bed and pointed to the open Bible. "May I ask what you were reading?"

"Nothing in particular. I found the Bible in the drawer and was hoping I might find some reassurance that God would forgive me. For everything. I've just made one big mess of things."

Maggie watched as Reuben picked up the Bible and expertly turned right to the passage he wanted, then read it aloud.

"'If we confess our sins, he is faithful and just to forgive us our sins, and to cleanse us from all unrighteousness.'" Reuben placed the emphasis on the word *all*, then read the verse through one more time for good measure. He placed the Bible back where it had been. "First John, one nine."

The three of them sat quietly for several minutes.

"I've done that," Charlotte said. "Confessed everything. But I still felt I needed forgiveness from the two of you. And from my parents. And Reginald."

"In time, Charlotte," Reuben said gently. "As God gives you the opportunity, you can make amends with those you need to. For now, you can have peace knowing you've done everything you can."

"I really do want what's best for my son. But how do we know what that is?"

"What does your heart tell you?"

Charlotte sat quietly for a bit, then spoke softly. "Darcy needs his mother." She looked out the window. "But he also needs a loving home, with two parents. I can't offer him that. Not yet."

A nurse came in to inform them that visiting hours were over. Maggie walked closer to Charlotte's bed and laid a hand on the girl's arm. "Things will work out. Get some rest."

Reuben smiled. "We'll come back tomorrow."

The drive to the Flannigans' home was a quiet one. After he parked the car, Reuben walked Maggie to the door. "That went rather well, I thought."

"Time will tell, I guess," Maggie said. "If it were up to me, I'd say Charlotte should keep that little tyke."

Reuben raised his eyebrows. "I'm shocked, Maggie Marshall."

"But even if she can't, he shouldn't go to his new family empty-handed."

"What do you mean?"

"I'd like to pick up a few baby things in the morning. Just essentials."

Reuben grinned. "You are just full of surprises."

Maggie simply shrugged. "Hope you get a good sleep tonight. And thanks. For everything."

Reuben nodded and opened the door for her, then stepped back. As he headed to his car, Maggie spoke her parting words in a voice too quiet for him to hear.

"You're a good man, Reuben Fennel."

CHAPTER 22

Charlotte couldn't sleep. She was certain the baby she heard crying nonstop was Darcy, and her breasts ached. A nurse had taught her how to express the milk to relieve the pain, but it wasn't enough. Hearing her tiny son's cry broke her heart, but she didn't dare mention it lest they move her to a different ward. She'd rather hear him crying than not be near him at all.

She sat up. Was it her imagination, or were his cries getting louder? They sounded closer. Then her door opened, and a nurse walked in, carrying the ravenous boy in her arms.

"We've tried everything," she said. "He will not accept the bottle, and he's keeping all the other babies and their mothers awake. That's some set of lungs on this kid."

Charlotte couldn't believe her eyes, but she wasn't going to question what was happening. She reached out for Darcy and soon had him nursing greedily, not just to his great relief, but also to her own.

"Are you going to be in trouble?" she asked.

"Perhaps," the other woman said. "But I'm head nurse on this shift, and for everybody's sake, this is the best call to make in the moment."

Charlotte knew her eyes must be glistening with unshed tears when she looked up. "Thank you."

The nurse just smiled and patted Charlotte's leg. "I'll be back to get him in a little while."

Charlotte studied the perfect little boy in her arms. Who was to say what was best for him? Clearly, in this moment, the best thing for him was his mother's milk. It didn't take any great education or special wisdom to know that. Why, he knew it himself!

Once he was full, he settled into a peaceful sleep, and Charlotte prayed the nurse wouldn't come back to take him for a long time.

Cradling him in her arms, she agonized over her dilemma. What was she going to do? Surely her parents could not force her to give this child up. Once they met him, they would fall in love with their grandchild too. They just had to! Her older sister, Helen, was married and had two children. Although her parents didn't go overboard with displays of affection, Charlotte knew they loved little Ricky and Beth. Charlotte figured she just needed to ensure they had the opportunity to meet Darcy. He would win them over.

"God," she prayed. "Thank you again for forgiving me for my sins. Thank you for this beautiful little boy. Please don't let them take him away from me. Please."

She was dozing off when the nurse came to collect Darcy. As soon as they were gone, she snuggled down and slept soundly until daylight.

Maggie was shocked when she walked into Charlotte's room during visiting hours the next afternoon. The baby was resting in her arms, and there was a smile of complete serenity on the girl's face.

"What's this?" Maggie asked. "I stopped by the nursery and they said I'd find Darcy here, with you."

Charlotte looked up, all smiles. "I'm feeding him again. They couldn't get him to take a bottle and were worried he was getting dehydrated."

The arrangement seemed most peculiar to Maggie, but she didn't have the heart to charge over to the nurses' station and start demanding answers. If it turned out that she and Reuben were taking both Charlotte and Darcy with them back to Winnipeg, it would certainly solve the feeding issue. And if he were left behind . . . Maggie couldn't bring herself to think about it.

"Did a little shopping this morning." Maggie opened the bag at her feet and pulled out a half dozen baby nightgowns, a dozen diapers, and some soft flannel blankets.

Charlotte gasped. "Oh, Mrs. Marshall!" She ran her free hand over the tiny garments. "You didn't have to do this!"

"I know. But I figured—whichever way this goes, we can't very well have this little nipper going about naked, can we? He needs a few things of his own."

Charlotte's face glowed as she smiled at Maggie. "Thank you so much."

Maggie took the baby from Charlotte and cuddled him. She wasn't sure she'd ever held such a tiny baby before, and the softness of him almost took her breath away.

"Where's Reverend Fennel?" Charlotte asked, still admiring the baby things.

"Helping out the preacher who found us a place to stay. His church is holding a Red Cross fund-raiser today."

"I suppose he's more comfortable there than here." Charlotte smiled.

"Feels more useful, too."

"He sure seems like a good man. Is his wife all right with him coming here?"

"Reuben isn't married." Maggie shifted Darcy so she could kiss his soft cheek. He kept his eyes closed but made tiny puppy squeaks at the disturbance. "Oh, you precious little thing, you."

She hoped Charlotte hadn't heard. But when she looked up, she knew she'd been caught in her tender moment. The girl was grinning, but said nothing. In fact, she quickly looked away and aimed her gaze out the window. Maggie was grateful.

"Has he ever been married?"

"Who?" Maggie knew full well Charlotte was still on the topic of Reuben Fennel, but felt the need to reestablish her tough exterior. "Oh, the reverend, you mean?"

"Yes."

"Not as far as I know."

"Isn't he kind of old not to be married?" Charlotte folded the baby clothes back into the bag.

"If he's old, I suppose I am as well. He was a year ahead of me in school, so that would make him about thirty-three, I guess."

Charlotte looked up. "Really? You knew each other when you were children?"

"Oh, sure. Went to the same church all our growing-up years. Same school for part of that time."

"What was he like?" Charlotte sat back against her pillows.

"Same as now, I guess. Nice. Different from the other boys." Darcy squirmed, and Maggie stood and began to sway slowly. "Why all the interest in the reverend?"

Charlotte picked up a hairbrush from her side table and began to brush her hair. "He was awfully kind to me yesterday. Like a pastor should be, you know? I went to church with my parents all my life, but we didn't have a minister like Reverend Fennel."

"He's one of the good ones, all right." Maggie focused her gaze on Darcy again.

"My pastor was the one who advised my parents to send me away." Charlotte lowered her voice to sound like a man. "'The church does not need this shame,' he told us. He said if we didn't keep it a secret, we would not be welcome to return. That our family had a duty to uphold its upstanding reputation and that other girls looked to me to set an example." Charlotte let out a snort. "Imagine. Me, an example."

Maggie studied the girl's face. "So deceit is the answer?"

Charlotte returned her brush to the table and lay back again. "Doesn't seem right, does it?"

Maggie continued to hold the baby after Charlotte dozed off. Her thoughts turned to Reuben. Charlotte made a good point. Why *wasn't* the man married? He'd make some woman a good husband. Some woman who knew how to be a good wife, and a good pastor's wife to boot. Maybe those kinds of women were even harder to come by than men like Reuben were.

A nurse came to collect the baby, and Maggie followed her out to the nurses' station. She watched through the nursery window as they laid Darcy in a bassinet alongside half a dozen other babies. He looked so tiny and alone, and she felt a dull ache forming in her chest. What would become of him? Did the adoption agency back home already have a family picked out for him? She didn't know. Would Charlotte's parents want to keep him if they had the chance to see him?

Nurse Dobson approached her. "Good news, Mrs. Marshall. Charlotte's doctor has agreed to release her early, under the circumstances. He says she and the baby are doing fine, and you can plan on taking her home Monday."

"That *is* good news. Thank you." The rush of gratitude and relief surprised Maggie.

"I apologize about the baby's feedings. Do you want us to try again?"

Maggie shook her head slowly. It occurred to her that if Charlotte's parents had any influence at all, she would never host another unwed mother again. She'd first breached their trust by letting the girl get away. Now the child had been born far from where he was supposed to be born, and the adoption authorities were completely unaware. Furthermore, she'd taken a road trip with a man who was not her husband and would be dragging Charlotte into the impropriety of it all for the ride home. There was no point in trying to salvage the situation now.

"No. Let's just leave things as they are," she said. "Let her nurse her baby."

CHAPTER 23

Reuben let the hood of the Plymouth drop into place with a thud. Fresh oil and other fluids, a tank of gas. Air in the tires. The trip home would be much different with Charlotte and Darcy along, and he didn't want to take any foolish chances. He'd also stocked up on jugs of drinking water, a bag of apples, and a box of crackers. Just in case.

"All aboard?" He surveyed the car's interior. Charlotte and the baby had taken over the backseat. Maggie tapped her foot in the front.

"All except you. C'mon! We're burning daylight."

Reuben climbed in behind the wheel and started the engine. "It's going to be a scorcher today."

"All the more reason for us to hit the road early. Too bad they wouldn't let you go any earlier this morning, Charlotte."

Reuben and Maggie had attended Pastor Cooper's church together on Sunday morning, then spent the remainder of the day visiting Charlotte and Darcy at the hospital. Leaving the baby in the nursery, they'd walked Charlotte around the grounds of the hospital and enjoyed a picnic on the lawn, at her doctor's suggestion. This morning, the color was back in her cheeks and she appeared happy to be traveling. Reuben knew this scene would look much different had they not been taking Darcy with them.

Reuben headed west out of Fort William and sped up as much as he dared when he reached the dusty gravel of the main road. It hadn't rained the entire time they'd been gone. Now that they were headed home, he allowed himself to think about his congregation. He prayed that no more soldiers from his flock were missing, killed, or maimed since he left. He wondered what Deacon Ellis had preached about the day before and hoped that he'd managed to challenge the people without wounding their hearts or loading false guilt on their heads. He knew that's exactly what would happen if Elder Mitchell ever took a turn in the pulpit, and hoped that day never came. The man believed in strict adherence to the rules at all cost. The problem was, the only one who seemed to know what "the rules" were was Elder Mitchell.

"I've been thinking about something ever since you two arrived at the hospital," Charlotte said from the backseat. "How did you know where I'd gone? What made you look for me in Fort William?"

Reuben could feel Maggie's eyes on him before she opened her mouth. "You gonna tell her, or should I?"

"Tell me what?" Charlotte asked.

"As you know," Maggie began when Reuben remained silent, "the reverend here talks to God. But did you know God talks to him too?"

"Really? God told you where I was?" Reuben could see the girl's big eyes in his rearview mirror.

"Not . . . exactly. Not directly," Reuben began. How to explain it? "I just get these—I don't know, dreams or visions once in a while. I get direction. In this case, I knew you were getting off the train at Fort William. But that's all I knew. I had no idea why."

"So then, how did you end up at the hospital?"

Maggie piped up. "The stationmaster who was there when you arrived helped us put two and two together, although we still weren't a hundred percent certain it was your trail we were following, until we found your room and that ugly old blue sweater of yours."

"Hey, I like that sweater."

"Well, you won't need it today, that's for sure." Maggie fanned her face. "How's that little squirt doing back there?"

"Good. He's starting to wake up. Probably due for a feeding before too long, but we'll be fine."

They rode in silence awhile, Reuben keeping his eyes on the road. The lush woods of northern Ontario were far easier to enjoy today than they'd been through the fog during the drive out. Every now and then, a deer appeared at the edge of the trees, then scampered out of sight. Rabbits, porcupines, and gophers all made appearances too.

As the day went on, the car got hotter. Charlotte spoke up again. "Why have I been smelling skunk all day?"

Reuben and Maggie exchanged a grin. "Be glad it's not worse," he said. "We hit one on our way out."

Maggie was scribbling on the back of an envelope with a pencil, using her purse as a desk. "What are you working on there?" Reuben asked her.

"Menu ideas for next week. If I don't hurry and get the restaurant open again, I won't have any customers left. Thought I'd get started now so I can hit the ground running when we get there. Speaking of skunks."

Reuben slowed, looking around. "Where?"

"Not here. In my restaurant."

"You're serving skunk in the restaurant?" Charlotte called out from the backseat. "I've never heard of anything so—"

"No, no, no. I was just thinking of my new business partner." Maggie kept her eyes on her list.

"What new business partner?"

Maggie half-turned in her seat and explained the situation to Charlotte. "So you see, it appears I may have a new, unwanted partner that I don't know how to get rid of. Like a bad case of skunk stink."

Reuben thought about Maggie's dilemma. If Earl Marshall was really a skunk, as Maggie seemed to think, he wanted to help her get free of him. But how? And if Earl really wasn't as bad as Maggie thought, maybe the best thing Reuben could do was help her give him the benefit of the doubt . . . which in turn would be a benefit to her, in the long run.

As the hot day dragged on, each traveler remained lost in his or her own thoughts. Midafternoon, they stopped in Dryden for a light meal and then carried on with their journey, this time with Maggie at the wheel and Charlotte in the front with the baby. Reuben noticed that the two of them were now talking more, but they kept the conversation light. It seemed no one wanted to bring up the topic of Darcy's future.

Reuben was just dozing off when the car started to slow down. Maggie managed to steer it over to the shoulder before it ground to a halt. Steam was rising from under the hood.

"Oh no." He jumped out of the car, and by the time he got the hood up, Maggie was at his side.

"What happened?" she asked. "I wasn't going too fast or anything. Are we out of gas?"

"No. Overheated, most likely." Reuben waved his hat over the top of the engine.

"So . . . we just sit and wait until it cools down?" Maggie asked.

"I don't know. There could be something else wrong." Reuben rolled up his sleeves, knowing in his heart he had no idea what might be wrong with the car or how to fix it. He poked at the various parts, wiggled tubes, and jiggled anything that would budge.

Charlotte climbed out of the car, Darcy resting in her left arm. "Any idea what the problem is?"

"I don't suppose you know anything about cars." Maggie took the baby from Charlotte.

"Not even how to drive one. How far are we from the nearest town?"

Reuben sighed. "I'm afraid the nearest town was the one we had lunch in, and that was more than an hour back. Sorry, ladies. It's been some time since this thing has been properly serviced. Why don't you try to get comfortable in that shady spot over there?"

"What are you gonna do?" Maggie asked.

"Pray. Feel free to do the same."

Reuben watched the two women cross the ditch and settle down with his old car blanket on some soft grass. He studied the confusing automobile parts again, then beseeched his master aloud.

"Lord, I should have learned a thing or two about cars before owning one. It's just irresponsible, and I'm sorry. Please forgive me. I'll take some kind of basic mechanics course first opportunity I get, I promise. And Lord, there's nothing worse than feeling like an incompetent man when you've got ladies and children under your care. Please, for their sake, bring help. Or show me what to do."

Reuben looked both ways down the long stretch of road, but saw nothing. How long had it been since they'd met another vehicle? He walked around the car twice, then stopped to look under the hood again. On his next trip around the car, he pulled drinking water out of the back and carried it to Maggie. He returned to the car and circled it once more. Then he got inside and tried to start it again, to no avail.

"Time to shout yet?" Maggie called from across the ditch.

"Huh?" Reuben thought he hadn't heard her right.

"You look like Joshua marching around Jericho. I think it's been seven times by now. Maybe you should shout."

"Very funny. I want it to start, not collapse."

Reuben had lost track of how many times he'd repeated the process of looking under the hood, circling the car, and trying to start it. He looked over at the women. Maggie appeared to have spotted some kind of wild berries and was picking them. Trust her to turn this delay into a practical pursuit. How could he let her down like this, now that they were halfway home?

The next time he raised his eyes to the horizon, he spotted a cloud of dust up ahead. Could it be?

"Oh, Lord, please let that be someone who knows a thing or two."

The cloud took a long time to get bigger. As the dust slowly grew closer, Reuben could see it came from a tractor. No wonder it was taking forever.

"Trouble?" A leather-skinned farmer with a bandanna around his neck called down from the seat of a faded red International Harvester. The machine throttled down.

"Yes, sir. Overheated, I think."

Maggie wandered over to join them. Reuben couldn't remember the last time he'd felt so humiliated. He was glad he hadn't worn his clerical collar. He didn't want to add to any stereotypical notions the farmer might have of pastors being pansies.

"Yer right about that," the man said after one quick look. "And here's your problem, right here. Broken fan belt. No wonder she overheated."

Maggie looked over at Reuben. "We got a spare one?"

Reuben shook his head.

"Got a pair of nylon stockings? I've seen them work real well in a pinch." The farmer spit on the ground. "Course, you're gonna need water for the radiator too."

"Water we have." Reuben turned to Maggie. "Nylon stockings?"

Maggie's jaw dropped. "Nylons? Are you kidding me? Do you know how hard those are to come by since this darn war started? I didn't even wear them to my own husband's funeral!"

The farmer looked from Maggie to Reuben and back again. "How about the other lady?" He had spotted Charlotte, who was crossing the ditch toward them.

"Charlotte, you got a pair of nylon stockings in that bag of yours?" Maggie asked.

"Me? No. Whatever for?"

When Reuben explained, the girl got in the car and began fishing through her bag.

"Will this work?" she asked, holding up a long strip of sturdy toweling from a public washroom dispenser.

CHAPTER 24

It was evening before they hit the road again in earnest. Maggie was restless to get home, but she did her best to keep quiet about the delay. Charlotte's toweling had done the trick as a makeshift fan belt until they made it to Lake of the Woods. There, a mechanic with a patch on one eye got them fixed up properly while the three travelers enjoyed a meal of fresh corn on the cob from a local stand on the other side of the road. While they ate, the conversation turned to theology as they discussed how Charlotte's towel could be considered a blessing from God when it had been, technically, pilfered.

"Do I need to confess?" she asked. "Send them money to cover the cost?"

"Do you feel guilty?" Reuben wiped butter from his chin. "Not that your feelings should be the only gauge."

"Not really. The towel saved our necks, didn't it?"

"You look entirely too pleased with yourself," Maggie said around a mouthful.

It felt good to be laughing. From there, things just got silly as the three of them discussed ways Charlotte could repay the railroad.

"With your waitressing experience, you could serve in the dining car all the way across Canada," Reuben suggested.

Charlotte rolled her eyes. "I'd rather clean the lavatories."

Maggie caught herself about to use the phrase *promise them your firstborn* when she realized how unfunny that would sound. They had let the matter drop when it was time to load back into the car and continue their journey.

By sundown, Charlotte and the baby were both fast asleep in the backseat. Maggie looked over at Reuben. "You doing okay?"

"Sure. Why don't you try to get some sleep? I'll pull over if I get tired."

"Well, if you do, wake me up so I can drive. I'm ready to get home."

But the next time she opened her eyes, the sun was peeking over the horizon behind them. Maggie couldn't believe it. She turned in her seat to see Charlotte and Darcy both fast asleep. "That baby slept all night? You drove all night?"

Reuben chuckled. "The baby was awake for feeding at least twice, and we stopped for relief once. You were dead to the world."

"My goodness. Guess I didn't realize how exhausted I was. Bet you could use a break."

Reuben pulled over. He stretched his muscles while Maggie found a thick bush to hide behind. When she was done, she climbed in the driver's side.

They reached Winnipeg by late afternoon and drove straight to the government adoption agency where Charlotte's arrangements had been made. The girl had been growing quieter with every passing mile. Maggie stood watching from the sidewalk as Charlotte climbed out of the car, clutching her baby close and biting her lip. Their slow procession up the cement stairs to the front door felt like a gangplank walk, even to Maggie, who could only imagine what was going on in Charlotte's heart.

"You'll need to make an appointment," the woman at the desk told them.

Maggie explained the situation with as much patience as she could muster. "You don't understand. This child was supposed to be adopted out, and he is already four days old." She looked at Darcy, snuggled innocently in Charlotte's arms, and felt like biting her lip too. How could they hand the little gaffer over to strangers?

"Miss Penfield's caseworker, Mrs. Shelton, is not in the office today. She's the one you'll need to talk to. I can book you in for tomorrow at eleven, if that works."

They agreed and headed out to the car. Maggie could read the relief in Charlotte's face and body at the reprieve. But she had to wonder: What difference would twenty-four hours make except to make things even harder?

"Maybe we can reach your parents before then," Maggie suggested when she noticed tears on the young mother's cheeks.

"They need to meet him," Charlotte insisted. "I'm certain they'll change their minds and let me keep him if they just get a chance to see how precious he is."

Reuben and Maggie exchanged a look as he started the car once again. For Charlotte's sake, she hoped the girl was right. But either way, Maggie would soon be saying good-bye to Darcy. As she looked at his sweet little face, she couldn't bear the thought.

"I'll take you home next," Reuben said.

"It's out of your way," Maggie protested. "We can catch a bus from your place, or from the church, wherever you need to go first."

"Out of the question. I intend to finish this adventure, and it's not finished until you and Charlotte are safely home."

Maggie said nothing as she tried to hide the grin that was attempting to take over her face. Instead, she studied the familiar sights along the Winnipeg streets. The shoe-repair shop she frequented when her faithful oxfords wore through. Competing restaurants she dared not step foot in, but was curious about all the same. Her lawyer's office. She supposed she'd have to revisit him soon and sort out the mess with Earl.

"Nervous about the next phase of your business?" Reuben asked.

Maggie stared at him. Could the man read her mind? "What makes you ask that?"

"You just gave a really big sigh."

"I did?" Maggie figured there was no point in denying it. "Yeah, I suppose I am."

"Have you given it more thought?"

No matter how she'd tried, Maggie hadn't been able to think of any way to get out of the pickle she was in. It wasn't as though she had a lot of options. "I guess I could give it a try with a skunk as my partner. Maybe it won't be all that bad." Even as she said the words, she recalled the leering Earl had done when he'd first been introduced to her during her engagement to Douglas. And after the wedding, the hand that had slipped intentionally around her waist and lingered across her buttocks. She blushed to even think about it; she wasn't about to mention it to anyone, ever. She'd rather die than tell Reuben.

They turned the last corner, only three blocks from her home. "Next time I take a holiday," she joked, "I'll try to go somewhere a little more—"

But her words were cut short. Maggie's jaw dropped and her heart began thumping so hard she thought it would burst through her dress. In the spot where Bert's Restaurant had stood for twenty-five years, there now stood a gaping, open hole with makeshift fencing stretched around it and DANGER signs posted every ten feet. As they got closer, she could see the smaller print on each one: DO NOT ENTER. DO NOT CROSS, UNDER PENALTY OF LAW.

"What the—" Reuben pulled over and parked across the street.

Charlotte pulled herself forward in her seat. "Mrs. Marshall! What on earth's happened?"

Maggie was speechless. She managed to climb out of the car, though she wasn't sure her legs would support her. She stood helplessly on the sidewalk, on the very spot she had so often stood to gaze with pride on her livelihood and her inheritance. It couldn't be! She looked to the neighboring businesses left and right. Both were still standing, as usual. Her garden shed, formerly hidden from the street, was still there and clearly visible. Her vegetables continued to grow, a sad tangle of overripe beans, corn, and weeds.

"My home," Maggie finally whispered. "Daddy's restaurant."

Suddenly, Arnold from Anderson's Drugstore was at her side. "Maggie!" he said. "I saw you pull up. They've been looking for you. Nobody seemed to know where you were."

Maggie looked up at the tall, lean druggist. "Who's been looking for me? What happened? When—? How?"

The man put a hand on her shoulder. "This happened Saturday night. I saw flames coming out the front windows and called the fire department. They got here promptly, but they couldn't save it. I'm sorry, Maggie."

"How?" she repeated. She was vaguely aware of Reuben and Charlotte on either side of her and of other neighbors who had joined them.

Bob McClellan, the baker, handed her a *Winnipeg Tribune*. Today's date was on top and the front-page headline read "Restaurant Burns. Owner Unaccounted For." Below that was a photo of her beloved home going up in flames.

Maggie could sense her knees weakening and felt strong arms beneath her elbows. When she looked up from the paper, she saw that it was Reuben who was supporting her. He helped her seat herself on the curb, then sat beside her, his face as distraught as she felt. He took the newspaper from her, scanning it quickly.

"The fire marshals don't know what caused it, or if they do, they're not saying," he said. "Because you and Charlotte were both missing, they fear you were both lost in the fire."

"Best you get down to the fire station as soon as you can," Arnold Anderson said. "They'll want to know you're okay and see if you can shed any light on what caused the fire."

"Police will want to be involved too," Bob McClellan said. "In case of arson."

"Arson?" Maggie slumped into Reuben. This couldn't be happening. It had to be a bad dream. Surely she'd wake up any minute and find herself still riding in Reuben's car down that dusty road. It just couldn't be true. And the idea that someone might have done this deliberately was unthinkable. Maggie thought she might vomit.

Suddenly she was aware of frantic sobbing behind her. Charlotte, still clutching her baby, was crying uncontrollably. "It's my fault. It's all my fault!"

Reuben stood up and went to her. He wrapped an arm around her shoulder. "Shh, Charlotte. It's not your fault. You weren't even here."

"That's just it. If I hadn't run away, this never would have happened!"

Darcy responded to his mother's distress by wailing, and Maggie watched Reuben take him from her arms. He tried to shush the baby while Charlotte sat beside Maggie on the sidewalk.

"I'm so sorry, Mrs. Marshall. I've brought nothing but trouble on you. You should go ahead and have me arrested. I deserve it. I deserve to be locked up, forever probably!"

The girl's display of dramatic nonsense served to set Maggie back on her usual course of determination.

"Don't be ridiculous. For all we know, you saved our hides by getting us out of here before it happened. We might have burned to death. Now come on." She hoisted herself to her feet and pulled Charlotte up after her.

"Reuben," she said, "can you please take us to the fire hall?"

CHAPTER 25

As soon as Maggie identified herself at the front desk of the fire hall, she found herself surrounded almost immediately by a half dozen people, all peppering her with questions. The fire chief cut through them, invited her into his office, and closed the door. Reuben waited in the lobby with Charlotte, who was still trembling and crying as Maggie walked away. Through the window in the fire chief's door, Maggie could see Reuben using the pay phone in the corner of the lobby.

"Mrs. Marshall," Fire Chief Bennet began. "First of all, let me say how glad we are to know you're okay."

"Okay is relative," she said flatly. "My home and my livelihood are gone."

"And I'm very sorry. We did everything we could." The big man reminded her of a giant teddy bear, with his curly hair and kind eyes.

Maggie nodded. "And I thank you. What caused the fire?"

"We're still working on that. I was hoping you might be able to shed some light on it for us." He pulled a sheet of paper from a file on his desk. "At your last fire inspection, there was only one order needing remedy. We understand your apartment doubled as a home for unwed mothers, but there was no means of escape from your upper-floor bedrooms."

"Yes. We had a fire escape added six months ago. Of course, we never needed it and weren't home to use it when we might have."

"And that could not have been the cause of a fire in any case. It appears you were meticulous about keeping your wiring and everything up to code."

"My father taught me that."

"Naturally we can't rule out arson until we can determine a cause. Was there any chance a stove could have been left lit?"

Maggie explained the events of the days leading up to her trip to Fort William, and watched the fire chief's eyebrows rise several times at her complicated story. He seemed satisfied by her testimony that the stove had not been used for at least twenty-four hours prior to her departure.

"I assume you have insurance? Is there anyone who might stand to gain by burning the restaurant?"

Maggie thought immediately of Earl. But surely even he wouldn't be foolish enough to think he had anything to gain from an insurance settlement when the paperwork was not even complete on his partnership. She shook her head. "I don't see how."

Chief Bennet sat back in his chair, his crisp white shirt tightening across his barrel-chested form. "Ma'am, from what you're telling me, you've had an incredible amount of stress in the past week, and you must be exhausted. I don't see any point in keeping you here longer at this time, but I'm afraid you will have to go see the police before you call it a day. I'm sorry." He gave Maggie a slip of paper with the name of the police officer assigned to her case, and she left his office.

"One more stop," she explained to Reuben. He nodded.

"I thought we'd stop by my boardinghouse and drop Charlotte and Darcy off there," Reuben said. "I've already called Mrs. O'Toole. She'll take good care of them until we can figure something out. She's got space for you, too."

Too overcome to speak, Maggie shot Reuben a grateful look. She hadn't even thought about where she and Charlotte would lay their heads that night.

At the police station, Maggie answered another round of similar questions. This time, Reuben remained at her side for support as they sat with an officer who had introduced himself as Detective Riley.

"Your neighbors informed me that you recently lost your husband, Mrs. Marshall," the young officer said. "I'm sorry."

"Thank you."

He continued. "This must come as quite a blow on the heels of so great a loss."

"It would have been a blow at any time," Maggie said quietly. Reuben put a hand on her shoulder.

"Of course." Officer Riley paused to clear his throat. "I want you to know that our department is doing everything we can to investigate this thoroughly. Now that we know your whereabouts, the matter *is* less urgent. Even if it turns out the fire was deliberately set, the possibility of manslaughter is ruled out. But that doesn't mean we will let it drop. We're working closely with the fire department and will keep you informed of any new developments."

"Thank you." Maggie still felt as if she might wake up any minute to a less harsh reality.

Reuben gave the police officer Mrs. O'Toole's telephone number and they left. It was a quiet ride to the boardinghouse, and when they pulled up behind it, neither was in a hurry to get out of the car.

Finally, Reuben spoke. "It's getting dark and I bet Mrs. O'Toole has supper for us. Think you can eat?"

Maggie sighed, then nodded. "I'll try."

"That's the spirit."

Maggie found Mrs. O'Toole's homemade bread and stew made from fresh garden vegetables did, surprisingly, manage to minister to her weary soul, as well as her body.

"The girl and the wee one are fast asleep," the landlady said softly. "Cried herself to sleep, the poor thing."

"Thank you for taking good care of them," Reuben said.

"It's what I'm here for, Reverend. And ma'am, if you'd like a nice hot soak in the bathtub, you just help yourself. Your bed is all ready for you. I laid out a nightgown you can use if you like, and if I can wash up some clothes for you, I'd be more than happy to."

So this is how it feels to receive the compassionate care of God's people, Maggie thought. *This must have been what Reuben meant about God doing his work through his people. If I'd been forthcoming about Doug's abuse, would I have experienced God's love after all?*

Maggie didn't know if her legs would carry her up the stairs, but she made it. She didn't stay in the tub long, fearing she'd doze off and drown. Once she had donned Mrs. O'Toole's nightgown, she handed the woman every stitch of clothing she had with her, suddenly realizing it was all she had in the world. She climbed between the clean cotton sheets and tried to relax. Remembering Reuben's habit of praying about everything, she decided to give it a try.

"God, I don't know if you listen to ordinary people like me. I've got nothing to offer you. Nothing. I'm completely empty. I have no home. No work. No family. I've done a rotten job with Charlotte. I wouldn't blame her parents if they file a lawsuit. I don't understand what's going on or how my life could come to such ruin so quickly.

"But God, if you're there, if you really see all, then you know the cause of the fire. Please guide the fire inspectors to it. And please show me what to do next." With that thought, Reuben's smiling face came to mind.

"And God, I thank you for Reuben. Thank you that we got Charlotte and Darcy safely back. And thank you for Mrs. O'Toole. Bless them all.

"And if you could have prevented my home from burning down, then I'm pretty mad at you right now. I hope you understand. Amen.

"Oh, and if you couldn't have prevented it, then I don't know why I'm bothering with you at all. Amen."

Talking to God was one thing, but surrendering her spunk was quite another.

CHAPTER 26

Charlotte lay on the twin bed Mrs. O'Toole had assigned her, Darcy snuggled closely at her breast. The landlady had kindly fashioned a little bed for him out of a willow laundry basket and several soft blankets, but Charlotte couldn't bear to be separated from him by even a few feet. She was exhausted, yet sleep refused to come. Just when she was convinced she'd shed her last tear, her crying would start all over again. One of the nurses at the hospital had told her it was common for new mothers to feel emotional, under even the best of circumstances, and Charlotte knew that hers were far from ideal. Her aching body, fatigue, and the pending doom of separation from her baby had been adding to her burden ever since his birth. But now, the load of guilt and loss was almost more than she could bear.

How could she have been so stupid? She had brought nothing but harm upon herself, her sweet baby, and Mrs. Marshall. Reverend Fennel had been inconvenienced beyond belief, yet remained so gracious. Now Mrs. O'Toole was providing for their needs, but who would pay? Charlotte had used the last of her money on that foolish train ticket, and for what? To try to reach a man who probably didn't even remember she existed. And although she'd tried twice this evening to telephone her parents, there was still no answer. She was certain they were still traveling, enjoying a holiday while her heart was breaking and her life falling apart.

The tears began again.

"Oh, God. If you really speak to people, I sure would like to hear from you now. How can I ever make it up to Mrs. Marshall? Where are Mother and Father, God?"

Her whispered prayers unsettled Darcy, and she worried his crying would disturb the others. She got out of bed and walked around the room with him, swaying gently when she stopped in front of the window.

"Shh-h. Shh-h, my little sweetheart. It's going to be okay."

She wasn't sure if she was saying the words more to the baby or to herself. How could anything ever be okay again? Everything she had imagined—the happy reunion with Reginald, getting married and becoming a real family—suddenly seemed like a naïve, adolescent dream. She felt incredibly foolish. Childish.

Charlotte wondered what it was like to hear from God the way Reverend Fennel did. Did he see a vision? Hear words? He'd said he couldn't describe it, he just knew he was being directed. That's what she needed: direction. She remembered seeing a Bible on the nightstand when she came to bed. Flicking on a lamp, she laid Darcy, now asleep, in his little bed and picked up the Bible.

As a child in Sunday school, she'd memorized verses and the books of the Bible in order, but it had all been just a game to her. If there was something in that book that could really apply to her right now, she'd need some kind of divine intervention for it to seep into her mind and heart. She flipped the book open to the approximate middle, not knowing where to turn but willing to absorb anything that might offer her strength or comfort or direction. Her eyes fell on the page.

She was not prepared for the eight words that touched her heart like soothing lotion on sunburned skin: *Be still, and know that I am God.*

At Mrs. O'Toole's breakfast table the next morning, Charlotte ate quietly with Reverend Fennel, Mrs. Marshall, and the other boarders. As they left one by one, however, conversation turned to plans for the day. Mrs. Marshall intended to visit her insurance agent first thing, and would meet Charlotte at the adoption agency at eleven o'clock. Reverend Fennel would drop Charlotte off there before going to work at his church.

"Once I get some insurance money, I will pay you whatever we owe," Mrs. Marshall told Mrs. O'Toole. "However much that turns out to be."

"No need to worry about that now. You have more than enough to think about." Mrs. O'Toole poured Reuben more coffee and carried the dirty oatmeal bowls into the kitchen.

"That could take a long time, Maggie," Reverend Fennel said.

Knowing Mrs. Marshall, Charlotte expected an argument. Instead, she simply said, "I know."

Reverend Fennel took a sip of his coffee. "Will you try to rebuild?"

Mrs. Marshall sighed. "I don't know. I may have to, in order to collect what's due me. But honestly, right now I don't have the heart for it. I'd just as soon get a job cooking for someone else for a while and not have the responsibility."

"Sometimes the wait for something provides the time a person needs to get their heart where it needs to be," Reverend Fennel said. "Working for someone else awhile might turn out to be good medicine. Especially if you have a good boss."

Charlotte absorbed the adult conversation with fresh eyes and ears. She had never had to worry about providing for herself before, but now that she had Darcy to think about, everything looked different to her. Even if she couldn't keep him, it would soon be time for her to think about what her contribution to the world would be—besides simply taking from it.

"Well, wish me luck." Mrs. Marshall rose from her seat and gathered her purse from a table by the front door.

"I'll do better than that," Reverend Fennel said. "I'll pray." He rose from the table. "Charlotte, let me know when you're ready to leave. I'll be in my room."

Two hours later, the reverend and Charlotte pulled up in front of the large redbrick building with GOVERNMENT SERVICES on the sign in front.

"Would you like me to come?" Reverend Fennel asked.

"Yes." Charlotte nodded. "Please." Gathering Darcy into her arms and as much courage as she could into her heart, she headed inside. She discovered Mrs. Marshall already in the lobby, giving a secretary their new telephone number. When Charlotte's name was called, all three of them entered Mrs. Shelton's office.

"Come in." The woman smiled. "Please, have a seat." She waved toward the chairs while she closed the door, and Charlotte took a seat between Reverend Fennel and Mrs. Marshall as they introduced themselves all around.

"So. There's been quite an unexpected turn of events, I hear?" Mrs. Shelton said, still smiling. "May I? Just for a moment, of course."

She held her arms out to the baby, and Charlotte handed him over with some reluctance. She'd met the woman only once before, when her parents first brought her to Winnipeg and arrangements were made for the adoption.

Mrs. Shelton walked around the desk to her own chair, snuggling Darcy closely and admiring him. "Such a sweet boy. You surprised us all, coming early, didn't you, little fellow?"

Then she turned to Charlotte with a warm smile. "He's beautiful, Charlotte."

"Thank you."

The woman stood and handed Darcy back to Charlotte across the desk, then sat down and directed her attention to a file folder.

"Now. As you know, the original agreement was for our adoptive parents to receive your baby as soon as he was born. Of course, circumstances have changed all that. How old is he now?"

"He was born last Thursday, so he's six days old," Charlotte said.

"Six days is a long time for a child to stay with his mother."

Charlotte only nodded.

"The parents are still very interested. However, there was one stipulation from the start. They requested that their own family doctor examine the child and that he be granted a clean bill of health before the adoption takes place."

"Wait a minute," Mrs. Marshall said. "That hardly seems fair. Parents who are expecting a baby in the usual way don't have that option. They get what they get."

"You're right, of course. Think of such conditions as a consolation prize for not being able to have a child in the usual way. We allow it."

Mrs. Marshall let out a *harrumph* and crossed her arms.

"In this particular case," the agent continued, "it may help you to know that the parents have already lost two children to genetic defects."

"Oh." Mrs. Marshall uncrossed her arms. "I guess that *is* different."

Charlotte felt instantly defensive. "The hospital staff in Fort William said he was perfect."

"I understand. Still, it is within the adoptive parents' rights to have him examined by a physician of their choosing. I'm sure it will be only a formality."

"How long will that take?" Reverend Fennel asked, glancing at Charlotte. "As I'm sure you're aware, the idea of separation becomes more difficult with every day that passes."

"Yes. And that's why I suggest we place the baby with a foster family until the parents are ready to take him. The foster mother could take him this afternoon. We have made an appointment for the doctor to see the baby tomorrow. He'll be run through quite a battery of tests, so there will be at least a two-hour wait for whoever takes him to the appointment."

To Charlotte, the woman's words were beginning to sound like they were coming through a long tunnel. "A foster family? No. Please!" She looked toward Reverend Fennel, willing him to side with her. To her surprise, it was Mrs. Marshall who spoke up.

"Now that just seems cruel. Bad enough the little tyke has to be handed to strangers. He shouldn't have to go through it twice."

Mrs. Shelton sighed. "It isn't required. But it is advised, for your sake, Charlotte."

Charlotte blinked hard to keep the tears at bay. "It will be hard no matter what. Please let me keep him until the parents are ready. I'm sure you can see that's best for Darcy."

She looked directly into the woman's eyes, and Mrs. Shelton held her gaze for several seconds. "You do realize he will be given a new name as well?"

Charlotte just nodded.

"Mrs. Marshall?" Mrs. Shelton said. "If I understand the arrangements that were made, until Charlotte's parents are located, you are still her guardian. Do you agree to support her until she is returned to them, even while the baby remains with her?"

Charlotte looked at Mrs. Marshall. How could the woman even consider offering Charlotte support when she was homeless and unemployed, recently widowed and probably penniless? And as soon as Mrs. Shelton knew all that, she wouldn't even consider letting Charlotte keep Darcy. This was going to be good-bye, she was certain. She couldn't bear to look at her little boy, but stared at her shoes, waiting for the final blow.

But Mrs. Marshall surprised her again.

"Yes," she said. "I will."

Charlotte looked up in grateful surprise, but Mrs. Marshall only looked at her out of the corner of her eyes.

"Very well." Mrs. Shelton slid a card across the desk. "Then see to it that the baby is at the office of this doctor tomorrow morning at ten o'clock. You'll hear from us again when all the results are back and the adoption is ready to be finalized."

Charlotte placed the card in her purse without looking at it. All that mattered was that she had been granted one more reprieve.

CHAPTER 27

Reuben couldn't believe it had happened again so quickly, after all these years. God had given him another directive, another vision. But this time, he was sure God was mistaken.

Long before they'd returned to Winnipeg, Reuben had recognized that he could never act on his childhood affection for Maggie Marshall. The very thought was ludicrous on every level. The woman's husband had been dead all of two weeks. The scandal that would result if he pursued her would be beyond recovery. Never mind that she'd given him no indication she felt the same about him. The way things had gone in her first marriage, she was probably done with men forever. And now she was in a boatload of trouble and grief. This was no time to be thinking thoughts of romance or making life-changing decisions. Even if by some miracle she did respond positively to a romantic overture, it would be only out of sheer desperation. That would be unfair to Maggie, and their partnership would be doomed to failure.

Besides, she'd make a miserable pastor's wife. If he could assist her and be a friend as she worked through the issues surrounding the fire, maybe help her get reestablished, then great. But nothing further could happen between them, Reuben had decided. This was only sensible.

Although they were all living under the same roof, over the past few days he'd seen Maggie, Charlotte, and Darcy only in passing or at meals—which he figured was probably for the best. After their visit to the adoption agent, Maggie had spent the next few days dealing with her insurance company, accompanying Charlotte and Darcy to the doctor, and looking for job openings, while Reuben had spent a day and a half visiting parishioners and two full days writing his sermon.

Both Maggie and Charlotte were planning to come to his church this Sunday. Both of them seemed to have a lot to sort out with God, and maybe he could help with that too. But not if there was any hint of something more going on in his heart.

But then, the dream.

It had come as he rehearsed his Sunday sermon. He'd often found that reviewing his sermons in his head as he lay in bed at night helped him to deliver them better. But this time, just as he reached the end and was ready to roll over and fall asleep, it happened. It came as clearly as anything he'd ever experienced, yet he could not accept it.

"That can't be right, God," he said aloud. "It just can't. You would never direct me to do something so crazy."

Besides, this time the vision wasn't like the others. For one thing, he was awake. At least he thought he was.

He rolled over and tried to ignore the message that came to him. But suddenly his room was filled with light, although it was still night. Time seemed to stand still—or to move very rapidly, he couldn't tell which. He closed his eyes tightly against the light. Was he asleep? He wrestled with God until he heard this:

How many times have you asked yourself what might have happened if you'd done the crazy thing I directed you to do back then?

Reuben knew exactly what this was about. He was eighteen years old when he'd received the direction to ask Maggie Sutherland to the spring dance. But back then, everyone knew Maggie was going with Douglas Marshall. They were practically engaged. Reuben could not bring himself to do it. It was the only time he'd failed to follow a directive, and he'd always thought that's why they stopped coming.

"Many. I've wondered countless times what might have happened," he confessed in a whisper. "I should have obeyed. I might have saved her untold grief at the hands of that man."

But this was different.

"God, I'm sorry, but this just seems wrong. I can't just jump into this. You'll have to give me something more, something that won't make me doubt this is from you and not just a longing from my own confused heart."

Is it that you're unsure it's from me? Or is it that your pride won't allow you to risk rejection?

Though Reuben couldn't hear the words with his ears, they were impressed upon his heart in a way that was new, yet undeniably powerful.

"It's both," he admitted, as much to himself as to God. "I don't want to feel like a fool. Besides, my plan to wait just seems a lot more godly and, well . . . *sensible*. Doesn't it?"

Silence.

Could the others in the house hear him? Was the stress of the past several days taking its toll, causing him to imagine things? Reuben heard nothing further, and the next thing he knew, the sun was up and the clock on his dresser said it was time to get up. He felt as if he hadn't slept for a minute . . . and he was quite certain that God had heard his *no* regarding a marriage proposal to Maggie Marshall.

Maggie and Charlotte sat side by side in a pew, Darcy asleep in his mother's arms. The little church was already warm on this early September Sunday, and ladies in hats fanned themselves with their programs. Not one of them had bothered to introduce herself or ask Maggie her name, though they looked at her with curiosity and something else Maggie couldn't name. Judgment? Pity? She was glad when the singing was over and Reuben stepped into the pulpit. She felt herself relax, eager to hear what he might have to say.

It was a good sermon. Reuben spoke with deep compassion to those who had lost family members in the war. He talked about his own losses in life and honestly shared what it was like to wrestle with God, to doubt God's love and power in the midst of one's pain. He was easy to listen to, and Maggie found the time flying by.

Although she herself had suffered two significant losses in recent days, it was the loss of her home and restaurant, not the loss of her husband, to which she applied Reuben's words. She felt great comfort when he pointed the congregation to Romans, chapter eight. Not just the pat-answer verse people liked to throw out about God working all things for good, but the entire chapter. In Reuben's telling of it, God assures his people that, though life will be hard, there is a coming glory that outweighs all our suffering. He pointed out that these verses compare our trials to the pain of a woman in childbirth, and the congregation chuckled when Reuben admitted he had no personal point of reference. But when he talked about the *glory* of a newborn infant diminishing the pain, there was a catch in his voice, and Maggie felt certain he was remembering the events of the previous week. She glanced over at Charlotte, who had tears on her cheeks.

Before she knew it, the service was over, the doxology had been sung, and they were walking home with Mrs. O'Toole while Reuben stayed behind to greet his flock.

Though his heart longed to follow Maggie down the street, Reuben knew he must shake hands and greet his parishioners after a week away. He ruffled the curly hair on top of Donny Robinson's head as the ten-year-old flew past, racing outside to enjoy the warm sunshine. As he shook hands with Donny's parents, he caught a glimpse of Elder

Mitchell approaching behind them, extra furrow lines surrounding his permanent scowl.

"Reverend," Elder Mitchell said. "We, the board, need to see you immediately. Please meet us in your office as soon as you've greeted the last person."

"Yes, sir." Reuben reached out, but the man did not shake hands with him. A sense of dread began niggling at him.

After he had wished the last straggler a good week, he closed the front doors and made his way to his office with heavy shoulders. It was not the board who awaited him, but only Elder Mitchell. He stood with his hands in his pockets, perusing the books on Reuben's shelf.

"Have a seat, young man," he said, but did not take one himself. Reuben sat in the chair behind his desk.

"I won't beat around the bush," the elder began. "When we couldn't find you last week, we contacted your landlady, who didn't know where you were either. She said only that you'd taken your car and had been gone two or three days already. When you finally telephoned Deacon Ellis and explained yourself, we called an emergency meeting of the elders board. By then, a few more details had come to light." Elder Mitchell leaned across the desk, his face so close Reuben could smell stale coffee on his breath.

"Is it true that you traveled halfway across the country with a single woman—a recently widowed woman, I might add—*without* a chaperone, *without* informing anyone of your purpose or your whereabouts, and *without* giving notice as to your pending absence last Sunday?"

Reuben shifted in his seat. "Well sir, we went as far as Fort William, which isn't nearly halfway across—"

"I don't need the details. Is it true or not?"

Though Reuben knew Mrs. O'Toole would never willingly betray him, the combination of her naïveté and chattiness had apparently done so as surely as any Judas. Denying these accusations would only make things worse. "Yes, sir."

The man stood upright again and began pacing the room like a courtroom lawyer. "And is it true that neither the woman you were accompanying nor the young pregnant girl you were chasing after are part of your own congregation?"

"Not yet, sir." He looked up at Elder Mitchell and nodded optimistically. "They were in church this morning, however."

"That hardly makes them church members."

"No, sir." Reuben slumped back into his seat.

Elder Mitchell stopped pacing and pivoted toward Reuben. "And is it true that you covered this little jaunt by using a special gas-ration card given to you in good faith by one of our deacons, for the purpose of emergencies arising within the congregation?"

Reuben merely nodded. Someone must have checked his desk drawer and put two and two together. *I'm doomed,* he thought.

"What do you have to say for yourself, young man?" Elder Mitchell had still not sat down and appeared to enjoy the power of his elevated position.

Reuben sighed. "You're right. I should have let someone know what I was doing, and I'm sorry. It was an errand of mercy, sir. Mrs. Marshall takes in unwed mothers. The girl she currently lodges had run off and Mrs. Marshall needed my assistance. I felt it constituted an emergency. There was no time to take it before the board."

"So you used your own judgment."

"Yes, sir. I did, but—"

"Well, your judgment was in very poor taste." The man placed his hands on his ample hips. "And, as you know, this is not the first time we have had to speak to you about using your time helping people outside your area of responsibility."

Tempted to challenge his broad use of the word *we,* Reuben swallowed hard instead. He knew the other board members had a habit of kowtowing to Elder Mitchell.

"And do you agree that the appearance of evil should be avoided by all Christians, but especially by those who set themselves up as leaders? That such behavior hurts the church?"

Reuben rose to his feet. "Sir, I'm certain our congregation would understand if I had the chance to explain—"

"Explain? And draw even more attention to your errancy? Absolutely not." Elder Mitchell crossed his arms over his bulging belly. "For these reasons, it is my unfortunate duty to inform you that the Elders Board of Smith Street Community Church has decided to let you go. We simply cannot afford this kind of scandalous behavior in a pastor. I'm certain that if you think about it long enough, you will agree you've left us no choice."

Reuben stared at the man, dumbfounded. He'd been expecting a reprimand, but would they really fire him?

"Just like that?" he asked. The shock made his knees weak, and he sank slowly to his chair once more.

"Please collect your personal items and vacate this office by noon tomorrow."

"But—" Reuben stammered. "Where are the rest of the board members?" But even as he asked the question, Reuben realized the other board members hadn't made eye contact with him that morning, which he'd noticed but dismissed. They were passive men who seemed all too willing to let Elder Mitchell do the dirty work, and it would do little good to appeal to any of them.

"It was a unanimous decision. If it makes you feel better, however, you are not without some friends on the board. If it had been up to me alone, you would not have been in the pulpit this morning. Some seemed to think it was only fair to allow you one more Sunday, though I don't know why. And surely even you can understand why we didn't inform you of our decision before this morning's service. You could have said anything."

Reuben couldn't help but wonder if it had simply been more convenient to let him preach one last time than to scramble for a last-minute substitute, but kept his question to himself.

"Will I have a chance to say good-bye?"

"Under the circumstances, that would be unwise. Any other questions?"

Reuben was too stunned to speak.

"If not, I'll be on my way. Mrs. Mitchell has a lovely roast in the oven. I would wish you luck in the future, but that is between you and the Lord. In spite of everything, I trust you to remove your items in a peaceful manner and not do anything spiteful or damaging to the Lord's property. Good day to you." He turned and walked out of the office without a backward glance.

Reuben sat motionless, staring at the surface of his desk for a solid ten minutes. His study Bible, the one he used for sermon preparations, still lay open to Romans, chapter eight. Instinctively, he knew the lesson he'd worked so hard to prepare was as much or more for him as it had been for his congregation. As his eyes began to well up, he read the following words, though they blurred before him:

"And we know that all things work together for good to them that love God, to them who are the called according to his purpose."

CHAPTER 28

On Monday morning, Maggie set out for her second visit to the insurance company's office, but her mind was on Reuben. As if all her other problems weren't enough, now she was worried about him. Something was wrong, and he wasn't saying what.

Over the past couple of weeks, Reuben had been the epitome of steadfastness, reason, and kindness, and she thought she'd gotten to know him quite well. But when he'd returned to Mrs. O'Toole's Sunday afternoon, it was as if a stranger had walked in the door. She had helped with lunch preparations, and everything was laid out on Mrs. O'Toole's long dining room table when he arrived. Fall flowers graced the center, the landlady's finest china laid out for Sunday's chicken and mashed potatoes. Mrs. O'Toole's insistence on waiting for "the reverend" had been met with mixed reviews by the other boarders.

When Reuben finally walked in, he crossed the entryway without a glance toward the dining room.

"I won't be eating today," he called over his shoulder as he headed up the stairs.

"But Reverend, we waited especially for you, lad," Mrs. O'Toole began. "'Twas a wonderful sermon! You must be famished."

That's when Maggie saw a side of the man she had not previously seen. He stopped on the stairs, turned, and faced his landlady. His face had a red hue to it, like he'd been in the sun too long, and his voice had an edge to it, making him sound like a parent whose last fragile thread of patience has snapped.

"Mrs. O'Toole, I have never asked you to wait for me, nor am I asking now, nor will I at any time in the future."

Poor Mrs. O'Toole looked like a lost kitten as Reuben turned and continued up the stairs. At the top, the door to his room shut with an extra-loud thud, and Maggie didn't see him the rest of the day. As far as she knew, no one else did either. The group ate their meal in silence. Mrs. O'Toole merely picked at her plate, sniffing occasionally and glancing toward the top of the stairs every five minutes.

Monday morning, Reuben had come downstairs while Maggie was helping Mrs. O'Toole prepare breakfast. He poured himself a cup of coffee, drank half of it, then left the cup on the counter and headed toward the front door. With his hand on the doorknob, he turned around briefly. "Mrs. O'Toole, I owe you and the others an apology for my behavior yesterday. I'm sorry." Without waiting for her reply, he left.

Clearly, something had happened after church on Sunday, and he wasn't ready to talk about it. Maggie's pride was wounded. She had already dumped so much on him. Surely he knew he could share his problems with her. Hadn't their friendship meant more to him than that?

That afternoon her bus stopped half a block from the insurance office, and she walked the rest of the way. It turned out that, just as she had thought, no funds could be released until the fire department declared that there was no suspicion of foul play—at least not by anyone who stood to gain anything as a result of the fire. At least there was no appearance of Earl's name anywhere on the paperwork. When the money finally came through, it would be hers alone.

Her next stop was the post office. They had been collecting her mail since the fire and now encouraged her to rent a mailbox to which they could forward any future mail until she was settled somewhere. She did so, sighing over the extra cost, and carried home the small bundle that had accumulated. On the bus ride home, she flipped through it. Besides bills, there was a letter for Charlotte from her parents and a note for Maggie from one of her former girls, Cornelia Simpson. Apparently, her last name was Baker now. Maggie read the note as the bus bumped along.

> Dear Mrs. Marshall,
> I thought you might like to know how I've been doing since finishing normal school. I got a teaching position at my childhood school here in Roseburg and will be starting my second year next week. It's challenging with eight grades all in the same class, but I love it! Better than that, I got married in July to Stuart Baker. Stuart is a teacher at the town school, so we have a lot in common. Life is going well—as well as can be expected with the war and everything. Of course, we all hope it is over soon. Stuart has been helping out with pulpit supply on Sundays. Sadly, our church is without a pastor right now. Pastor Johnson, the man who married us, was called away to care for his aging parents after the death of his younger brother overseas. Stuart is wonderful with children, but does not truly feel led to teach or preach to adults!
> I think of you often as I tend my garden and prepare some of the recipes you

taught me to make. I hope you and the restaurant are doing well and that your husband will soon be home.
Sincerely,
Cornelia (Simpson) Baker

Maggie read the note two more times. Among all the girls she'd sheltered, Cornelia stood out. She was the hardest worker and the most levelheaded, by far. The most ambitious, too, finishing high school by correspondence while she worked in the restaurant and waited for her baby to arrive. Even with all that on her plate, she also took the most interest in learning cooking and serving skills and in doing her work with integrity. It was surprising that a girl like that would even find herself in such a position in the first place. But Maggie never asked, and the girls rarely volunteered the circumstances surrounding their confinement. Most of them, like Charlotte, held high hopes that their babies' fathers would come galloping in like knights in shining armor and make everything right. They never did.

So, Cornelia had saved up her restaurant earnings and gone on to be a teacher. Maggie was not surprised to hear she was doing well and had already married. She was a pretty girl, and pleasant—even in the face of Maggie's cold treatment. She supposed she should write back and inform Cornelia of the loss of the restaurant, in case she was ever in the city and came looking. One could always hope.

But there wasn't time for such things now. Maggie picked up a newspaper at the stand next to the bus stop and walked to Mrs. O'Toole's in time to help with lunch preparations. It was the least she could do, since Mrs. O'Toole insisted she wasn't charging either Maggie or Charlotte room and board until they could get their situations settled.

Reuben did not return for lunch.

After the dishes were cleared away, Maggie spent the first hour of the afternoon looking for job ads in the paper, and the remainder of the day visiting four different restaurants that were looking for cooks and waitresses. At the first three, she introduced herself to the manager on duty and each told her the same thing: They were not hiring.

The last restaurant she visited was in the Fort Garry Hotel, the grandest hotel in Winnipeg. Lots of famous people had stayed there, including Sir Arthur Conan Doyle and King George and Queen Elizabeth. Maggie had been there once, for a wedding, and thought herself awfully bold to be approaching the imposing building now—especially with the dinner hour only a couple of hours away. But what did she have to lose?

The maître d' looked Maggie up and down when she explained why she was there. She was certain he was about to dismiss her when, to her surprise, the manager walked up behind him and asked a point-blank question.

"Did I hear you say Bert's Restaurant?"

Maggie nodded. "Bert Sutherland was my father."

"That place has a reputation for great pie. You the baker by any chance?"

"Yes, of course." Maggie tried not to stammer. "And chief cook."

"If you can crank out ten pies in time for tonight's dessert cart, and if they meet our standards, you might just have yourself a job."

"N-now?" Maggie did stammer this time.

"Our pastry chef enlisted in the army and didn't show up for work. I'm desperate. You willing or not?" The man said most of this without looking up from the clipboard he carried.

"Uh—sure. Can I just make one telephone call?" Maggie fished through her purse for Mrs. O'Toole's number.

"Show her the phone, Marcel, then show her the kitchen," the manager said to the maître d', before turning away so he could tackle his next dilemma. He hadn't even given Maggie his name, nor had he asked for hers.

CHAPTER 29

Charlotte stared at her reflection in Mrs. O'Toole's full-length mirror, slightly tilted on its stand. Despite her new matronly figure, she still looked like a child. Her long, sandy blond hair had not been trimmed in over a year and hung to the middle of her back. The skirt and blouse she wore were offerings from Mrs. O'Toole's attic and tragically outdated.

She knew she should feel grateful, and she was trying. The truth was, Mrs. O'Toole was rapidly becoming her only companion. Mrs. Marshall was busy with business affairs and job hunting. Her new friend, Reverend Fennel, who had seemed so kind and trustworthy, was suddenly distant. She still had not succeeded in reaching her parents by telephone. She had called her friend Rose, who was eager to hear whatever Charlotte might know about the fire, which was nothing. Rose expressed no interest in Charlotte's baby, but was excited about starting her last year of high school this week.

With little else to do, Charlotte spent her time caring for Darcy. Mrs. O'Toole taught her how to bathe him and what she could do to prevent diaper rash. And today she had shown Charlotte how to wash the diapers, which Charlotte declared the most disgusting job in the universe. But she had to admit, when she brought them inside from the clothesline where they'd hung in the morning sunshine, the clean, fresh smell filled her with a sense of accomplishment. What would her girlfriends back home think of her now?

When Mrs. Marshall returned at lunchtime, she handed Charlotte a letter from her parents. It had been sent from somewhere in British Columbia a week earlier. Finally! She laid a sleeping Darcy in his laundry-basket bed and opened the envelope. Her mother's familiar handwriting filled half a page.

Charlotte:

We have been trying repeatedly to call you. Is Mrs. Marshall's telephone out of order? What is going on? I left our travel itinerary with the Piersons back home, who were also collecting our mail and such. David Pierson managed to track us down at our hotel in Vancouver. He said a telegram arrived for us at home, which he signed for. It was from someone named Marlajean Olson and it makes no sense whatsoever. It says, CHARLOTTE EXITED TRAIN FT. WILLIAM. BABY COMING. CONTACT MCKELLAR HOSPITAL ASAP.

Charlotte, this makes no sense at all. Did the baby come early? Why on earth would you be in Ft. William? We called the hospital and they said they had no record of a Charlotte Penfield having been there. Was this Olson woman some kind of kook? Why is there no answer at Mrs. Marshall's? What hospital are you to have the baby at in Winnipeg? We couldn't remember.

We also contacted the adoption agency, but the secretary we spoke with had no information and Mrs. Shelton has not yet returned our call.

The letter closed with a phone number for the place where her parents expected to be by the time Charlotte received the letter, a hotel in Calgary. With Mrs. O'Toole's permission, Charlotte placed the long-distance call, only to be informed her parents had checked out that morning. Would their next stop be Winnipeg?

Returning to her room, Charlotte picked up her sleeping baby and held him close. She was tempted to run away again, but told herself that was not the answer. She'd learned that the hard way, causing much grief and loss to others in the process. It was time she started behaving like a grown-up.

"Sweetheart, it's going to be okay," she sang as she rocked Darcy gently and studied his tiny face. "Your grandparents are going to fall in love with you, just wait and see. How could they not? They'll take us both home with them and then . . . then . . . well, I don't know what then. But it will all be okay. We have to believe it will all be okay. You believe it, don't you, my sweet son? I know you do."

It was late afternoon when she heard a tap on her door. "Telephone for you, Charlotte," Mrs. O'Toole called from the other side of the bedroom door. Charlotte hadn't even heard it ring.

She opened the door. "Is it my parents?"

"Not unless they're in town. It's a local call, love."

Charlotte was half-expecting, against the odds, for it to be her father on the line. Instead, she heard the crisp voice of Mrs. Shelton, the adoption agent. Her heart sank. This could only mean it was time. Darcy's new parents were ready to take him home.

"Good afternoon, Charlotte. How are you today?"

"I'm well, thank you." She swallowed hard. *Whatever is best for Darcy.*

"I'm calling to ask when you might be able to come to my office for a consultation, the sooner, the better."

"A consultation?"

"Yes. There's been a turn of events we need to discuss. Have your parents arrived?"

"No, ma'am."

"Then you'll need to bring Mrs. Marshall with you. Is she there with you now?"

"No, ma'am." Mrs. Marshall had called Mrs. O'Toole earlier to say she would be tied up through the evening.

"Can you come first thing in the morning?"

"I can. I don't know about Mrs. Marshall."

Mrs. Shelton cleared her throat. "If she cannot come with you, please have her call me. But you come regardless, please. It's important."

They said their good-byes and Charlotte returned to her room, where Darcy had awakened and was ready to be changed and fed. As she snuggled him close, she wondered what this turn of events could possibly be. How would she get a moment's rest tonight, wondering and imagining the possibilities?

At dinner that evening, Reverend Fennel apologized to the whole group for his behavior of the previous day. Once the meal was cleared away and the others had left the room, he asked Charlotte about her day and what the latest word was on her parents. He even held Darcy and suggested Charlotte might want to go for a walk around the block to get some fresh air and a little break. "Not too long, though," he added. "I sure like this little guy, but I won't know what to do if he gets fussy."

Charlotte hesitated. Her doctor had recommended walking as a great exercise, and she hadn't been apart from the baby since leaving the hospital. Perhaps it would do her good. Reverend Fennel seemed like his old self again; at least he was sure trying to be. But she just couldn't bring herself to leave her son in his care when she'd seen another side of him. She saw the irony in this. How could she ever turn Darcy over to complete strangers if she couldn't even trust this man who had become a friend and, in a way, her rescuer?

"Can I ask you a question first?" She couldn't believe she was being this bold, but perhaps motherhood changed a person.

"Sure."

"Are you always . . . well . . . out of sorts . . . after church on Sunday?"

Reuben sighed. "No, Charlotte. I'm not. Yesterday was an exceptional day. Let's just say I got some difficult news, and I'm still sorting it out. I'm sorry you had to see that."

That satisfied Charlotte enough that she was able to take a lovely walk and enjoy the sights and sounds of the neighborhood. Even though it was still early September, some of the trees were turning brilliant colors and the evening air was beginning to hold the promise of cold days ahead. She wrapped her old blue sweater around herself and breathed deeply.

"God," she prayed. "If this is my last night with my little boy, I need you desperately. See me through this somehow."

CHAPTER 30

Reuben handed Charlotte the milk bottle across the breakfast table. "Has anyone seen Maggie this morning?"

"All's I know is she said she'd be in late last night." Mrs. O'Toole took her place at the foot of the table and added brown sugar to her porridge. "Her hat's on its hook, I checked for it. Probably exhausted, poor thing."

"I hope she's up soon. She's to go with me to see Mrs. Shelton this morning." Charlotte ate her breakfast with her right hand, holding a sleeping Darcy closely in her left arm.

"Does she know that?" Reuben stirred his cereal to cool it.

"Haven't had a chance to tell her yet, but Mrs. Marshall isn't one to sleep in."

"Haven't had a chance to tell me what?" Maggie came down the stairs, buttoning the cuffs on her sleeves.

"Oh, there you be, love!" Mrs. O'Toole jumped up to retrieve the coffeepot from the kitchen, but Maggie patted her shoulder.

"Sit. I can get my own coffee."

Everyone at the table watched as Maggie returned with her cup and took a place at the table. She dished up oatmeal and added milk and sugar before realizing all eyes were on her. "What?"

"You tell us." Reuben smiled at her as he buttered a piece of toast.

Maggie grinned. "Well, if you must know, I got a job."

Mrs. O'Toole looked at Reuben, then back to Maggie. "That was quick."

"It seems Bert's Restaurant has a reputation in this town for excellent pie. You're looking at the new pastry chef at the Fort Garry Hotel."

Mrs. O'Toole let out an impressive whistle. "That's grand! Congratulations."

"Thank you. I worked my first shift yesterday, and they want me back today at one o'clock. It's only temporary, of course, until I can get my own place up and running again."

Reuben knew he was staring, but he couldn't stop himself. Maggie had not allowed herself one moment to mourn her husband, to recover from the draining trip to Fort William, nor to grieve the loss of her business and home. He knew she was surely exhausted, but she didn't look haggard. On the contrary, there was a warmth and inner light to her that hadn't been there before. Still, he couldn't help but worry.

"Are you sure this is what you want to do, Maggie?"

"I'm not sure of anything, Reuben. All I know for sure is the offer was made, and I'm in no position to refuse it. They even provide a uniform, which is jolly good luck for a woman with only two outfits to her name, don't you think?" She turned her eyes toward Charlotte. "For heaven's sake, Charlotte, what's all the fidgeting about?"

Reuben could see the distress on Charlotte's face, but the girl said nothing. "Charlotte's had a call from the adoption agency," he prompted.

"Oh." Maggie looked at the girl. "Well?"

"Mrs. Shelton wants me there first thing this morning, and asked that you come too."

"I see. Well, that shouldn't be a problem. We can make it back here before I need to leave for work and if not, I'll take the bus from there. Did she say what it was about?"

"Not exactly, only that it was important. But there's more. I've heard from my parents. They received word about the baby. They'll be here soon, maybe today."

"I'm free today, Charlotte." Reuben swallowed the last of his coffee. "Just let me know where you need to be and when."

Maggie spoke around a mouthful of toast. "How did your parents hear?"

"Marlajean, the lady from the train, sent a telegram. Our neighbor accepted it, and when my parents called him, he relayed the message. But they won't know to find me here."

"It'll be quite a shock if they show up at Bert's. Seems like the only connection they've got now is the adoption agency. Best we head over there." Maggie spooned up the last of her oatmeal and swallowed it as she rose from the table. "Thanks, Mrs. O'Toole. Sorry I can't stick around to help you today. You know I'm going to make all this up to you, right?"

"I don't want to hear another word about it." Mrs. O'Toole started gathering dishes. "And those are the same words I said to that gossipy old Edith Osten when I ran into her at the grocery store yesterday too. Makin' up stories about ya, Rev'rend. Says you've been reprimanded by the board and won't be back. I put her in her place, let me tell you I did. The nerve. 'I don't want to hear another word about it,' I said."

Reuben watched her head for the kitchen. He glanced at Maggie and Charlotte, but they were already on their way up the stairs, tuning out Mrs. O'Toole's chatter.

"Would you like me to come along?" he called up the stairs.

"Thank you, Reverend Fennel. I would like that very much," Charlotte called. "We'll be right down."

"I'll drive you then. Let me bring the car around to the street." Glancing toward the kitchen again, he sighed and headed out the door to start his car.

In Mrs. Shelton's waiting room, Maggie turned to Reuben. "You sure you don't need to be at work? We can manage."

"This *is* my work." Reuben held his hat in both hands, flipping it around as he leaned forward, elbows on his knees. He wished he had the courage to tell Maggie the truth.

"Well, not technically, since we're not part of your congregation. Yet." Maggie reached toward Reuben's lapel as if she was going to pull off a piece of lint, but then stopped. When he caught her eye, she pulled her hand back. "No meetings today? Sermon preparation?"

"Look, if you want me to leave, just say so." Reuben placed his hat on his head.

"Of course I don't want you to leave. I'm just saying—"

"Miss Penfield? Mrs. Shelton will see you now." The receptionist opened the door to Mrs. Shelton's office, and the trio filed in.

Maggie and Charlotte took the only two chairs opposite Mrs. Shelton's desk while Reuben stood behind Charlotte, hat in hand once again. The girl was trembling, and he laid a hand of support on her shoulder. The receptionist closed the door, and Mrs. Shelton took her time shuffling through a file of papers before her.

"Good morning, Charlotte. Mrs. Marshall. And Reverend . . . ?"

"Fennel. Reuben Fennel."

"Right. I do wish your parents were here, Charlotte, but I see no reason to drag this out any longer. We've had a highly unusual turn of events. But then, this case has been unusual for some time now, hasn't it?" She looked down at the stack of papers again. "I'm not sure how to tell you this, Charlotte, but it seems your son's doctor has found an abnormality with his heart."

Charlotte gasped. "His *heart*? He's all right, though, right? I mean, he's perfectly healthy."

"He does *appear* perfectly healthy." She nodded. "The diagnosis is a ventricular septal defect, also called a hole in the heart."

"A hole?" Charlotte's hand flew to her own chest, and she clutched Darcy even more closely.

"Now, it's not at all uncommon in newborns, and often it will grow closed on its own."

"And if it doesn't?" Maggie asked. Reuben thought she sounded as distressed as Charlotte.

"It won't necessarily cause problems. Dr. Monroe said it's a good sign that his skin does not have a bluish color, one of the most obvious symptoms when the defect is serious. That means his blood is not oxygen-poor." Mrs. Shelton looked down and read from the notes. "'Many people with small ventricular septal defects lead normal, productive lives with few related problems.'"

"So let me guess." Maggie shifted in her seat. "The adoptive parents don't want to take the risk."

Mrs. Shelton paused, and Reuben wondered if she was searching for the right words. "They have decided to forfeit this opportunity and will wait for a healthy baby."

Reuben could feel Charlotte's shoulders sag beneath his hand. Was it from relief or despair? Baby Darcy lay awake on her lap, his innocent eyes gazing up at her.

"I can't believe it," she whispered. "He's so perfect. Are you sure it wasn't a mistake?"

"I'm afraid not." Mrs. Shelton tapped a stack of papers together neatly.

Maggie cleared her throat. "So what happens next?"

"I want to keep him!" Charlotte pleaded. "More than ever, I want to keep him." The tears were flowing in earnest now, and Reuben again found himself offering the girl his hanky. Truth was, he was having a difficult time keeping his own emotions in check.

Maggie took Darcy from Charlotte's lap. "Now, Charlotte. You'll never convince your parents you're mature enough to be a mother if they see you blubbering like this."

"But you don't understand," the girl sobbed. "I can't let him go now. He needs me! I know him. I know his cries, and he knows my voice."

Reuben was reminded of the Bible story about Solomon and the two women who both claimed a baby as their own. How he longed for Solomon's wisdom now. A knock at the door made them all turn their heads. Mrs. Shelton's receptionist stuck her head in.

"Sorry to interrupt, but the Penfields have just arrived, inquiring about Charlotte. Shall I send them in?"

"Please!" The relief in Mrs. Shelton's voice was palpable.

Reuben watched as a middle-aged couple walked in and looked around the room. It was apparent from Mrs. Penfield's pink silk suit and matching hat that they were well-off. Her husband towered over them all, a striking figure in a double-breasted pinstriped suit and an unfortunate choice of facial hair that reminded Reuben of Adolf Hitler.

The receptionist left, closing the door behind her. The little office was now overly crowded, and Reuben wondered if he should volunteer to leave. But his curiosity kept him pinned to the spot.

"Charlotte!" Mrs. Penfield's face was as white as the wall behind her. "What on earth is the meaning of all this?"

Mr. Penfield took up the cause next. "There you are, Mrs. Marshall! I hope you have a good explanation for what has occurred here over the last week."

"I do indeed, sir." Maggie stood and trained her eye on him. "Your grandson was born, that's what occurred. I should think any grandparent would be thrilled to know their daughter was safe and sound and had delivered a robust child. I would think that after such a long absence, they would want nothing more than to hold their daughter in their arms again and see their newborn grandchild. *I would think—*"

"What you think has nothing to do with it!" The man's face was turning crimson, and Reuben didn't know whether to fear more for his immediate health or for Maggie's safety. As Mr. Penfield's volume rose,

Darcy began to whimper. "You were hired to watch over our daughter and to ensure the child was delivered as promptly as possible into the hands of his new parents via the adoption agency. From what I can see, you have failed in the most miserable way imaginable—"

"Mr. Penfield, if I might have a word?" Reuben figured he should jump in before the man blew a gasket, and he used his most commanding voice to address the taller man.

"And who on earth are you?"

But Mrs. Shelton spoke first. "Please. Mr. and Mrs. Penfield, the only way we'll settle this is if everyone stays calm. Perhaps it would be best if Mrs. Marshall and Reverend Fennel waited in the other room for the time being."

"Nothing doing! I want explanations, and I want to hear them from her!" Mr. Penfield pointed his finger in Maggie's face.

To Reuben's surprise, Maggie ignored the man and turned instead to Charlotte's mother. "Please, Mrs. Penfield. Take my seat. Meet your grandson. Speak to your daughter. Reuben and I will be right outside if you need us."

With that, she placed Darcy in Charlotte's arms and left the room. Reuben followed, shutting the door on the sounds of Mr. Penfield's protests, Charlotte's continued sobbing, Darcy's wails, and Mrs. Shelton's exasperated pleas for everyone to calm down.

CHAPTER 31

If Charlotte had thought labor and delivery were difficult, she now saw them as nothing compared to the agony she faced at this moment. Her father looked as if he would rip Darcy right out of her arms and toss him out the window. Her mother refused to look at the baby, though she remained calmer than her husband as she stared at the surface of Mrs. Shelton's desk. While blowing her nose hard, Charlotte managed only to make Darcy cry harder. She wiped her eyes, took a deep breath, and focused on settling her baby.

"You can have my chair, Father." She got up and began gently swaying like Mrs. O'Toole had taught her. "It's okay, little Darcy. Mommy's got you," she whispered close to his ear. "Shh-shh. It's okay."

Her father took the seat but ignored his daughter. "Mrs. Shelton. I daresay you and your agency are as much to blame as Mrs. Marshall. Would you mind telling me why this infant is not now in his own home with his proper parents?"

"And why he wasn't born here, in Winnipeg," Charlotte's mother added.

Her father leaned forward in his seat, one hand on his hip and the other wagging a pointer finger at Mrs. Shelton. "And I hope you realize you've completely lost any chance of receiving a favorable reference from us in the future."

Charlotte wondered why anyone would ever have occasion to ask her parents for a reference when the whole situation was all such a big secret. Who would know to ask? But she held her tongue, thankful that Darcy had quieted.

Mrs. Shelton looked up at Charlotte. "To begin, you'll have to ask your daughter what she was doing in Fort William when she knew the baby was due in a few weeks. What do you have to tell your parents, Charlotte?"

Drawing upon everything in her, Charlotte managed to hold back the flow of tears that were threatening to spill. She knew Mrs. Marshall was correct. Emotion would not work in her favor at this point. The only hope she had of winning her parents over was to show them a contrite heart, a humble attitude, and the truth. She sent up a quick prayer for strength and took a deep breath.

"Father . . . Mother . . . I am so sorry. I behaved very foolishly, I see that now and I could not regret it more. I just—I thought if I could just get to Reginald's camp, if he knew about the baby, everything would be okay. He would marry me as soon as he was released, and we could be together. So I caught a train for Petawawa, but the baby started coming before we reached Fort William, and they put me off the train."

"I don't understand." Her father shook his head, still angry. "Why did Mrs. Marshall approve of this?"

"She didn't, Father. She didn't know. It's not her fault."

"You ran away?" her mother gasped. "Do you have any idea how dangerous—"

"How could you have run away when Mrs. Marshall is supposed to be supervising you? Where was she?"

"She was at her husband's funeral." Charlotte felt so ashamed, remembering how she'd taken advantage of the situation. How could she have done such a thing? Although Mrs. Marshall still had her rough edges, in the days since the funeral, Charlotte had seen another side to her, and now she found herself wanting to defend the woman who'd shown her such commitment since this nightmare began. She knew Mrs. Marshall had grown fond of Darcy too.

"Her husband's . . . *funeral?*" Her mother sounded incredulous.

To Charlotte's relief, Mrs. Shelton jumped in. "A lot has occurred in the last couple of weeks. It's unfortunate that none of us were able to reach you. I'm afraid Mr. Marshall was killed in action. Apparently the funeral provided Charlotte the opportunity she believed she needed to seek out the baby's father. But as you can see, her plans were derailed. Pardon the pun."

No one was amused.

"So you had the baby in Fort William, and then what? Why is he here with you?" Charlotte's mother put a hand to her head. "I'm getting a headache just trying to sort all this out."

"Marlajean, the lady who befriended me on the train, sent you the telegram. When Mrs. Marshall discovered I was missing, she came after me. She and Reverend Fennel. I don't even know how they knew where to find me, but they did."

Mrs. Shelton spoke up. "By the time Mrs. Marshall found Charlotte and Darcy, they were—"

Charlotte's father raised a hand. "Wait a minute. Who on earth is Darcy?"

"Your grandson." Charlotte held the baby up for her parents to get a good look. "And he's wonderful. Would you like to hold him, Father?"

"Certainly not! He is not my grandson. There are no doubt two perfectly good sets of grandparents waiting to coddle this . . . this . . . child. Why are they not already in this picture? Where are his parents?"

More than anything, Charlotte wanted to scream, *I am his parent!* But she held her tongue.

"Unfortunately, the adoptive parents have changed their minds," Mrs. Shelton explained.

A sputtering sound escaped the lips of Charlotte's father. "They can't do that!"

"They were quite within their rights. I can show you the paperwork if you like."

"No need for that. I just don't understand on what grounds they could back out, and why didn't they say something sooner?"

Charlotte shot an entreating look at Mrs. Shelton in hopes that she wouldn't say anything about Darcy's health issues yet. Surely, if her parents would just take a good look at the sweet boy, if they'd hold him, they would fall in love with him as she had. Before Mrs. Shelton could speak, however, her father launched into another tirade.

"Well, you'll just have to find another set of parents, that's all there is to it. And in the meantime, find someone else who can care for the child. We came to collect our daughter and take her home, and that is exactly what we mean to do. We should be nearly home by now." He stood and moved toward the door. "Come along, Charlotte. Leave the baby with Mrs. Shelton."

"But Father . . . !"

"No buts. This organization has been grossly negligent, and it will bear the consequences. Come along, Laura."

But Charlotte's mother remained in her seat, wringing her hands. "Edward, please. Be reasonable."

"Reasonable? I'm being perfectly reasonable. We hashed all this out months ago, and we are sticking with the plan, regardless of who else proves their incompetence. Can we help it we lucked into a bunch of numskulls that can't keep track of one young girl?"

Charlotte's mother waved one hand toward the baby and looked up at her husband with pleading eyes. "Whether you acknowledge it or not, Edward, this *is* your grandson. *Our* grandson. We can't just dump him here and expect the agency to deal with it. He could end up with anyone!"

Charlotte felt hope surge in her heart and held Darcy toward her mother. "Do you want to hold him? Isn't he sweet?"

Her mother glanced at the baby, then at her husband's fierce glare. Finally, her eyes settled on the floor. "No sense in getting attached, Charlotte. This reminds me of when you were little and were forever dragging home stray kittens."

"Stray kittens? Mother, how can you say such a thing? Darcy is my son, and now that I know what it is to be his mother, you can't make me give him up." Charlotte took the chair her father had vacated.

Mrs. Shelton cleared her throat. "If I may say something . . . ?"

"Well, I wish you would." Charlotte's father didn't move from the door.

Mrs. Shelton removed her eyeglasses and pressed two fingers against the bridge of her nose. "The events surrounding Darcy's birth are most unusual, I will grant you. And you still have not heard the entire story." She replaced her glasses. "When Charlotte and the baby returned to Winnipeg with Mrs. Marshall and the reverend, they discovered that Mrs. Marshall's home and restaurant had burned to the ground. Their world has been in turmoil, to say the least."

Charlotte watched her father's jaw drop. "Burned? On purpose?"

"We don't know yet, Father. But just think, it could have happened while we were there, asleep. Then all truly would be lost." Surely now her father would muster a little compassion.

But he only gave her a withering glare. "More likely it wouldn't have happened at all had you been there."

It felt like a blow to her midsection. How could he know how much that very thought had plagued her?

"Edward, that's unfair." Charlotte's mother folded her hands across the top of her purse and addressed Mrs. Shelton. "What do you propose we do?"

Mrs. Shelton shuffled through the growing stack of papers from Charlotte's file. "I may be able to find another set of parents, but it would take at least a month, maybe two, to arrange. With the war on, it's not like there are young married couples lined up at my door. Ordinarily I would suggest foster care for Darcy in the meantime. However, I've never been a believer in shuffling children to another caregiver after they've bonded with the first. In truth, I have fought hard to prevent that. If you could see clear to allow Charlotte to keep him until he can be placed in the care of his permanent—"

"Certainly not." Her father's voice was quiet, but firm. "Not for another minute."

"Father! You're not listening. I won't let him go, I don't care if King George himself wants to adopt him."

"It's not for you to say, young lady."

"I'll just run away then. I'll do it."

"Well now, isn't that mature? You're certainly proving yourself a grown-up, aren't you?"

Charlotte let the tears flow now. There was no point. Once again, Darcy started to cry and Charlotte knew he had to be getting hungry. Without a word, she lifted her blouse and began taking care of her baby's need.

"What are you—? Oh, my Lord. Tell me this is not happening." Her father turned his back, folding his hands together behind it.

Charlotte's mother rolled her eyes. "How did you think she was feeding him, Edward? There has to be some way to work this out, Mrs. Shelton."

With a quick glance at Charlotte, Mrs. Shelton took a deep breath and let it out. "There's also the matter of Darcy's health. We would have to disclose everything to any potential parents, of course."

"His health? But Mrs. Marshall called him robust." Charlotte's mother looked at Darcy.

"And he certainly is, from all outward appearances. But his doctor has diagnosed a heart problem that may or may not bring future complications. The couple we were working with has already lost two children and did not want to assume the risk. I'm sorry."

"He's going to be just fine, Mother," Charlotte cut in. "Chances are very good this will never be a problem, especially if he stays with me and keeps getting my milk."

"Oh, for heaven's sake. What kind of circus is this?" Her father's posture was beginning to show signs of defeat.

"I think Charlotte is exaggerating on those last points," Mrs. Shelton said. "There is nothing in the doctor's report about that . . ."

Charlotte's mother nodded. "I thought as much."

"But she *could* have a point," Mrs. Shelton continued. "Doctors don't know everything. I've always thought mother's milk was best for a baby."

"It's not your place to have an opinion, Mrs. Shelton." Charlotte's father placed his hat firmly on his head. "Now this argument has gone on long enough. I'm sure you have other clients. We'll be back tomorrow, and I do want this settled by then. Charlotte, please take the baby and get in our car. We'll stop wherever you're staying, gather your things, and take you to our hotel with us."

With that, he strode out the door and through the waiting room without a backward glance.

CHAPTER 32

After she and Reuben removed themselves to the waiting room, Maggie knew she should feel a weight lifted from her shoulders. Charlotte's parents were here. For better or worse, they'd have to work things out as a family, and the matter was no longer her responsibility. Instead, her heart felt only heavier. She could see how devoted the girl had become, the bond between her and her baby an obvious one. She saw the change that had occurred in Charlotte, the kind of growth that can only result from someone loving another more than self. Maggie's own heart would break for Charlotte if the girl were forced to say a forever good-bye to Darcy. For the first time, Maggie wished she'd been more empathetic with the other girls who'd given up their babies. In truth, she couldn't bear the thought of saying good-bye to Darcy herself.

Reuben sat, hat in hand, leaning forward with his elbows on his knees. Was he praying or merely studying the pattern of the floor tiles? Maggie recognized that this might not be the best time to approach him about what was eating him, but then again, there might never be a good time.

"Thank you for being here, Reuben," she began. He acknowledged her with only a slight nod. "If you need to get to work, we'll all understand."

"I don't need to get to work." He continued staring at the floor.

"Is there something you want to tell me?" When he didn't respond, she tried again. "Look, I've leaned on you so much in the last while. Now I know something's going on with you, something beyond Charlotte and the baby. You're not yourself. I wish you'd trust me with it."

Reuben lifted his face, but gazed only toward the reception desk. "I trust you, Maggie."

"Well, then . . . ?"

The sigh that escaped ended in a slight tremble of his lips. "Let's just say I am no longer pastor of Smith Street Community Church."

Maggie wasn't sure she'd heard correctly. "What?"

"I need to start looking for a new job."

"Since when?"

"Sunday. After service."

"You mean you just up and quit?" Maggie hoped with everything in her that he'd say *yes*. Instead, a sense of foreboding entered her heart as she remembered the trite comments she'd made about him losing his job after taking off across the country with her. Surely it wasn't that. But she could tell Reuben was struggling with his answer.

"I am very tempted to lie to you right now." Finally, he looked at her. "But no. I did not quit. I've been given the boot. Please don't ask why."

"I don't think I need to."

Another sigh. "The thing is, I don't know why I feel so bad about it. Those aren't the sort of people I want to work with anyway. I just wish I had been able to help make them more compassionate people while I had the chance. Honestly, I probably should have quit a long time ago. But I liked the security."

Maggie stared at Reuben's profile and found herself resisting an urge to touch his back, to stroke his hair. "How hard is it for a pastor to find a new job? Don't you have some kind of higher-ups who can appoint you elsewhere?"

"Only if I'm not fired. The assumption is, a fired pastor finds another line of work. I've been thinking of talking to Robert Broadford."

"Isn't he one of Mrs. O'Toole's boarders?"

"Yes." Reuben sat up straight in his chair and looked at Maggie. "He works for the Greater Winnipeg Victory Loan Organization. Perhaps I could be useful to them, do my bit for the war effort."

Maggie didn't hear what Reuben said next. She was trying to recall where she'd heard recently about a church in need of a pastor. Then it came to her. She reached into her purse and pulled out the letter from Cornelia Simpson.

"Have you ever thought about getting out of the city?" She unfolded Cornelia's letter and found the sentences she was looking for.

"What do you mean?" Reuben's gaze moved to the paper in Maggie's hand.

"A little church in Roseburg is without a pastor. I know someone there."

"Roseburg? I don't even know where that is."

"Not sure myself, but we can find it on a road map easily enough. I don't have many details." She handed the letter to Reuben. "I'd put in a good word for you, though."

When Reuben just looked at her, she added, "I'd tell them you understand what being a shepherd is truly about."

"Thank you, Maggie." She watched him jot down the names *Stuart and Cornelia Baker, Roseburg* on the little notepad he kept in his pocket, and then he handed the letter back to her.

As she tucked it into her purse, Maggie found herself instantly flooded with regret and hoped Reuben would forget all about the opportunity. Her heart was not ready to let him go.

Two hours later, dressed in her new pale blue uniform with white apron, Maggie was again rolling pastry dough at the Fort Garry. It felt good to be doing something she was competent at, something she could do practically in her sleep. Having only the baking to focus on was a breeze compared to running an entire restaurant, and she had plenty of time to think as she worked. The police and fire departments were still investigating; the insurance company still withholding funds. When Maggie had tried to contact Earl, there was no answer at his home. She and Mrs. O'Toole had returned to the property to clean up the garden, and Reuben had moved the contents of the toolshed to Mrs. O'Toole's shed. Until something further happened, Maggie's hands were tied. Soon Charlotte and Darcy would be gone; Reuben could be moving away. She was grateful for work to keep her busy. Maybe, she figured, she could even learn some new things from this classy joint to incorporate once she reopened Bert's. *If* she reopened Bert's. Or maybe the Fort Garry could learn a thing or two from *her*.

"We've always added a hint of nutmeg to our maple-pecan Danish here," said Carl, the head chef, when he saw Maggie mixing her filling.

"Well. Now we don't." She sniffed and picked up her rolling pin to continue her work.

CHAPTER 33

Reuben dropped his envelope into the mailbox and began the walk home in the darkness. He had prayed about Maggie's suggestion throughout the afternoon, then spent the evening composing his letter. Unable to sleep, he'd decided to step out for some fresh air and drop off the letter for the early morning pickup. How long would it take his query to reach Roseburg? His twenty-five-dollar monthly room and board was paid until the end of September, and he sincerely hoped he wouldn't have to come up with October's. Maybe Maggie was right. Getting away from Winnipeg and starting over might be the best idea. If he applied anywhere in the city, his references would be checked, and Elder Mitchell would be only too happy to supply his unhelpful opinion.

"Lord, I admit my heart doesn't like the prospect of putting a hundred miles between Maggie and me. But I want to walk through every door you open and not try to force open any you are holding shut," he had prayed. "You've given me the name of a town that needs a pastor. So far, that's an open door. If Roseburg is not where you want me, please close that door."

Why God should answer his prayer when Reuben was ignoring his directive regarding Maggie, Reuben couldn't say. But he knew of nowhere else to turn. Besides, it wasn't like he had completely dismissed the directive. God hadn't indicated *when* he should propose marriage to Maggie, only that he should. It was too soon; anyone with any sense knew that. *Wasn't it?*

Besides, she was sure to refuse, and then he wouldn't even have her friendship. Far better to put some distance between them first, let things settle down, and then see what happened. But even as he formed that thought, it seemed like flimsy reasoning. *You're a coward, Reuben Fennel,* he thought.

On an impulse, and with nowhere else he needed to be, Reuben took a much longer route home so he could walk past Maggie's former restaurant and home. From the sidewalk, he stood surveying the sad sight. It was even gloomier by the light of a lone streetlamp. He secretly hoped Maggie would sell the property and move on with her life, but it was not for him to say.

Suddenly a movement in the backyard caught his attention, and he noticed the door to the garden shed hanging open. He could have sworn he'd replaced the padlock after removing Maggie's tools. Had he left it unlatched, or had some troublemakers been poking around?

When he approached the shed, he could see the hasp had been pried off, leaving the padlock still closed and dangling from the useless shackle. Someone must have been awfully disappointed to put out all that effort to get inside, only to find the shed empty. Perhaps it would have been less damaging to leave the shed unlocked so would-be thieves would move on after seeing there was nothing to take. Reuben chided himself for not thinking of this before.

He wasn't sure why he bothered looking inside, but when he did, he got the surprise of his life. Someone had removed most of the floorboards and was now digging a hole in the dirt below! Whoever it was hadn't detected Reuben's approach, and Reuben quietly backed off and moved around the corner of the shed. He waited, listening to the grunts of the man as he worked. He'd been waist-deep in the hole, a large pile of dirt growing in one corner of the shed.

Reuben couldn't imagine what was going on. Who was it? Should he confront the man or call the police?

Before he could decide, he heard the ping of metal on metal, followed by the man's low voice muttering, "There you are." A few more grunts and pings, and Reuben gathered that whatever the man was digging for must have come free. "Thank you, Duggie, ol' boy."

Without thinking, Reuben swung himself around to the front of the shed and blocked the doorway with his body. "What are you doing?" he demanded.

"What the—" The man dropped the box and picked up his shovel with both hands.

Reuben quickly realized he was at a disadvantage with the light behind him, highlighting his silhouette in the doorway. But if he moved to the side, the man might get away. Given the absence of further options, he lunged forward just as the shovel swung at what would have been Reuben's head, catching the man across the middle and propelling both of them into the hole. He felt something snap in his side as he continued to struggle, trying to hang on to the invader as the man's fist made contact with Reuben's face. He hadn't been in any sort of scuffle since he was thirteen, and that had been nothing more than a fairly anemic playground brawl, engaged in during the light of day. Reuben figured it would be to his advantage to make as much noise as possible, and he started hollering even as he tried to keep a firm grip on the man.

"Who are you? What are you doing here? What's in the box? This property belongs to Maggie Marshall, you've got no business here."

The man continued to grunt and fight, but did not respond to Reuben's questions. He managed to clamber out of the hole, kicking Reuben in the face as he did so. With one last-ditch effort, Reuben reached out and grasped the man's ankle and hung on as tight as he could while bracing his own feet on the wall of the hole. The dirt began to give way, sucking him farther in. The man's foot kept kicking, but Reuben refused to let go.

Suddenly, the shed was filled with light.

"Police! Stop what you're doing!" A bright flashlight lit up their surroundings. Reuben relaxed his grip, and the man lunged for the box. Once he had it securely tucked up against his body, he made a dive for the door and tried to get past the police officer blocking it. Dust flew everywhere, giving the air a foggy glow in the light. Reuben tried to breathe but could only cough weakly as a pain in his ribs drove him to his knees at the bottom of the hole. He wiped a hand across his eyes to clear his vision, and when he pulled his hand away, it was covered in blood. Reuben could just make out the silhouette of a second police officer and was relieved to see his assailant had not gotten away.

Once the man was in handcuffs, the first officer turned toward Reuben. "Get outta there," he said. "You're both coming with me for questioning."

Obeying orders as best he could, Reuben clumsily began to climb out of the hole. That's when he recognized the face of his attacker. He'd met the man only once before.

But he was certain the handcuffed man was none other than Earl Marshall.

CHAPTER 34

Charlotte lay awake on the soft hotel bed, staring at the ceiling. As long as she lived, she would not forget the conversation she'd had with her parents that evening.

After leaving Mrs. Shelton's office, her father had called his attorney, who referred him to a reputable colleague in Winnipeg. The lawyer agreed to see Mr. Penfield that afternoon, and he'd been gone for three hours. Meanwhile, Charlotte and her mother settled into their hotel suite.

When her father returned, he announced that he was taking them all to dinner in the hotel restaurant and did not wish to hear another word about their situation until they'd had a chance to eat a fine meal. He then called the front desk and ordered the professional nanny service offered by the hotel.

"Oh, really, Edward, that's not necessary," her mother had tried to intervene. "We can take the baby with us. All he does is sleep."

"Laura, you have no idea how far my influence reaches, do you? We can't risk being seen with an infant we have no wish to explain. Besides, I'm sure Charlotte could use the break. Couldn't you, darling?"

Charlotte looked up from the corner of the room, where she was changing Darcy's diaper. Her father had not called her *darling* since she was a little girl.

"Not really," she said. "I love taking care of him."

"Nonsense." Her father straightened his tie and began putting on his suit jacket. "You think that now, when he's a newborn. Newborns are easy. But every mother needs a break."

Charlotte's mother let out a most unladylike snort.

Within minutes, a uniformed childminder had knocked on their door. Charlotte left instructions to have her paged in the restaurant if Darcy required feeding, and secretly hoped that he would, although she had just finished nursing him. She followed her parents to a table, where Edward Penfield ordered for all of them.

Charlotte ate the grilled salmon and baked potato without really tasting it. Her parents tried to make pleasant conversation, but all she could think about was her baby and what the future held in store for him. She ached to return to their room to make sure he was all right. When her father ordered three pieces of cherry pie for them, she thought she might bolt. Her mother noticed her fidgeting and placed a hand on Charlotte's arm.

"He's in good hands, sweetheart."

"Of course he is. Relax, darling." Her father smiled at her.

Why was he being so nice? Something had changed since they left the adoption agency. Her father was acting as if he had everything under control once again. What was going on?

When their desserts arrived, Charlotte recognized the unmistakable *M*-shaped vent hole carved into each slice. She had all but forgotten they were in the very hotel where Mrs. Marshall worked. Would she ever see the woman again? Suddenly an idea struck her.

"Excuse me, I need to use the powder room." She rose from her seat and headed in the direction of the washrooms before her mother could offer to accompany her. As soon as she rounded the corner, she checked over her shoulder to make sure her parents weren't watching and changed course, heading for the kitchen instead. She pushed the swinging door open and looked around the room for Mrs. Marshall.

"Charlotte! What are you doing here?"

Charlotte swung around. Mrs. Marshall was just donning her gloves, and one arm was looped through the handle of her purse.

"Looking for you," Charlotte said. "Are you off duty?"

"Just. Are you staying here?"

"Yes. I never had a chance to say good-bye this afternoon and wanted to see you. Just in case . . . well, you know. Just in case I don't see you again."

"Where's Darcy?" Mrs. Marshall's brows creased.

"In our suite with a sitter. Do you want to say good-bye to him?"

Charlotte was surprised when Mrs. Marshall's eyes began to well with tears. She hadn't thought it was possible. The woman nodded without a word. Charlotte grabbed her by the arm and led her down the hallway to the elevators and up to the Penfields' suite. Inside, they found the nanny sitting on the sofa, reading, while Darcy slept soundly.

Charlotte dismissed the sitter while Mrs. Marshall scooped the sleeping baby up and sat on the sofa, crooning to him in a tiny voice. As she watched, she felt mesmerized by the transformation. Maggie's work uniform, cinched in at the waist, was stylish compared to her usual attire, and with the sweet expression on her face, the woman looked pretty. And much younger. She looked up at Charlotte.

"Do you know yet what's going to happen?"

Charlotte shook her head. "No. But my father saw a lawyer this afternoon and is acting very differently. I'm afraid, Mrs. Marshall. I don't know what's going on. I'm not ready to say good-bye to you, and I'll never be ready to say good-bye to Darcy. But I'm so glad I saw you. I really wanted the chance to say thank-you. For everything."

Mrs. Marshall sighed. "I'll do whatever I can to help you, Charlotte."

"When I ran away, I was certain you'd be glad to be rid of me. I never dreamed you'd come after me." Charlotte bit her lip to keep from crying. "I'm glad you did."

Mrs. Marshall studied Charlotte's face a moment, nodded, and then returned her gaze to Darcy. Softly, she said, "I'm glad I did, too."

They were interrupted by Charlotte's parents walking in the door.

"There you are!" her mother said, taking in the whole room. "Why didn't you tell us you were coming back here? Where's the nanny? Why is Mrs. Marshall here?"

Mrs. Marshall placed Darcy in Charlotte's arms. "I'll be leaving. I just wanted an opportunity to say good-bye." She glanced at Charlotte. "If this *is* good-bye."

"Actually, I'm glad you're here," Charlotte's father said. "We need to have a serious conversation with our daughter, and some of what we learned today might be beneficial to you if you continue your—um, *hospitality program.*"

Charlotte hoped Mrs. Marshall didn't pick up on her father's sarcastic choice of words. "Can you stay?"

Mrs. Marshall looked at Charlotte, then at her father. "Yes, I can stay."

Once again, her father took charge. "Have a seat, both of you."

Mrs. Marshall returned to the sofa, and Charlotte sat next to her. Her parents took the chairs beside a small round table, and they all watched while her father pulled a small portfolio out of his interior jacket pocket and laid it open on the table.

"Charlotte, your mother and I have come to a decision. Technically . . . legally, we cannot force you to give the baby up for adoption."

"You can't?" Charlotte could hardly believe it. Why wasn't she told this in the beginning?

"The decision is ultimately yours."

"Then my decision is easy—"

He raised one palm toward her. "Let me finish. As I said, we cannot force you. We can, however, hope that you will respect our wishes as your parents, as the people who have provided for you these seventeen-plus years. Keeping in mind that we are older and wiser than you, you can see why we believe it's in your own best interest—and the best interests of the child—for you to surrender him to a family who can care for him properly. Think of it as your sacrificial duty to your son and to your parents. Surely you can see it that way?"

Charlotte looked down at her little son, but couldn't answer.

Mrs. Marshall spoke up. "That's a lot of pressure, Mr. Penfield."

"I'm not finished, Mrs. Marshall." Charlotte's father rose from his chair and paced across to the window, where he stood looking out across the city. "You have two choices, Charlotte. You can place the baby back with the adoption agency and return home with us to resume your life as normal. You can finish school and go on to do whatever you would like. We will support you all the way and celebrate your successes just as we would have done had this never happened."

"What's the second choice?" Charlotte's voice was barely a whisper, but Darcy sensed her distress and began to squirm.

Charlotte's father glanced at his wife, then turned toward his daughter and straightened to his full height. "If you refuse to give the child up, you're on your own. It's as simple as that." Then, in a slightly more gentle tone, he continued. "I'm confident you'll make the right choice. You're a smart girl."

"I can't make this decision without talking to Reginald." Charlotte tried to sound firm as she stood and began swaying to calm the baby. "He has the right to know he has a child. Darcy has the right to a father. I want to at least find out where we stand before I make this decision."

Charlotte's parents exchanged a look. "Do you want to tell her, or shall I?" her father asked, his voice cold.

Charlotte's stomach began to churn. "Tell me what?"

"You tell her," her mother said, staring at the floor. "If you think we must."

"What? What am I missing?" At the urgency in Charlotte's voice, Darcy began to squirm.

Her father moved from the window over to where Charlotte stood rocking the baby and looked her in the eye. "We wanted to spare you further hurt, Charlotte. I wish you had trusted me to recognize the character of that boy."

Charlotte looked at her mother, then back at her father. "What are you not telling me?"

"Reginald *does* know that he has a child."

Charlotte waited for more, but it was not forthcoming. "How does he know? How do you know he knows?"

"He just doesn't know about *this* child." Her father kept his eyes on Charlotte's, but pointed one finger toward Darcy.

Charlotte didn't understand. "What do you mean?"

Her father continued with a sigh. "I mean, Reginald has another child. A daughter, born about three months after you left for Winnipeg. Her mother is Vera Dugald."

Charlotte stared at her father. She'd never heard of anything so ridiculous in her life. Her parents had stooped to a new low, fabricating this monstrous story and agreeing to lie just to convince her not to contact Reginald.

"You're lying."

"I wish we were, Charlotte. Show her, Laura."

Charlotte's mother reached into her handbag and pulled out a newspaper clipping. She unfolded it and held it out to Charlotte. It was a wedding announcement for Reginald Wilson and Vera Dugald, complete with photo. It was dated two weeks after Charlotte had arrived at Mrs. Marshall's.

Charlotte slumped onto the sofa, and Mrs. Marshall took Darcy from her arms before holding one hand out to take the clipping so she could read it too.

"I'm so sorry, Charlotte," her mother said softly. "We truly wanted to spare you."

The four of them sat quietly while the news sank in. Charlotte felt no need to suppress tears, for they didn't come. She felt only numb. In her mind, she was doing the math. It didn't take a genius to calculate that Reginald had been seeing Vera and her at the same time.

It was Mrs. Marshall who spoke next.

"So . . . it sounds like you regret not telling Charlotte this in the beginning, am I right? You wish you had?"

"Well, yes," her mother said. "Now we do. Perhaps trying to spare her the pain wasn't in her best interest, in hindsight."

"Then with all due respect," Mrs. Marshall continued, "how can you be certain that the choices you are giving her now are truly in her best interest?"

Charlotte appreciated Mrs. Marshall's boldness but knew it would have little effect on her father, who lifted his chin in Mrs. Marshall's direction. "Do you have any children, Mrs. Marshall?"

"You know I don't," Mrs. Marshall said. "But if you're implying—"

"Then you are in no position to have an opinion, much less express one. I invited you to stay merely so that you could hear the entire story and understand the legal limitations we face. We hoped you might help Charlotte understand the necessity of what we're asking her to do. Should you continue in your so-called service to young women—and I hope you don't—this information could be useful to you . . . perhaps keep you from misleading other young girls. From letting them believe some fanciful notions about parenting."

Charlotte wanted to rise to Mrs. Marshall's defense, but she didn't have a chance.

"What if there is a third option?" Mrs. Marshall moved Darcy to her shoulder and rubbed his back gently.

"Like what?" A vague glimmer of hope rose in Charlotte's heart.

Mrs. Marshall spoke slowly. "What if both Darcy and Charlotte can stay in foster care, together, until she reaches the age of majority?"

"What are you getting at?" Charlotte's mother asked.

"I'm saying, if someone like me was willing to keep them both, then Charlotte wouldn't be on her own."

Charlotte's father glared at the woman. "You're delusional if you think we'd pay you, Mrs. Marshall."

"Yes. I can see how that would be delusional, and that is not what I'm suggesting."

"Are you saying you'd be willing?" Charlotte was practically holding her breath.

Maggie turned toward Charlotte. "Only if you're absolutely certain. Once your choice is made, there would be no going back. You'd be signing on for a lifetime of responsibility to raise this little boy."

Charlotte's mother spoke up. "I don't see how you're in any position to make that sort of offer, Mrs. Marshall. You don't even have a home." Charlotte detected jealousy, insult, and judgment all rolled into her mother's tone.

"Or a husband, or a steady means of support." Charlotte's father walked to the door, opened it, and waited for Mrs. Marshall to walk through. "Your idea is ludicrous, and your time here is done."

Mrs. Marshall returned the baby to Charlotte's arms and left without another word.

Now Charlotte lay sleepless, knowing she had to give her parents her decision tomorrow. She wasn't sure which hurt more, Reginald's betrayal or her parents' lack of love for her and Darcy. Would they truly shut her out of their lives if she chose to keep him? Surely her father was bluffing.

But then, she recalled the women who sat at the country club with her mother, and the pastor who had encouraged Charlotte's retreat to Winnipeg. She knew that her mother could never bear the gossip she'd have to endure when the truth came out and that her father was quite serious.

Maggie Marshall's words kept coming to mind. *"If someone like me was willing to keep them both . . ."*

To think that such a short time ago, Charlotte couldn't wait to run away from Grumpystiltskin. Never in all her dramatic fantasies had she imagined herself longing to run back.

CHAPTER 35

Maggie walked the three blocks from the bus stop to Mrs. O'Toole's boardinghouse with a heavy heart. Had she made a mistake in offering to take Charlotte and Darcy in? Mr. Penfield was right: She really had nothing to offer the pair. It was obvious he had been trying to make the choice as clear-cut as possible so that Charlotte would choose to go home with him and her mother. Now Maggie had muddied the waters by suggesting a third option that she wasn't even sure she could provide. Perhaps she'd done more harm than good. She had just wanted Charlotte to know she needn't be alone.

With a sigh, she carried herself up the steps and through the front door. Mrs. O'Toole was on the telephone.

"She's just walking in the door now, Rev'rend. Hang on." Mrs. O'Toole held the receiver out to Maggie. "It's for you, love. Rev'rend Fennel."

Maggie dropped her purse by the telephone table and held the receiver to her ear. "Hello, Reuben."

"Maggie, it looks like I'm the one who needs help now. Can you come down to the police station?"

"To the—"

"Sh-shhh! I don't want Mrs. O'Toole to know where I am. She's still standing there, I'll bet."

"Why are you there?" Maggie turned her back to Mrs. O'Toole as casually as she could, but nearly tripped over Sheila, who let out a meow. Mrs. O'Toole picked up the calico and carried her into the kitchen, where the woman no doubt stood listening from behind the door.

"It's a long story, and I'll explain it all when you get here, but they're going to want to ask you some questions too. It involves your restaurant property and Earl Marshall. I need you to vouch for me before they'll let me go."

"Okay. I'll be there as quick as I can, but this better be good. The buses have stopped running for the night."

"Bring my car, Maggie. When we're done here, I'm going to need a ride to the hospital. I've got a cut on my head that could probably use a stitch, and I'm pretty sure I've got a cracked rib."

"What on earth? Reuben!"

"Just come."

Maggie walked up the front steps of the police station for the second time in only a few weeks. She found it ironic that before the fire, she'd never come here even once, despite contemplating that action often during the time when Douglas was beating her. Why had it seemed like such a shameful thing to admit what was happening to her? "You made your bed, now lie in it" had been the popular train of thought in her home as she grew up, and the implications of that phrase ran deep.

She pushed open the door, wondering what on earth Reuben had to do with Earl.

As soon as she explained the reason for her visit, she was swiftly led to a room where Reuben and two policemen waited. One introduced himself as Inspector Radcliff. The other, Constable Morris, told her that he had been called to the scene by Maggie's former neighbor, who saw someone sneaking around Maggie's shed. He explained that Earl Marshall was being detained in a separate room.

"Do you know this gentleman, Mrs. Marshall?" Inspector Radcliff asked.

"Yes, I do. This is Reverend Reuben Fennel, my friend and pastor." Whatever trouble Reuben was in, it couldn't hurt his case to call him her pastor.

"Mrs. Marshall, can you explain why this box was buried under your garden shed?" He showed her a heavy box made of metal, its green paint chipping and rust forming at the corners.

"I've never seen that box in my life," she said. "May I ask what's in it?"

"Nothing, at the moment. The contents are in our evidence room— nearly fourteen pounds of amphetamines."

"Amphetamines?" Maggie had only the vaguest notion what amphetamines were. "What on earth—?"

"Do you have any idea how they got there, Mrs. Marshall?"

Maggie's thoughts turned immediately to her late husband. In the days before Douglas had enlisted, he was always "wheeling and dealing," as her father put it. It was nothing for him to trade valuables, from jewelry to vehicles, always looking for a profit and frequently locking things in the garden shed. Between his gambling and his drinking, however, Douglas had never succeeded in his quest to grow rich. But Maggie had often wondered how many of his deals might be illegal and how long it would be before his misdeeds caught up with him. She'd stopped worrying about that when he went off to war.

"Mrs. Marshall?" the inspector repeated.

"I'm thinking," Maggie said. "One of my late husband's poker buddies is a custodian at the St. Boniface Hospital. I heard him brag more than once about the money to be made on the streets from some of the drugs he could get his hands on. I asked Doug about it once. He assured me that Buster was 'just blowing smoke. He'd never have the guts to do anything like that,' he said."

By midnight, the police had taken down Maggie's full report about Earl inheriting Douglas's half of the property. It was obvious that Earl had known about the drugs buried there. That was reason enough for the police to arrest him. They were satisfied that Reuben had happened by innocently and, after warning him not to intervene in such a way again, they released him and told Maggie she could go, too, after she gave them Buster's full name: Howard LeBlanc.

Now Maggie sat in the hospital waiting room while Reuben got his ribs wrapped and his forehead stitched. A light rain had begun on their way over, and she now heard thunder rumbling in the distance. The approaching storm echoed what was going on inside her—everything rumbling and roiling. Trouble seemed to follow her like a dark shadow, and now she'd dragged Reuben into it. Kind, innocent Reuben, who only wanted to help.

I am making everyone's lives worse instead of better, Maggie mused. *And I'm exhausted. God, if you listen to folks like me, please help me. Show me how to help Reuben. And Charlotte. Even if that means removing myself from their lives so they can get on with their own.*

She pulled from her purse her treasured note card from Cornelia Simpson and read it again. *At least I know I helped someone in my life,* she thought. *One person. I made a difference to one person.* It was something to hang on to.

Reuben came out of the examining room holding one hand against his ribs, a white bandage on his forehead. "I'm so sorry about this, Maggie." His face registered pain, and his posture was slightly slumped.

"*You're* sorry? *I'm* the one who's sorry. You never would have gotten into this mess if it weren't for me. You'd still have your job if it weren't for me."

"You can stop that right now. I made my own decisions to get involved, Maggie. Give me some credit." He nodded toward the card in her hand. "What have you got there?"

Maggie looked down at the card and sighed. She saw no reason not to share it with Reuben. "This is the young lady whose church is looking for a pastor." She held the card toward him. "You should apply." This time, she said it with complete conviction.

Reuben read Cornelia's words and handed the card back. "I already did."

CHAPTER 36

On Sunday morning, Reuben and Maggie lingered over breakfast at Mrs. O'Toole's dining room table while the landlady hovered over them like a mother cat with a dog lurking nearby. Two days had passed since his confrontation with Earl, but Reuben had not seen enough of Maggie for him to initiate a follow-up conversation.

"What's on your agenda for today?" Maggie asked as she stroked Sheila, curled on her lap.

"With no sermon to deliver, I'm footloose and fancy-free." Reuben raised his steaming coffee to his lips.

Mrs. O'Toole scowled at Reuben's flippancy. "I'll not be returnin' to that church," she announced. "After what they did to you. It's a cryin' shame."

Reuben sighed. "Mrs. O'Toole, whatever you may have heard about what they did, you did not hear it from me, and the last thing I need is to be the cause of a church split. You've been a faithful member since I was a boy, and it's important that you continue to attend. Please?"

She considered his request with a frown. "Well. Since you put it that way. If you think that's what's best, I'll do it."

"I do."

"Then I best be changin' into my Sunday dress." She set the coffeepot on the table and headed upstairs.

Reuben turned to Maggie. "Are they giving you the day off?"

"Yes. I won't be going to church, though."

"I'm not suggesting that you do."

Maggie took a deep breath and let it out again. "Reuben, I'm afraid I've done a really impulsive thing."

"Should I find that shocking? From you? The girl who took off halfway across the country with me, chasing a runaway?"

Maggie's eyes widened. "First of all, I am hardly a 'girl,' and secondly—"

"—it wasn't halfway across the country." They said the words together and laughed—as much as Reuben could laugh with the pain in his ribs.

As he listened to Maggie relay the conversation that had taken place in the Penfields' hotel suite, Reuben wasn't shocked to hear of the firm stance they'd taken with their daughter. He'd met their kind before and knew the deep-rooted power of pride. He was surprised, though, at the offer Maggie had made to shelter Charlotte and the baby.

"I don't know what I was thinking," she said. "I should have stayed out of it. But I know that girl, Reuben. She's completely attached to that little nipper, and I know she'll never choose to give him up now. I can't stand the thought of the two of them on the streets."

"It seems Charlotte's not the only one attached to that little nipper," Reuben observed.

Maggie turned her gaze toward a sunbeam that cascaded through the window, making Mrs. O'Toole's hardwood floor gleam. "I won't deny it. But that doesn't give me the right to butt into family business."

"You don't need to feel bad about it, Maggie. I've seen a real change in you, for the better. That little boy wormed his way into your heart very quickly. Before you held him in your arms, you couldn't wait for the Penfields to show up so you could wash your hands of the lot of them."

"Guess I can't deny that either."

"You're a better person for it, Maggie. Your offer was made out of kindness and compassion, and those things are never wrong."

"Thank you." Maggie stayed focused on the cat in her lap. "Sounds like you can take the pastor out of the pulpit, but you can't take the pulpit out of the pastor."

"Sorry. I don't mean to preach."

"You're not preaching. You're shepherding. And I appreciate it."

For the next half hour, they discussed the events of the horrible night when Reuben had confronted Earl, and they speculated about how the drugs could have come to be buried in Maggie's shed.

"Douglas and Earl were in cahoots, I'm sure of it," Maggie said. "The box was probably put there by Doug himself. I'll bet you anything he told Earl about it before he shipped out, and I'll bet you anything that's why he changed his will. Of course, I have no way to prove anything. But I'll be seeing my lawyer just as soon as I can. I hope the police can press enough charges against Earl to keep him in custody a long time. And when he gets out, maybe he'll stop and think before he causes me any more trouble."

"Do you think he'd come after me?" Reuben raised one hand toward his still painful rib.

"Hard to say. Earl's a basic coward, and not really all that bright. Did he think no one would notice something going on when he broke into the shed and just started digging?" Maggie shook her head. "Still, it wouldn't hurt to beware of the man."

"Maybe if they can get a conviction, your insurance money can be freed up, and you can think about rebuilding. If you want to."

"I hope so." She nodded.

"Do you think you will?"

Maggie sighed. "I'm not sure anymore. One of the things that made that restaurant so special is that it was my father's. Even if I rebuild, even if I call it Bert's—it wouldn't really be Bert's." Sheila jumped down to the floor and wandered in the direction of the kitchen and her dinner dish. "And these few days of working for someone else have been pretty enjoyable, actually. I'm going to get a paycheck, and my first thought won't be about making sure the restaurant's expenses are covered. I've never known what that was like."

"There's a lot to consider." Reuben nodded.

"Yes, there is. Especially in these uncertain times. And especially given that reckless offer I made Charlotte."

"You haven't heard from her since the other night?" Reuben sat up straighter to relieve the ache in his ribs.

"No. I hope that means she's on her way home with the baby *and* her parents, that they came to their senses and she'll have the best of both worlds. What kind of people could just walk away from their own like that?" Maggie shuddered.

Mrs. O'Toole had just started down the stairs and was pulling white gloves over her work-worn hands when the doorbell rang. Maggie and Reuben both moved toward the archway between the dining room and front entrance, but Mrs. O'Toole beat them to the door and pulled it open.

On the doorstep stood Charlotte Penfield, Darcy in her left arm and a large suitcase in her right hand.

CHAPTER 37

Did you mean it, Mrs. Marshall?" Charlotte spoke before anyone else had the chance. She watched as Reverend Fennel stepped forward and opened the door wide to bid her enter, and then as he sent a confused-looking Mrs. O'Toole down the sidewalk in the direction of the church. An angry bruise swelled around a stitch in the minister's face.

"What happened to your forehead?" Charlotte asked.

"Long story. Let me take that bag, Charlotte." He set it down on the hallway floor. Charlotte stepped into the parlor and took a seat on Mrs. O'Toole's sofa. Her arms ached from carrying her load from the bus stop.

Mrs. Marshall walked straight to her and took Darcy in her arms. "Let me take this little one." She took a seat on a chair, and both women looked up at the reverend.

"Would you like me to stay?" he asked.

"Yes," Charlotte said.

"But you're not obligated," Mrs. Marshall quickly added. "Getting involved with us has cost you dearly already."

"It's too late. I'm already involved." He took the other chair, and the three sat looking at one another for a moment. No one seemed eager to start.

"I came to see if you meant what you said, Mrs. Marshall," Charlotte finally began. "Can Darcy and I stay with you?"

Mrs. Marshall cleared her throat. "I fear I may have made a rash promise, Charlotte. Your parents are right; I have little to offer you."

"It's my parents who have little to offer me." Charlotte blinked hard to keep her emotions under control. "They barely looked at Darcy even once. They refused to hold him. But you have given him only love and care since you first laid eyes on him. That's worth everything."

Those tears Charlotte felt sure she had seen welling in Mrs. Marshall's eyes at the hotel reappeared now, but the woman quickly turned her attention to Darcy and did not let them fall.

"I've already told my parents I won't part with Darcy under any circumstances, and they're on their way back to Ontario. They gave me enough cash for the train fare home if I change my mind. I won't."

Charlotte had rehearsed this speech throughout a sleepless night and now delivered it with confidence. "If you're convinced you made a mistake with your offer, Mrs. Marshall, I will use the money for train fare. But not to go home. Whichever direction I head, I'll be taking Darcy with me."

"Would you have reached the same decision had I not spoken up the other night?" Mrs. Marshall asked.

"Yes. I wouldn't be sitting here right now, but I definitely wouldn't be going anywhere without Darcy." Charlotte looked at Reverend Fennel, whose eyes still held that kind look in them she'd seen when they first met. "I know the two of you have troubles galore, and I'd give anything if I could ease them instead of adding to them. But right now you're the only friends I have in the world—you and Mrs. O'Toole. I had to start somewhere."

"You don't know the half of my troubles," Mrs. Marshall muttered.

"I suppose that's true. I know I have nothing to offer you right now, but if you rebuild your restaurant, Mrs. Marshall, I'll gladly work for you again."

"Pretty hard to work in a restaurant and care for a baby at the same time," Mrs. Marshall reminded her gently. "Even harder to work in a restaurant and care for a toddler at the same time."

Charlotte hung her head. This wasn't going to work. Why, oh why, did she ever run away? If she'd stayed, the restaurant might still be thriving. If only her parents had told her the whole truth about Reginald in the beginning, she'd never have run. Then again, if only she hadn't allowed herself to become swept away by Reginald's charm, none of this would have happened in the first place. But then there'd be no Darcy.

She could "if only" herself to death.

"I want to tell the two of you a story," Mrs. Marshall said suddenly. "About something that happened when I was younger than you are now, Charlotte. I had a dear friend named Susan. We loved each other like sisters, and when Susan became pregnant at sixteen, I swore to myself I'd stick by her and support her in any way I could."

Mrs. Marshall took a deep breath before continuing. "Susan's parents insisted that she have an abortion. But before one could be procured, Susan chose to end her life. I was away on a trip with my mother when she did it. By the time I got home, there was nothing I could do. She was gone." The last three words were barely discernible as Mrs. Marshall's voice quivered and then rose again.

"Her child would be nearly your age now, Charlotte. I bet Susan would be happily married and the mother of more children. She always aspired to be a nurse, and she'd have been one of the best. So full of cheer and life. Do you remember Susan, Reuben?"

Reverend Fennel nodded. "I do. The two of you were inseparable. I thought she died of influenza. I'm so sorry, Maggie."

"I wanted to be there for her, no matter what." Mrs. Marshall gazed out the window behind Charlotte.

"I'm sure she knew that," he said. "She'd have done the same for you. Her choice was not your fault. You know that, right?"

Mrs. Marshall nodded, though she said nothing. But a light had switched on for Charlotte. She finally understood why Mrs. Marshall had opened her home for pregnant girls. It was the only way she could find to "be there" for her friend. Charlotte understood something else too. Mrs. Marshall's reluctance to show feelings and kindness to the girls in her care stemmed from her pain, not from a lack of caring.

"I'm telling you this now to help you understand why I may have made an irrational offer to step up." Mrs. Marshall locked eyes with Charlotte. "I can't bear the thought of you ever becoming that desperate, Charlotte. Not if it's in my power to help somehow. But if you're going to stay, we need to work together."

Hope surged in Charlotte once again. "I understand. I'd do whatever you say."

"No." Mrs. Marshall spoke firmly. "I don't want you to do whatever I say. I mean we'd be partners, like two adults who respect each other's opinions and consider each other's needs. We'd have to figure things out together."

"Oh. I don't know what I can contribute just yet." Charlotte bit her lip. "But I'm more than willing, Mrs. Marshall."

"Well, for starters, you can stop calling me Mrs. Marshall. I'm Maggie."

Charlotte tried to suppress a smirk. "All right then. Maggie. Does that mean Darcy and I can stay?"

"I hope you will."

The two grinned at each other, and the reverend was the first of them to rise. "While we're at it, can I please just be 'Reuben'? Now, I'll carry that bag of yours upstairs and leave you two to work out the details."

"Not with that cracked rib, you shouldn't," Mrs. Marshall called out.

"Cracked rib?" Charlotte knew her mouth hung open but felt powerless to close it.

"Long story," Reverend Fennel repeated. "I'm sure Mrs. O'Toole will be happy to have you and Darcy here, Charlotte." He picked up the bag and disappeared around the corner, where Charlotte could hear him taking the stairs with a slight *mmph* sound on every second step.

CHAPTER 38

Thursday morning, Maggie once again made her way to the offices of Jones, Brighton, and Jones, Attorneys at Law. She sat in the waiting area, scanning the *Winnipeg Free Press* dated September 14, 1942. Headlines like "Battle of Edson's Ridge in Guadalcanal Rages" and "U.S. Defeats Attacks by Japanese; Heavy Losses for Japanese Forces" reminded her that the whole world was at war. Maggie preferred not to think about it. There was enough war raging inside her heart.

Her Sunday had been spent helping Charlotte and Darcy get settled back in at Mrs. O'Toole's. The landlady welcomed them warmly after Maggie assured her she'd cover their room and board through the end of October. She didn't want to admit how difficult that commitment would be to keep. She and Charlotte had agreed that after October, they'd need to reevaluate and see what was what.

Before returning to work on Monday, Maggie had escorted Charlotte and Darcy to the doctor for a follow-up appointment, at which Charlotte was declared healthy and it was determined that Darcy was putting on weight. The doctor felt confident that the hole in his heart would grow closed by the time he was four years old. "I've seen this before," he said.

On Tuesday, Reuben had received an invitation by telephone from the Elders Board of Roseburg Community Church to come for a visit and interview for the pastoral position. He'd caught the train that very afternoon and expected to return today.

Maggie turned to the entertainment page and saw that a motion picture called *The Major and the Minor* with Ginger Rogers was playing. She wondered how her hair would look styled like Ginger's. While perusing the fashion section, she imagined herself buying a new outfit for the first time in years. Would Reuben like it?

Then she shook her head. What difference did it make? Reuben was a good friend, nothing more. Soon he would no doubt be back in the pulpit where he belonged, and surely the God he served so faithfully would lead him to the right woman to stand by his side and greet parishioners week after week. Maggie couldn't imagine which would be worse—having to smile while wearing too-tight shoes or shaking hands with people whether she liked them or not.

"Hello, Mrs. Marshall. Come on in." Theodore Jones welcomed her from the door to his office and gestured for her to take a seat. "What can I do for you today?"

Maggie sat in the chair indicated and removed her gloves. "There have been some new developments in the situation with my restaurant," Maggie said. "Specifically, it isn't there anymore."

"I heard. Actually, I took a drive by there one day to see for myself. I'm awfully sorry. Fire is a nasty thing."

It took a good thirty minutes for Maggie to explain where things stood with the property, what had occurred with Earl, and why he'd been arrested. All the while, she kept an eye on the clock hanging on the attorney's wall and wondered how much this consultation was going to cost.

"I'm also hoping to find out from you today what to do about my former charge, Miss Charlotte Penfield, and her son, Darcy." Maggie needed another ten minutes to describe that situation.

"It's not as complicated as you think," the man assured her. "By law, Miss Penfield reached majority when she gave birth to a child. She's emancipated from her parents and no longer requires any legal guardian or custodianship. And she is the legal guardian of her son. She is as free to live how she chooses as you are."

"She is?"

"Yes. Although without parental support, I suspect financial limitations will be a burden. But neither her parents nor you are under any legal obligation to provide for her."

This was news to Maggie, but it confirmed what she'd already told Charlotte—that they needed to relate as two adults if this relationship was to continue. Maggie determined that she would do her best to provide until such time as Charlotte could contribute, but the fact was, the girl was free to leave at any time, and it was important that she know that.

She rode the bus to the Fort Garry for her afternoon shift with a lighter heart than she'd had in weeks.

Reuben sat at Stuart and Cornelia Baker's farm table enjoying corn on the cob, fresh garden tomatoes, and cucumbers for lunch. The young couple was newly married and both taught school, she at a one-room country school next door to their house and he in town.

So far, Reuben loved everything about Roseburg and its people. He'd never lived beyond the city limits of Winnipeg, and he found the small town charming. He felt the interview with the elders had gone well the previous evening. Stuart Baker served on the church board and had driven him around the community before bringing him home for the night. Reuben had spent an hour alone after dark on the Bakers' front porch, praying and looking up at the night sky, seeing in it more stars than he ever knew existed.

Looking out across the field ripe for harvest, Reuben watched the stalks of wheat swaying in the moonlight like ghostly figures. As he watched, the heads of grain seemed to grow faces, the stalks developed arms that bid him come to them. Though he'd never farmed a day in his life, when he closed his eyes, he felt himself drawn toward the wheat, sickle in hand, ready to harvest it. This might have seemed a grisly picture, except for Reuben's familiarity with the words of Jesus in Matthew, chapter nine: "But when he saw the multitudes, he was moved with compassion on them, because they fainted, and were scattered abroad, as sheep having no shepherd. Then saith he unto his disciples, 'The harvest truly is plenteous, but the labourers are few; Pray ye therefore the Lord of the harvest, that he will send forth labourers into his harvest.'"

As quickly as it had come, the vision was gone. But Reuben knew something exceptional had just taken place.

Now, he buttered his corn thoughtfully.

"I'm so glad I mentioned our need for a pastor to Mrs. Marshall," Cornelia said. "It was merely news. I never dreamed she'd send us an applicant. How do you know her?"

"We go way back." Reuben sprinkled salt on the corn. "Grew up together at school and church. We parted ways for a while, but became reacquainted recently when her husband was killed in action."

"Oh? I'm so sorry! That must be terrible for her."

Reuben didn't know how much to say. Although Cornelia admitted only that she'd met Maggie when she lived briefly in the city, he gathered she had been one of "Maggie's girls." It wasn't likely that Maggie had shared anything about her marriage with the girls in her care.

"She's had a lot of adjustments to make in an extremely short time," Reuben said. He thought it best under the circumstances not to mention the burned-down restaurant. That was Maggie's news to tell, and there were still too many unanswered questions.

After lunch, Stuart took Reuben to the train station. Before they got out of the car, however, Stuart handed him an envelope. "Reverend Fennel, the board met early this morning. I'm pleased to tell you that you'll find an official offer of employment in that envelope. We'd be happy to welcome you to Roseburg and hope you'll call us with your decision by the end of the week."

Reuben looked at the envelope and recalled his vision of the wheat field. It would be hard to say good-bye to Maggie, but his answer was clear. "I can give you my decision now," he said. "I believe with all my heart Roseburg is where God wants me."

CHAPTER 39

Just as Reuben had predicted, Mrs. O'Toole had been more than happy to embrace both Charlotte and Darcy. Now, as Charlotte busied herself with the newspaper, Mrs. O'Toole carried the baby up the stairs, cooing and talking to him all the while. "I prayed you'd come back to me, my pretty wee one." Then, with a quivering and slightly off-key falsetto, she launched into song. "'Tis so sweet to trust in Jesus, just to take him at his word, just to rest upon his promise . . ."

Charlotte watched the pair disappear around the corner of the landing and smiled as the words broke off into humming and tra-la-las. She turned her gaze back to the *Winnipeg Free Press* spread out before her on the dining room table. With Reuben gone to Roseburg, Maggie working, and Mrs. O'Toole happy to help with Darcy, Charlotte had had plenty of time to peruse the job ads. Women were being hired for all sorts of positions formerly held only by men. With her limited experience, she couldn't afford to be picky, but she wanted to earn as much as she could and still have as much time with Darcy as possible.

One ad in particular caught her attention. It said that in Fort William, where Darcy had been born, barracks had been built to house women willing to come to work for the Canadian Car and Foundry Company. The company had been contracted by the Royal Canadian Air Force to produce Hawker Hurricane planes, but because so many of its welders had gone to fight, they were now hiring and training women. Even its chief engineer was a woman, the famous Elsie MacGill! The ad promised twenty dollars a week, twice what Charlotte could earn in Winnipeg as a nanny or waitress. She tried to imagine herself as Rosie the Riveter, but it was difficult. The money her father had left her would more than buy her train fare to Fort William. But what about Darcy? The ad encouraged "all single women" to come, implying no children. Charlotte sighed and turned the page.

There she read that the women of Winnipeg were leading the way by creating a Volunteer Bureau and enlisting thousands of women in myriads of ways for the war effort. Volunteering would allow Charlotte to choose her own hours and gain experience, but she wouldn't earn any money. There had to be some way to care for her little boy and contribute to the newly formed household in which she found herself. It was too much to expect Mrs. Marshall—Maggie—to keep supporting her. The poor woman had trouble enough!

Then another ad caught her eye:

Wanted: Childminders.

The Government of Canada is subsidizing child-care costs for preschool children of mothers who are directly contributing to the war effort. Programs include activities, outings, fresh air, and exercise. Childminders needed for eight-hour shifts. Contact . . .

Charlotte grabbed a pair of scissors and cut out the ad. If she could land a job in one of these care centers, perhaps she could bring Darcy to work *with* her! After all, she'd be contributing to the war effort, just like the mothers she'd be serving! The possibility seemed too good to be true.

She ran upstairs. "Mrs. O'Toole, can I leave Darcy with you while I go see about this job?" She showed the woman the ad.

"Of course, love. If you go now, you can be back before his next feeding."

Charlotte grabbed her hat, gloves, and purse, and headed for the streetcar.

The address was easy to find. The building was the former Wrigley Elementary School, now known as the Wrigley Children's Center. As Charlotte made her way to the front door, she saw at least two dozen small children playing in the sandbox and on the swings. They were supervised by four women wearing identical dresses. Uniforms would be an added bonus, as the only clothing items Charlotte owned were maternity dresses and some outdated things Mrs. O'Toole had provided.

"I've come to apply," Charlotte told the redheaded young woman at the front desk. "My name's Charlotte Penfield."

"Certainly." The girl handed Charlotte a form and a fountain pen and indicated a corner table. "You may sit there and fill this out. I'll check with Mrs. Hudson. She may want to meet you right away."

Charlotte had never applied for work in her life. Where the form asked for experience, she mentioned her waitressing work and wrote that she loved children and had been caring for one around the clock for the past six weeks. She didn't know whether it would work in her favor to say she was a mother or not. For references, she wrote the names *Mrs. Maggie Marshall, Rev. Reuben Fennel,* and *Mrs. Mary O'Toole.* The fact that all three shared the same address would no doubt raise questions, but with any luck, she could sell herself before that part was noticed.

"Mrs. Hudson will meet with you now, if that suits you," the red-haired receptionist said.

"Yes, of course!" Charlotte stood and saw a tall, slim woman standing in the doorway of a nearby office. She wore a crisp suit and a warm smile.

"Hello, I'm Ruth Hudson." The woman held out her hand and Charlotte shook it, feeling very grown up. She was making her own way in the world! Mrs. Hudson ushered her into the little office, where they both took a seat.

"Have you always lived in Winnipeg?"

"No, ma'am. I am fairly new here, but I plan to stay. I intend to raise my son here and am looking for work so I can provide for him."

"I see. Are you a war widow?"

"No, ma'am."

"Is . . . your husband overseas?"

"No, ma'am."

Mrs. Hudson waited for Charlotte to continue. Remembering where deception had gotten her so recently, she decided to just blurt out the truth, come what may. But first, she sent up a silent plea for help. *God, if you see me here—please help me! I need this job!*

"I'm not married. My baby is only six weeks old, and I was hoping that if I could work here, he could come with me to work. I'm good with children. I have a vivid imagination and can dream up all sorts of fun games and activities. Why, just give me a bag of old clothes and I can keep young children entertained for hours! I can play the piano and sing, too. Musical instruction is important for little ones, don't you think?"

Charlotte stopped. Had she said too much? Ruth Hudson was making notes on the application form before her.

"Most young women in your position are encouraged to give up their babies for adoption."

"I was as well. I have chosen to raise him." Charlotte could feel her bravado beginning to slip, and raised her chin a notch.

"You realize that's going to take a great deal of courage?"

"Yes, ma'am."

"People will call you all kinds of things. 'Fallen woman' and far worse."

"Yes, ma'am."

"They will call your son names too."

To this, Charlotte had no reply, though an urge to defend Darcy rose within her at the mere suggestion. Then Mrs. Hudson surprised her.

"How do you know Maggie Marshall?" she asked.

Truth—come what may, Charlotte reminded herself. "I lived with her and worked in her restaurant during my pregnancy. I live with her still."

"I see. And, may I ask, how did you find her to work for?"

Charlotte swallowed. Would now be the time to bend the truth? Maggie had been horrible, there was no other way to say it. But now Charlotte understood why. She couldn't betray their newly formed friendship, but she felt bound to be truthful. And if she admitted to having run away, she'd never get the job! *God, how do I say this?*

"It was a challenge, and there were times I behaved impetuously. But I feel I learned a lot from Mrs. Marshall and have come to value our relationship and appreciate her work ethic."

Mrs. Hudson smiled. "Before the war, I was a regular customer at Bert's Restaurant. Anyone who can work for Maggie Marshall should get along just fine with us, Miss Penfield. Your little son would be enrolled in our nursery program, and you would not be assigned to that department."

"I understand." Charlotte knew any mother would be tempted to give her own child more attention than the others.

"We pay ten dollars a week, one of which would be deducted for his care—the same rate as our other clients pay after subsidy. If you can live within those parameters, you've got the job."

"I can!"

Mrs. Hudson tapped the application papers together on her desk. "We need someone for the seven a.m. to four p.m. shift. You get a half hour for lunch."

"May I visit my baby during my lunch break?" Charlotte began calculating the hours between opportunities to nurse Darcy.

"Certainly. But lateness will not be tolerated. Can you start tomorrow?"

"Yes, ma'am!" Charlotte stood to shake the woman's hand.

"Stop and see Miss Stephens on your way out. She will outfit you with a uniform and a copy of the employee manual. She can also register your son for the nursery. Welcome aboard, Miss Penfield."

Charlotte smiled all the way home on the streetcar. She'd done it! Just like a real grown-up, she had gone out and found a way to support herself and Darcy—without Reginald and without her parents' help! *But not without God's,* she remembered. *Thank you, Lord.* And somehow, Maggie had been part of this, too.

As she hurried up Mrs. O'Toole's sidewalk, she could hear Darcy squalling to be fed. She opened the door, dropped her purse, and took the infant from the frantic woman.

"Thank goodness you're home, love! He's been fussing for the last hour!"

Charlotte settled into the parlor chair with its back to the doorway. "Sorry for the trouble, Mrs. O'Toole! But I got the job! Tomorrow he'll be going with me."

"Oh, gracious, child! Are you sure you're ready for that?"

"I need to be, Mrs. O'Toole." Darcy began to nurse greedily, his little face still red from distress. "We'll make it work."

"Well, that's grand. I'll go fix us a pot of tea."

Charlotte watched Mrs. O'Toole walk to the kitchen, then looked down at her tiny son. "We'll make it work, won't we, Darcy?" Even as she found herself brimming with hope, Charlotte sensed this new chapter might be her most challenging yet.

CHAPTER 40

Maggie couldn't believe it. First Charlotte had declared her independence. Now Reuben was leaving for good.

I know it's for the best, she mused, watching through the kitchen window as Reuben loaded his belongings into his car. *He needs a job. The church in Roseburg needs a pastor. He'll be a perfect fit.* So why did it feel like a piece of her insides was being removed?

Returning for one last box, Reuben turned toward Maggie.

"Well, I guess this is it." He laid the box on the counter near the door and took a couple of steps toward her. "I want to thank you for putting me in touch with the Bakers. I really needed this position, and I think it'll be good to get away from the city. They seem like lovely people."

Maggie nodded, trying to ignore the lump forming in her throat. "You're welcome. It's not like I didn't owe you anything, though. I can't begin to make up to you everything you've done for me."

"Just trying to be a friend." Reuben's brown eyes held her gaze.

"And you've been a good one. The best. I'm sorry our friendship cost you so dearly."

"I'm not." Reuben glanced toward the hallway, then back at Maggie. "I might have stayed at that church for years, bowing to the whims of arrogant hypocrites and losing my very soul in the process.

Our situation forced an end that needed to come. I hope they find a leader who can wake them up, stir up some compassion and genuine faith. I wasn't that man."

"I hope your new congregation appreciates what a good man they're getting, that's all I have to say." Maggie tapped Reuben lightly on the chest with the palm of her hand. "Now you better hit the road if you want to get there before dark."

"You and Charlotte should come visit sometime. After I'm settled."

Maggie paused, trying to imagine it. "That would be a little awkward, Reuben. Don't you think? Best if we leave things be."

"Will you write?"

Maggie studied his face and saw the hope in his eyes. Her heart longed to continue the friendship, but where could it possibly lead? He needed a life partner, a wife. And once he found her, their friendship would become more awkward still. Better to end things now, for his sake.

"A Christmas card, for sure," she said, though her heart cried *Don't go!* "I'll let you know how we're managing."

Reuben nodded, then looked down at his shoes and back up at Maggie. "I'll look forward to it. And you can watch for one from me as well."

"Let's hope the war is over by then."

"Reuben! Are you leaving?" Charlotte hurried into the kitchen with Darcy in her arms. "I haven't said good-bye!"

"I wouldn't have left without saying good-bye, Charlotte." Reuben held his hands out to take the baby, but Charlotte rushed into his arms, sandwiching Darcy between them in a familial hug. "I don't want you to go!"

"Now, Charlotte," Maggie warned. "That's not helping."

When Charlotte pulled away, tears ran freely down her face, as bold as brass. Maggie sniffed. When would that girl learn to keep her emotions to herself? Why, it was like hanging your undies on the line outdoors instead of drying them inside, like any lady knows to do.

"You three have helped me more than you know," Reuben said. "May I pray for you before I leave?"

"Oh, yes, please!" Charlotte smiled up at him, the tears still dripping off her face and onto Darcy's blanket. Maggie said nothing, but allowed Reuben to lay one hand on her shoulder while his other rested on Darcy's head. The baby began to fuss.

"Lord," he began. "Bless and protect my friends Maggie, Charlotte, and Darcy. Provide for their needs, Father. Keep them healthy and safe and happy. Show them the path you want them to walk, and grant them peace. Amen."

With that, he bent to kiss the top of Darcy's head, and Charlotte moved in for one last hug. "I'll walk you to the car," Charlotte said. Darcy was crying in earnest now.

"Here, give me that child." Maggie coaxed Darcy out of Charlotte's arms. "It's getting cold out there, and he's not dressed for it."

As she turned to leave the kitchen, Mrs. O'Toole swept in, her arms flapping like a giant goose preparing for takeoff.

"Oh, Rev'rend! How I hate to see you leave! It's been a joy, lad, an absolute blessing to have you in my house." The woman's eyes glistened. It was almost more than Maggie could take. *What is with these weepy women? Let the poor man do what he needs to do!*

"It's been a joy for me as well, Mrs. O'Toole. I will dearly miss your wonderful meals."

As she carried Darcy up the stairs, Maggie could hear Reuben still reassuring Mrs. O'Toole with his gentle voice, and Mrs. O'Toole whimpering on with her loud one. Without looking back, she headed straight to Charlotte and Darcy's room, where a rocking chair stood in one corner. She sat and began rocking him and he settled almost instantly.

She heard the kitchen door open and close, then the slamming of the car door. The engine roared to life and she heard the wheels crunch on the gravel as the car pulled away and continued down the back lane.

She wished she'd had the courage to offer a prayer for Reuben the way he had prayed for her.

For whatever my prayers are worth, Lord, bless that man. Watch over him. Make him a blessing to the folks in Roseburg. Bring him the woman he needs.

The kitchen door opened and closed again, and then the chatter of Charlotte and Mrs. O'Toole broke the silence in the house. Maggie rose and laid Darcy gently in his bed, kissing his forehead.

That's when she realized her own cheeks were wet with tears. She brushed them away impatiently. It was time for her to catch the bus for the Fort Garry to start her afternoon shift.

CHAPTER 41

Reuben placed his last pair of socks into the dresser drawer and closed it. Then he tucked his empty suitcase onto the top shelf of his bedroom closet. The boarding room the elders had arranged for him was small but adequate. The retired couple who owned the house had been members of the church since immigrating to Canada as newlyweds.

"Let me explain you, Reverend," Mr. Schmidt had told him that evening at supper, his German accent thicker than his wife's. "Our church owns parsonage right next to church. But it is big enough for family of ten. You are just one man, so better church rent it out for top money and you pay for us room and board, yah?"

This did seem reasonable to Reuben, although he would have appreciated being included in the decision.

Hilde Schmidt chimed in. "You will feel yourself so much happier here by us. I do cooking, washing, cleaning, yah? You just be the minister."

"And church makes little bit profit," her husband added. "Everybody wins!"

Reuben smiled. "Indeed. I do appreciate your fine cooking already, Mrs. Schmidt."

The woman beamed. "Please. You call us Heinz and Hilde. And it will not be long, you will see. You will meet a young lady to marry, and then you can move into the parsonage and fill it with children up!"

"Do not rush the man, Hilde," Heinz scolded. "Sorry, Reverend. You go the stairs up and settle in. If you need anything, holler."

It hadn't taken more than twenty minutes to "settle in," and the November sun was rapidly taking its bow for the evening. Reuben grabbed a jacket and hat and descended the stairs two at a time. A brisk walk around his new community would do him good.

Knowing he'd be walking south toward the church come morning, he chose to go north. Roseburg was a bit of an anomaly, a town two miles long and sixty feet wide, it seemed. It consisted of one long main gravel road. He walked past two general stores, a post office, school, Catholic church, filling station, and a community hall. A barbershop doubled as a billiards room. The only thing that appeared to still be open was a combination café, hotel, and beer parlor.

At the town center, three side streets led off the main drag to the east, forming a grand total of four square blocks, each lined with two-story houses on big lots. Most had large gardens, now surrendered to the frost, and outhouses in the backyard. Reuben's loop around these residential blocks raised a chorus of dogs, all tied to posts in their respective spaces. No fences existed anywhere he looked. The barking brought to the windows the faces of a few dog owners, curious to see what the ruckus was about. One front door opened, and out stepped a beanpole of a man. He was dressed in trousers and a white undershirt, both suspenders hanging down below his waist, where they remained as he pulled a warm jacket on over it all.

"Evenin'," he called out.

"Good evening."

"Nice night for a walk."

Reuben approached the man. "Yes, it is." He reached out a hand. "I'm Reuben Fennel, the new pastor at Roseburg Community Church."

"How'd you do? Name's Rogers. Bill Rogers." The man rubbed one hand across his well-whiskered jaw while shaking Reuben's with the other.

"Do you by any chance run Rogers General Store?" Reuben asked.

"That's me all right. Store was my dad's before me. You stayin' at the Schmidts', then?"

"That's right."

"I heard. Good people. Regulars at my store. Always pay up, every month. You'll do fine there. Don't pay attention to what you hear."

Reuben chose to ignore the last sentence, although he couldn't help wondering what it meant. "Good to know. Well, I'll be on my way, Mr. Rogers. Maybe we'll see you in church."

"Don't usually go myself, 'cept at Christmas. Don't see the need. But the missus takes the kids regular. They need to learn what's in the good book. You'll see them."

"I'll look forward to it." Reuben noticed no fewer than four faces in the window then, sandwiched between the edges of the curtains: a woman, two boys, and a girl. They instantly disappeared when Reuben looked directly at them, the curtain swaying closed once again. He smiled and carried on around the bend.

The third street to cross the main drag was a mile-marker road and continued on in both directions, beyond town and toward farms—including the Bakers' farm, where he had stayed on his initial visit.

By the time he returned to the Schmidts' house, darkness had fallen in earnest. The back-porch light had been left on for him, and as he came around the corner, he saw something he had not noticed on his way out. A swastika the size of a frying pan had been painted on the side of the Schmidts' home in red paint.

"Welcome back, Reverend!" Reuben was greeted with two wide smiles as he walked in. "Have a cup of tea with us. Did you enjoy your walking?"

"Yes, thank you. Roseburg is lovely, isn't it?"

"Oh, yes. We have lived here since thirty years, and it is home now. Our youngest son, Otto, was born here. He is in the army, fighting with other Canadians." Heinz offered Reuben the newspaper that lay in the center of the table. "This paper is a week old, but you are welcome to it."

Reuben recognized the same issue he'd seen several days before in Winnipeg. "No, thank you." He pulled out a chair and sat. "May I ask you a question, though?"

"Certainly."

"Are you aware the side of your house has been defaced?"

"Defaced?" Heinz raised his brows and looked up at his wife, who poured Reuben's tea.

"He means the paint." Hilde returned the pot to the stove and sat across from her husband. "Yah, we know. It started the same time as the war. We paint over it, they come back. We paint again, they come back again."

"Finally, we just leave it," Heinz said. "It is easier this way. We have no use for the Nazis or for Herr Hitler, but we have been lumped in with them because we are German."

"Do you have any idea who has been doing this?" Reuben asked.

"Oh, sure. But we do not want to make trouble. We say nothing. It is better that way. When the war is over, it will be forgotten. Yah?"

"I hope you're right, Mr. Schmidt."

"Heinz."

"Heinz. Have there been other forms of mistreatment?"

Heinz looked at Hilde again. "He means have people been unkind to us," she said. She turned back to Reuben. "Most treat us just like they did before the war. Half the people came here from other countries— Norway, England, Italy, Iceland. Even Syria."

"The Haddads," Heinz explained. "Good people, all of them. Just looking for better way of life. We are welcome at church and grocery store. Our kids always fit in at school."

Hilde set her teacup down. "But now. Well, there is just one problem—"

"Hilde." Heinz's voice was firm. "We do not wish to paint ugly picture for the reverend. We do not want to be—what the word is? Gospel?"

"Gossips."

"Yah, gossips."

Hilde crossed her arms. "I was not going to gossip. I was just going to tell to him the truth, so he would know."

"He will know soon enough, if he needs to know."

"I'm sure you're right." Reuben swallowed the last of his tea. "If you'll excuse me, I'll be turning in now. It's been a very long day."

Before crawling under the covers, Reuben sat on the edge of his bed and opened his Bible. His eyes skimmed over a psalm, his mind barely taking in the words as he considered the vandalism on what was now his home and what its presence there meant.

Apparently little Roseburg was not as idyllic as it seemed.

CHAPTER 42

Charlotte looked around the nursery where Darcy would be spending his day. Four women wearing pale pink uniforms identical to hers buzzed about, settling babies up to two years old. One wall was lined with stacking cribs that reminded Charlotte of monkey cages she'd once seen at the zoo. The walls were stark white, the only splash of color being where the rules and regulations hung on bright yellow paper. It was not the environment she would have chosen for her son, but everything was clean, and the worker to whom she handed Darcy smiled reassuringly, as if she could sense the lump in Charlotte's throat.

"See you later, sweetie." Charlotte kissed Darcy on the forehead, smoothed the front of her uniform, and hurried off to the opposite wing of the building to begin her new job. The bus ride from Mrs. O'Toole's had taken a little longer than she anticipated and she had no time to lose.

This room was much larger than the nursery, but more crowded with women dropping off their toddlers. Some of the mothers wore overalls, their hair covered with kerchiefs, lunch buckets in their hands. Others wore skirts or dresses. Charlotte knew that they would all earn more money at their office or manufacturing jobs, piecing together munitions and even aviation parts, than she would caring for their children. But she didn't mind. This was the only way she could remain close to Darcy and continue nursing him.

"Hi, I'm Becky." A dark-haired woman held out a hand toward Charlotte. "Welcome aboard."

"Thanks." Charlotte followed her to a counter where children were being handed over and checked in by their mothers.

Becky walked Charlotte through the procedures, and Charlotte checked off names in a logbook. One by one, the mothers filed out. Some of the children headed straight for the books and toys displayed along one end of the large open room. One little girl sat quietly weeping in a corner while others wailed outright until their mothers were out of sight. Then they settled down.

After the last mother had gone, Becky announced it was time for a game. She pulled a box out from under the counter and began distributing toy tambourines, kazoos, cymbals, and drums. The children lined up single file behind her, and she began marching around in circles, clapping her hands to create a beat. Charlotte followed suit, bringing up the rear of the line and joining in the fun. When the game was over, she glanced up at the door to the hallway. Through the large window she saw Mrs. Hudson, the woman who had hired her, observing from the other side. Charlotte raised a hand in greeting and Mrs. Hudson smiled back, then walked away.

This was followed by some Simon Says, storybook time, twenty minutes of outdoor play, a snack consisting of soda crackers and peanut butter, and free play. Charlotte helped several children to the bathroom, placed a bandage on one boy's skinned knee, and rocked a little girl to sleep. Before she knew it, her lunch break had arrived.

Darcy was beside himself with hunger, and Charlotte wasted no time finding a corner in which to nurse him. Feeding the baby and eating her sandwich at the same time was not the simplest trick, but she'd have to master it or go hungry herself. Half an hour later, she returned to work so that Becky could take her break.

After lunch, the children napped for a full hour while their caregivers used the time to tidy up and prepare for the remainder of the day. Another venture outdoors followed, then an arts-and-crafts time and more stories. Charlotte couldn't believe it when the mothers began arriving to pick up their children. The day had flown! After she returned to Darcy, she had to stop and feed him again before they headed off to catch the bus home.

As Charlotte sat in the nursery feeding her baby, a middle-aged worker approached, buttoning her coat. She studied Charlotte briefly before speaking.

"I'm Vivian. Darcy did just fine today." She smiled warmly.

"That's good to hear. I'm Charlotte."

"How did things go at your end?"

"Good. So many cute little kids. I think I'm going to like it here." Charlotte lifted Darcy to her shoulder to burp him.

"Your hubby overseas?"

There it was. Charlotte had wondered how long it would be before the subject surfaced. She'd almost made it through her first day. She realized that it might be much easier to outright lie. Who would know the difference whether she had a husband or not? It was one thing to endure the judgmental glares of casual acquaintances, but she'd have to face Vivian and her other co-workers every day, all day long. She remembered the unkind words she herself had freely exchanged with her old school chums when their classmate Tilly Munroe dropped out of school and had a baby. Was that really only a year and half ago? *God, forgive me. I can bear to be called a whore if I must, but I can't bear to have Darcy considered "illegitimate."*

"His father is stationed in Ontario," Charlotte said. It was the truth. "And you?" Perhaps by diverting attention from herself, she could keep the charade alive without causing damage.

"We've got two boys in Europe—France, last time I knew—and my youngest is stationed near Petawawa, chauffeuring officers around. Where in Ontario is your husband?"

Well, that didn't last very long. Charlotte bit her bottom lip and sent up a silent plea for courage.

"Petawawa also—"

"No kidding! Hey, I bet they know each—"

"—but . . . he's not my husband."

Vivian stared at her, waiting for more. "But I thought you just said—"

"I said Darcy's father is there. He's a cook at the base. We're not married."

Vivian stared some more. "When are you getting married?"

Charlotte sighed. Might as well lay it all out there and get it over with. Maybe Vivian would prove to be kind, like Mrs. Hudson. "We're not. He's . . . he's married to someone else now."

"Good Lord." A look of disgust changed Vivian's face, but Charlotte couldn't tell if the sentiment was directed at her or at Reginald. Maybe both.

"How old are you, anyway?"

"Almost eighteen."

The woman's head moved back and forth almost imperceptibly, her lips closed tightly as she studied Charlotte and the baby.

"What on earth is this world coming to? How did you ever get this job? Did you think they wouldn't find out?"

Charlotte could feel her jaw drop, but no response would come. Vivian wasn't finished.

"Don't you think the parents are going to raise a stink when they find out their children are being looked after by an unwed mother?"

"I—I don't think they really need to know."

"Oh, you don't. That's fine for you. You probably couldn't care less who looks after *your* kid. But real mothers care, I can tell you that. You know there are plenty of good girls who would love to get this job? How can you sit there, nursing your little bastard, bold as brass?"

"She's nursing him because he's hungry."

Charlotte and Vivian both looked toward the source of the voice. Mrs. Hudson stood in the doorway, her tall frame an imposing figure. "She can sit there feeding him because he's hungry, as any mother would. I don't believe it's any concern of yours, Vivian."

Vivian glanced at Charlotte, then at Mrs. Hudson. "Are you aware this young mother isn't married, never has been?"

"Did you have any trouble with the baby today, Vivian?"

"N-no."

"You seemed quite enthralled with him when I checked in earlier. I saw you rocking and singing to him. It was downright heartwarming."

"Well, that was before I knew—"

"Precisely. Now don't you have a bus to catch?"

With a huff, Vivian grabbed her purse and gloves and headed out the door. She never looked back at Charlotte.

Mrs. Hudson watched her leave, then turned to Charlotte. Darcy still nursed greedily, oblivious to his mother's pounding heart.

"I'm sorry, Miss Penfield. I will do my best to make sure this won't happen here again."

Charlotte was still too stunned to respond.

"But I may as well tell you. This is your new life, and there are plenty of Vivians out there. Not all will speak up, but many will think the way she does. Or say it behind your back. You'll need a thick skin. Did Maggie Marshall warn you about that?"

"Not—not really."

"Well, she should have. She can't be around all the time to protect you from it, and neither can I. You'll need to learn to stand up for yourself and your son, or he'll grow up believing what he hears."

"Yes, ma'am."

Her tone turned to something warmer. "I'm sorry your first day had to end like this. Otherwise, did things go all right?"

"Oh, yes! I can't thank you enough for giving me this chance, Mrs. Hudson." Charlotte wrapped Darcy tightly in his blanket and stood. "I will learn to deal with people like Vivian. For Darcy's sake."

"See you tomorrow then." Mrs. Hudson turned to leave. "You can leave the lights on for the cleaners."

Charlotte rode the bus home in silence, the occasional tear escaping down her cheeks. The childhood taunts of "Charlotte, the harlot" surfaced in her memory. Back then, she wasn't even sure what a harlot was, but she knew from Sunday school that there was one in the Bible, so she had figured it must be something good. She felt mortified when her friend Connie explained.

Had her parents been right all along? She'd just experienced a taste of what they wanted to protect her from, what they wanted to protect *themselves* from. Would she have to deal with this sort of thing forever? Would it go away if she married one day? But who would marry her now? The thought of Reginald's wife happily married and enjoying her new life with Reginald's child crossed Charlotte's mind, but she quickly dismissed it when she looked down at her little son, contentedly nestled in her arms.

"We can do this, my darling boy," she whispered near Darcy's ear. "With God's help, I know we can do this."

CHAPTER 43

Halloween had passed, and winter was definitely here to stay. Snow lay piled high between the streets and sidewalks, making navigation a challenge for drivers and pedestrians alike. The famous "windiest intersection in Canada"—Portage Avenue and Main Street—was to be avoided at all costs. Maggie had purchased a used but warm winter coat from the Goodwill store, along with boots that fit right over her shoes. These kept her feet dry, but did nothing to protect against the cold. Mrs. O'Toole had knitted hats, scarves, and mittens for her and Charlotte.

"No point waitin' for Christmas. You need these now!"

"Oh, Mrs. O'Toole! These are beautiful," Charlotte had gushed, running her hands over the bright red needlework. "When did you have time to do this?"

"What else have I got to fill my time, love? And it's not all that much. I unraveled some jumpers of me ol' Patty's, that's how I come by the wool. Didn't cost me a penny."

Maggie's set was a more subdued grayish-blue color trimmed in white, and the idea that Mrs. O'Toole had unraveled her late husband's sweaters to make them brought a lump to her throat. What was wrong with her? If she wasn't careful, she'd soon be as silly and sentimental as Charlotte. God forbid.

She walked up the steps to the boardinghouse, one hand on the rail to keep her from slipping on the icy concrete. Darkness was settling in, and she was tired from another day of baking at the hotel. Working within the restraints of food rationing was difficult but not impossible, and for some unexplainable reason, she enjoyed the challenge.

The warmth of the house and the savory smell of something in the kitchen welcomed her like a soft blanket around her shoulders. She hung up her coat and purse and checked the small table under the telephone in the hall. A note with her name on it said to call her lawyer, Theodore Jones, when she got in. Two telephone numbers were neatly written at the bottom.

"Mrs. O'Toole?"

"Oh, there ya are, Maggie." Mrs. O'Toole came around the corner from her sitting room. "I see you found your message. Quite important he said it was, and not to wait for office hours. The bottom number is his house and you can call him there."

Now what? Maggie wondered. As a self-protective measure, she had given instructions at the police headquarters and fire hall for all new information to go straight to Jones first. She wasn't sure she could handle any more bad news. Was Earl out of jail? The thought sent a shiver through her.

Her lawyer picked up on the first ring. "Theodore Jones."

"Good evening, Mr. Jones. It's Maggie Marshall. My landlady said it was all right to call you at home."

"Oh, yes. I'm glad you did. There have been some major developments in the case, Mrs. Marshall."

"Bad news or good?"

"Some of both. As we suspected, the fire commissioner has determined that an accelerant was used, meaning it was arson that destroyed your home and restaurant. I am sorry. These kinds of losses are even harder when you know it was deliberate."

Maggie sighed. "I hope that's not the good news."

"It's not. You need to know this has all happened unusually fast. Arson is one of the most difficult criminal cases to prove in a court of law, because of the many elements needed to support the points of the crime. In this case, your arsonist wasn't too bright. It turns out that someone was actually seen pouring fuel around the base of the building the night of the fire."

"Really? And they've only just come forward with this information?"

"It happens. The better news is, police have enough evidence against Earl Marshall to keep him in custody until he goes to trial."

Maggie sighed in relief. "Any idea when that might be?"

"At least another month, I'd say, but since that takes us into Christmas, it could be next year. You will probably be called to testify, based on your history with your late husband."

Maggie felt panic rise to her throat. "Why? How can any of Douglas's activities affect Earl if I can't prove a connection?"

"Leave that to me, Maggie. I'd like to meet as soon as possible and have you tell me your whole story from the beginning. Are you up to it?"

"I guess I'll have to be, won't I?"

"Don't worry. I will coach you all I can so you're ready when the time comes."

They made plans to meet early the following week, and Mr. Jones instructed Maggie to be thinking about and jotting down anything that came to mind regarding the relationship between Earl and her late husband and the questionable activities she suspected had taken place.

"Even if it seems trivial, write it down," he said. "It may turn out to be important."

Her appetite ruined, Maggie picked at her supper. She could hear Darcy kicking up a fuss in an upstairs bedroom and wondered what was upsetting the usually contented little tyke. The telephone rang again, and

Maggie could hear Mrs. O'Toole discussing a sugarless-cookie recipe with her friend Lydia, who was hard of hearing even when the connection was a good one. Tonight, apparently, it was not a good one.

A fire engine sounded its siren a few blocks away, which instantly reminded Maggie of her burned-down home. The wail kicked off a chain reaction of barking dogs throughout the neighborhood. This was followed by at least one neighbor yelling at his dog to shut up. How could Maggie be expected to think in all this ruckus? And it wasn't like she wanted to think very hard anyway.

If she testified at Earl's trial, how much would her history with Douglas come into it? Would she have to describe his abusive treatment and how long she had endured it? It would feel like being stripped naked in front of everyone. A woman could only take so much humiliation.

A newspaper lay on the kitchen table, reminding her that it was Thanksgiving time in the United States: "Victory Prayers Voiced in Service at White House: President and 200 Leaders Ask Peace for World: Divine Guidance Invoked."

Maggie stared at the headline a long time, not bothering to read the story. How could peace possibly come to a world where it couldn't even be imagined in individual homes? Though no air raids had sounded and no bombs dropped in Canada, it seemed to Maggie this house had been far less peaceful since Reuben Fennel left it. Could it be that he had been "invoking divine guidance" on this household's behalf and now they were on their own?

Maggie carried her plate over to the sink, washed and dried it, and placed it with the others in a cupboard. Then she wandered into the sitting room. Mrs. O'Toole was off the phone and had gone upstairs to help Charlotte settle the baby. The sirens had faded away and the dogs had been silenced. Maggie had never paid much attention to the décor in this room, but now she looked around her. A picture on one wall depicted Christ on the cross, surrounded by Romans who held him in contempt and loved ones who wept grievously. She studied it, trying to imagine the pain, the hatred, the utter vulnerability of being in that position. Naked and nailed to a cross. Could a person feel any more exposed? A new thought struck her: *He was humiliated too.*

She noticed a record of Christmas carols that had been placed beside Mrs. O'Toole's gramophone. She pulled it from its sleeve and settled it on the turntable, carefully placed the needle in the first groove, and slid the switch to the On position. Immediately, scratchy sounds began to emit from the speaker, followed by the strains of a philharmonic choir accompanied by a symphony orchestra.

Maggie wandered to the window. More snow was falling, which meant she'd be shoveling again in the morning. Sometimes one had to wonder why anybody lived in Manitoba. Ice and snow all winter and mosquitoes all summer! But as the music played on, she pushed her difficulties out of her mind and watched the gentle snowflakes make their way to the ground. It was her favorite Christmas carol, and the irony that it originated in the very country blamed for the start of this dreadful war, the homeland of Mr. Hitler himself, was not lost on her:

> Silent night, holy night
> All is calm, all is bright.

Maggie knew that in a world so torn, she was blessed to live in the relative peace and safety of this home. She had much to be thankful for, even as she had much to trust God for. As they so often did, her thoughts turned to Reuben Fennel.

"I miss that man, Lord," she whispered against the cold glass of the window, her breath creating a patch of fog. "You probably already know that, so I may as well admit it. I wish he were here to talk to. But he's not, and I need your help and guidance. You've gotten us this far. Please don't let them call me to testify, but if they do . . . show me what to say."

Holy infant, so tender and mild . . .

Again, a picture rose to her mind of that awful night when her husband's blows ended the life of her unborn child.

"But, oh God, please . . . please don't make me say any more than I absolutely must."

CHAPTER 44

Reuben knew his first sermon in Roseburg would be among his most important, no matter how many years he stayed. While it was tempting to pick the best of the messages he'd delivered in past years and deliver it again, he instead spent his walks to the church every day in conversation with God, asking for guidance. This congregation was different than the one he'd left behind in the city, and he didn't know them yet. But God did. *Show me what they need, Lord.*

The fear surrounding the war seemed less tangible here, though there were certainly many young men from the Roseburg community who'd enlisted, and its people had experienced their share of loss. In general, Reuben's observations told him people here were content with less, more committed to hard work, and less self-contained than their city counterparts. Everyone knew everyone, and for the most part a genuine, caring atmosphere prevailed. The only person in town he'd met so far who was less than friendly was Mr. Wittenstock, who ran the post office. He wasn't unkind, exactly. He just didn't go out of his way to be pleasant when Reuben stopped in to inquire about obtaining his own mailbox and key.

"You can have a mailbox, but they don't even have doors on 'em, let alone locks," he'd said. "No need for a key. If you don't figger you can trust folks, I can keep your mail back here and hand it to you over the counter. Them's your options, take it or leave it."

"I'll take a box, please," Reuben had said with a smile. "No reason not to trust anyone."

The man didn't return the smile. "Never know who you can trust with this war on. Could be spies anywhere."

Reuben paused, trying to decide whether the man was serious. "I'll take my chances."

"Your call. You can have number 57. It's been available since ol' Mrs. Rankin passed. That'll be seventy-five cents for the annual rent, please."

"Really?" Reuben hadn't heard of such a thing before, but paid the man without argument.

Mr. Wittenstock filled out a receipt, stamped it *Paid*, and slid it across the counter. He watched Reuben stuff it into his wallet, return the wallet to his pocket, and reach the door before he said, "You have a letter."

Reuben looked up, his hand already on the door handle. "I do?"

The man moved to the back of the room, found the envelope he was looking for, walked slowly to the mailboxes, and slid the letter neatly into box number 57. Reuben found the slot on his side and pulled out a plain white envelope with Charlotte Penfield's name and Mrs. O'Toole's address written in the corner.

"Well, I'll be. Thanks, Mr. Wittenstock!"

The postman nodded almost imperceptibly, and Reuben could feel him watching until he closed the door behind him. He carried the letter with him to the church, where a corner room served as his office. His books already lined the shelves on one wall. A small window framed in white lace looked out onto the Roseburg cemetery, buried under five inches of snow. His simple desk held Reuben's most prized possessions—his Bible, his typewriter, and the fountain pen his father had given him when he graduated from seminary. He took a seat on a rickety wooden office chair and opened his first letter from what he still considered home:

Dear Reuben,

It still feels funny to call you that. I trust you're finding Roseburg to your liking and meeting lots of good people there and that you aren't too lonely. We miss you here.

I took your advice and asked God for guidance and I'm now working at the Wrigley Children's Center, caring for preschoolers whose mothers are working for the war effort. Darcy comes with me and stays on the infants' side, where I can visit him on my lunch breaks. It's working out well, and I wanted to thank you again for all your support. I hope I can pay it back to you some day. I am learning that a lot of people are not as kind as you are and I have to learn to let their comments go. I am trying.

Darcy is growing more each day and is beginning to smile and coo. Sometimes I am certain he really thinks he's talking to me!

Maggie and Mrs. O'Toole both say hello. They are doing fine.

Yours sincerely,
Charlotte

Laying the letter aside with a smile, Reuben went to work on his first sermon.

On Sunday morning, Reuben stood in the pulpit and scanned the room. Bright winter sunshine beamed through the stained glass windows, coloring the ivory of the pump organ's keys. The wooden pews were half-filled. Several of the faces were already familiar and most smiled up at him encouragingly.

"I don't need to tell you that our world is at war," he began. "We may not hear the air-raid sirens or see the bombed-out buildings. We don't watch the constant movement of military personnel. No enemies are demanding our homes and farms for refuge. We don't see the wounded and dying around us. Thank God we don't."

Several heads nodded in agreement, giving Reuben courage.

"But we *have* felt the pain of loss in this community. Many of our young men are away, as is true for every town and village across this vast country. You have suffered. Many have felt the deepest pain a family can know, as some have already made the supreme sacrifice. None of our soldiers will come home unchanged.

"Even more than that, though, is the war that continues to rage right here at home. A war no one can see because it is spiritual in nature." Reuben paused to find the right page in his Bible. "In Ephesians, chapter six, the Bible says, 'We wrestle not against flesh and blood, but against principalities, against powers, against the rulers of the darkness of this world, against spiritual wickedness in high places.'"

He looked up at his congregation; most appeared to be listening intently. "Our enemy is real and active and seeks to destroy us in the very core of our being. In times like these, he will use every trick he can find to make us hateful and suspicious of one another. If we give in to that, he wins the war."

Reuben pulled a white handkerchief from his pocket and held it high. "How many of you men carry one of these? Go ahead and pull it out." He waited while several men cooperated.

"Ladies, do you have a hanky in your purse? I have one here that Mrs. Schmidt was kind enough to loan me." He held up a dainty scrap of white linen embroidered with delicate yellow flowers. The women in the congregation followed suit with their own handkerchiefs, then looked up at Reuben expectantly.

"When I was six years old, my father fought in the Great War. During that time, he was taken prisoner and held captive for many weeks. He was badly mistreated. Which nation's army did this to my father is not important. What they did to him is not the main thing.

"What matters most is the *attitude* my father chose. He was returned to us, thankfully. He was never the same, physically or emotionally. But I say with confidence that my father came home a stronger man in every way that matters. Why? Because he chose to forgive. 'The enemy can take away our land, our way of life, our families, and our dignity,' he used to say. 'He can torture us, maim us, and even end our lives on this earth. But there is one thing he can never do, and that is to make us hate him. The day we do, he wins.'"

Reuben paused to make eye contact with as many as he could.

"My friends, don't be fooled. You are engaged in a battle every bit as real as our young men in the thick of the fray overseas. And every time you allow hatred or prejudice to cloud your thinking, you are waving a white flag of surrender." Reuben waved both hankies to illustrate his point.

"The enemy wins when you say a malicious word about your neighbor. He gains ground each time you think a suspicious thought or voice an unfounded opinion. His munitions are reinforced when you pass judgment based on others' ethnicity and forget we are all made in the image of God."

His hands came down and the little white flags ceased their waving.

"But when we allow love to rule our hearts and ask God to direct our ways, the enemy flees and cowers, for he cannot stand against it." As he spoke, he folded the hankies and returned them to his pocket.

"The most powerful thing you can do right here, at home in Canada, to help win this war is to love one another. To stand united with your brothers and sisters, to lend a hand to all who need it. By God's grace and by his power, we not only can stand firm against the destroyer, but we can also advance against the kingdom of darkness. He's given us that privilege; the weapon he's given us is called *prayer*. And when you engage, the Bible tells us, our enemy has to flee."

A large man near the back let out an *amen*, and several others followed suit.

"Let's not let him win, folks. Let's not sit idly by, for to do so is to wave that white flag. Let's be diligent, prayerful. Let's watch our actions and rein in our tongues. Allow God's army of holy angels to move into our community, to make Roseburg a beacon of light that no spirit of darkness can hide in, knowing he will be exposed. Let's stand united in love and compassion and grace.

"I challenge you with this in the coming week: Each time you pull out your handkerchief, let it serve as a reminder of the battle we're in and of the powerful weapon called prayer we've been given. Instead of waving that white flag, pray. One day, God will show us what happens in the spiritual realm when we pray. For now, we need to trust in what we cannot see. It's called faith."

Reuben closed with a benediction blessing, and as the organist began the strains of the doxology and the congregation rose to sing, he made his way up the aisle. In the foyer, he stood at the doors and greeted each person, matching many more names to faces and hearing "Fine sermon, Rev'rend" repeatedly, until the last individual had exited the building.

He could only hope and pray his "fine sermon" had reached more deeply than their ears.

CHAPTER 45

Christmas had come and gone. The war had taken the briefest of truces but now raged again until it seemed no country, no family had been left untouched. It almost seemed as if it would continue forever, until no human beings remained on the planet. Nineteen forty-three was rung in without fanfare and arrived without the prayed-for announcement of peace.

Reuben had finally received a letter from Maggie Marshall, and a most intriguing letter it was.

> Dear Reuben,
> I'm sorry this isn't a proper Christmas card, but they come dear nowadays. I hope you are enjoying Roseburg and finding your work there fulfilling. Please give my greetings to Cornelia when you see her.
> I am still working at the Fort Garry and have had to fill in for one of the cook's helpers a time or two in addition to my baking. How people can still afford to eat at that grand place, let alone stay

there, is beyond me. I can't help being of the opinion that some folks, somewhere, are making money on this dreadful war, though I can't explain how.

Can you believe it? Earl is being charged with arson with the intent to murder. Maybe that's not the correct legal lingo, but my lawyer hopes to convince the jury that Earl believed I was at home in my bed the night he set fire to my house. Naturally, all of this has given me cause to ponder. If you and I hadn't been chasing down Charlotte ("halfway across the country"), I most certainly would have been in my bed that night.

It's not an easy thing to know someone wants you dead.

You might be surprised to know I went to church last Sunday. Not your old church, of course. And not that big old monstrosity of my in-laws, either. There's this little church I pass on the way to work each day. I noticed it from day one. Finally stopped in one weekday, just to poke my head in the door. It was open, though no one was around. I sat in the back pew awhile and somehow felt quite peaceful there.

I stayed long enough to realize that I spent much of my adult life wanting someone else dead. Now that he is, my troubles have not ended, and I began to see that they won't as long as I keep carrying bitterness around in my heart.

So I guess you could say the good Lord's working on me. I can't tell you I experienced any fancy sudden transformation, and I'm pretty sure bits and pieces of hate and resentment still linger in the dusty corners of my life. But I've asked God to shine his light into those corners and sweep them clean. I hope he does.

I am still waiting to hear whether I will be testifying at Earl's trial. I appreciate your prayers and your friendship.

Charlotte and Mrs. O'Toole send their love. Darcy is growing like a bad weed. He can roll over by himself now and the little stinker does so every chance he gets.

Sincerely,
Maggie

It was lunchtime in the Schmidt family kitchen when Reuben walked in the kitchen door, stamping snow from his boots. The warmth of the room and the delicious smell that suffused it filled him with anticipation. This place was beginning to feel like home and these people like family. With a wooden spoon, Hilde stirred a big pot of borscht on the top of her wood stove, then laid the spoon down and opened the oven doors to reveal four loaves of bread. As he removed his coat, Reuben watched her set the fragrant loaves on a side table, then he stepped over to close the heavy oven door for her.

"Thank you, Reverend. Lunch will be ready in three minutes. Two, if you set the table for me."

"Be glad to." Reuben grabbed some bowls from a shelf and began laying them on the table. As he was pulling spoons and knives from a drawer, Heinz Schmidt entered by the back door and repeated the snow-stamping, coat-removing ritual Reuben had followed.

"More snow coming down," Heinz said. "Maybe we should—"

But his words were cut off by a loud knock at the front door. *"Ach. Wer ist da?"*

"How should I know?" Hilde removed her apron and slung it over a kitchen chair as she walked toward the front hallway. "Nobody ever comes to our front door. Maybe we will have another guest for lunch."

Heinz and Reuben followed.

Standing on the front step was the postman, Mr. Wittenstock. Like a statue, he neither moved nor made eye contact with anyone, but delivered his message in one word.

"Telegram."

The only sound was a faint gasp from Hilde. Heinz took the piece of paper from the man's hand, and Mr. Wittenstock turned and walked slowly away. Heinz closed the door, then rested his forehead against it. He reached his hand out in Reuben's direction. The telegram hung from his fingers, as if daring someone to open it and discover its contents, which could not possibly be good news. Reuben could clearly see the words *Canadian Pacific Telegraphs—World Wide Communications* printed across the top in white print on a blue background.

"Maybe he is coming home!" Hilde sounded like she was trying very hard to sound hopeful.

"They would send him home only if he is badly wounded." Heinz continued to hold the paper at arm's length.

"Maybe you should sit down," Reuben said. He took the telegram and guided Hilde to a sofa in their sitting room. Heinz sat next to her.

Reuben took a seat on the closest chair, inhaled deeply, and quickly glanced through the paper's contents while the couple watched his face and held on to each other.

Mr. & Mrs. Heinz Schmidt

Roseburg, Manitoba 1943 Jan 17 AM 10:17

10711 MINISTER OF NATIONAL DEFENCE DEEPLY REGRETS TO INFORM YOU THAT A107953 PRIVATE OTTO HEINZ SCHMIDT HAS BEEN OFFICIALLY REPORTED KILLED IN ACTION SIXTEENTH JANUARY 1943 STOP IF ANY FURTHER INFORMATION BECOMES AVAILABLE IT WILL BE FORWARDED AS SOON AS RECEIVED.

DIRECTOR OF RECORDS

"Please tell us he is only missing," Hilde whispered.

Reuben looked up at their distraught faces. *How do you inform someone their son is dead?* He shook his head.

"I'm so sorry, Hilde. Heinz. Your boy has given his life."

CHAPTER 46

Maggie picked up the copy of the *Winnipeg Free Press* that lay on a small table next to her chair in the waiting room of Jones, Brighton, and Jones. The front-page headline announced that Princess Juliana of the Netherlands had given birth in an Ottawa hospital. Holland's royal family had taken refuge in Canada in 1940, following the occupation of their homeland by Nazi Germany, and Princess Margriet Francisca had been born January 19, 1943. The article went on to explain that the Canadian government had temporarily declared the maternity ward "extraterritorial" to ensure the newborn would be solely Dutch. Otherwise, the potential heir to the Dutch throne, by virtue of her birth on Canadian soil, would have become a Canadian citizen. Given the way the war was raging on, Maggie wondered whether it really made any difference. Would the princess and her family have a country to return to?

She laid the paper aside with a sigh. What news would Theodore Jones have for her today? The man seemed to be half lawyer and half private detective, digging for any bits of information about Earl he could use in Maggie's interest.

She pulled from her purse her most recent letter from Reuben Fennel and opened it for at least the tenth time. It never failed to bolster her courage:

Dear Maggie,

Thanks for your letter. I am pleased to hear of the work God is doing in your heart and feel privileged that you chose to share it with me. I am praying along with you that you will not be called upon to testify at Earl's trial, for your sake. But I also know that if you must, God will be with you and give you strength and courage for the task. He will guide your words if you ask him. Sometimes an experience like that can even bring healing and a newfound peace, because you are no longer alone with your secrets. Does that make sense? And whenever light is shed on truth, it is always a good thing. So you see, Maggie, God can turn this hard thing to good, and he will, in the end. That doesn't make the journey an easy one, but he will see you through it. Trust him. You might find the book of Esther will encourage you.

I have had to conduct the most difficult memorial service of my career to date. The Schmidts, the couple with whom I board, have become quite dear to me. Their son, Otto, was killed in action and they have been completely distraught. Hilde has taken to her bed and Heinz is beside himself with worry for her. I am doing what I can on a practical level—shoveling snow, splitting *wood, and so on. But my training for the pastorate did not fully prepare me for this level of despair and I feel useless to relieve her grief. I pray and read Scripture at her bedside daily, but she neither acknowledges my presence nor asks me to leave. Thankfully, the community has rallied around with provisions of meals, but I don't know how much longer they can keep it up and I am not so handy in the kitchen. On a positive note, when we returned home from the church following the service, the swastika on the back of their house had been painted over.*

"Mrs. Marshall?" Theodore Jones stood in the doorway to his office. "Come on in."

Maggie tucked Reuben's letter into her purse as she took a seat in the inner office. She checked her watch. "Let's get right to the point, Mr. Jones. I need to be at work in an hour. What new information do you have?"

The attorney shuffled some papers on his desk and kept his eyes cast down. "It's not what we'd hoped for. Earl Marshall is out on bail."

"What?" Maggie was certain she'd heard wrong.

"Apparently they didn't have enough evidence to detain him until his day in court. Which, by the way, has been set for . . . March 15."

"March 15? But that's over a month away! What happens until then? Is anyone keeping an eye on him? Who knows what he could do between now and then?"

"Oh, I don't think we need to worry. He'll be on his best behavior if he knows what's good for him. It will all be over for him if he does anything to draw attention to himself, and he knows it. But Maggie, I do think it's going to be important for you to tell the courts about his association with your late husband and about what you know of your husband's activities."

"So you said."

"I know it's not something you're keen on. You don't want to drag your husband's name through the mud, and that's understandable. But—"

"That's not the issue." Maggie couldn't have cared less about the reputation Douglas left behind.

Mr. Jones looked at her a moment. "If it's a fear of public speaking, I can assure you almost everyone has that fear. But it's not what you might be imagining from the picture shows, where the courtroom is crowded with people. The trial would actually be quite small."

That wasn't the issue, either, but Maggie was not yet ready to voice her real concerns to this man. Let him believe she merely had stage fright. Surely she could find a way to outline Douglas's criminal involvement with Earl without dragging in his treatment of her. None of that had anything to do with Earl's charges anyway. That testimony would never stand up in court, so why even mention it?

For the next half hour, Maggie talked while Theodore Jones took notes. She described the late-night card games, the drinking and gambling her husband and brother-in-law had done together.

"They were inseparable," she said. "Where you saw one, you saw the other. Earl was best man at our wedding, and Douglas was best man at his."

"I didn't know Earl was married."

"Only briefly. He married a young lady named Edna Campbell in '31, and she left him in '32." Maggie wished she'd been as courageous as Edna.

"That's worth noting," the lawyer said. "Did Earl and Douglas ever fight with each other?"

"They argued." Maggie recalled the time she'd seen them come to blows. Ironically, it had happened after the one occasion when Earl was foolish enough to follow his brother's example and threaten Maggie.

Earl had entered the restaurant kitchen, drunk, and begun poking around in the icebox. Maggie was in the midst of the supper rush and ordered him out.

"I don't have time for your nonsense, Earl, and you're in the way. Get out of here."

Earl turned and looked at her with bloodshot eyes. "Don't you dare order me around, Maggot."

He raised a hand to slap her just as Douglas came around the corner. Douglas grabbed his brother before he could lay a finger on Maggie, swung him around, and punched him twice. Earl sagged against the icebox, then slid to the floor.

"Just because you can't keep a woman of your own doesn't give you the right to knock mine around. Go sober up." Douglas kicked his brother toward the door and waited in the doorway until he'd recovered enough to stand and leave. The irony of Douglas coming to her rescue made Maggie want to throw up, but she knew better than to say anything in the moment. At least she'd been spared that time.

But she was not yet prepared to share this episode with her lawyer.

Instead, she listed every prized item she remembered Douglas bringing home—whether it had been won in a poker game or some backstreet deal, she had no idea—to store in their shed until he and his brother could find a way to profit from it. She explained how it appeared to her: that Douglas and Earl rarely made money on anything and lost far more than they gained, including a valuable heirloom necklace of her mother's.

She didn't tell him about the beating she'd endured, fighting for that necklace.

CHAPTER 47

Charlotte's first paycheck was just enough to cover her room and board, and she paid Mrs. O'Toole with a glad heart. Her second was for more because it represented an entire month's work. She and Maggie visited the thrift store and chose some clothes for Darcy. There were mornings when Charlotte felt certain Darcy had outgrown his nightgown while he slept. With her third month's pay, she sent the Canadian Pacific Railway a money order for three dollars to cover the toweling she had stolen from the station in Fort William. They hadn't replied. With that off her conscience, she purchased a used dress for herself. Her mother would be appalled to know she had stepped foot inside a secondhand store, let alone that she'd become a regular customer.

Charlotte studied her reflection in the mirror. After weeks of wearing Mrs. O'Toole's old clothes and gradually cinching them in as her body returned to its pre-pregnancy size, she felt downright beautiful in this new-to-her royal blue dress with white buttons down the front, from collar to waist. Her preference would have been the cherry red one that zipped up the back, but the buttons allowed for easier nursing, and Darcy's needs came first. Still, this was so much more attractive than what she'd been wearing, and she was proud that she'd earned the money to buy it. She would wear it when she went to church with Maggie.

Since her confrontation with Vivian, word of Charlotte's unwed-mother status had spread throughout the care center. Just as quickly, her co-workers had sorted themselves into two obvious camps: those who snubbed her and those who demonstrated compassion. The snubbers made Charlotte wish she had simply lied and said her husband was killed in action. War widows were all too common, and she saw the respect and sympathy they received. It would have made life much easier.

But there were two or three whose treatment of her made Charlotte feel, if not respectable, at least human. One younger worker named Elsie favored Darcy like her own private pet and seemed to go out of her way to speak with Charlotte whenever the opportunity arose. Meanwhile, Vivian went out of *her* way to avoid both Charlotte and Darcy.

Charlotte was learning to ignore the looks of contempt aimed in her direction whenever she walked in the door carrying Darcy. Silently she recited the words of a letter she'd received from Reuben Fennel:

"*. . . enduring this now will make you a stronger person in the long run, Charlotte, and a stronger person means a more resilient mother for Darcy—which is what he is going to need. God will help you. Hold your head high. Not in an arrogant way, of course, but in knowing you and your son are beloved children of God.*"

Those words provided a soothing balm the day she overheard two of the mothers discussing her circumstances as they helped their children into coats and snow boots at the end of the day.

"What kind of name is 'Darcy,' anyway?"

"That kid is four months old already. How much you want to bet she'll be popping out another one before the year is out?"

"That's usually the way it goes with her type."

. . . beloved children of God.

The words calmed her mind while she emptied a potty after helping one of her toddlers use it. "Charlotte should clean all the potties," Rachel had joked, "since she obviously loves to get herself dirty."

. . . beloved children of God.

"Where is your boyfriend taking you tonight, Charlotte?" Laurel asked loudly one Saturday as the workers filed out of the building. "Or is he staying home with his wife for a change?"

Elsie came to stand alongside her. "Don't pay any attention," she said. "C'mon, I'll walk you to the bus."

That evening, Charlotte and Darcy sat home alone as another snowfall came steadily down. The other boarders were gone for the weekend, as usual. Maggie was filling in for a line chef at the Fort Garry, and Mrs. O'Toole was away visiting her sister. The Irish woman had been teaching Charlotte how to tear old clothing into long strips, braid them together, and then stitch the braids into rugs that could be sold for extra income. While Charlotte worked, her baby lay on a blanket on the floor, kicking his arms and feet until he would gradually roll over onto his tummy, and then he'd begin the whole process over again until he rolled onto his back. Charlotte kept up a running commentary, and Darcy jabbered in response.

"This is not how I ever thought I'd be spending a Saturday evening, Darcy." She sighed. "Not that I don't love you beyond words—I think you're tops. It's just that, here I am, only eighteen years old, and already looking back to the days when I felt like the belle of the ball. You should see some of the pretty spring frocks in my closet at home." She could hardly form the word *home*. What did it even mean anymore? If home was where people loved you and cared for you, then the house where her parents lived was definitely not home.

"One of every color, at least. My favorite was the peach one with the white collar—I wore it only twice. First time was to my friend Miranda's sixteenth birthday party and the second was to a dance with your—with Reginald."

The thought of Reginald filled Charlotte's heart with sadness. "My parents were right about one thing, Darcy. I should have steered clear of that boy. He did not have my best interests at heart. Why didn't I see it?"

Darcy agreed with a single "goo" that melted her heart.

"But I wouldn't change anything, because then you wouldn't be here." Charlotte picked up a new strip of fabric and began weaving it into the braid on her lap. "Still, I confess, I do get lonely. My days of going out and having fun with other young people are over. There's a new picture show in town I'd love to see, but who would I go with, and what would I do with you? And it would feel like a terrible waste of my hard-earned money.

"But that's all right, my baby. Spring is coming. You and I will go for long walks in the park and discover playgrounds and baby squirrels and birds' nests—"

She was interrupted by a loud knock at the front door. She laid aside her work and opened the door to a man she didn't know. Suddenly she wished someone else were home with her. The man seemed polite enough, though, as he remained outside on the doorstep with snow landing on his broad shoulders.

"Good evening, young lady," he said. "I'm here to see Mrs. Maggie Marshall. I'm a relative of hers."

"I'm sorry, but Maggie's working this evening. I'd be happy to give her a message when she returns."

"Oh. I'm sorry to hear that. Is she still working at the Fort Garry?" The man had a nice smile. "Yes. By the time you get there, though, she'll probably be done for the day. She should be here in a half hour, maybe less."

"I've come quite a distance and it's important that I speak with her. I'll tell you what." The man picked up the snow shovel leaning against the wall. "How about I shovel your steps and sidewalk while I wait?"

"Now that's just silly." Charlotte wanted to close the door before the cold draft reached Darcy. "No point in shoveling snow while it's still coming down. Why don't you come inside and wait where it's warm?"

Charlotte opened the door wider, and the man stepped in. "Why, thank you, that's very kind. Oh, what a handsome baby! Are you babysitting?"

Anybody with enough sense to notice her son's fine looks was bound to be a good person, Charlotte decided. With pride, she announced, "This is my son, Darcy."

"Well, he's a strapping fellow. Congratulations, Mrs.—"

"Penfield. Charlotte Penfield. And you are—?"

The man put out his right hand to shake Charlotte's. "Earl Marshall."

"Nice to meet you, Mr. Marshall. Here, let me take your coat so you can have a seat. Maggie shouldn't be long. Can I offer you some tea?"

"Yes, thank you. It's a chilly night."

Charlotte moved to the kitchen, where she put the kettle on and pulled the tea down from the cupboard. When she returned to the sitting room, she found Mr. Marshall crouched in front of Darcy, talking to him. The baby responded with smiles and excited kicking of his feet. Charlotte watched, smiling. She wasn't sure how Earl was related to Maggie, but hoped his presence meant good news for her. Such a nice man.

She returned to the kitchen when the kettle began whistling, and as she poured it into the teapot, she heard someone at the front door. *Mrs. O'Toole must be home already.* Charlotte replaced the lid on the teapot and hurried to the front door. To her surprise, Maggie was hanging up her coat and studying the one Earl Marshall had hung on a hook beside it.

"Maggie! You've got a guest." Before Charlotte could say more, she heard the man's deep voice.

"Hello, Maggot."

Charlotte turned to see Earl Marshall in the sitting-room doorway, leaning casually against one side, his arms folded. Had she heard him right? The friendly and polite timbre of his tone had changed to something cold. Charlotte turned to see that Maggie's face had paled.

"What are you doing here?" Maggie's voice held a tremble Charlotte had not heard before.

"I came to see *you*. My dear sister-in-law. I wanted to extend my condolences on the loss of your restaurant. Excuse me, *our* restaurant."

Maggie pulled the man's coat and hat from their hooks and held them out toward him. "This is not the time nor the place, Earl. You should leave now."

"Oh, I'm not going anywhere. We have unfinished business. As you well know. I'll leave once you and I have reached an understanding about a certain upcoming trial and exactly what you're going to say."

Charlotte suddenly regretted allowing the man inside. "I'm sorry, Maggie, I didn't—"

"Charlotte, take Darcy and go next door to wait for Mrs. O'Toole," Maggie instructed.

Charlotte tried to obey, but the man stood between her and her baby, who had begun to cry.

"Nobody's going anywhere. Who is Mrs. O'Toole?"

Charlotte tried to push past the man to pick Darcy up, but he grabbed her by the shoulders. "I said, who is Mrs. O'Toole?"

"She's our l-landlady. Let me past!"

"Let the girl go, Earl," Maggie said. "This has nothing to do with her." Maggie stepped toward Earl, and Charlotte felt him tighten his grip with his left hand while he reached inside his coat with his right. He pulled a pistol out and waved it in Maggie's direction.

"Don't you move," he said.

Charlotte screamed.

"And you, shut up." He pointed the gun at Charlotte. "Both of you, sit down on that sofa."

Charlotte felt paralyzed, but when the man yelled "Now!" she sat. Maggie followed suit, but Earl was still between them and Darcy. The baby was wailing.

"Sit there until I tell you otherwise."

Maggie put an arm around Charlotte. "Earl, be reasonable. Let her calm the baby down, he'll only get louder until you can't hear yourself think—"

Earl stepped forward and slapped Maggie hard across the face. "Don't you try to order me around, you worthless little maggot."

Charlotte saw her opportunity and made a dash toward Darcy.

"Charlotte, don't . . . !" Maggie yelled.

The man was too fast. Charlotte felt a hard kick to her hip that sent her sprawling into the wall. A lamp came down on top of her, and by the time she was able to look around, Earl had scooped up Darcy with one hand. With the other, he held a gun to the baby's head.

"You *will* listen to me, both of you, or you can say good-bye to this kid."

CHAPTER 48

Reuben stared out the train window, wondering if he was truly losing his mind. Months had passed since his last message from the Lord, the one that convinced him he should propose marriage to Maggie Marshall. But since then, he and Maggie had gone their separate ways and their letters were growing more infrequent. At least two eligible young women from his congregation had made their interest and availability known without any hint of shyness. If he had any sense, he'd choose one of them for courtship and marriage and settle down to his calling in Roseburg. Although Hilde Schmidt was showing significant improvement, Reuben feared she would never be the same woman she'd been before the death of her son. With Heinz once again managing the outside chores, Reuben felt more of a burden than a help now. If he married, he could move out.

So why couldn't he get Maggie out of his mind?

Then last night, just when he was asking God for guidance about the situation, he was nailed with another clear impression: He saw a picture of Maggie, pounding furiously on a heavy door and glancing over her shoulder in fear. Was she in some kind of trouble?

He had tried to shake the image off at first. When that didn't work, he tried to argue. "God, she's a hundred miles away. She's safe now, and she is rebuilding her life. She's made it pretty clear she's not interested in having another man in her life, messing everything up."

But the vision remained, as clear as if Maggie were in the same room. He had no idea what it was about, only that he'd be catching the next afternoon's train for Winnipeg.

He disembarked at the Winnipeg train station and looked around at the familiar surroundings. *Now what, Lord?* He could see the Fort Garry Hotel just a short walk up Broadway Avenue, but Maggie would surely be home from work by now. He shouldn't just stop in unannounced and empty-handed, though, should he? He should at least pick up something for Mrs. O'Toole.

No. Just get there. The instruction was clear.

So Reuben made his way quickly to the first trolley that would get him within walking distance of his old boardinghouse. Snow was falling heavily now, and he thrust his hands deep into his coat pockets as he trudged down the sidewalk. He saw lights glowing through Mrs. O'Toole's sitting-room window and realized his heart was pounding hard at the thought of seeing Maggie in mere moments. As he let himself through the little gate and walked up to the front door, he could hear a baby crying in full force. Darcy's lungs had definitely grown stronger since he left! The child seemed to be in deep distress.

Reuben knocked and waited. Darcy kept wailing on the other side of the door, but no one answered it. Couldn't they hear him over the baby's cries? He knocked again, then tried the doorknob. Locked. Clearly, somebody was inside, even if it wasn't Maggie. He moved around to the sitting-room window and tried to peer in, but the curtains were closed.

Reuben made his way around to the back door, each step breaking through snowdrifts a foot or more deep. The door to the porch was open and he stepped in and stamped as much snow off as he could. He could still hear Darcy wailing. The kitchen door was unlocked, and he stepped through to see abandoned tea preparations. Between the baby's cries, Reuben could hear a man's voice coming from the sitting room. He moved toward the front entry and listened. The voice was vaguely familiar, but it wasn't until he heard Maggie's voice that he was certain who it was.

"Earl, just tell me what you want and let the baby go."

"I want cooperation at my trial, Maggie. You'll say exactly what I tell you to."

"Absolutely, Earl. I'll do whatever you say. Please just let Charlotte take the baby and go upstairs. Then we can talk in peace and quiet."

"Shut up!"

Earl sounded drunk or confused. Reuben wished he could find a way to see them without being seen himself. Clearly Earl was somehow endangering Darcy, but which direction was he facing? What was he armed with? The telephone sat just inches from Reuben's elbow, but there was no way he could speak into it without alerting Earl to his presence. Thanks to Darcy's screaming, however, he found he could remove the receiver from its cradle without detection. He laid the receiver down gently on the table, then waited another moment before pushing the crank just enough to connect to an operator.

"I'll let the kid go as soon as you tell me where Douglas stashed the rest of the stuff, Maggie," Earl was saying.

"I don't know what you're talking about, Earl." Maggie's voice sounded surprisingly strong.

"Don't lie to me, Maggot. If you already sold it, I swear I'll shoot this kid and you too."

Earl had a gun. Reuben knew he had no time to lose, and that he held the advantage of surprise. With one long stride, he stepped around the corner into the room. Earl Marshall stood facing Reuben, with the howling Darcy tucked under his left arm like a football. Earl swung the gun in Reuben's direction, shock registering on his face. Reuben made a wild lunge for the man's knees. He heard Charlotte scream and

Maggie's cry of "Reuben!" Then the loudest crack he'd ever heard in his life. A gunshot. The baby's wails grew even louder, if that was possible.

Reuben hit the floor, his arms wrapped tightly around Earl's knees. He became acutely aware of a knife-sharp pain in his left shoulder, but he saw Maggie dive for Darcy and wrestle him from Earl's grip. Another shot fired. *Earl must still have the gun.*

Reuben scrambled to climb on top of Earl and pin him facedown to the floor. From the corner of his eye, he thought he saw Maggie flee the room with the baby, but where was Charlotte? Had she too escaped? He clamped one hand down on Earl's wrist and tried to pry his fingers off the gun with the other. That's when he realized his own sleeve was soaked with blood, which had begun to seep out onto Mrs. O'Toole's rug. He managed to pin Earl's left hand behind his back, but his arm was weakening rapidly and Earl was building momentum, kicking so hard that Reuben rocked back and forth like a rodeo cowboy. Still, the gun remained tightly in Earl's hand. Another shot cracked the air, deafening Reuben, and then all was eerily silent as the struggle continued. With every ounce of strength, Reuben leaned hard into Earl's back, willing him to lie still.

Maggie ran back into the room, this time without Darcy. She dashed straight for the two wrestling men and knelt on the floor. With one knee on Earl's head, she clamped both her hands over his arm, freeing Reuben's hands to finally pry the gun loose, though he felt certain he was breaking Earl's fingers in the process. He slid the pistol across the floor as far as he could, but it hit the wall just short of the doorway and stayed in the room. Maggie was moving her lips and saying something to him, but he couldn't hear her words, or anything else. He moved to Earl's feet and held them down, then looked around the room.

Charlotte lay facedown on the floor, a pool of blood forming around her midsection.

CHAPTER 49

Maggie couldn't believe this was happening. Why, oh why hadn't the authorities kept Earl Marshall in custody? He was clearly unstable, and now at least four lives were in danger. She heard another shot fired as she reached the bedroom Charlotte shared with her baby. She laid Darcy in his crib, closed the door behind her, and dashed back downstairs, wondering if she would find Charlotte and Reuben both dead and Earl waiting, gun in hand, to finish her off too.

The telephone receiver lay off its cradle, and Maggie could hear a voice coming from it. She picked it up. "This is the operator; I hear gunshots and screaming. Please give me your address. I can send help. Please give me your—"

Maggie cut her off by quickly stating the house address, and then laid the receiver on the table again.

The scene as she rounded the corner into Mrs. O'Toole's sitting room was like something from a war zone. Charlotte lay slumped near one corner of the room while the two men continued to tussle. She ran to assist and practically sat on Earl's head, yelling at Reuben to wrench the gun away. It seemed hours passed before she finally saw it slide across the floor and hit the wall with a thud. She noticed that Darcy's wails were becoming high-pitched screeches and then realized it wasn't the baby she was hearing but sirens, coming closer. *Thank you, Lord!*

"Can you hold him?" Maggie asked Reuben.

He stared at her with an uncomprehending look in his eyes. His shirt and Earl's were both soaked with blood, but whose blood was it?

"Take care of Charlotte," Reuben yelled.

The sirens were right outside now and someone was banging on the door.

"Police! Open up!"

Maggie ran to the door, unlocked it, and swung it open wide, admitting two police offers with guns drawn. She pointed them toward the sitting room, then ushered in two more officers. Another two had entered through the kitchen. She looked out to the street where three police cars and an ambulance were parked, their lights flashing. A handful of neighbors stood in the snow, watching.

One of the policemen ran back outside, past Maggie toward the ambulance. A second approached her. "Where's the baby?" he asked. Maggie led him upstairs.

"Is there anyone else in this house?" he asked.

"No." Maggie turned into Darcy's room and picked him up. The baby was clammy with sweat, his face soaked with tears.

"Stay here and try to calm him," the officer instructed. He closed the door on his way out. Maggie moved to the window and watched as two medics carried a stretcher into the house while the police officer spoke to the gathered crowd, which then dispersed quickly. She rocked back and forth until Darcy finally began to settle down, an occasional sob escaping his exhausted little body. Maggie knew he was probably long overdue for a diaper change but didn't want to risk setting him off again. What was happening downstairs?

Looking out the window again, she saw Earl being escorted away in handcuffs by two police officers. They pushed him into the rear seat of one car and drove away. Next came Reuben. He was walking, but leaning hard against a medic who appeared to be applying pressure to his shoulder. Reuben had been shot! Maggie could feel hot tears on her cheeks but didn't bother to wipe them away. Reuben crawled into the ambulance unassisted, and two more medics came out the door carrying Charlotte on a stretcher. Maggie caught her breath. The girl's face was as white as the sheet she lay on. She watched while they loaded her into the ambulance and then it, too, drove away. Maggie heard footsteps on the stairs.

"Ma'am? Are you all right?" The police officer who had come upstairs with her earlier now stood in the doorway.

"Is Charlotte alive? Will she be all right?" Maggie held Darcy so tightly he began to squirm again.

"They're taking care of her, ma'am. A neighbor told me you and she are both boarders in this house, is that correct?"

"Yes."

"Could you come downstairs with me and explain what went on here this evening? You can bring your baby with you, it's safe now."

Maggie didn't bother to explain that the young woman in the ambulance was the baby's mother. "Let me change him first?"

"Certainly. Then come downstairs, please, but let's sit in the kitchen. The other room will be off-limits until we know if the young lady is going to—"

His voice trailed off. Maggie stared. *The young lady is going to what? Live?* Charlotte might die! *Oh Lord.* Charlotte might die, and it would be all her fault. She should have made the girl go home with her parents. She should have insisted.

The officer left the room without another word. Maggie changed Darcy's diaper and noticed red welts and the beginnings of bruises on his little arms and legs. She could still see the crazed look in Earl's eye as he gripped the baby, and she felt certain that the child might be dead now if not for Reuben's intervention. Her hands shook as she dressed him in a fresh nightgown and cap. She wrapped him in a clean blanket, then carried him down to the kitchen. She had just sat down when Mrs. O'Toole entered.

"What is going on in my house?"

Maggie met the shaken woman at the door, took her coat, and steered her to a chair. "Sit down, Mrs. O'Toole. You might as well hear the story too."

By the time Maggie had finished telling her version of events, the police officer taking notes and asking questions the entire time, Darcy had fallen asleep. How long until he became hungry? Maggie wondered.

"Officer, I must get to the hospital and find out how Charlotte and Reuben are," she said. "Mrs. O'Toole, can I leave Darcy with you?"

The woman nodded. "I've got canned milk and a baby bottle left from when Charlotte was job hunting. I can get more milk in the morning if we need it. You go."

"The hospital is my next stop," the policeman said. "You may ride with me if you wish."

Maggie climbed in beside the police officer and tried to breathe deeply. It was nearly midnight. She felt exhausted and riddled with guilt. Why did she bring trouble wherever she went? Reuben and Charlotte had nothing to do with Earl Marshall, but now they both had suffered wounds at his hand. What if Charlotte didn't pull through? *Oh, Lord, I can't bear the guilt. Please let them both be all right. Darcy needs his mother. I need her.*

I need Reuben too.

She recalled the moment earlier in the evening when Reuben had entered the room. Even amid all the confusion and terror of the moment, she had felt joy surge in her heart at the sight of him. What had brought him to Winnipeg now? His infrequent letters indicated he had settled into his position in Roseburg and felt called to stay. Had something happened? Of all the moments for him to walk back into their home!

Maggie followed the police officer into the emergency ward of the hospital and waited as he inquired at the desk. Though he was given permission to see Charlotte and directed to the room where she was,

Maggie—to her frustration—was instructed to wait. Just as she was taking a seat on a hard wooden chair in the waiting area, she saw Reuben being wheeled down the hall toward her. A nurse pushed the chair. Reuben's left arm was in a sling, but he appeared to be all right otherwise. When he spotted Maggie, he assured the nurse he could walk from there, but she persisted in pushing the chair all the way.

"Regulations," she said.

Maggie stood as he approached, but could barely find her voice. "Are you all right, Reuben?"

"I'll be just fine. My shoulder was only grazed." Reuben abandoned the wheelchair, took Maggie's hand, and pulled her onto a chair as he sat next to her. "They won't let me see Charlotte. Have you heard anything?"

"No." Maggie wanted to reach out toward Reuben's wounded shoulder, but refrained. "Does that hurt bad?"

"Could be much worse." He held up a bottle of pills. "Painkillers. And you'll need to speak into this ear for a while." He pointed to the left side of his face. "Can't hear out of the other, but they tell me it'll come back. Have you given your statement to the police?"

Reuben and Maggie sat together in the waiting area and compared notes. Each of them had heard three shots fired, though which of the shots had struck Charlotte, they didn't know. Maggie explained how Earl had been released from jail and was waiting for her at the house when she'd arrived home. She told Reuben, as she'd already told the police, that Earl had been threatening her regarding his upcoming trial and seeking information about the whereabouts of some valuables he and Douglas had no doubt hidden somewhere and which he could not find.

"Is it possible Douglas double-crossed his own brother?" Reuben asked.

"I wouldn't put anything past either of them."

Maggie could feel Reuben's eyes on her. She looked up into his face and saw tender concern and love there, which only added to her guilt.

"Reuben, I am so sorry you got dragged into this. I've brought nothing but trouble to you since that day you innocently stopped by to offer your condolences. I never should have asked for your help with Charlotte or with any of this. I'm so sorry—"

"Maggie. Stop it."

"It seems like every time I turn around, I'm facing some new calamity. Do you think I'm cursed or something?"

"Of course not."

Maggie hoped he was right. "What brought you back anyway? And tonight of all times?"

Reuben said nothing at first. Maggie watched the expression on his face turn to something she couldn't decipher.

"Hard to explain," he said. "I just knew I needed to come. Quickly."

Maggie studied his face. "God really does speak to you, doesn't he?" How she had grown to love him, despite her efforts to deny the feelings that had been deepening in her heart.

"Yes. He does. I almost never obey quickly enough, though. I question everything. I'd make a lousy soldier, Maggie. Maybe if I'd gotten on an earlier train, the very next train after he told me to come to you . . . maybe Charlotte wouldn't be lying there now. When am I going to learn?"

"If you hadn't come when you did, we might have lost Darcy," Maggie said. "Instead, he's roughed up a bit, but he'll be fine."

"I wonder what's taking so long?" Reuben rose to his feet and paced the small room, then sat down again. His face was pale.

Fresh anxiety rose in Maggie's chest and she gripped the edge of her chair. "What if she doesn't pull through, Reuben? I won't be able to bear it. I should have urged her to return home with her parents."

Reuben turned to face Maggie. "And never see her son again?" He shook his head slowly. "That would have killed her more certainly than any bullet."

CHAPTER 50

Charlotte wondered how she'd landed in the beautiful meadow. Never in her life had she been surrounded by such beauty and peace. There wasn't another soul in sight. The sun shone warm on her skin, the sky a brilliant azure. She turned and looked around. As far as she could see, in all directions stretched fields of wildflowers in every color she'd ever seen and more. Their fragrance dizzied her, and she closed her eyes and lay back on the soft grass, breathing deeply. She could hear birds twittering and the faint buzz of a bee as it flittered from flower to flower. She didn't feel hungry or thirsty. Nothing hurt. If only she could stay here forever.

But where was Darcy?

Then suddenly, it was as if she were being sucked backward through a narrow tunnel against her will. *No. Let me stay!* The sunlight darkened to a cold, gray haze. The sounds of the birds morphed into sounds that were almost human in nature, but the words were indiscernible. The flowers faded to white and then disappeared altogether. Gradually, Charlotte became aware of every muscle in her body, as one by one they began to hurt. Her head pounded, her back ached. Her arms and legs felt pinned to the ground. A pain near her ribs made her want to cry out, but she hadn't the strength to do so. *Oh, please let me go back.*

"Charlotte?"

She heard her name. The voice was familiar, but she couldn't attach it to a face. She tried to open her eyes, but the weight of her eyelids was too much.

"Charlotte, it's Maggie. Can you hear me?"

Maggie? Did she know anyone named Maggie? Charlotte tried to remember. When her eyes still refused to open, she tried to speak. A low moan escaped her lips, then everything went black again.

Charlotte had not returned to her beautiful meadow, yet once again she felt herself being sucked through that dark tunnel. Forward, this time. Where was she going? The pain was returning. *Make it stop!* Though her eyelids still refused to open, she was aware of light on the other side of them. Her eyes hurt. Everything hurt.

She slowly became aware of sounds again. Voices she didn't recognize somewhere down around her feet. She strained hard to understand the words.

"Her vital signs are stable, Doctor."

"And it's been how long? Ten days now?"

"Yes, sir."

Charlotte managed to open her eyes into a blurry squint. She saw a white ceiling and a bright light above her head. She looked toward her feet and saw two shadowy figures in white. Angels? She hoped not. If she were in the presence of angels, surely she wouldn't feel this overwhelming pain.

"She's waking up, Doctor."

The white figures moved closer to her head, one on either side. Charlotte was aware of someone touching her hand.

"Miss Penfield? I'm Dr. Glendale. You're in the hospital."

The man was saying more, but his words grew garbled and slowly became no more than a buzz. Charlotte found herself back in the meadow. But instead of warm sunshine, this time she was covered in a blanket of snow. Everything was white as far as she could see, yet she wasn't cold. Just very, very tired. She closed her eyes and let herself sleep.

"Charlotte? If you can hear me, squeeze my hand."

This time, Charlotte didn't experience the sensation of being sucked through a tube. She could hear a voice, quite close by. With great effort, she concentrated on her hands. She couldn't tell which one was being held. Maybe both?

"It's me, Charlotte. Maggie. Can you squeeze my hand?"

Charlotte wished this Maggie person would tell her which hand to squeeze. She didn't know if she had the energy to move them both, but she focused hard and squeezed both her hands as tightly as she could.

"I think I felt something," the voice said. "She's responding!"

Someone else must be in the room. Who?

"Charlotte, I felt that. Good work! Now I know you can hear me. Can you open your eyes?"

Charlotte tried hard to lift her eyelids. It seemed to her they were open, but she couldn't see anything.

"Reuben's here with me, Charlotte."

"Hello, Charlotte." A man's voice. Deep and gentle. Charlotte tried to remember who Maggie and Reuben were.

"We'd sure love for you to wake up, Charlotte." The man again. His voice sounded so kind and made her want desperately to respond.

Once again, Charlotte could see blurry whiteness and knew her eyes had to be open this time. She blinked until the blurriness resolved into two distinct figures, one on either side of her. She kept focusing. The man on her left. Plaid shirt. This must be Reuben, the one with the kind voice. She moved her eyes to the right. A woman. Blue dress. What had she called herself? It started with *M*. Her voice was not as kind. It made the speaker sound weary, maybe even a little gruff. The face came into focus. It was surrounded by a wild tangle of red curls.

"Hi, Charlotte. Atta girl, you can wake up now." The woman smiled at her. Maybe this *M* person wasn't harsh after all. "You've been in the hospital a long time. Six weeks. But you're getting well. We're all waiting for you to get better so you can come home."

Who was "all"? Charlotte turned her head toward the man again. He spoke.

"Do you know us, Charlotte? I'm Reuben. And this is Maggie." *Oh, yes: "Maggie." Now I remember. I was right, it started with an* M. *But who is she?* These two weren't nurses or doctors. Apparently Charlotte lived with them. But she was certain they weren't her parents. She remembered her parents. Mother and Father. Where were they?

"Darcy's going to be so happy to see you, Charlotte," Maggie said.

Darcy. Instantly, Charlotte felt a surge of warmth at the name. *Think. Who is Darcy?* She squeezed both hands again, with all her might.

"I felt that this time." The man's voice. Reuben.

"Me too. She's trying to tell us she wants to see Darcy."

Charlotte felt exhausted from trying to think so hard, but she wanted desperately to know who Darcy was. Why wasn't he there? Maybe if she could see his face. Whoever he was, she knew he was important and extremely precious to her. She tried to force her eyes to focus on the woman, but they snapped shut and refused to budge. As she drifted away again, the last words she heard were from the man.

"Lord, please bring complete healing to Charlotte's body and mind. Show us what to do for her. Darcy needs her, Lord. We all do."

And she was lost again in the blissful warmth of sleep.

CHAPTER 51

I don't understand." Maggie sat across from Dr. Glendale's desk. "If the bullet went into her rib-cage area and came out the back, why is Charlotte's brain damaged?"

The doctor cleared his throat. "Tests indicate that there's swelling on her brain, which we believe happened after she fell. There is evidence of a very tiny fracture on the left side of her skull. This tells us she must have hit the floor hard.

"Secondly, her body is pouring all its energies into survival and into healing its damaged parts—the laparotomy showed us that most of the damage from the gunshot was to her liver, always a serious wound. That's the reason she's been in a coma. It's the body's way of shutting down so it can heal and survive."

"It's an amazing thing, the way our bodies were created," Reuben said from his seat next to Maggie.

"It is indeed." The man nodded. "I've been at this for thirty years, and I learn more with every case. For Charlotte, this could have been much worse—so easily fatal. But somehow, the way she fell actually put pressure on her wounds and helped stem the bleeding at a critical time. We were able to make the repairs we made only because she was hemodynamically stable—"

"Wait. What does that mean?" Maggie leaned in toward the doctor.

"Hemodynamics is simply a way to explain the physical laws that govern the flow of blood. Our blood vessels are extremely complex, with many ways for blood to enter and exit them, a necessity under constantly changing conditions. As serious as this incident was, Charlotte needed everything to go as well as it possibly could in terms of her hemodynamic response. And it did."

"Would you call it a miracle, Doctor?" Reuben asked.

"*Miracle* isn't a word I throw around, but I would say she is a very fortunate young lady. As for her memory and muscle responses, I'm certain all of that will return gradually—possibly even quickly—once her body gives her brain the go-ahead, for lack of a better term. These things are largely out of our control, but we can monitor her for infection, keep her hydrated, and drain away the excess fluids. All of that helps."

Maggie looked into the doctor's weary face. "Any idea how long it'll be?"

Dr. Glendale paused. "I've seen patients take months, even years, to return to full cognizance. Other times it happens seemingly overnight. The timing is impossible to predict, but of one thing I'm certain: There *will* be significant improvement."

"But there may be some things she never remembers?" Reuben asked.

"That will depend largely on how determined she is to get well." The doctor rested his elbows on his desk and tapped his fingertips together. "You've told me she has a baby son at home. Once she improves enough to remember him—and I'm fairly confident she will—he could prove highly motivational for her."

Reuben and Maggie returned to Mrs. O'Toole's feeling encouraged. In the six weeks since Earl Marshall had invaded their home, life had changed considerably. Naturally, Maggie had contacted Charlotte's parents to inform them of what had happened. Just achieving this much had taken a great deal of work, since all her files and address book had been lost in the fire. Only by digging through Charlotte's personal belongings in her room at Mrs. O'Toole's did they finally find an address for the Penfields. It was on a sealed envelope addressed in Charlotte's own hand, and it was Reuben who found it.

"I'm glad you're here with me," Maggie had confessed. "If I were alone, I'd never have the self-control to leave it sealed. I'm a nosy one."

"You're an honest one to admit that, Maggie." Reuben smiled. "And I love that about you. I'm curious too. But until there's a good reason to do otherwise, let's respect Charlotte's privacy as much as possible."

Two days later, a return telegram arrived for Maggie from Charlotte's father:

1944 FEB 23 AM 9:20

MRS. MARSHALL. WE DO NOT HAVE A DAUGHTER NAMED CHARLOTTE. EDWARD PENFIELD.

Reuben had watched the indignation rise in Maggie, turning her face red. Just as quickly, the anger subsided and her eyes welled with tears. She turned to Reuben.

"Even now, he won't budge. How can anyone be so heartless?"

"Pride is a powerful thing."

"I guess it's up to me now." Reuben could see the fear behind her teary eyes.

"It's up to *us*, Maggie," he said, pulling her into a warm hug. "I'm not going to abandon you with this."

Reuben had returned to his congregation in Roseburg, where Mrs. Schmidt had sprung to life at the opportunity to care for her wounded reverend.

With his shoulder healing and his hearing slowly returning to normal, he made midweek train trips to Winnipeg to visit Charlotte and help Maggie in any way he could. She and Mrs. O'Toole were doing a remarkable job of caring for Darcy under the circumstances. The little guy was now eating solid foods—mashed fruits and porridge—and was showing signs of trying to crawl. He would soon be a much bigger handful than Mrs. O'Toole had energy for, however, even just during the brief hours Maggie was at work.

Reuben had helped Maggie work through the legalities of her situation. Earl Marshall had been convicted of attempted murder, along with a long list of other charges, including drug trafficking and arson. His lawyer was still working toward reducing his sentence, based on his insanity defense, but even if he succeeded, Earl would remain institutionalized and was no longer a threat to Maggie or anyone else. For that, Reuben felt grateful and deeply relieved. He had not completely succeeded in protecting her, but Maggie had survived and was a more confident woman because of it. Though it had pained him to hear the firsthand accounts of the abuse she had suffered, Reuben had watched with growing pride while she took the stand at Earl's trial and told her story with quiet dignity.

Maggie had even found a buyer for her commercial property—another amazing answer to prayer. Between the war still raging in the world, and the battle being waged in Maggie's heart over how to handle her father's legacy, the sale seemed to Reuben nothing short of a miracle. She had downplayed her decision, though.

"It's just a piece of dirt, really," she'd said the day she told him. "What my father gave me lives on, right here." She placed a fist over her heart.

"Do you have plans for what you will do with the money?" he asked.

"Promise you won't laugh?"

"No." Reuben grinned. "If it's funny, why would I cheat myself of a good laugh?"

"Then forget it." Maggie picked up their teacups and moved to the sink without a word.

"You're a stubborn one, Maggie Marshall. All right. I won't laugh."

Maggie turned around and stood with her back to the sink, her hands gripping the edge of the counter. "Running a restaurant is what I know how to do, and I love it. But the girls I've taken in over the years—well, I never let myself get close to any of them, not before Charlotte. I know I came across as cold and heartless to protect myself from the pain when they left. But I cared about each one. I really did."

"I know you did, Maggie." Reuben thought his heart might burst with whatever it was he was feeling.

"I wish I could go back and be a better friend to them. Would it have killed me to try?"

"You did more than a lot of people would." Reuben walked over to Maggie and took one of her hands in his. "But if you're being eaten up by regret, you can change that. Tell God about it. He already knows you were operating out of a heart filled with pain . . . the loss of your childhood friend, the loss of your baby, your husband's abusive treatment."

"None of that excuses me, Reuben. I've been so callous."

"And yet, God is crazy about you, Maggie. He loves you. And he loves nothing better than to forgive his children and give them a fresh start."

Maggie nodded. "That's what I want. A fresh start. That's what I want to do with the money. If I could do anything in the world, I think I'd like a chance to influence young girls *before* they get in trouble. Maybe somehow help prevent some of the sad stories I've seen."

"I can easily see you doing just that, Maggie. And the need is great. One day soon, I hope, this war will be over. But twenty years from now, we'll see young men and women who grew up without their fathers because they died in battle or because they returned home too damaged and scarred to be what their children need them to be. Young women will turn to young men to fill that hole in their hearts, and young men—today's little ones, like Darcy—may not have what it takes to rise up and be men."

"You're painting a pretty bleak picture."

"I simply mean that there will always be plenty of opportunities to help youth, Maggie. And God loves your willing heart. He will open doors and show you the path you're to follow if you trust him with it."

Maggie was looking at her feet. Reuben saw a tear form on her cheek and brushed it away with his finger.

"Marry me, Maggie." Even Reuben was startled by the words that came out of his mouth. Had he really just said that?

She looked up at him, surprise written all over her face.

"*Marry* you?" She kept her eyes on his, but turned her face to the side. "That's kind of out of the blue, isn't it?"

Reuben bit his top lip. "It kind of slipped out. I've been wanting to ask you forever, but not like this. You deserve a little more romance."

Maggie laughed. "Romance? Me?"

"But it's out now. I might as well charge ahead. Will you?"

"You're serious."

"Of course I am. You can't tell me it hasn't crossed your mind."

Maggie grinned. "You're right, I can't. It has. But . . . it's just . . . *me*? A pastor's wife? Have you seen me with people?"

"This isn't about being 'a pastor's wife.' I want you to be *my* wife. Could you see your way clear to do that? Just once, could you look at me and see Reuben, and not 'the reverend'? The man behind the pastor is even more smitten with you now than when he was a boy. Besides, the church could use a little shaking up."

Maggie laughed out loud at this. "And you think I'm the one to do it? Shake up the church?"

Reuben enfolded both of Maggie's hands in his. "All I know is, you're the most hardworking, honest, and caring woman I've ever met."

"Caring? Me? I have a funny way of showing it."

"I miss you like crazy when we're apart, and if I don't kiss you pretty soon, I might explode."

Maggie smiled and leaned closer, and Reuben took this as permission. With one hand, he caressed her mass of red hair, and with the other he lifted her chin. Their lips gently met, and then he closed his eyes and kissed her again before enveloping her in a warm embrace. "I love you, Maggie. Please say yes."

Maggie's arms had slipped around his neck, and now she stretched as far away from him as she could without letting go. "You have no idea what you're getting into."

"Is that a yes?"

Maggie smiled and nodded.

"Hallelujah!" Laughing, Reuben tightened his grip around Maggie's waist and swung her around the kitchen. "I was just sure you'd refuse!"

"Well, it may not be my smartest move," Maggie teased, "but you've stood by me through thick and thin already—how stupid would I be to say no?"

CHAPTER 52

Maggie stirred the oatmeal bubbling on Mrs. O'Toole's stove. She'd hardly slept and had spent the previous night trying to sort through everything going on in her head. Had Reuben really proposed? Had she really said *yes*? What on earth had she been thinking? She couldn't simply quit her job and run off to Roseburg to be a pastor's wife! Could Reuben even support them both on his wartime salary in a small town? What about Charlotte? She couldn't just abandon Charlotte and Darcy.

"Ow!" A splash of hot cereal landed on her finger. She dropped the wooden spoon and let her finger fly to her mouth.

"Now you don't need to be cookin' all day at the Fort Garry and here too." Mrs. O'Toole bustled into the room and tied an apron around her ample middle. "Let me do that. Sit down and I'll pour you a cup of coffee."

Maggie wearily obeyed. How was she going to get through her work shift?

Mrs. O'Toole studied her face while she filled Maggie's cup, then her own. "You look like me Grandpap O'Brien's ol' sheepdog after a night of chasin' badgers."

"Didn't get much sleep, that's all. I'll be fine." Maggie took a long drink.

"If you're worryin' about the wee one, he's going to be just fine. And if you're worryin' about Charlotte . . . well, I'm prayin' for a full recovery, just like that doctor said. She'll be right as rain soon."

"I hope you're right. Can I ask you a question?"

"You can."

"If, um . . ." Maggie paused. "If Reuben Fennel were to ask me to marry him . . . well, what would you think?"

A smile broke out across Mrs. O'Toole's face. "I'd be thinkin' it's about time the man came to his senses!"

"And if I were to agree to it?"

"Then I'd be sayin' you've finally come to yours as well! Are you tellin' me he did? And you did?"

Maggie just smiled, and Mrs. O'Toole rose to her feet and danced an Irish jig right there in the middle of her kitchen. "Glory be! I knew the man loved you from the day I first saw the two of you together. We're goin' to have a wedding! Praise Jesus!"

Maggie walked the corridor toward Charlotte's hospital room with a lighter step than she'd known herself to take since childhood. She had no idea how things would play out for Charlotte and Darcy, but Reuben Fennel loved her and wanted her to be his wife. *I don't deserve the man, God. But if you're giving him to me, I'll do all I can to be worthy of him, I promise.*

When she rounded the corner into the room, another wonderful surprise greeted her. Charlotte was sitting upright in a wheelchair. A nurse was fitting clean sheets on the bed.

"Charlotte!" Maggie stopped short. "You're up!"

Slowly, a smile spread across the young woman's face. The words that followed were slower still, but clear. "You're Maggie. Am I right?"

"Yes. Yes! I'm Maggie. You remember!"

The nurse walked over to Charlotte and placed a protective hand on her shoulder. "Careful, Mrs. Marshall. Charlotte's still extremely fragile.

She's been speaking clearly since last night and talked us into getting her up. But her memory still hasn't gone back to before the . . . um, incident."

"But you remember me, Charlotte, right?" Maggie prompted the girl. "You knew right away who I was."

"You were here before," Charlotte said. "You told me your name."

"Oh. I see. Well . . . that's good. That's a great start, Charlotte!"

"That's exactly right," the nurse said. "Things can only get better from here. Charlotte, would you like Mrs. Marshall to take you for a walk? It's a beautiful day out there."

Charlotte nodded, and Maggie pushed the wheelchair down the hall and out a side door that led to a small cobblestoned atrium. Too early in the year for flowers in Manitoba, the small plots between walkways lay filled with black dirt, ready for planting. A cluster of three evergreen trees provided a patch of color against the pale sky. Charlotte took a deep breath and sighed in appreciation. Maggie took a seat on a bench facing her.

"I know that you are Maggie," Charlotte began. "And I know Reuben is the man who was here with you. But I don't know who you are, really. I know you're not my parents. Why aren't they here? And who is Darcy? I have so many questions."

The speech had taken Charlotte a full two minutes.

Maggie sighed. She knew nothing about these kinds of injuries. Surely dumping the whole load on Charlotte at once, explaining the past year or more of her life in one fell swoop, would prove too overwhelming.

"It will all come to you when you're ready, Charlotte. Be patient. For now, just know that Reuben and I are your friends. We love you very much."

"Is he your husband?"

Maggie smiled. "Not yet. Soon, though."

"And Darcy? Does he love me, too?"

"Very much."

Charlotte tilted her head to one side. "Why hasn't he been to visit me?"

"Soon, Charlotte. We'll ask your doctor when it might be all right. You're in good hands here. You just need to focus on getting stronger. It will all come to you, in time." Maggie tried to sound as confident as she could, as much for her own sake as for Charlotte's.

The puzzlement was still obvious on Charlotte's face. "I don't understand why my parents aren't here. Are they alive?"

Maggie cleared her throat. She thought of the sealed envelope she and Reuben had found in Charlotte's room, addressed to her parents. "Yes. They're alive. They're home in Ontario and you're here in Winnipeg, with us now. I have something at home that may help you remember—a letter you wrote to them but hadn't posted yet. Shortly before your accident, I think."

"Accident? I know it was a gunshot wound, and I know it was no accident. I just don't recall who did it or why."

Maggie feared Charlotte was going to start demanding more answers than she was ready to handle.

"Charlotte, for right now, it doesn't matter. Today is a day to celebrate! You're up and you're speaking and you're outdoors! That's an awful lot for one day. Let's be glad and let your memories unfold how they will. Now, I don't know about you, but I'm getting a bit chilly. Let's head inside."

Charlotte's face had paled. "I *am* getting tired."

Maggie returned the girl to her room, where a nurse helped her tuck Charlotte into bed. She was asleep before Maggie could pick up her purse.

On the trolley to Mrs. O'Toole's house, Maggie rested her head against the window. A restless night triggered by yesterday's proposal, followed by today's work shift and a visit with Charlotte, had made for a really long day. Now it was time to go home and relieve Mrs. O'Toole by watching Darcy for the evening. How long could they keep this up?

She hoped that maybe she could put the baby down early and get to bed herself before it got too late.

It had been hard to focus on anything but Reuben since last night, though he'd caught a train to Roseburg and she wouldn't see him for five more days. They'd agreed to put their wedding plans off until Charlotte was stabilized, but they wanted it to happen before next fall.

"I'm confident she'll recover," Reuben had said. "But if it's not meant for her to have a full recovery and she needs our care, we'll be in a far better position to do that as a married couple. Don't you agree?"

It made sense to Maggie.

"Meanwhile, I'd like to tell my congregation about the engagement as soon as possible. I want to introduce you to them, Maggie. When can you come?"

Maggie had made no promises until after she talked the matter over with Mrs. O'Toole. In the end, they'd agreed that both women would catch the train for Roseburg—with Darcy—weekend after next. They'd leave Saturday morning and return Sunday evening, so as not to abandon Charlotte any longer than necessary.

What an unusual romance! But then, these were unusual times. She studied the headlines of the newspaper being read by a man in the seat in front of her. Two thousand bombers and fighters from Britain and another thousand from Italy had launched an attack on German plane plants in Germany, Bucharest, and Ploiesti. Surely the war would end soon. How much longer could it go on?

Maggie closed her eyes to shut out the headlines and tried to close her mind to the war. Instead, she remembered Reuben's sweet kisses and how wonderful it had been to feel his arms around her. How safe and right. Regardless of what was going on in the world, regardless of what unfolded with Charlotte, regardless of how bad a preacher's wife she'd make . . . Maggie knew in whose arms she wanted to be. Forever, if she could.

CHAPTER 53

Maggie and Mrs. O'Toole stepped down from the train onto the wooden platform, Mrs. O'Toole holding Darcy, and Maggie carrying two bags. Bright sunshine made the day feel filled with hope and possibilities. When she saw Reuben's tall figure approaching, she couldn't help but break into a smile. He gave her a quick kiss and took her bags.

"How's my little man?" Reuben put his face close to Darcy's. The baby laughed and placed a pudgy hand flat across Reuben's face. "Good trip?"

"'Tis an adventure we're havin'." Mrs. O'Toole was all smiles. "I haven't been out of the city since before the Depression. It's grand to see some green countryside!"

"Hope you're both up for a bit of a walk. My boardinghouse is up this way." Reuben pointed the way with his chin, and the ladies followed.

"Absolutely. Been sitting too long." Maggie took Darcy from Mrs. O'Toole and looked around at what would soon be her hometown. It appeared far from prosperous, its buildings run-down and in need of paint. Yet pansies or marigolds bloomed in nearly every front yard they passed. Reuben pointed out various business establishments and homes of his parishioners. He greeted children who peered curiously from their front steps as they walked past, and even said hello to a puppy named Rusty in front of one home, setting down the suitcases in order to give the pup a quick rub behind the ears.

"Darcy, come meet the doggie." Reuben took the little boy from Maggie's arms and held him close enough to pet the puppy, whose tail wagged so hard Maggie thought it might slap Darcy in the face. The baby squealed with delight.

Reuben picked up their bags again. "How's Charlotte?" he asked as they resumed walking.

"Better each day," Maggie told him. "I explained to her what we were doing this weekend, and that I wouldn't see her for a few days."

"And what did she have to say about that?"

Maggie did her best impression. "She said, 'Oh, how romantic!' It was the old Charlotte back. A little glimpse of her, at least. She's happy for us, Reuben."

Reuben's smile lit up his whole face. "I'm happy for us, too."

They stopped in front of a tall house that Maggie took to be the Schmidts'. Reuben led them to the front door, but it swung open before he could grab the doorknob. There in the doorway stood a plump woman in her fifties, her lips smiling, though a hint of loss clouded her eyes.

"Mrs. Schmidt," Reuben said, "I'd like you to meet Mrs. Mary O'Toole. The two of you have a lot in common—you both know how to take very good care of me!"

The two women shook hands, smiling. "And this," Reuben continued, placing an arm around her, "is my beautiful Maggie."

Maggie could feel her face heat up. "How do you do?"

"It is lovely to meet you both," Mrs. Schmidt said. "Welcome! And this must be Darcy!" The baby hid his face in Maggie's shoulder.

Mrs. Schmidt ushered them into her home, and Reuben carried their bags upstairs to the bedroom Maggie and Mrs. O'Toole would share. In one corner of the room, a crib had been set up for Darcy. A bouquet of lilacs, nestled in a vase on the bedside table, filled the room with a sweet fragrance as a gentle breeze fluttered white lace curtains at the open window.

"Make yourselves at home, yah?" Mrs. Schmidt said. "I have lemonade ready when you come down. And a little surprise for you, Maggie."

"For me?" Maggie saw Mrs. O'Toole and Reuben exchange a grin and knew they were in on it, too, whatever it was.

When they walked into Mrs. Schmidt's parlor a few minutes later, the first thing Maggie noticed was an old gray work dress draped over a sewing machine in the corner. She spotted the dress immediately because she had one just like it at home.

"Surprise!" Mrs. Schmidt pulled a clothes hanger down from the window curtain rod. On it hung a lavender-and-white dress, just as stylish as some of the dresses Maggie had seen in the window of Eaton's store in downtown Winnipeg.

"This is for you, Maggie." Reuben took the dress from his landlady and held it out to her. "Mrs. Schmidt thought you might like something new to wear to church tomorrow."

Maggie could feel her jaw hanging loose but felt powerless to close it. She hadn't had a brand-new dress since . . . well, years. She turned to Mrs. O'Toole.

"You knew about this?"

The older woman was grinning from ear to ear. "The reverend asked me for your dress size, love. I figured the best way was to let him bring Mrs. Schmidt this old thing." She picked up the gray dress.

"So that *is* mine! I wondered where that went." Maggie had been looking for the garment the previous weekend when she helped Mrs. O'Toole wash windows. "I thought I was losing my mind!"

She held the new dress against her body and gazed down on it. "It's beautiful! I don't know what to say."

"The color suits you beautifully, Maggie." Mrs. O'Toole smiled, then turned to Mrs. Schmidt. "You're a grand seamstress, dear."

Maggie performed a little twirl with the dress, feeling fourteen again. "Thank you so much!" When she looked up at her audience, she wasn't sure who was beaming more—Mrs. Schmidt or Reuben Fennel.

Maggie sat on the hard pew, the Schmidts to her left and Mrs. O'Toole to her right. Darcy had warmed to Hilde Schmidt and now sat on her lap, nearly dozing.

"I should hold the baby through church," the woman had declared that morning at breakfast. "If I need to carry him out, I know just where to go. Besides, I already the reverend's sermon heard. He likes to practice in his room."

Reuben had grinned sheepishly while the others had a chuckle at his expense.

"Not that it is not worth again hearing," she added.

The first person to greet Maggie at the church when they arrived had been Cornelia Simpson, now Baker. She'd embraced Maggie with a warm hug. "I confess I'm a little nervous about your living here," Cornelia had whispered. "I've never told anyone—"

Maggie looked the younger woman in the eye. "It's not my story to tell," she said. "Ever."

"Thank you." Cornelia smiled with relief.

Now Maggie tried to concentrate on the church service, though her thoughts bounced from one to another.

I love this new dress.

When is Reuben planning to introduce me? Will I need to shake everyone's hands? Her palms got sweaty just thinking about it.

Please don't get fussy, Darcy.

Is it a sin to love this dress so much?

Lord, help Reuben as he preaches.

I wish Charlotte could be here.

What if people think I always dress this nicely? They might think I'm too fashionable for this role, for this small town. What if they think I'm a snob?

Oh Lord, I don't know if I belong here. I wonder where we'll live?

Maybe I should have just worn my old dress.

Lord, help me get my mind off myself and listen to the sermon.

Reuben was talking about the omnipresence of God. "The Lord is here in this room, of course. It's not hard to believe it when we stand and sing his praises together. We can feel him."

Reuben was in his element, and Maggie felt proud as she sensed the congregation's rapt attention to his words.

"But he is just as present when you leave this place. He is with you in your home, in your garden, in your school, in your business, in your fields, and in your barn. When you're on the train or on your tractor. And he is most certainly with your sons on the battlefield."

Maggie heard a rousing *amen* from somewhere behind her.

"Think how joyful you'd feel right now if you stood in your kitchen and your soldier son walked in, home at last. I want you mothers to remember that to God, this planet is no larger than your own kitchen. He can see your boy, he is watching over him, and he will not allow anything to happen to him that he cannot use for good."

Maggie stole a sideways glance at Mrs. Schmidt and noticed tears on her cheeks. Compassion rose in her heart for the bereaved woman, and she reached for her hand and held it tightly while Reuben continued.

"'Yea, though I walk through the valley of the shadow of death, I will fear no evil,' the Scriptures say in Psalm 23. 'For thou art with me.'

"And in Psalm 139, the psalmist says to God, 'Whither shall I go from thy spirit? Or whither shall I flee from thy presence? If I ascend up into heaven, thou art there: if I make my bed in hell, behold, thou art there. If I take the wings of the morning, and dwell in the uttermost parts of the sea; Even there shall thy hand lead me, and thy right hand shall hold me.'"

It's true, Maggie reflected. It seemed she had made her bed in a sort of hell years before, and God had sought and found her there. She looked at Darcy, now asleep in Mrs. Schmidt's arms. He was the closest thing she'd ever had to a son. She tried to imagine him grown and off fighting a war and how difficult it would be to trust God with the outcome. She glanced around the room. Several young women filled the seats, along with their parents, grandparents, and younger siblings. Reuben shouldn't have left them out. If she'd had a chance to see Reuben's sermon ahead of time, she'd have suggested he remind the girls that God was with them too. How many of them were overburdened with worry for big brothers or sweethearts far away? Did they feel responsible to fill the gaps left behind? Did they feel less important, with their parents so focused on the sons? Someone needed to tell them they mattered as well.

I'll have a little talk with Reuben later, she thought. Then the words came to her:

You *do it.*

Where had that thought come from?

You can tell the girls yourself. Soon.

But Maggie had no time to dwell on the suggestion because the congregation was standing to sing a closing hymn. As the organist cranked out the introduction on an old pump organ, Maggie managed to find the right page in the hymnbook for "If Jesus Goes with Me." Together they sang:

> It may be in the valley, where countless dangers hide;
> It may be in the sunshine that I, in peace, abide;
> But this one thing I know—if it be dark or fair,
> If Jesus is with me, I'll go anywhere!

As the song continued, Maggie thought over the changes about to take place in her own life. She would soon be part of this congregation, this community. Not just a part, but a leader. Never in her wildest imagination would she have considered such a thing. *But if you go with me, Jesus, I'll go.*

When the hymn ended, Reuben asked everyone to sit down again.

"Before I pronounce the benediction, I have an announcement to make," he said. "Most of you know that I have recently become engaged to be married. Today I want to introduce you to my bride-to-be, Maggie Marshall. Maggie, would you join me, please?"

Maggie thought she'd faint, but somehow one foot kept moving in front of the other until she stood at Reuben's side.

"You'll have an opportunity to welcome Maggie on your way out this morning as she joins me by the door. Our wedding date is set for July 12th and will take place right here. You are all welcome to attend, of course."

While Reuben prayed God's blessing over the people, Maggie took the opportunity to look around the room. Here were parents, husbands, and wives who needed strength and comfort. Youth who needed guidance and encouragement. Precious people who would be looking to her to set an example, to show the way.

Oh Lord, she prayed. *Are you sure you know what you're doing?*

As Reuben ended his prayer and escorted her up the aisle to the front doors, where they would stand together greeting congregation members, the pump organ reprised the chorus of the last hymn. Maggie drew in a deep breath and smiled at the faces turned toward her.

If Jesus goes with me, I'll go. Anywhere.

CHAPTER 54

Charlotte pulled the navy-and-white polka-dot dress over her head and studied her reflection in the bathroom mirror while she buttoned the front. Today was the day! Maggie and Reuben had promised to bring Darcy for a visit. With the doctor's permission, they'd had a frank talk and caught her up on the details of the past year.

How ironic that her parents had wanted her to forget her son's existence, and now she had. If they had come for her in recent weeks, she'd have gladly returned home with them—no questions asked. No questions, that is, until the day came when her memories began to return. Then she likely would have thought her imagination had run completely amok, perhaps even assumed she was going crazy.

As it was, she still had a hard time believing any of it. Apart from their hospital visits, she had no recollection of Maggie, Reuben, or Mrs. O'Toole; neither had she any remembrance of Darcy. Her memories of Reginald were vague. She recalled his *inviting* her to the movies and to a dance, but not the events themselves. She did remember being at a party with him at his cousin Nancy's house. These vague recollections, combined with the changes to her body and the fact that her parents had not shown themselves, all gave Maggie's story credibility.

But what if it wasn't true? What if her parents were really dead and everyone was keeping it from her, for fear of a setback? Reuben had told her to ask God to reveal the memories she needed, as she needed them. So she had. And now, in a few short minutes, she would meet her son.

A nurse walked Charlotte down to the waiting room where they had agreed to meet. The first person she saw was Reuben, seated in one of the chairs facing the door. His eyes were trained in the direction of the window, where Maggie stood, looking out. In her arms she held a baby boy, who also gazed out at the May sunshine. Charlotte stopped and watched.

"See the kitty?" Maggie was saying. "Nice kitty. Kitty says 'meow.'"

The baby placed a chubby hand on the glass and pressed his forehead against the window. *Darcy.*

Charlotte thought she might pass out. The nurse helped her ease into a seat as a flood of recognition poured over her like a warm shower. "Darcy," she said.

Maggie and the baby turned toward her. Reuben came over and knelt in front of her.

"Charlotte!" Maggie said. Slowly she began to walk toward Charlotte, who kept her eyes fixed on the baby. "This is Darcy."

"I know. Oh! I know!" Charlotte was laughing and crying all at once. "I remember! Oh, my baby!"

She held her arms out to take him, tears streaming down her face. Darcy looked uncertain. He turned his face toward Maggie, who smiled and nodded. "It's okay, sweetheart. This is your mommy."

Darcy allowed Charlotte to hold him, but kept his eyes on Maggie. She moved in close to reassure the little boy.

"Is it all coming back?" Reuben asked.

"Not everything," Charlotte said. "I-I . . . can't think how he got here . . . I don't remember birthing him, or . . . or . . . I don't know! I just know he's mine and I love him. I love him so much!"

"Relax, Charlotte," the nurse said. "Just hold your baby and don't try to force the memories."

For the next hour, Charlotte renewed her acquaintance with her little son. She, Maggie, and Reuben took him outdoors and let him play on a blanket on the ground, but he kept crawling off the edge. When he reached Maggie's deck chair, he pulled himself to a standing position, never letting go of the chair.

"He's so big!" Charlotte was amazed. Little by little, a more complete image was coming to her, like a window blind being lifted an inch at a time. She could recall individual rooms in Mrs. O'Toole's house, but not the woman's face. She could envision the children's care center where she had worked, but not the names of her co-workers. She remembered addressing the letter to her parents Maggie had mentioned, but couldn't recall its content.

"Did you bring the letter?" she finally asked.

Maggie and Reuben exchanged a look. "I did. It's in my purse."

"I think I'd like to read it."

"You've had a lot for one day. Are you sure you're ready?" Reuben asked.

"No. But none of us knows what it says, do we? If I can see what it was I wanted to say to my parents, perhaps things will start to make more sense."

Maggie pulled the envelope from her purse and handed it to Charlotte. She recognized her own handwriting on the front and her home address in the Lawrence Park neighborhood in Toronto. Should she open it now, with Maggie and Reuben present, or save it for when she could be alone?

As though reading her mind, Reuben asked, "If you'd rather have some privacy, we can leave."

"Reuben!" Maggie scolded. "Don't make me leave! I've been dying to know what's in that letter since we found it over two months ago!"

Charlotte laughed. "It's all right. I want you here. Both of you."

Darcy had worked his way around their little circle and now began to fuss, his hands on Reuben's knee. Reuben picked him up and cuddled him close as he began to walk back and forth. Charlotte watched in wonder as the little boy rested his head on Reuben's shoulder. As far as she could remember she had never seen a man do this with a baby, especially one that was not his own. Her eyes welled with tears again.

Sliding her fingers under the flap of the envelope, she tore it open and pulled out a single sheet of stationery. The page was filled with her own delicate handwriting, written in blue ink. She stared at it a moment without actually reading the words.

"I remember writing this," she said with wonder. "I remember asking Mrs. O'Toole for the paper and using the fountain pen at her little desk in the corner of her kitchen."

"Do you remember what you wrote?" Maggie asked.

Charlotte sighed. She looked away from the page and thought for a moment. "No-o. But let's find out." After another glance at Darcy, whose thumb was in his mouth and whose eyes were dropping closed, she turned to the letter and began to read aloud.

Dear Mother and Father,

I thought I should let you know what's become of me since you left Winnipeg last fall and let you know I am all right. Mrs. Marshall and Mrs. O'Toole graciously allowed me to return to the boardinghouse and are helping me care for my son. I found work at Wrigley Children's Center, created for mothers who are working toward the war effort. The job allows me to take Darcy to work with me each day. It's tiring, but I love it. Remember how you used to tease me about my overactive imagination? It comes in handy when telling stories to the preschool children. Most of all, it pays for our room and board and a *little extra. It was literally an answer to prayer. I suppose it will close its doors when the war ends and the women can return home, but I am learning to trust God for my provision.*

Charlotte stopped reading and looked up at Maggie and Reuben, who were listening intently. Though she remembered her workplace, she hadn't been able to recall its name or why it existed. Now the gaps were being filled in and the memories becoming clearer.

My co-workers have not all been kind to me and I've learned firsthand the pain of ridicule and prejudice, often directed at my innocent son. I can see where you were right about that, and what it is you wanted so desperately to protect me from. But I also want you to know I have grown through these challenges. When I first came to Winnipeg, I was still a little girl—completely absorbed in my own romantic notions and daydreaming about the life I thought I wanted. A life no one truly gets to live.

I can see how childish and selfish I was. I am truly sorry for disappointing you as I did and I want to ask your forgiveness.

But I also want you to know I forgive you. And I forgive Reginald. I will not be attempting to contact him, lest I jeopardize his new marriage and family, but I need to write the words down and share them with someone. Reginald's betrayal is not the most painful thing in this story. You may not think I have anything to forgive you for, that I deserve whatever has happened. And perhaps you are right. But your rejection of me and your grandson has hurt me more deeply than I can describe.

I am choosing to forgive you because of something I'm learning from Maggie Marshall—who is learning it from Rev. Fennel. When we don't forgive, we are only feeding ourselves a slow poison. I don't want to do that. I want to be the best person I can be, the best mother for Darcy, and I can't do that if I am poisonous myself.

I don't know whether we can ever be part of each others' lives again. That will be up to you. If I don't hear back, I will not contact you again. Regardless of what you choose, know that all is forgiven. I hope you can find it in your hearts to forgive me too. As for me, I am free. With God's help, I am free to follow his leading and raise my son with as much love and guidance as I can. And I am strong. With his help, I can withstand the judgmental looks and comments directed my way.

I never knew it was possible to love someone so much as I love my son. Now I know, and I would not trade him for anything in the world.
Sincerely,
Charlotte

Charlotte slowly folded the letter, then looked up. She was surprised to see tears streaming down Maggie's face. The woman quickly pulled a hanky from her purse and wiped her eyes. Reuben, one arm folded around the sleeping baby, reached into his pocket and pulled out his own handkerchief. When he blew his nose, the baby startled in his sleep, which made Charlotte chuckle.

"Good for you, Charlotte." Reuben's voice was just above a whisper. Maggie simply nodded.

"I suppose I should add an update. Let them know I'm going to be okay. I know they might only ignore it, but at least I'd know I did all I could."

"That's very mature of you, young lady," Reuben said. "Your parents will come around, you'll see. Maybe not today, but one day. And in the meantime, we're here if you need us. Aren't we, Maggie?"

Maggie nodded again. Charlotte had never seen the woman overcome with emotion before and sensed her embarrassment.

"Here you are!" Dr. Glendale let the door fall shut behind him and joined Charlotte's circle in the atrium. "I've got great news for you, Miss Penfield. You're ready to go home."

Charlotte smiled up at him even as she was biting her bottom lip. Was she really ready?

"When?" Maggie asked.

The doctor looked at Maggie and Reuben, then Charlotte. "How does today sound?"

CHAPTER 55

Reuben stood at the front of his own church, but not behind the pulpit this time. That spot was being temporarily filled by Reverend Morgan Lee, an old friend from Bible school who had happily agreed to perform the marriage ceremony.

The church was filled to capacity and beyond, with a few men standing along the walls on both sides and in the back. Heinz Schmidt stood nearby as best man. "You are like son to us now," the man had declared when Reuben asked him. "I will be honored to stand off with you."

As Mrs. Borthistle began the wedding march on the old pump organ, a hush came over the congregation, and all turned toward the back of the room. Charlotte walked down the aisle first, looking lovelier than Reuben had ever seen her in a taffeta dress the color of peaches and carrying a bouquet of homegrown white daisies in her hands. She smiled graciously, enjoying her moment in the spotlight. Her long blond hair had been pulled into some kind of updo and arranged with tiny white flowers. Reuben couldn't help thinking what a lovely bride she would make.

But then his breath was stolen away by the real bride.

Maggie had warned him ahead of time. "Don't expect nothing fancy," she'd said a few weeks before the wedding. "Mrs. O'Toole has agreed to make me a new suit that will double as my Sunday best as a good pastor's wife for years to come. There's a war on, you know."

So Reuben was shocked when tears began to form in his eyes at his first sight of Maggie. Her new suit was the color of fresh sage grass. Adorned with fine white piping and formfitted to Maggie's slim figure, it flattered her completely. The copper shimmer had returned to her mass of red curls, which were now gathered on top of her head and held in place with jeweled combs that caught the light of the July sun streaming in through the stained glass windows. A few loose tendrils curled softly around her face. She carried a white Bible in her gloved hands, and on her feet were new tan-colored shoes that Reuben suspected were the closest thing to frivolous Maggie would ever allow herself.

But it was her face that held his gaze. Never one for makeup, Maggie must have submitted to Charlotte's enhancing touch to her eyes, cheeks, and lips. Reuben had performed several weddings and had thought he understood the term *radiant bride*, but this was beyond his experience. Surely everyone in the room could feel the glow emanating from his Maggie.

He reflected back on the day he first walked into her home and saw a world-weary and soul-dead woman who greeted him stoically just days after becoming a widow. He'd suspected then that her callousness had to be a cover, and he had been right. In the months since that day, Maggie had been through enough versions of hell to make her an even more bitter person. Instead, she'd allowed God to heal her heart. The result was this beautiful woman who now stood smiling before him, a slight tremor in her hands the only evidence of her nerves.

God, thank you for not letting me say no to this.

CHAPTER 56

April 1946. Roseburg, Manitoba

Maggie hung the last of the garments on the clothesline and stretched, taking in the bright blue sky. The warm spring sunshine felt wonderful on her face. Nearly a year had passed since VE Day. Victory in Europe. Maggie remembered joining the Schmidts around their radio to hear the official announcement. Three months later, Japan surrendered.

Meanwhile, Reuben and Maggie had moved into the parsonage while Charlotte and Darcy had stayed on at the Schmidts'. Now three years old, the little boy visited "Aunty Maggie and Uncle Reuben" often. And during this time, Maggie had come to feel a true part of the community.

She and Charlotte both worked part time at the Roseburg Café, the town's only restaurant. Business had picked up significantly since the war ended. The soldiers had started trickling home, married men first, in the fall of 1945. Most made it home by Christmas, with two more groups arriving in February and March. Today the citizens of Roseburg would celebrate together with a parade, a grand welcome home, and a ceremony to honor the fallen.

As the single boys returned, more than a few of them began to take notice of Charlotte. One of them, Ross Jackson, had not been put off in the least by the presence of Darcy. He had become a dear friend to all of them, and Maggie hoped it wouldn't be long before the friendship blossomed into romance and marriage. From what she'd seen so far, Ross would make a wonderful husband and father.

Like Reuben.

Running a hand over the small bulge growing under her apron, she wondered how much longer she would stay on at the café. The work had provided an excellent opportunity to get to know people in the community, especially those who didn't attend church. But her real work took place at the club for girls she and Charlotte had started. They met Tuesdays after school at the church for various activities, from learning new skills like gardening and crocheting, to raising funds for the playground—all efforts initiated by the girls themselves and carried out with youthful enthusiasm under Charlotte's energetic leadership.

It had taken Reuben's intervention to convince a couple of parents that a single mother like Charlotte could be a role model for their daughters, but Maggie still remembered with pride how Charlotte had humbly and bravely maintained her dignity until she earned their trust. Each club session ended with a short Bible lesson led by Maggie. Preparing for the lessons taught her far more than she was teaching the girls, and she was stunned by the good questions they raised—causing her to return to her Bible and to Reuben for further guidance. She was also amazed by how frequently the girls asked to speak privately with her and then poured out their hearts. As if she weren't the most cold-hearted woman they'd ever met. As if she had any empathy or wisdom to offer. As if she were safe.

When and how had she and Charlotte, the most unlikely candidates, become these people? God surely did have a sense of humor!

Turning toward the house, she spotted Reuben coming around the corner, returning home for lunch after a morning of visitation with various veterans. He smiled warmly at her. Maggie knew he had heard horrific stories from these young men in the past several months. Several of them met together weekly under the guise of studying basic mechanics. But Maggie knew that although Reuben was finally learning a few useful things about maintaining a vehicle, the real purpose of the group was emotional and spiritual support.

The men leaned on one another because of their shared experience, and they leaned on Reuben simply because of who he was. He provided a compassionate heart, a safe place to cry, and strong arms to hold them while they did. Sometimes he turned around and cried, too, in Maggie's arms at the end of a long day, but his tears were always for these boys who'd seen far too much suffering and bloodshed. Still, he said he couldn't imagine himself anywhere else or doing a more important job. And their little church was filled to capacity every week.

She greeted him with a kiss. "Soup's on."

Reuben wrapped an arm tightly around Maggie's shoulders and walked her to the door. "I can smell it from here and I'm starved, Mrs. Fennel. How did I manage to marry the best cook in the world?"

"I thought Mrs. O'Toole was the best cook in the world."

"Not even close."

"Liar."

Reuben laughed and kissed her temple. "You're going to be the best mother in the world, too. I'm so glad you rode halfway across the country with me that time."

Maggie just grinned and rolled her eyes. Together, they sat down at their little kitchen table to her vegetable soup and homemade bread. Reuben reached across the table for her hand, bowed his head, and began to pray.

"Lord, thank you for our lives. For bringing us together, for this roof over our heads and this food on our table. For the little one who will soon join our family. For the work you've called us to do, the people you've called us to serve. Make us worthy, dear God. Most of all, thank you for what this day represents. As our community finally meets to celebrate, may it truly be with thanksgiving in every heart—even for those who are still mourning their losses. Thank you for bringing peace to our land and to our hearts through your precious son, Jesus. Amen."

Maggie squeezed Reuben's hand and echoed his *amen*. She smiled up at her husband with joy she had not dreamed possible.

The war was over.

ACKNOWLEDGMENTS

Special thanks to:

My late stepfather, John Klassen, for his insights into life in Winnipeg in 1942.

Marci McCowan, for her medical advice.

Mike Hurlbert, for the details about Fort William (now Thunder Bay).

Peter Ralph, for sharing his expertise in auto mechanics.

Fire Chief Phil Carpenter, for the arson investigation advice.

Barb Knott, for her knowledge of legal fees.

Jim Hamlett and Clarice James, my first reviewers. Check out their books!

Jessica Kirkland, Agent of the Year and God's gift to me.

My editors at Waterfall Press, especially Shari MacDonald Strong, for challenging me to make a good story better.

Jon, Nate, Dara, Mindy, Kevin, Reuben, Jill, Mom, and Shanon. It's tremendous when family and cheerleaders are one and the same.

Wendy and Dale Olson, my sister and brother-in-law, for use of the cozy gazebo in their beautiful yard for a weekend writing retreat. Every writer should be so blessed!

All the readers who praised my first book enough to make this one possible!

Most of all, my thanks are due to my redeemer, Jesus Christ, master storyteller and main character in the greatest story ever told.

ABOUT THE AUTHOR

Photo © G. Loewen Photography

Terrie Todd is an award-winning author who has published eight stories with the Chicken Soup for the Soul series and created two full-length plays with Eldridge Plays and Musicals. Her bestselling debut novel, *The Silver Suitcase*, was a finalist in the 2011 and 2012 Christian Writers Guild's Operation First Novel contest.

In 2010, she served on the editorial advisory board for the anthology *Chicken Soup for the Soul: O Canada*. She lives with her husband, Jon, on the Canadian prairies, where they raised their three children. By day, Terrie is an administrative assistant at her local city hall. She enjoys acting and directing with her community theater group, the Prairie Players, and being grandma to four little boys.